APPALACHIAN TRAIL

A NOVEL

Darren Drevik

APPALACHIAN TRAIL

Published by Maridar Publishing, a division of Maridar LLC.

For information, address: Maridar Publishing, 125 Mountain Road, Stowe, Vermont 05672

ISBN 978-0-9908647-0-7

Library of Congress Card Catalog Number: 2014917180.

"Unclouded Day," by Rev. J.K. Alwood. Reprinted under creative commons license.

"The Precious Jewel," by Roy Acuff. Copyright 1943 Sony/ATV Acuff Rose Music. All rights administered by Sony/ATV Music Publishing LLC. 424 Church Street, Nashville, TN 37219. All rights reserved. Used by permission.

To Marilyn, my white blaze

When April with his showers sweet with fruit
The drought of March has pierced unto the root
And bathed each vein with liquor that has power
To generate therein and sire the flower;
When Zephyr also has, with his sweet breath,
Quickened again, in every holt and heath,
The tender shoots and buds, and the young sun
Into the Ram Aries one half his course has run,
And many little birds make melody
That sleep through all the night with open eye
So Nature pricks them on to ramp and rage
Then do folk long to go on pilgrimage,
And palmers to go seeking out strange strands,
To distant shrines well known in sundry lands.
And specially from every shire's end
Of England they to Canterbury wend,
The holy blessed martyr there to seek
Who helped them when they lay so ill and weak.

- The Canterbury Tales

1
KATAHDIN

Nate Townsend loved sunrises, but prayed every night he would never see another. The first moments of daybreak over the ocean to Nate were always as subtle and unnoticed as the last moments of consciousness before drifting off to sleep. Every night, as the sun inched closer to the shoreline behind his home in Maine, the light was at first imperceptible. Within seconds, nearby objects – once invisible – suddenly gathered enough illumination to gain attention. Just as quickly, wisps of clouds tens of thousands of feet up in the atmosphere began collecting the umber and yellowing shades of sunlight. Finally, the whole sky was bright, although the sun still had yet to tip its hand as to where on the horizon it would breach the dissipating darkness. Even before it peeked out, the day had clearly arrived. Rocks, crashing waves and evergreen timbers – invisible only minutes before – were clearly illuminated. Finally, just when it seemed as though it would never arrive, that heavily anticipated slice of red and orange sun slit parallel to the horizon, and the surf finally got the chance to directly reflect the light that has been teasing it for the past half hour. Once the fireball itself broke free and is bisected by the horizon – and then separated from it entirely – it was all anticlimax. At this point, the real magic had already passed, and the sunrise now became cliché, the subject of paintings, poems and Instamatic snapshots. Only those who had been awake an hour earlier had seen the entire show.

On this morning, Nate had witnessed every moment of the shoreline's visual serenade. His kitchen window front-row seat overlooked the rock-and-sand coastline of Seal Island, Maine, and his view of the whitecaps that lived beyond the shoreline, had until recently been a comfortable one. He poured a third cup of coffee into his chipped black ceramic mug and slowly walked away from the window, through the cluttered, carpeted living room and toward the front of his house. There, scattered on top of the dining room table, was a jumbled assemblage of clothing, freeze-dried food, pocket knives and toiletries. Centered on the table amidst all the various items was a new fully stuffed backpack, fluorescent orange, as if to scream out its virginity to all the other backpacks it might come across. The loose items strewn across the tabletop were the also-rans, the hiking accouterments that had not made the grade. Just like beauty pageant runners-up, they had been accorded respect but clearly would not be treasured and shown off.

The packing had been difficult. Nate's experience should have made the task easy, and yet he had agonized over his inventory late into the previous night, questioning which toothbrush would be lighter on the trail, and which backpacking stove and fuel combination would be the most effective. At 1 a.m., when he caught himself weighing his four pocket knives with a scale to find the lightest one, he realized the absurdity of his obsession, and turned in for the night.

When the alarm sounded barely four hours later, he awoke to the five seconds of disorientation that had become routine during the past six months. The bedroom was familiar, the soft sound of the waves brushing the shore was the same as it had been for most of his life, but the silence in the room, the pink walls and the confinement of the single-size mattress momentarily confused Nate. Once awake, he quickly rose, showered, and scuttled into the kitchen.

Now he waited. In silence. After studying the sun's arrival off the coast, he turned and stared at the orange backpack and all it represented. Slowly panning his eyes around the dining room, Nate looked further, into the living room where he could see the walls scarred by nail holes that once held nails, nails that once held frames, frames that once held photographs, photographs that held too much pain, and thus had been removed. There were several larger holes in the walls. Those had been slathered with plaster, but never painted over.

The sunlight was now bright enough to begin filtering across the kitchen and into the dining room. Nate looked at his watch in time to see the second hand tick off the last few moments that were 5:45 a.m. on this chilling mid-April morning.

Nate slowly worked his way around the three-bedroom ranch, switching off lights and thermostats. When he finally returned to the dining room, he slid the pack off the table and gently swung it around on his left shoulder, flipping off the final light switch and pushing through the door leading to the garage. With an overstated swing of the shoulder, Nate plopped the pack into the passenger seat of his SUV and hit the button for the garage door opener.

The drive along the rock-littered shore from his house to downtown Freeport took twenty-five minutes, but it twisted and turned its way through evolving scenery. It began with the remote, craggy forest around his house, then cut through small, more-developed subdivisions before finally arriving at the outskirts of the city proper. At this time of the morning, on a Saturday, there was no traffic along the road. Given Nate's preoccupation, it's doubtful he would have noticed any.

When he arrived at the parking lot in Freeport, he saw his friend David Sumner's fading green sedan waiting for him. Nate pulled up alongside the car and stared at the rumpled, pudgy figure wearing a pale-blue hoodie and slumped behind the steering wheel, apparently asleep. Nate gave a sharp honk of the horn, startling the inhabitant into convulsions.

"Not funny," grunted David, rubbing his eyes. "I knew you wanted to leave early, but this is ridiculous. The roosters are still sacked in, for God's sake."

Nate watched as David slowly locked up his sedan and walked around to the passenger side of Nate's vehicle.

"This is just clinically stupid," David continued to grumble. "I mean, you're going to be on the trail for six months, so how would a couple of extra hours of sleep matter?"

David had been Nate's friend in Freeport for more than two decades, since Nate's family first arrived in Maine. The two had been inseparable in elementary school, drifted apart during their junior high years when girls, boys and hormones did battle, and then cemented the bonds of friendship during their final two years of high school. The fact they ended up working together at the same company was no surprise to those who knew them as children.

"I figured you accountants didn't have anything to do during the weekend," Nate said, smiling. "The banks are closed and there's no money moving back and forth for you to count. You guys have no life."

"What are you talking about? I have a remarkable life. I'm chock full of personality."

"For an accountant."

"For an accountant," David agreed.

Nate sat still behind the wheel, staring forward silently. David studied him and then realized why his friend hadn't restarted the car. He grunted as he reached around and pulled the seatbelt across his waist and snapped it. Once David's seatbelt was on, Nate slipped the car into gear.

"That's really an annoying habit," David said.

"Tell me all about it after the airbag deploys someday," he said.

Nate wheeled toward the parking lot's exit, taking a quick glance around, making a mental census of how many RVs were camped along the periphery. Nate and David both worked at L.L. Bean, and they had chosen to make the company's outlet store their meeting point. Counting cars and RVs had become a habit for Nate, ever since he'd been placed in charge of the company's outlet stores four years ago. He received the promotion after a successful stint as the company's marketing director. His claim to fame was developing the company's second outlet operation, designed solely to sell clothing and accessories for small children. In retrospect, it had been a fairly simple idea, which came to him one afternoon while watching the thousands of retirees scouring Freeport for something – anything – to purchase that would further overstimulate and over-spoil their coveys of grandchildren.

Since it was a weekend, today would be a big day for the retail operation. A dozen RVs were already ringed around the edges of the parking lot, their generators humming in unison. Nate took stock and then headed toward the main highway. David took a quick glance around, ran some quick numbers in his head and speculated aloud that it would be the outlet store's busiest sales day to date.

"Good day not to be on the floor then," Nate agreed.

Within five minutes, the two were on Interstate 95 racing north. The town of Freeport quickly vanished in the rearview mirror, replaced with lines and lines of evergreens running parallel to the roadway. Maine in the middle of April was slowly beginning to spring back to life. Everywhere else in the United States, warm weather had already brought forth greening trees and flowering plants. Maine was just now rediscovering warmth and snatches of color. The long winters and glacial advances and withdrawals made for a rather barren landscape, lined with granite and fir. It was not surprising that such a Spartan landscape yielded an equally Spartan people. Maine is a land of little color, little excess. Likewise, the people of Maine waste little, be it resources or words.

Thus, it was obvious to all each time they stopped for gas or snacks that neither Nate nor David was a true son of Maine. They were far too chatty, both between themselves and to the clerks. On the plus side of the Mainer scorecard, however, both did buy Moxie sodas rather than Cokes or Pepsis. The drink, invented in Maine in the 1870s, has a distinctive taste similar to root beer that made it popular at the turn of the twentieth century. By the 1950s, however, it had been overtaken by more hyper-sugared sodas.

After two hours, one refueling stop and two bathroom visits – "This coffee is going right through me," David apologized – Nate reached his exit, turned left and began driving away from the coast and toward the rapidly growing mountains to the West that formed the spine of the state. David began making mental notes, because he would be making the return trip by himself.

"You have no problems with me using your car for six months, right?"

"That was the deal," Nate reminded him.

It seemed more than fair to David. Nate had offered, in return for David shuttling him all the way north to Baxter State Park, to let David use his car for the time he was gone hiking the Appalachian Trail. David had been told that the trip would take anywhere from four to eight months, depending on how fast Nate hiked and what obstacles he met with on the way. Unknown to David, Nate had placed the signed title for the car transferring ownership to David into the glove box. At some point just before his journey's end, he would mail David a letter letting him know that he was giving him the SUV.

"Not that I don't like my car," David promptly lied. "My goal is to get it to 300,000 miles. That'll be impressive. We'll have a party."

As an accountant, David's obsession with his car was actually a love affair with numbers. He kept a spiral-ringed notebook in his glove box and logged every fill-up. He would spend five minutes after topping off the tanks calculating and analyzing variations in his miles-per-gallon before pulling away from the pumps. Should there be a drop in performance, or should it need a quart of oil a week earlier than he had calculated, he would immediately take the car into the shop. David's ability to be easily distracted might result in the SUV being in an accident, Nate thought, but the car certainly would be well-maintained.

The mountains were much closer now, and as they entered the town of Millinocket, they wheeled into the gravel parking lot of a general store that looked more like a giant log cabin. Stepping inside, Nate quickly saw the store's clientele fell into two groups: Locals, who came in for groceries and other sundries, and hikers and hunters, who came in supplies, food or overpriced equipment and ammo that they may have forgotten to bring with them.

Nate picked up would likely be his last Moxie and then strolled through the huge building, looking over tents, titanium cook pots and food packets, comparing what he saw to what he had loaded into his pack the night before. He blinked as he stumbled upon a wooden sign with huge, carved black letters:

NOT ALL WHO WANDER ARE LOST

He stared at the sign.

NOT ALL WHO WANDER ARE LOST, the sign continued to shout.

It was a quote from *Lord of the Rings*, but since Nate had never read any of Tolkien's books, he didn't recognize it. He quickly changed his focus to hiking poles, making a snap decision that he needed a set. He grabbed the first pair he could reach, a garish, neon red set with rubber handles and graphite bullets at the points, designed to survive millions of impacts against rocks, water and soil along the hiking trail.

When the clerk rang up the poles, Nate was briefly startled at the $175 price. He hadn't bothered to look at the tag, but checked himself, realizing he had every dollar he owned tucked inside his wallet, and that the exorbitant price the store was charging wouldn't even put a dent in the bankroll he was carrying for supplies and food along the 2,100-mile trail. As he and David returned to the SUV, he jammed the poles into the back hatch.

"Let me drive the rest of the way, Nate," David said. "Since I need to backtrack out of here, I'd better remember the way."

Nate settled into the passenger seat, then watched as his best friend nestled a tall cup of overburnt coffee into the driver's-side cup holder. As the car idled, David began to play chemist, carefully adding the right amount of sweeteners and creamer from paper packets to turn the stale liquid into something drinkable. While David took several sips of his drink to make sure his additives were correctly proportioned, Nate just stared, entertained. After several coffees and Moxies during the first three hours, the idea of drinking anything else now seemed unwise. After more three more minutes of pouring and mixing, David was finally ready to pull out.

As they changed roads and left Millinocket, the landscape also changed. Roads transformed from relatively straight ribbons into winding, twisting trails. Softer hills now became steeper, and the mountain range that had been closer to the horizon now loomed large. The mountains were a balanced mixture of green and brown, both forested and craggy. The green tended to hug the lower levels, while the barren, brown rocky sections tended to be at the higher elevations, where Nate knew the combination of bitter cold, high winds and thinner air made trees unwelcome. Nate stared at the deeper green sections of mountains, as he leaned his head against the passenger-side window. The green was comforting, primal, reaching deeper and deeper into his psyche.

"Na-than!"

Nate was staring at a different set of tall, green mountains, these curved into a smooth ridgeline rather than craggy and jagged at the top. Still, they were impressive, reaching altitudes over 6,000 feet. The mountains, while quite different from the brown-capped peaks of Maine, boasted a thousand varying hues of green that were equally dazzling. The mountain tops, however, were partially obscured by fog and haze, making it impossible to discern individual trees along the sides and the ridgeline. Still, their size and familiarity brought comfort to an eight-year-old Nathan, who stood transfixed by them.

"Nathan! Get in the car, honey. We've got to go," a woman's voice shouted.

Nate didn't want to turn his gaze from the mountains, fearing he might never see them again. He tried to memorize each small valley, slowly tracing its outline from the thin, whispering line that began just below the ridge and following it down as it grew and wound its way down to the base. He knew from roaming them that each valley held the small stream that had dug it out over many millennia, starting as a spring at the top and gradually becoming a moving, burbling waterway as it abandoned the rocky mass of its birth and moved out into flatter, less dramatic geography.

"Nathan!" The voice was now much closer and much more insistent. He turned and saw his mother towering over his right shoulder. "I swear, Nathan, sometimes I think you're as deaf as a post. Honey, it's time for us to go. Run an' jump in the car."

Nate obeyed, piling into the back seat of the dirty white Dodge Dart. He adjusted himself, pulling his short pants down as far as they would go so that his bare skin wouldn't touch the clear plastic seat covers his father had installed. The seat covers made his skin sweaty and uncomfortable, and after a few hours of baking in the midmorning sun, they were uncomfortably hot. The seat, however, was nowhere near as hot as the metal-clasp seat belt, which he avoided and hoped that his mother would forget to remind him to fasten. His father was already in the car, chain-smoking and waiting for Nate's mother to settle into the front seat next to him.

"C'mon, honey," he said to his wife. "It's already so hot the hens are laying hard-boiled eggs."

The Townsend family's belongings were all stacked on top of a flatbed trailer the underpowered Dodge was going to drag all the way from East Tennessee to Maine. Old furniture, abused steamer trunks, a few plastic children's toys and other aged household items were all tied down with rope, covered with bleached-out sheets. It looked like a scene from *The Beverly Hillbillies*, and more than a few drivers who passed them on the road laughingly made that comparison. Nate was too young and too oblivious to be embarrassed. He'd never watched television.

His father worked at a vegetable canning plant nestled at the foothills of the mountains where his family had managed to scramble and survive for six generations. Juter Townsend was the first in his family to give up trying to grow vegetables out of the rock-strewn ground, and instead found a job putting them in cans. He was hard-working – those in this region who weren't hardworking didn't live well or long – and the manager of the canning plant recommended Juter as his replacement when he retired. This was an unusual and brave step, because the canning company, based in New Jersey, assumed that everyone who worked in their rural plants was too stupid or too uninspired to lead others. Almost every manufacturing operation that set up its operations along the Appalachian spine assumed that the locals were nothing more than illiterate rabble, barely capable of doing the manual labor assigned them. To think that a hillbilly could manage a business was a radical notion. Still, the company's managers from Cleveland, Pittsburgh and Atlanta had all balked at the thought of moving themselves and their families to the wilderness of Roan Mountain, Tennessee. So out of desperation, they handed Juter the post and continued to look for a manager, assuming Juter would fail within a few months.

Juter surprised them, improving productivity and suggesting during inspection visits several additional local vegetables besides beans and corn that the company could can and sell. His homespun sayings mixed necessary candor and humor in equal measure, which made the orders easier to swallow. He said one vendor who couldn't seem to keep his company's equipment running was "as sharp as a bowl of mashed potatoes," and complained the corporate efficiency expert's visits were "as welcome as an outhouse breeze." Rather than resent him, his workers gave him extra effort because they knew he was one of them.

Juter's ability to reduce expenses came from his thrifty Scot-Irish attitudes,supplemented by an ancient and rudimentary business textbook he had traveled to Knoxville to buy one weekend. After several years of pleasing the powers-that-be in New Jersey, the company discovered that one of its plants in Freeport, Maine, needed someone who could control costs and innovate. Dare they send Juter? Desperation is often the father of opportunity, and thus Juter found himself offered the Faustian bargain of abandoning his home, family and the South in return for a substantial raise. It was a difficult decision, but his family had arrived in the Appalachians generations earlier because they had fled Scotland and Ireland for the financial opportunity of America. Uprooting and moving, while painful, came naturally to his people. No jobs meant you moved. Poor soil meant you packed up the family and headed west for better ground. So Juter's decision, while one his family regretted, was not one that hadn't been made many times before over the past three centuries.

When first told of the move, Nate initially considered it a great adventure and had no understanding of the distances involved. Maine was another state, just like North Carolina. North Carolina was just a twenty minute hike over the ridgeline, so traveling to a different state was an easy thing to do. How could traveling to Maine be any different?

But now that the family's belongings were packed and the permanence of the move was becoming apparent to him, Nate's reluctance about the move grew as rapidly as the thunderheads on a hot summer afternoon. By the time his parents were calling him, the mountains had hypnotized him, calling out for him to plant himself in the ground as firmly as a hickory stump. As a the car pulled out and aligned itself west and then north, away from the family's house, Nate remembered crying, the first time he had done so without stubbing his toe or somehow injuring himself.

The Maine roads were really winding now, and a sharp turn slammed Nate against the passenger-side window and woke him. David was trying to navigate the sharp curves leading up to Baxter State Park too quickly, and Nate considered asking him to slow down. He thought better of it, remembering that David had despised backseat drivers ever since the two of them had learned to drive at the age of sixteen. Nate calculated they had already passed the isthmus that ran between Ambajesus and Millinocket Lakes and were close to the park entrance.

Baxter State Park held the tallest peak in Maine, and the northern starting point for the Appalachian Trail, which wound its way across the spine of the Appalachian and Blue Ridge mountain ranges until it ended at Springer Mountain, Georgia. The Penobscot Indians had named the craggy peak Katahdin, which means "The Greatest Mountain." Unlike many of Maine's smaller mountains, created by ancient glaciers digging out valleys around them, Katahdin was formed by volcanic action, with the glaciers coming later to polish it and amplify its height by digging out the smaller peaks and lowlands around it and creating the Penobscot River, whose two forks curl around both sides of the peak. The park that held the peak was somewhat of an anomaly, created in the 1930s due to the generosity of then-Governor Percival Baxter, who donated much of the land himself. While most national and state parks have relatively modern plumbing and other facilities, Baxter was relatively primitive, using old-style privies and avoiding the construction of modern-looking welcome centers and buildings, which contributed to the continued decline in the number of visitors each year.

Once inside the park, David noticed immediately that the paved road ended and he was navigating along a dirt roadway with more than a few ruts from the winter runoff. He followed the signs to Daicey Pond camping area, barely able to top twenty miles per hour on the washboard road. When he finally reached the campsite, he pulled off, getting a giggle from the sign warning that cell phones and two-way radios were banned in the park. The odds, he thought, of getting a cell signal out her had to be somewhere between slim and none.

"Wow," David said. "I've heard of getting away from it all, but I don't think anyone around here has even heard of 'it all.' What the heck could you call and tell someone about?"

Nate took a quick glance and after seeing or hearing not a single soul, declared it "perfect." It was so early in the season that no one appeared to be occupying any of the twenty or so rustic cabins scattered around the site. Nate dragged his gear out of the back of the vehicle and found the small cabin he had reserved for the night. David continued to marvel at how remote and barren the area was. Governor Baxter had insisted in buying and donating land for the park that it was to be kept forever remote and undeveloped, and David would have emphatically told the governor his wishes were still being honored. Still, even a jaded accountant had to admit that the sight of Katahdin rising and reflected in the still waters of Daicey Pond was worthy of any postcard.

The plan was relatively simple. The campsite was at the ten-mile mark on the AT, so Nate would drop all his gear except for a snack and water, spend the day hiking to the mountain's peak, and then follow the Appalachian Trail back down to the campsite and cook dinner. David chose to sleep most of the day, vowing he would never climb any mountain, much less one that rose thousands of feet in just a few miles. "I don't climb mountains unless I'm chased," he kept insisting.

Nate made sure he had laid out bags of potato chips, crackers and six cans of soda for David before striking out. He didn't want his friend rummaging through the expensive, freeze-dried food he had stocked up for the first leg of his hike. Given the park's remoteness, it was irreplaceable without a long drive back to Millinocket. Plus, he would have to endure an evening of complaints about the taste.

Cheetos and two-liter Pepsi in hand, David waved as Nate started down the trail.

"Bye, Grizzly Adams! Make sure you kill something delicious for dinner!"

Nate's first two minutes of solitude revalidated his decision to undertake the pilgrimage. The trail quickly led away from the campground and snaked its way along the shoreline of Daicey Pond. He could see the lake's placid, wide surface reflecting budding plants, evergreens and mountain peaks. As the trail slowly twisted away from the pond, it was quickly framed with tall birch and soft maples. None seemed wider than ten inches in diameter, and more than a few were laying on the ground or leaning askew, victims of previous years' winter storms.

After less than an hour, the trail met and followed part of the roadway Nate and David had driven on, before reaching another campground and then leaving the roadway yet again. This campground was called Katahdin Stream, a set of sites located closer to the peak. Initially, Nate had considered spending the night here, but feared the lean-to shelters were too rustic for a friend who considering "roughing it" to be staying at a Hampton Inn rather than a Hyatt.

After leaving the campsite and roadway, the climb intensified. The trail itself, which had begun as a finely groomed, three-foot-wide pathway through the woods, now was littered with three-foot to eight-foot-wide boulders, little gifts to hikers left 12,000 years ago when the last of the glaciers receded. Until now, the hike had been nothing more than a good stretch of the leg, but at this stage Nate began to breathe more heavily as he pushed himself forward and upward. Good grief, he thought. If this is getting tough for me with nothing but water on my belt and snacks in my pocket, what's going to happen when I'm carrying forty-five pounds on my back?

Katahdin always gives something to its visitors, and right now it was giving Nate doubts. Doubts about his abilities, doubts about his plan that had seemed so logical just five miles ago along Daicey Pond. Climbing Katahdin demanded a healthy dose of trepidation. Unlike hiking in more developed and tourist-friendly areas, hikers occasionally died trying to reach the mountain's peak. It was not by accident that each hiker trying to summit Kathadin had to register before heading above the tree line. If someone didn't come down, the rangers wanted to know whose name to call out during the search – or the name of the body they might find later. Hiking in April was rare – normally the park did not even open until May 15. Had the state not opted to open the park early due to an extremely mild winter and early spring, Nate would be breaking the law hiking to the peak this early. Most southbound through-hikers – those hiking the Appalachian Trail in one continuous trek – waited until June to begin. Nate hoped his early departure and choice of the less-popular southbound direction would mean fewer people joining him along the route.

Each day at 7 a.m. the rangers would determine the level of danger in trying to climb the mountain. Their class system had four levels, clearly posted at the trailhead:

> Class 1 – Open. Weather conditions favorable for day use and climbing.
> Class 2 – Open but not recommended for climbing.
>   Weather conditions favorable but changing.
> Class 3 – Open but not recommended; one or more trails closed,
>   trails closed to be named by Ranger
>   when setting the class day.
> Class 4 – Mandatory closure of all trails at the trailheads.

Even in May and June, Class 3 and 4 days were the most common, but when signing in, Nate noted today would be a Class 2 day. As he slowly climbed his way above the tree line, he wondered what the changing conditions might be, and why he hadn't bothered to ask. He scanned the sky as he reached a clearing and saw no indication of gathering clouds or other dangers. He pushed on, noticing the trees themselves were adjusting to the altitude changes. The deciduous trees, still three weeks or more from budding their leaves, had vanished and were replaced almost exclusively by firs, which were themselves thinning out as the soil vanished and nothing more than rock and hardscrabble gathered underfoot. Quickly, hiking had ended and climbing began. Sections of the trail went from a two-percent grade to a 40-degree scramble over individual rocks and boulders. The trail, which earlier had followed Katahdin Stream and even presented a scenic twenty-foot waterfall along its path, now had left the stream and had grown increasingly barren. The last five miles to the top would rise from 1,000 feet above sea level to 5,267 feet. By 3,500 feet, the trees had vanished.

After one agonizing two-hundred-yard section of climbing, Nate stopped to swig some water and looked to his left to see a craggy peak 500 yards away. This was The Owl, he knew, and was an indication that he wasn't far from Katahdin's peak. No longer protected by trees, and now at serious elevation, he shivered. The temperature had dropped dramatically, he finally noticed, and the winds had arrived with authority. He had prepared for cool weather but not for the sudden blast of cold winds quickly chilling him. His choice to wear only light hiking pants and not heavier ones was now evolving from a dumb decision to a potentially fatal one. Moving was a better choice than standing still, so Nate quickly began climbing again along the spine of the ridge. He was walking up one of three ridge lines that met at the top to form Katahdin's peak. The other two were more prominent and had earned the nickname "Knife Edge." As he surveyed this, Nate wheeled to take in the panorama and finally saw the clouds he had been looking for. Except they weren't in the sky. They were below him. They had been gathering 500 to 800 feet below where he was standing. At first, he mistook them for simple fog, but the next time he turned and look, he quickly realized they were coalescing, clumping and darkening.

Katahdin's peak was close now. The hike now was little more than climbing a rock pile in a quarry. There were occasional green clumps of four-foot fir sprigs desperately wedging themselves between boulders, but this was now mountaineering, not walking, and the cool breeze was now cold, constant wind. Nate was shaking now, but he had no idea if it was exhaustion of his muscles or involuntary shivering from the cold. Keep moving, he told himself. People don't die if they're moving. The thought spurred him to climb, but it didn't reassure him. "Stupid, stupid, stupid," he said aloud to himself. Six months of hiking planned, and you're going to die of exposure on the first day. He scanned up and down the trail, trying to find another hiker. Earlier he had wished for solitude on the trail. Now he was wishing for another hiker to provide him a potential rescue should he need it – and it was rapidly starting to look like he might. It's there! I can see the top, he said to himself. It was still high up there, and still a good twenty minutes of climbing, but it was there. Do I turn around and head back to the tree line and shelter from the wind? I can go down faster than up. That makes sense. But I'm close! I've got to start this trip from the beginning. A pilgrimage has to start from the beginning. Can't desecrate this at the beginning. I made a vow. I made a promise in the night to their memory, he told himself.

Nate's thought processes were now breaking down. He was debating which way to turn, not realizing that his body had already made the decision for him as it continued to climb. Through inertia and habit, each knee bent and each booted foot planted itself a little higher and a little closer to the peak. His mind was skipping like a record, and minutes of his memory began disappearing. By the time Nate realized what was happening, he was within 100 yards of the summit. He blinked, turned to see the spot on the trail where his brain thought he was standing. It was easily 1,000 feet lower and more than a half-mile behind him. What happened? There's the top! Get there and then get down, he told his body, which was pleased to have his brain back for the last 300 steps of the trip. Now each step was punctuated with a shout as he exhaled the word with force. "I'm. Going. To. Do. This. I. Don't. Want. To. Die. Today!" As he shouted out "Today" he reached the top pile of boulders and saw the brown sign that marked the top of the peak. "KATAHDIN" the sign barked in thick, white-painted letters. "Northern Terminus of the Appalachian Trail."

The sign was the only thing Nate could see now. The clouds that had stalked him from below were now upon him, coating and saturating the mountaintop with moisture and obstructing all views. There would be no scenic vistas to take in. There was only a wall of gray, wet and cold. The fog of the mountaintop was replicated in his brain. It became even more difficult to make decisions. After an interminable delay, he finally realized he'd reached his objective and turned from the sign taking perhaps twenty steps before stopping again. When he had envisioned this pilgrimage months ago, he had planned to sit on top of the mountain, look southwest toward his eventual goal, as if he could see Georgia from Katahdin's 5,268-foot elevation and meditate on the events that had brought him here. That reflection would have to come later. He couldn't even pretend to see 2,000 miles over the horizon. He knew he was rapidly freezing to death, and his brain was beginning the process of shutting down, making meaningful reflection impossible. Now, a new concern arose. He had walked away from the sign, and realized he was standing amidst a rock pile with no idea which direction to walk. He knew that the trail ran along the spine in three directions, but in the fog of pending hypothermia, he was unsure which direction to walk. The Appalachian Trail is a well-marked trail, with white blazes, rectangles four inches wide by eight inches long painted on trees from Maine to Georgia, and these blazes were also painted on rocks. In the white cloud and fog, however, they were impossible to find.

Great, he thought. I'm trapped on a mountain. I'm going to die on this mountain before even starting down the trail. I work for a sporting goods company, and I'm going to die and become the biggest laughingstock in the history of hiking.

Nate sat down and pulled out the last of his water. He had brought two one-liter Nalgene bottles, but after a final swig both were now empty. He stared into the white milkiness of eternity and continued to shiver. His thoughts drifted off, occasionally focusing for brief moments on incidents from the past, only to be unable to hold the recollection for more than a second. Memories briefly appeared and then blew out into the haze in front of him. Finally, his mind was able to hold onto a single thought, a single memory. A forgotten song from his childhood. Now, as sections of his brain shut down, old sections rallied back into action, dredging up forgotten snippets of his youth. In the last stages of life, physicians report elderly patients often recover memories from childhood as the brain begins its decay and older, long-ago-used sections reactivate. Nate was experiencing a similar phenomena.

A song. An old, old song. It was from his childhood in the mountains, but it was far older than that. Where had he heard it? Was it a song his mother had sung? He remembered hearing a guitar accompanying the song, and no one in his family played a musical instrument. So where had he heard it? A fiddle. He remembered a fiddle, too. It was clearly a song he'd heard more than once, to remember it so clearly. The melody was simple, but relatively fast. The words. What were the words? Clouds. It involved clouds, because that's what had triggered the memory in the first place. Mountains. Clouds. How did it go?

Oh they tell me of a home where no storm clouds rise
Oh they tell me of a home far away

He couldn't remember the rest. He just knew he wanted to go where the storm clouds didn't rise. Storm clouds meant misery. He hated the storm clouds now, the storm clouds that blinded him and sapped his energy. Suddenly, his knees buckled and he found himself on all fours. The fog had gotten worse, and now the moisture from these low-hanging clouds was soaking him. There was no reason to pull out his rain gear – the water permeated the air. Every breath felt like a fifty-fifty mix of oxygen and water. He was swimming on top of the mountain, and he began to crawl along the rocks. He didn't feel like he could even pull himself to a standing position, so he didn't try. Like a Maine crab, he worked himself along the knife edge, focusing on small rocks and scraps of tiny trees jammed between them. Suddenly, he found something different. On one four-foot diameter light brown rock was covered with a patch of white. It wasn't natural. It was man-made, and his brain fired up long enough to realize it was a trail blaze. He continued to crawl, and after another 100 yards he saw another white rectangle painted on a large boulder. His arms and back were screaming in agony, and he painfully pulled himself erect. He looked down. He could still see the blaze. He looked around and saw that the clouds and fog were still thick, but visibility had improved to the point where he could see the six feet necessary to recognize blazes painted along the rocks. He picked up his pace slightly, continuing to walk at a safe clip to avoid tripping on the rocks, but eager to see another blaze. In a world of nature and certain death, the blazes were the only calling card of the man-made world, and he had determined that at least for now he wanted to be part of that world.

More blazes. His calves were starting to hurt now, and he realized it was because he was descending the mountain, and most of his weight was being carried by the backs of his legs as he worked his way down the trail. His pace was clearly faster on the descent, and he rapidly discovered the tiny tree sprigs growing in size. After another hour, he rejoined Katahdin Stream. He violated every backpacking rule he knew and drank the water from the stream untreated. The cold water chilled his insides, but he could feel the air temperature rise as he descended, and his rapid pace had helped to generate body heat. His brain was also picking up energy, and he began to realize how close to death he had come on top of Katahdin. He shivered, and for the first time it was an emotional rather than a physical reaction.

By the time he reached the trailhead check-in, he was in much better shape. He did his best to hide his shivering and paleness from the rangers, who were just happy that the one sole hiker who had ascended the mountain was now accounted for, so they wouldn't be making a call to Bangor for search teams.

By the time he reached the campsite, Nate had made dozens of resolutions to himself. He would always hike with more cold-weather gear than he needed. He would not take risks. He would carefully monitor any weather information available. All good precautions, but he knew there was one risk he was taking that he would not compromise on. He still planned to hike the trail alone, much more dangerous than hiking with a partner or in a group. He wanted nothing to do with people. This was to be a solo journey. He would not compromise on that point.

David was asleep in the cabin when Nate arrived around 4 p.m. Nate noted that his friend had heavily raided the stash of snack foods, desert cakes and sodas he had brought from Freeport. The junk-food frenzy apparently had forced David into the bunk for an hours-long sugar coma. Nate unrolled his sleeping bag and settled it on the bunk frame. He dug out two chemical heating pads, each three inches square, that, once opened, began generating heat that would keep Nate warm in his bag for up to eight hours. Nate slid into the bag without waking his friend and began quickly drifting off, even as the heat began to radiate along his feet and legs. He had done battle with the clouds and won, but he knew that Katahdin had almost been victorious. He had persevered only by determining that he had wanted – for now at least – to walk away from the stormclouds. His last conscious thought, as the sunset began washing through the trees outside the cabin, returned to the song from his childhood:

Oh they tell me of a home where no storm clouds rise
Oh they tell me of a home far away

Where did the song come from? He couldn't remember. Now exhausted but warm, however, he had recovered its second line:

Oh they tell me of a home far beyond the skies
Oh, they tell me of an unclouded day

And in that home, he slept

2
THE ONE HUNDRED MILES

"You promised me dinner."

Nate opened one eye and looked around, disoriented. His eye seemed to be coated with a film, and the cold air rushing over his eyeball only made the occlusion worse.

"I didn't get a dinner."

Dinner? What time was it? Nate saw light blaring in through the open cabin door, but it seemed the wrong color, and much brighter than it should be.

He returned to his inquisitor, by now realizing it was David, encased in a giant ski parka on the top half of his body, and nothing but long underwear below.

"I didn't hear you come back. I waited for a long while, and then I just ate some food I'd brought with me. I woke up about an hour ago and realized we'd both slept through the night."

David stared for a long moment, awaiting a response. Nate had none, as he was just now finally realizing it was morning, not evening.

"You promised me a dinner," David said one more time, adopting the tone of a spoiled child who didn't get cotton candy at the fair.

"OK, I've got that part," Nate finally croaked, shocked at how raspy his voice sounded. The cold overnight air had fogged his eyeballs and wrecked his voice. He was afraid to pull himself out of the sleeping bag to see what other tragedies nature had perpetrated on his body. "I can cook you breakfast. If you want, I'll cook you dinner for breakfast. If you're really hungry, I can cook you dinner and breakfast for breakfast. Your call."

David pondered this, scratching his tussled hair, which was

standing at attention after 14 hours of uninterrupted sleep. "Let's start with breakfast. But if I'm still hungry, I want dinner too."

Fortunately, after a large hot breakfast of eggs, bacon and hash-browned potatoes with a pot of night-black coffee, thoughts of a second meal vanished. This would be the last heavy meal Nate expected to eat. Everything in his backpack was dehydrated or freeze-dried. He had packed a second cooler of traditional (and thus heavy and perishable) foods to give the two of them a couple of final sendoff meals. He would send the leftovers, including the untouched food from the previous night's unprepared dinner, back in the car with his friend. Once on the trail, the eggs would be powdered and the bacon would be just a fond memory to trigger a Pavlovian response in his salivary glands. As breakfast progressed, Nate noted that the mood shifted as the moment of their departure neared. Joking conversation quickly ended, and an uncomfortable quiet descended on the campground, which was already eerily silent as no other campers were to be found in the two dozen or so cabins.

"So," David said, finally breaking the silence, "you're not going to go native on us and never return, are you?"

He had meant it as a joke, but David had quickly cut to the heart of the matter without realizing it. There was no planned return. Nate would not be bounding back into his office in Freeport with funny tales of blisters and bears. His house was closed up and utilities shut off. He had chosen to give away his car. Most of his retirement and savings were either stuffed in his left pocket or were within an ATM's swipe should he need it along the trail. This was a real goodbye, not an au revoir or see-you-soon. Only one of the two men sitting beside the small campfire knew it, though. Nate didn't want his last conversation with his best friend to be a bald-faced lie, so he quickly changed the subject.

"Listen, do me a favor and drive by my place every month or so," David said, giving the impression that he still had any interest in the building that had housed so much happiness and horror. "You don't need to go in, just make sure it hasn't burned down or anything. You know. Just a quick look."

"Sure. Anything else you need me to handle?" He knew Nate would have left nothing unplanned, so he understood the emptiness of his offer.

"No, everything's taken care of."

The silence returned. The campfire's small flames had now evaporated into small clouds of gray smoke that drifted up, changing direction and occasionally forcing one of the two men to shift their camp chair to avoid it.

"Look," David said, afraid to broach the subject, but feeling compelled by the agonizing silence that threatened to ruin their breakfast. "I know the last six months …" He stopped, unsure how to phrase the question in a way that wouldn't tear at the emotional stitches that were holding his best friend together.

"I know a lot of people think this hike and Marie are somehow linked, but they're not." Nate suddenly realized that despite his best efforts, he had indeed just lied to his friend. "I talked about doing this long before…" he let the second lie drift off, hoping that somehow it would not be as odious because he had left it unfinished. David misinterpreted the pain of lying to his friend as the pain of loss.

"Nate," he said, desperately seeking to escape from the awkwardness he had initiated. "Why don't you go ahead and get going? The sun's been up for more than an hour, and I can certainly clean this up and head back. Heck, I may just throw the pans in a garbage bag and run them through the dishwasher when I get back."

One of the pans was cast-iron, and Nate was about to explain what would happen if it was washed in a dishwasher, but he decided his friend's confusion and irritation after the fact would be a pleasant notion for him to enjoy along the trail, and so he said nothing.

The two stood and hugged briefly. Nate reached into the cabin and grabbed his backpack, and with some effort slung the heavy burden onto his back. He adjusted the shoulder straps as tight as they would go and then fastened the padded belt that wrapped and hugged his hips. He took one last survey of the campsite.

"You're sure you can get out OK?"

"Yeah. Just drive like you, but backwards and a lot faster."

"Sounds about right. I'll send you a postcard from somewhere."

"Make sure it has a picture of a pretty girl on it. And none of those granolas with foot-long armpit hair, please."

"I'll make sure they bathe before I take the picture."

With that, Nate gave his childhood friend a big hug. It was unexpected, and somewhat longer than David was comfortable with, but Nate had his reasons. Forty steps later, he spun and added an informal wave before turning and heading out of the campsite and down the trail.

The drive north had taken the Townsend family five days. Nate's father had wanted to make the entire trip in two, driving through the night and taking one- or two-hour naps only when needed. His wife, Sarah, however, had believed that the trip should be viewed as an educational opportunity for her son, who had never traveled more than ten miles from his birthplace on Roan Mountain. While Juter had plotted out the most direct route to Maine, his wife had scratched out his dark line on the Esso roadmaps he had collected and redrawn them with red ink, signifying the final route she expected him to adhere to, in her role as chief navigator of both the car and their family.

Coming down the mountain, Sarah cautioned Juter about his speed as a morning mist thickened.

"Juter, dear, be careful about the fog."

"Yes, honey," Juter agreed, then smiled. "It's so bad the birds are walking."

As they wheeled the battered Dodge Dart and trailer onto U.S. 19-E and pointed it northward, the family began unwrapping the breakfast that Nate's grandmother had prepared for them to eat on the drive. Nate quickly placed the napkin on top of his husky-size blue jeans, making sure the crumbs from the rapidly disintegrating biscuit fell into his lap and not onto the seat or floorboard of his father's car. While the car was weathered and battered, its inside was immaculate, and the family was trained to treat the plastic-covered upholstered bench seats like church pews. Nate watched the steam come off his biscuit as he peeled back the wax paper, soaking in the smell of his grandmother's art. Coupled with the scent of butter and bread was the freshly cooked salty country ham tucked between the biscuit's two halves. The car bumped briefly as it hit the Watauga River bridge in Elizabethton, and Nate had to reach his hand up to keep his food from flying into the air. The river flowed just below the Watauga Dam, finished more than a decade earlier. The Tennessee Valley Authority dam existed because then-President Franklin Roosevelt had read a story about a flash flood destroying much of Elizabethton.

Breakfast finished and all crumbs and wax paper safely secured in the plastic Piggly Wiggly bag brought along for the task, the car and trailer sliced their way through the mountain range that separated Elizabethton from the Holston River Valley. That valley would cut a diagonal northeasterly course to Bristol, and then up into Virginia. They stopped briefly in Bristol to pick up groceries, secured them in a green solid-metal Coleman cooler and then wheeled the car onto U.S. 11 for the trip out of Tennessee. There was no sign heralding their entry into Virginia. Either it had been vandalized or Nate simply didn't notice it. Since Bristol straddled the state line, it most likely was a small unobtrusive sign, easily missed. He could have been distracted when it passed, but given that his only distraction on the trip would be four stacks of books his mother had placed on the back seat with him for the journey, that seemed unlikely.

Virginia itself seemed no different to him. U.S. 11 gently weaved its way through a long, linear valley, with the Appalachians crowning up outside the left window, and the tops of the Blue Ridge bobbing and weaving their way up and down along the right. The names of the cities on the mileage signs – Abingdon, Wytheville, Roanoke – were like undiscovered countries to him, but he got to see little of their alien societies except through the car window, or on rare occasions exploring their gasoline station restrooms. Lunch was a beside-the-roadway experience, as his mother took the bread and lunchmeat from the Bristol stop and added her own homemade potato salad. They chewed quietly, sitting on top of a picnic table conveniently placed a hundred yards off the roadway. His father, constantly thinking like a plant manager, spent his lunchtime poring over the maps, looking at his two-dollar Timex wristwatch and calculating whether they were ahead of or behind schedule.

Sarah had no such concerns. She was busy explaining the geography and geology of the foothills and mountains to Nate, noting that the New River they were about to cross over was one of the few rivers in the world that ran south to north, and that it would soon be leaving this flat valley and cutting a swath through the rugged mountains of West Virginia hundreds of miles away.

By early afternoon, they had left U.S. 11 and turning east arrived at Appomattox Courthouse, and Nate received instruction on the end to the War Between the States. Sarah never used the term "Civil War." During her childhood, a teacher had pointed out that the term was an oxymoron. The topic of the War Between the States was a touchy one in the southern Appalachians. Where the South had almost unilaterally supported the Confederacy and the North was essentially pro-Union, families scattered along the spine of the Appalachian Mountains had been deeply divided a century ago. Most wanted to avoid the issue, in keeping with their longstanding Scotch-Irish desire simply to be left alone. Most of the residents were pro-Union, but being represented in Southern statehouses in Nashville, Raleigh, Columbia, Richmond and Milledgeville, their opinions carried little weight. Once the Confederacy became a reality, homegrown militias quickly cropped up, and families found themselves involved in brutal, bloody and costly insurrections that were anything but civil. Nate's ancestors had been caught up in such divisions. The battles of Chickamauga and Shiloh were large, noisy and spectacular, Sarah would explain, but they were ballroom dances compared with the brutality that took place in the hills and hollows of the Appalachians. Nate had ancestors who had joined both the Union and Confederate armies, Sarah explained. He had relatives who had hidden in caves to avoid being impressed into service for units they did not want to join. He had a great-uncle who had been shot in the back outside his home one night for his pro-Union stance, and one of his great-grandfathers might very well have been the pro-Confederate home guardsman who pulled the trigger. As a result, the war was rarely discussed in his household, and when mentioned at all, everyone employed euphemisms. His grandmother constantly referred to the War Between the States as "the recent unpleasantness."

Thus much of the information Nate was receiving off the National Park Service maps and his own mother's lectures was new to him, and the fact that he had never heard his mother speak so openly about the issue gave it all a sense of furtive secrecy and danger.

Appomattox itself was somewhat unimpressive. Designed to show the rustic style of houses and farm structures used in the 1860s, the buildings looked no different from any Nate had grown up around. One teenage girl from New Jersey with a Pepsi bottle in her hand was marveling out loud about the lack of plumbing in the houses, shocked that everyone had to go outside in the elements to go to the bathroom or collect water. Nate couldn't understand why this was so confusing to the girl.

The remainder of the day was spent driving northward through the center of Virginia, along two-lane serpentine roads that either allowed them to race at high speed as they bisected farms covered either by corn or cattle, or slowed them as they passed through the occasional one-traffic-light townships with bizarre names like Toga or Alpha, Arvonia and Dixie. In Dixie, they stopped at a roadside restaurant and shared a set of meals. His mother and he split an order of fried chicken, while his father pulverized an entire plate of country-fried steak. "Driving is hard work," Juter kept saying, right before shoveling another forkful of gravy-coated meat into his mouth. "Harder than a deaf man learning Latin."

Sarah finally managed to pry the road maps out of Juter's hands and studied them. "We're not that far now, Juter," she said, smiling as she kept her eyes focused on the road map. Nate kept looking at the map's cartoon tiger, unable to discern the secret behind the squiggly red and black lines. "Should we find a motel here or further north?"

"We may just stay in the car tonight." Juter's plan to save money was to minimize the number of nights spent in roadside motels, which he called "bedbug factories." His strategy was to alternate, spending one night sleeping in the car and then bedding down in a motel the second night. "Most people can go one day without a shower – few can go more than two" was his rationale.

Later that evening, Juter pulled the Dodge Dart off the side of Hwy 53 and into a field well off the roadway. He pulled a roll of electrical tape out of the trunk and began taping up the back lights of both the car and the trailer. Juter had read a story once about a family who had pulled off the side of the road in a fog, only to have another car plow into the back and kill everyone, the driver thinking he was following the car in front of him. Juter was determined to protect his family from a similar fate, and once done he even added a bit of insurance by taking a falling tree branch and laying it behind the trailer, partially camouflaging it from cars driving down the road.

After Sarah spread a wool blanket across the back seat of the Dodge, Nate settled in with a pillowcase filled with clothing as his pillow. He was so tired from the day's events that he quickly nodded off to sleep. Early the next morning, well before sunrise, he awoke confused and disoriented, taking several moments before realizing why he was spread across the back seat of his father's car. He listened in the darkness to Juter's snoring and rose just enough to see that his father was sleeping slumped against the driver's side door with Sarah pressed against him, her long legs stretching across the width of the car to the passenger-side door.

Nate needed to go to the bathroom, but he didn't want to wake either of his parents. He pulled down on the stainless steel door handle, moving it as slowly as an ant crawled so as not to make a loud sound when it disengaged the door lock. He pushed the door open, glad that there was no squeaking of hinges. There was no dome light to illuminate, and for that Nate was grateful. He carefully closed the door and then struck out a hundred yards away from the roadway toward the tree line. When he reached the woods, he carefully worked his way down a slight slope. It was darker here, and he didn't have as much moonlight to help him find his way. He quickly relieved himself and then looked around. Just a little further down the slope, the tree line ended, and Nate thought he saw a small building beyond the branches. He carefully stepped in that direction and cleared the second tree line to see a huge pasture of rolling and waving grass, gradually rising toward the base of a tree-lined mountain no more than three hundred yards away. In the middle of the pasture was a very small brick structure, no more than ten feet square, whose purpose Nate couldn't discern. He looked back in the direction of the tree line and the car beyond it, and then struck out slowly toward the structure.

This was always a beautiful time for Nate. While many children enjoyed sleeping late or feared the dark, early-morning hours that signified the last moments of night always held a special magic for him. They were quiet. They were solitary. Nate could imagine he was the only living person in the world as he stared out at the empty world, laid out and painted with moonlight just for him. His father had taken him hunting for possums several times during the past year. Nate didn't enjoy shooting at the nocturnal creatures, because they shared his love of the late night and early morning. He had enjoyed the time of day, however, and the chance to share it with his father, whom he adored.

Even after reaching the brick structure, Nate still couldn't figure out its use. Only after prying open the two-foot-tall door on its back side did he realize it was a spring house, a structure used to protect a well that had been dug to provide fresh water. He had seen spring houses, of course, but never one built so formally, as if the water itself deserved its own mansion. He surveyed the field around him, looking at how the moonlight danced off the ridges and ripples of grass. He lay down on the ground and took in the pinpoints of light above him, matching up clusters of stars into the constellations his mother had taught him. Orion. Ursa Major. Virgo. Gemini.

"What are ya doing here?" a deep bass voice boomed out, startling Nate and causing him to leap to his feet instantly. Nate found himself dwarfed by a six-foot-four tower of a man who was almost invisible to him due to his blackness. His face and hands were dark, making it impossible to discern any of his features. Likewise, he was wearing a black woolen jacket over a dark shirt and work pants that were at the very least deep brown. The man could have just stumbled upon Nate, or been watching him for the past twenty minutes. There was no way of knowing. His natural camouflage, coupled with his attire, made him imperceptible.

In taking the time to size up this specter, Nate suddenly realized he hadn't answered the giant's question. What was the answer? That he had to take a leak? No, that wasn't what he wanted to say to a stranger, especially one that looked like he could crush him between his thumb and forefinger. That he was out for a walk? That was better, but presented more questions than it answered. Nate decided for a more truthful, if less plausible answer.

"I was just looking at how pretty it is."

For the giant, it was an unexpected answer, especially coming from an eight-year-old boy. He studied the boy's face for signs of deception but found none. He made sure he hadn't misjudged the age of the boy – he had certainly miscalculated his maturity, but he came away uncertain. The boy had spoken a kindred language to him, and the giant man decided to respond in that tongue of nature.

"Pretty? It's that. But it's more."

Nate took this in. It was certainly one of the most adult conversations he'd ever participated in. But what did it all mean?

"Where is this place?" It was a stupid and ill-structured question, and Nate knew this when he uttered it. But it was out there.

"It's a special place. But first of all, where'd you comes from? Do you live nears here? Where is your house?"

Nate didn't want to tell the giant of his parents or their car parked on the side of the road less than a mile away. He wasn't sure they weren't trespassing, and he didn't want to get his parents in trouble with someone this large and forbidding.

"My house is a long way from here. In Tennessee."

"You lost?"

Nate surveyed the fields, the moonlight, and the gently curving mountain ridges. "No, I'm just wandering."

"There's an old sayin': Not all those who wander is lost," the giant said, then smiled, flashing Nate the first part of his body to reflect moonlight – his giant smile. "Let me show's you around, then when the sun comes up we can figure out where you needs to be."

They began walking slowly up the rolling hills toward the curved mountaintop, and as they walked the giant talked as he kept an eye on his new tiny charge.

"My name's Eston King," the giant began. "I work here at this plantation as the night groundskeeper. It's more of a watchman's job than a groundskeeper, but I am supposed to keep all the night critters from doing damage to the house and the farm. It's a very busy house and we get lots of visitors during the day, but most of what I do is during the night when it's nice and quiet."

"I like to be out at night when it's quiet and you can be by yourself, too," Nate volunteered, hoping to build a rapport with this giant named Eston. By now, Nate had realized that Eston was no giant, just a very tall man. Never leaving the hollows of the Tennessee mountains, Eston was the first black man he had ever met, and he seemed foreign, unusual and slightly frightening to the young boy. While slaves had been common in the deep South, very few in the Appalachians had owned them, and thus the black population of the rural mountains was small. But the more Eston talked, the less frightening and friendlier he became.

"Yes," Eston replied. "I prefers being alone to being around lots of people. Especially around here. Most of the time when people talks to me, they's tellin' me to do something. So being alone in the quiet and dark is much better."

The two had now reached the tree line at the base of the mountain, and Nate didn't even hesitate walking into the shadowy undergrowth with Eston, their connection of friendship being constructed of a joint love of solitude. After five more minutes of uphill walking, they arrived at a small cemetery with a metal fence surrounding it. There were a variety of tombstones, but one at the far west end of the cemetery stood out. They walked around the fence and stopped in front of it. Along with a large slab with words carved into it, there was a fifteen-foot obelisk on top of the structure that made it tower above the other markers in the cemetery. Nate tried to read the words on the slab through the metal gate, but there was not enough moonlight to read the name, the dates or the other words carved below them.

Eston watched Nate peering through the slats in the fence, and supplied some answers.

"This is an ancestor of mine. In fact, he's the only ancestor of mine buried here. They won't let us bury any other ancestors in here. We have to bury our folks somewhere else. But this was the big man of the house. Very powerful. Very rich. Leastwise, everyone here thought he was til he died. Then we found out otherwise. They sold everybody and everything off after he died and it took a long time to get it all back."

"Was he your grandpa?"

"No, lordy no. We're talking a long time before that. I'm not even sure. Maybe my grandpa's grandpa. But I knows we's related. My mother made sure I knew that. But I'm not allowed to tell anybody here that. They don't want to think that people like me could be related to the man of the house."

Nate wasn't sure what Eston meant by "people like me." Was he talking about giant people? Black people?

"Come on, I'll show you his house."

They walked further up to the top of the mountain, which suddenly shed its deep tree growth at the top and exposed a giant, green lawn and large, brick and glass house that saddled the mountain's top. It was the largest and prettiest house Nate had seen in his life to that point, and it was certainly the most unique, with sections that were both square, round and other strange shapes, with odd corners. It seemed to point north, and provided a clear view of a small town at the bottom of the mountain, and various farms scattered in all directions. The lights of the town were still flickering in the night sky, but the warming light of an impending dawn was beginning to illuminate the farms.

"I can'ts let you go inside, but I thought you'd like the view."

The view was impressive. It quickly cemented an opinion

Nate had held since his early childhood on Roan Mountain: An unobscured view from above brings clarity. To understand what's happening around you, and to understand yourself, a mountaintop provides vision and understanding. Whenever he had wanted to ponder a difficult moment in his life, a hike to the balds above his parent's cabin had given him time to think. Here, watching life slowly start to move on dozens of tiny farms below him, standing next to Eston, he understood that his love of solitude was not unnatural, that it was shared by others. Like him, others appreciated the insight and understanding that came from being above everything else.

Off in the distance, the rumble of car wheels brought him back to the present, and as the sound increased, Eston turned to him.

"Now it's time to figure out where you belongs," he said, smiling downward at the boy. "That's the overseer coming up the road. He'll help us gets you back. One thing, though. Don't tells him what I said about the man of the house and me. As I tolds you, they won't like it."

Nate promised as the white Chevrolet truck cleared the tree line and pulled up next to the house.

The overseer was an overweight, short white man with jowly cheeks and a Camel cigarette tucked in his mouth, dangling out the right side. He exited the truck with some difficulty, walked up to Eston and then surveyed Nate.

"Friend of yours, Eston?"

"Well sir, Mr. Todd, at first he was just a lost little boy, buts now we's seems to be gettin' on jus fine." Nate couldn't help but notice that Eston's grammar had gotten worse, and his tone was much less self-assured, more deferential, even slightly timid. He couldn't figure out why this small man had made such a change in the giant.

"Where'd you find him? Does he have a name?"

"I founds him down by the highway, and he says his name be Nate. I asked him where he lived, and he be telling' me he's from Tennessee."

"Hmm. Tourist. Son, do you know where your folks are at?"

Nate figured trespassing or no, a direct answer was called for. If Eston was afraid of this man, perhaps he should be, too.

"Yes sir," he said. "I can show you if we walk back down the mountain." He managed to avoid, for now, telling about his parents' car.

"Well then, Eston, why don't you walk him back down and reunite him with his folks. If you don't find them, bring him back and we'll call the authorities." The pudgy man thought about providing a long lecture about separating from your parents, but decided he had too much to do this morning and kept it short. "Shouldn't ever wander off," he pontificated. "Nothing good ever comes of it."

Nate and Eston cut a glance at each other, sharing a slight smile at Mr. Todd's apostasy. Nate managed a "yes sir" before they turned and started back down the mountain.

They finished the hike back to Nate's car in silence, both enjoying the quiet of the early morning and the sound of birds waking and squirrels rustling the branches overhead as they leapt from one tree to another. When they reached the final tree line, Nate could see that both of his parents were still fast asleep in the front seat.

"My folks are there," Nate said, pointing to the two unconscious figures in the front seat.

"Is they ... alive?" Eston asked. "They's wasn't in no accident, was they?"

"Oh no, no, no. They're just sleeping. We were sleeping in the car." Nate paused. "Do you have to wake them and tell them I wandered off?"

Eston thought for a moment and decided he didn't want to talk to any more white people than he had to. "No, I guess not." He shook Nate's hand and then gestured for him to walk back to his car.

"Don't pays no attention to Mr. Todd, now," he said as Nate began walking. You and I, we're part of the wandering brotherhood. Don't never be afraid of it."

Compared to the climb to the top of Katahdin, the first 11 miles of trail heading southbound were nothing more than a leisurely stroll. Nate found himself enjoying the walk, with gentle inclines, but mostly modest downhill stretches. For a while, he paralleled a small stream with the huge name Nesowadnehunk Creek, but it eventually left him. Toward the end of the day, after crossing two other small streams, he reached Abol Stream, which signified he was leaving the environs of Baxter State Park. Shortly thereafter, he came to a main road and a small grocery store.

This was Abol Bridge, a major crossing point for the trail. It marked the beginning of The One Hundred Miles, the longest, most remote section of the trail. For eight to ten days, there would be no road crossings, no small stores and no major campgrounds. For southbounders, Abol Bridge was where you loaded up with food – there would be none available for more than a week. You made sure you had first-aid supplies, because if something happened there was no one to help you out – indeed, there was no way anyone would know where you were. The Appalachian Trail was by its nature a remote passageway, but the truth was you were rarely more than a day's hike from a roadway where you might flag down help. The One Hundred Miles, by comparison, was pure solitude, pure joy and pure danger. Hiking alone, as Nate was, amplified that danger. Fracture a leg, especially this early in the season, and you'd have to drag your body one hundred miles down a rocky trail or die.

The Maine Appalachian Trail Club, which maintained the entire AT in the state, had erected a greeting for those hikers approaching The One Hundred Miles. The sign did its best to dissuade unskilled hikers, and then capped itself off with a cheery sendoff:

> IT IS 100 MILES SOUTH TO THE NEAREST TOWN AT MONSON. THERE ARE NO PLACES TO OBTAIN SUPPLIES OR HELP UNTIL MONSON. DO NOT ATTEMPT THIS SECTION UNLESS YOU HAVE A MINIMUM OF 10 DAYS SUPPLIES AND ARE FULLY EQUIPPED. THIS IS THE LONGEST WILDERNESS SECTION OF THE ENTIRE A.T. AND ITS DIFFICULTY SHOULD NOT BE UNDERESTIMATED.
> GOOD HIKING!
> MATC

The store at Abot Bridge always did a brisk business. Either the hikers who came in were southbounders like Nate who loaded up fearing they would perish in The One Hundred Miles, or they were ravenous northbounders, who in the fall would emerge from the wilderness starving or simply hungry for something not freeze-dried, like a hamburger or steak.

After loading up on more freeze-dried packets, Nate walked the short distance to the campsite, paid his fee and pitched his tent.

This was the first time he had put up the tent, and he was thankful that he'd arrived before nightfall. Tents erected in the dark always looked pitiful compared with those put up in the daytime, and Nate had time to make sure he had hammered in all of his stakes at a proper distance to ensure taught guy lines. He scanned the campsite for other tents and smiled as he saw none. He unwrapped and ate the two hamburgers he'd picked up from the store and then tossed his garbage into a nearby trash can, washed his hands in a nearby stream bed and settled into his tent for the night. The ground was hard, and the egg-carton-shaped pad between his sleeping bag and the tent floor wasn't providing anywhere near the comfort he was seeking. Well, he thought, maybe after a few days it will feel better. The sun was just beginning to set, but Nate could already feel the temperatures dropping. The sound of the nearby river he would cross tomorrow was rushing through the trees, and it provided an enjoyable lullaby as Nate drifted off to sleep.

The next morning, Nate rose at first light, quickly rolling up his sleeping bag and pad. He rolled up his tent and packed it away. He pulled out his new camp stove and attempted to attach it to the silver fuel canister. After four false starts, he finally threaded the screws properly and twisted the stove on. He opened the fuel line and clicked the button that sparked and then fired up the stove. It sounded initially like a rocket engine to Nate, and he set it on the ground and placed a small metal pot filled with stream water on top. While he waited for the water to boil, he surveyed the campground. None of the deciduous trees had greened yet, and so he was able to see a good distance, all the way back toward the grocery and ahead toward the bridge over the river he had heard the previous night. The water quickly boiled, and Nate measured it out in a flat, metal cup and then poured it into the plastic bag that held his dehydrated eggs with bacon chips. He sealed the bag, shook it vigorously to ensure all the bizarre yellow-and-brown mixture was coated, and looked at his watch to time the "cooking." After the required four minutes, he opened up the bag, plunged a plastic spoon inside and took his first taste of backpacking food.

He immediately wondered what time the grocery opened, and if they would laugh at him for ordering a hamburger for breakfast.

It was not that the food tasted bad. It was that there was so little taste at all. The photograph on the outside of the package promised a bacon-and-egg omelet that would rival any provided at the finest hotels in Boston. It was the disconnect between what Nate's brain had been conditioned to expect and what his taste buds were registering that made him think about hamburger breakfasts and dinners. As he chewed, he began to manage his expectations more effectively, and by the time he finished the meal he decided the eggs, while slightly gritty, were perfectly acceptable, and the small chips of bacon were little bonus buds of flavor that he hunted out with his spoon.

After washing off his spoon – the convenient thing about backpacking cooking is that only one implement, the spoon, needs to be washed – Nate disposed of his trash, packed everything away and hoisted his pack onto his back. The added weight of ten days of food immediately bent his shoulders and knees, and he struggled to right himself. He pointed himself toward the sound of the river and moved out.

Abol Bridge, a narrow structure with separate, dedicated lanes to separate the hikers from the massive, rumbling lumber trucks, crosses the west branch of the Penobscott River. Despite the distance, Nate could clearly still see Kathadin's peak reflected in the river's surface. The Penobscott is a welcome sound to northbounders fleeing The One Hundred Miles wilderness, but to southbounders it is a fond farewell to civilization. The entire area of The One Hundred Miles – indeed most of this section of Maine – had been devoted to logging during the past two hundred years. Much of the nation's lumber during the nineteenth century had come from this section of Maine, with loggers cutting the giant timbers down with nothing but axes and hand saws, and floating them down the Penobscott to waiting lumber mills downstream. While logging continued to be a major industry in the area, timber management policies minimized the clear-cutting that had initially decimated the forests in the 1870s and 1880s.

Nate didn't dread The One Hundred Miles – he had done his research and planning – but his encounter with Katahdin made him wary. Sure, he had planned, but had he fully understood what was needed to survive The One Hundred Miles? In a little over a week, he'd know.

For now, he was a southbounder. And he was wandering.

The first day's hike had been a downhill stroll. The second day began as a modest climb until midday, when Nate ran straight into the Rainbow Ledges, a twin-peaked mountain that began to wreck the muscles inside his calves and thighs. He was pushing his 205-pound frame up the incline, along with more than fifty pounds of backpack and equipment. At first, he began to slow as his muscles revolted. Then, finally, he was taking a single step and then stopping, trying desperately to catch his breath. He would hold in place for a minute and then start walking again only to find that after a few steps he had to stop. It took him more than two hours to climb the two miles to the top, and he was so exhausted he didn't even notice that back over his shoulder was another stunning view of Katahdin. He was no longer a hiker and a wanderer. He was simply a beast of burden. The only joy was that he now had a downhill stretch that would lead to a shiny, blue Rainbow Lake.

The downhill stretch was no better, however. While his calves and thighs were tortured on the uphill climb, now his knees were screaming as the entire force of his pack's weight was jammed onto his joints as he stepped down the rocky side of Rainbow Ledges toward the lake. By the time he'd reached the lake, he knew he was done. He had only hiked eight miles, and the campsite he had planned to sleep at was more than three miles away, but he could walk no further. He dropped his pack in a clearing near the trail and collapsed on the ground. He would camp here tonight and ponder his inauspicious start to The One Hundred Miles. It was his first day, and he was already behind schedule.

The next day brought less-challenging terrain, but the damage done to his legs and the continued weight of his overstuffed pack made it just as painful. The scenery – the trail wrapped around Rainbow Lake for most of the day – was stunning, but Nate couldn't appreciate much of it. The sun was bearing down on him, and it wasn't until late in the day – too late, unfortunately – that he realized he hadn't packed any sunscreen. He quickly pulled a shirt from his pack and rigged it to cover the top of his head and the back of his neck, but before long he knew the damage had been done. By the end of the day, he had hiked only another eight miles, and settled into a lean-to at the edge of the lake. He had planned to hike a minimum of ten miles a day and had been hopeful he could do twelve or fourteen. Completing only eight miles a day meant he would run out of food long before he exited The One Hundred Miles. He pulled out his maps and began calculating how he could get back on schedule, or failing that, how he could make sure that his food lasted until he could escape the wilderness. He briefly considered turning back, knowing that he was just two days from a fresh hamburger, but the thought of re-climbing Rainbow Ledge had no appeal for him.

The next day, Nate found himself climbing yet another steep mountain, this one called Nesuntabunt. Like before, he staggered under the weight of his equipment, and his climb was tedious and slow. He stopped every 100 yards. Frustrated, he began yelling at himself and grunting as he took every step. "Why is this so difficult? Am I in such bad shape? Go! Climb! Climb!"

As before, once he got to the bottom, he was walking along another lake. He checked his map in the late afternoon, and continued walking until dark, trying to catch up on his timetable. Finally, he stopped and checked his map. He had managed ten miles, but was falling further and further behind. He was still seventy-four miles away from getting out, with just seven days of food and plenty of mountains still ahead of him. He was less than a mile from a lean-to shelter, according to the map, so he dug the headlamp flashlight out of his pack, strapped it to his head, and continued in the growing darkness down the trail.

Arriving at the shelter, he dropped his pack. A quick inspection showed the shelter was littered with droppings from some small animal, and so Nate quickly dug out his tent. Even with the lack of light, he was able to erect it with more ease than he had the day before. He dug out some dried beef jerky and decided to make that his dinner, refraining from the formality of boiling water and cooking something freeze-dried. He pulled the map again from the plastic bag that protected it from the elements and studied it. Monson, Maine, was the end of The One Hundred Miles. It could have been the Sea of Tranquility on the moon considering how much map there was between it and Nate's shelter.

Running out of food was a big concern, but fortunately water was not an issue. The cornucopia of lakes he was passing provided plenty of fresh water, and Nate had two ways to purify it – either by using his hand-pumped filter, or by simply plunking an iodine tablet into his one-liter water bottle. The latter was easier, but gave the water a slightly brown coloring that looked distasteful but had no effect on the flavor. Nate rationalized that running out of food a day early, while certainly not ideal, would not be fatal. Running out of water, however, was not recommended. The rule of threes suggests that a human being can't live more than three minutes without air, three hours in the cold without shelter, three days without water, and three weeks without food. Nate had no desire to test any of these theories. He took out a pencil and circled all the water sources between his shelter and Monson, committing them to memory so he wouldn't get caught short.

The next morning, two days of hiking in open sunlight had finally caught up with him, and his skin felt hard and raw as the sunburned flesh took on the texture of his jerky. The tops of his ears were the worst, but his forehead, cheeks and the back of his neck were also blistered and screaming in pain. While boiling the water for his instant coffee, he rummaged through his backpack and looked for something he could use as a hat. He took a long-sleeved shirt and wrapped it around his head, tying off the sleeves so that the shirt covered his ears and dangled over the back of his head to shade his neck.

For the next four days, the routine varied little. The uphill sections continued to terrorize his back and leg muscles, although he noticed it was taking less time to reach the top of the peaks. Was this because the peaks were smaller? Was he acclimating to the trail? Or was it because every day there was slightly less food in his pack? He didn't know, but each night he popped three ibuprofen tablets so he could drift off to sleep without thinking of the pain he felt in his legs and back.

Most nights, he had slept inside the lean-to shelters scattered every ten miles or so along the trail. Most had names designating where they were located – Wadleigh Stream, East Branch – but occasionally he would come across a named shelter. Who the heck was Carl A. Newhall, and why did he merit a memorial shelter, he wondered.

On the tenth day, as predicted, his food ran out. He had tried to ration out the food to stretch an additional day or two, but his hunger each day after ten to twelve hours of hiking was as demanding as an irate boss, and he honored its power by eating a full meal. Tonight was no different, so he took the last bag of dehydrated beef stew and wolfed it down. Cleanup, as usual, took less than a minute, and after stashing his gear inside the lean-to, he sat in the dark staring at the modest four-stick campfire he'd built.

At this point, he thought starvation was the only challenge he faced. Suddenly, a voice out of the dark enlightened him.

"Ya stink!"

3
A VOICE IN THE KNIGHT

After almost two weeks of silence and solitude, the voice startled Nate, and he fell off the rock he was sitting on. The light of the modest campfire made it impossible to see into the night, and he squinted and craned his neck, trying to spot where the speaker stood. The voice again barked, clearly a man's voice, as it noted "I mean, I could smell ya half a mile before I got here."

This was something David would say, but there was no way his friend could have made it to this campsite, even if he had followed one of the rare gravel logging roads that cobwebbed the area. The voice was lower, and seemed scratchier than his snarky friend.

"I don't mean to be rude, but I figured ya'd want to know." The voice was getting closer now, and Nate considered whether he should take steps to protect himself. He had no weapons, and his pocket knife would hardly ward off a charging man or animal. He stood, but was still unable to see the source of the disembodied voice.

"You're the first backpacker I've met with this year," the scratchy voice said, as Nate began to see a wispy figure materialize along the side trail he had used to enter the campsite only an hour earlier. Finally the voice provided a body to accompany it, a rail-thin man wearing a traditional red-and-black plaid wool shirt and green full-length pants. He wore round-rimmed metal-frame glasses and clearly was in his late fifties, two factors that led Nate to abandon thoughts of self-defense or flight. The figure loosened his left backpack strap and let the weight roll off his back with a smooth motion that indicated he'd done it thousands of times before. Nate couldn't help noticing the pack was easily one-fifth the size of his orange monstrosity. The man instantly imparted an air of sartorial breeding that stood in stark contrast to the remote wilderness location.

"I'm sorry, I should have given ya more heads-up that I was coming down the trail." He smiled as he searched the campfire's perimeter and found an acceptable rock to serve as a seat. "I'm Kenneth Knight," he said, grinning widely. He didn't offer his hand, either because he thought it unnecessary or the odor he had alluded to made him want to keep his distance. "I work for the timber company that owns much of the land on either side of the trail. Well, in point of fact, I'm part of the family that owns it."

"Nate. Nate Townsend. I'm from Freeport, and as you figured out, I'm hiking the trail."

"Through-hiker or just section-hiking?"

The question was an instant litmus test of the seriousness of Nate's venture, and one he would come across each time he met someone along the trail. Section hikers attempted to complete the trail's 2,100 miles one section at a time, hiking for a few days and clicking off anywhere from ten to fifty miles before returning to their normal lives. Some section hikers took decades to finish the entire trail, while others took several weeks each year to knock off larger sections of the trail. While anyone hiking the trail was respected, the fraternity of through-hikers who attempted the entire Maine-to-Georgia or Georgia-to-Maine journey in one continuous effort were considered hiking's nobility.

"Through. Started at Katahdin about twelve days ago."

"Obviously haven't taken a swim in any of the lakes since then," Kenneth said with an even-wider grin.

"Too cold. In too much of a hurry."

"Do ya like looking at wildlife?"

"Sure"

"Bet ya haven't see much on the trail, have ya?"

"No," Nate admitted, not having considered the matter. "Too early in the season?"

"No," Kenneth laughed. "It's because they smell ya coming!" He giggled an high-pitched machine-gun giggle, clearly amused with himself.

The commentary was quickly crossing from a good laugh into being downright insulting, Nate thought. Sensing this change in mood, Kenneth quickly backtracked a bit.

"I don't mean to tease ya about that. It's just when you're out here alone for a while, ya don't realize how important hygiene becomes. It can affect your health. Here's a tip: It'll also affect whether ya can get someone to drive ya into town when the trail crosses a main road."

"So you seem pretty dainty," Nate said, trying to find something to needle his visitor with. "Are you bathing every night in the lakes, or do you carry a portable shower with you?"

"Actually, I just got dropped off this morning," Kenneth replied, oblivious to Nate's effort to suggest effeminacy. "I do little one- and two-day surveys of our holdings all along here. I take a spray-paint can and mark deadfall or other trees that need to be cleared for our crews. I was dropped off along one of the logging road crossings earlier today. I'll spend the night here and then get picked up tomorrow in Monson."

Monson! It was a just one day away? Nate had calculated that it was two full days away on his map. Now this stranger was telling him he could have a shower and hot meal by tomorrow.

"How many miles is it from here? I calculated it was around twenty to twenty-two."

"It is. It's twenty-one to be exact."

"So you'll do twenty-one miles in a day?" Nate was incredulous.

"Most of a day."

"That's impressive. I'm hoping to work up to that, but I'm not there yet."

"Well, if it's taken ya almost two weeks to get here from Katahdin, you're certainly not there yet."

Now Nate was becoming annoyed. Kenneth Knight clearly had a superiority complex, and physical prowess and family fortune be damned, Nate wasn't going to tolerate it.

"Well, I'm carrying a little more weight than you are."

"I can see that. Are ya going to be one of those hikers holding a garage sale at Monson?"

"Excuse me?"

"Happens every year. Hikers start out at the northern end of the trail. Make their way through the One Hundred Miles wilderness. By the time they get to Monson they either quit or realize they don't need the overpriced, expensive and heavy gear they've lugged through The One Hundred Miles. I have a friend who owns a consignment sporting goods store in Bangor who sends a kid up here every June to buy people's castoff gear at ten cents on the dollar. Makes a killing. Surely you've found some equipment you're tired of lugging up and down the MUDs."

"MUDs?"

"Mindless Ups and Downs. Hiker lingo."

Nate did a quick mental inventory of the contents of his backpack, and admitted to himself that he had far too many clothes for the trip. He had packed five of everything – shirts, pants, socks – and except for the socks, he had realized that he could easily rinse out the previous day's clothes in a stream and make do with only two sets of clothes. Likewise, he was carrying a $300 GPS unit that was of little use because the maps and trail signage gave him a good indication of where he was – and where he wasn't.

"My sporting goods friend always says 'when it comes to taking weight off a pack, just whittle off the ounces and the pounds will take care of themselves.'" Knight went on to explain, as if Nate was incapable of discerning the obvious message. "If ya can get rid of four small things that weigh four ounces each, suddenly you've taken a whole pound off your back."

Nate continued to bristle at the condescending tone, but since it was likely he would be sharing a campsite with this professor of packing, he decided to let it lie. Unfortunately, just as nature abhors a vacuum, Kenneth Knight abhorred silence and did his best to fill it.

"Give ya an illustration," he said, pulling out a clear piece of plastic from his knapsack and them dumping the pack's contents on top of it. Nate craned closer to see what had spilled out in the campfire's slowly dimming light. Kenneth began picking up items at random, displaying them as if they were treasured artifacts from an archeological dig. He waved what looked like half a toothbrush in the air. "This toothbrush, for example. I sawed off the bottom half of the handle. Why carry the extra ounce when I can still brush my teeth with just a two-inch handle?" Next he pulled out what looked like a white biscuit. "These crackers have tons of protein, but they weigh far less than any camp food. I get more energy for less ounces that way." He rummaged through his gear, and Nate began noticing what was missing rather than what was splayed across the plastic.

"Where's your sleeping bag?"

"Don't have one." Kenneth grinned again. "I have this thin quilt-like blanket. Filled with nothing but down. Very, very light, but it insulates great. I just wrap myself in it at night, and if I get cold hiking I can just drape it over my shoulders."

"What about a tent? Do you stay just in the shelters?"

"Yeah, I try to, but sometimes in the late summer they're filled up. You're looking at my tent. It has all my gear on it."

"That thin piece of plastic?"

"Yep. Just run a string between two trees. Then put a small rock in each of the corners and wrap string around them and then tie them off and stake them. Ya've got a nice pup tent that'll keep ya dry if it rains. If it doesn't rain, I prefer sleeping under the stars."

Nate was calculating the difference between a six-ounce piece of plastic and the eight-pound tent he had carried for days up 2,000- to 4,000-foot climbs. Kenneth was annoying to listen to, but regardless of how sourly his words were seasoned, they were edible words for a hungry, inexperienced hiker. Nate was realizing that because of his job he was extremely knowledgeable when it came to hiking gear and clothing – but he clearly was not an experienced hiker.

"Actually, my pack is a little heavier than normal because it's so early in the season. I carry more cold-weather gear this time of year just to be safe."

Nate vowed to cast a critical eye toward his backpack's contents once he got to Monson, but he was also determined not to be a cliché by casting off gear willy-nilly. He watched as Kenneth stowed his gear on an upper bunk of the lean-to and lay down in the bunk underneath, careful to make sure he was as far away from Nate's gear as possible. And upwind.

"Tomorrow there's a great waterfall a couple of miles down the trail. You'll love it."

"Worth taking a picture of, is it?"

"No. Worth taking a shower under."

And with that, Kenneth stretched out and was immediately snoring.

Nate's mental photographs of the Tennessee mountains began fading from his memory less than a year after his arrival in Maine. At first, the edges along the sharper peaks were sanded down in his mind, becoming smoother. Then the mountains of his memories themselves began to shrink, becoming more like the rolling hills around his Freeport home. Eventually they became nothing more than fuzzy mounds of green, losing all their majesty and towering strength as he focused on the geography of his new home. Tides crashing along craggy rocks replaced thunderheads crashing headlong into 6,000-foot peaks.

His father had not failed in Maine, but rather thrived. The Presbyterian stoicism of Juter's mountain roots had dovetailed perfectly with the calm, quiet Congregationalist mentality of his new home. Workers at the nearby blueberry canning plant had initially been skeptical of a plant manager from the South. Aside from his first name, however, they found little in Juter that conformed to preconceived notions of Southerners. He was smart. Perhaps not well-read, but possessing an intelligence that surprised anyone who dared underestimate him. He was unemotional. They were happy to discover that he was fair. If someone made a mistake, he was willing to let it slide as long as the offender faced up to it, learned from the error and then never repeated it. Those few workers who had caused difficulties in the plant – actions that initially had brought Juter to Freeport – quickly found him unwilling to accept substandard work. He was tested, and as often happens, it was those doing the testing that ended up with failing grades. In less than six months, the plant was exceeding its production quotas. Juter was wise enough to sandbag his quota increases for the subsequent years, so that, repeatedly, his reputation as a miracle worker was kept intact.

Sarah's acclimation to Maine was less easy. She found it difficult to make friends with the other wives who lived in and around Freeport. Maine may have been one of the northernmost states, but the cliquishness of the women there would rival the most exclusive of Charleston country clubs. Like many Southern women who had come from poverty and suddenly found themselves dropped into the middle- to upper-middle class, Sarah overcompensated and as a result gained a reputation as somewhat of a showoff, a worse sin in the eyes of Mainers than being poor. It was not until the fourth summer in Maine that she found a confidante in the mother of Nate's new friend David Sumner. Nancy Sumner was also a transplant, but from the corn farms of Indiana. Her husband was a mechanical engineer and had moved to Freeport for a job in one of the nearby factories. In some ways, Nancy's acclimation to the topography of Maine was more difficult – the rocky soil was as foreign to a native of Indiana as the moon. Nancy and her husband, William, had moved into a house just 200 yards away from the brick ranch the Townsends had built near the cliffs off Merepoint, one of many peninsulas that hung like stalactites off the state into the Atlantic Ocean. David and Nate had quickly discovered each other, and once the proper parental introductions were completed, it was clear that Sarah and Nancy were kindred souls, trapped in a storm of standoffishness and maple syrup. They quickly clung to each other to withstand the winds of others' indifference.

For Nate and David, the social trials of their parents went unnoticed. The two quickly became inseparable and spent the warm months wandering and exploring the woods and craggy coastlines surrounding their homes, which served as the epicenter of their daily adventures. One day they would stand along a cliff with handmade flags, attempting to signal the incoming and outgoing crab boats. Another day they might be using giant sticks to clear new trails through the thickets for future use. They were explorers, blazing new ground as if they were the Lewis & Clark of Maine's coast. It was rare to find them indoors, even on a rainy day, unless they were refueling with a warm lunch served by either Sarah or Nancy.

By the time he began classes at Brunswick High School, Nate's memories of the southern Appalachians had become romanticized and inaccurate. While he was still far too gregarious and outgoing to be recognized as a native Mainer, his southern Appalachian accent inherited from Juter and Sarah had all but vanished, replaced by a nondescript newscaster style of speech that confused his classmates as to his true origins. Indeed, David didn't think of his best friend as a Southerner any more than Nate thought of his friend as a native of the Midwest. They were kindred spirits of Maine, and if they spoke or acted slightly different from their classmates, it was of no concern to them.

The first day of high school was the day that would set Nate cascading down a path that would eventually lead him down the East Coast's longest trail. It began uneventfully, with Nancy driving the two boys the fifteen miles to school – she never trusted school buses to deliver schoolchildren on time – and wishing them both well as she handed them brown sacks with packed lunches. As soon as the car was out of sight, both Nate and David found the closest trashcan and ditched their lunches. High schoolers, they had been told, didn't bring their lunch, and so they had pocketed four quarters each from Sarah's dresser to make sure they had the "cool" hot lunch. After homeroom, they split up to race to their respective first-period classes.

American Government was a social studies class required of all students, and its instructor was Colonel Randolph Barry. No one was sure whether Barry had been a real colonel, but no one dared address him as anything but "Colonel Barry." The Colonel was one of those who felt that America was a grand experiment that had gone horribly wrong the moment Alexander Hamilton's Federalists had been usurped by Thomas Jefferson and his Republican views about democracy and the wisdom of the people. While most textbooks of the period lauded FDR, The Colonel did little to hide his disdain for the New Deal, constantly peppering filmstrips and readings with his editorializing about the evils of big government.

"Does anyone know what the term 'Medicare' means?" he bellowed to his new students, who were instantly stunned into silence. At age 15, each of the students were more than four decades away from ever needing it – so of course none of them knew what it was.

"Medicare is an example of the most insidious plot to destroy American civilization since fluoridation," The Colonel continued, and Nate instantly deduced that the towering, imperious teacher never actually wanted answers from his students. He had all the answers. The rhetorical question was The Colonel's crosier, and he wielded it as effectively as any bishop walking amongst his flock.

The Colonel continued, telling his students that Medicare was the first step to the government taking over every aspect of American life. He produced a 33 rpm vinyl record, with a black-and-white photograph of an old actor Nate recognized. Nate listened as the well-monotoned voice on the record explained to the students why Medicare would lead to the government telling doctors where to work, and by extension, eventually telling every American where they could live and work. "Once Medicare becomes law," the voice concluded, "Americans will spend our sunset years telling our children and our children's children what it once was like in America, when men were free." After the record ended, The Colonel continued to rant about how America was turning into Russia. Nate's mind quickly began to wander around the room. He took inventory of his close friends in the room – there were at least six – and they tallied up the others in the classroom whom he at least recognized.

Most of the students seemed as bored by American Government as he was, an impressive accomplishment for The Colonel, considering it was just the first day of class. Nate then went desk by desk, sizing up those he didn't know. When his gaze wandered down the far right row at the desks lined up against the beige-painted radiating heaters along the back wall of the classrooms, his eyes stopped on the blonde girl sitting in the middle of the row. He could only see the left side of her face in profile. It was an impressive profile, and he took the time to study it. Her eyes were blue, and her eyelashes were longer than those of most of the other girls in the classroom. Her nose was slightly upturned at the end, slightly porcine but in a flattering, not cartoonish way. Indeed, the slightly upturned nose gave her an air of class and distinction among the more raw and roughened faces of her classmates. Her figure was extremely feminine, and the brown sweater that clung to it surely held mysteries within. Where had this girl come from? She didn't carry the normal, more roughened traits of a Maine girl, and her build was a tad too delicate for her to be a local.

As The Colonel's rant began to digress into a litany of what they would be studying this year – the evils of the labor movement, the evils of FDR, of how Teddy Roosevelt started out well but eventually became evil – Nate tried to create a history and story for this mystery girl from his imagination. He was no Sherlock Holmes, but he'd already deduced that she had to have moved to the area within the past twelve months because he had never run across her. She was blonde. Perhaps she was from Sweden or some Norwegian country. Probably not, although she could have ancestors from there. The upturned nose made him think she might be from Boston. She still looked a tad too thin and frail to survive many Northern winters. She also seemed a bit more tanned than most. The South? Florida, perhaps? Maybe even California, although the thought of relocating from California to Maine, while a moving company's dream, was too far-fetched to consider. Nate decided he needed to speak with her to determine how effective his deductions had been. This presented a problem, as speaking to girls was an area where he had no discernible skills and very little practicable experience. Oh, he could tell a joke to one, or tease one. A serious, mature conversation with a member of the opposite sex?

No.

Still, curiosity and a maturing realization that there was more upside than downside in starting a conversation with a girl emboldened him. After an hour of listening to The Colonel, a conversation about anything besides the separation of powers would be welcome. As the bell rang, Nate bolted from his desk to make sure he was outside the classroom door ahead of his quarry.

"Are you new here?" It was hardly scintillating, but it was the best opening line he could produce. He had been formulating it for the past thirty minutes, weighing its plusses and minuses, and he had elected to go with it. It would pay off.

"Yes," came the shy answer, and the accent immediately let him know his instincts were good. It was a lilting drawl. It was "Gone With the Wind" packaged into a five-foot-eight blonde girl whose charms and beauty were transmitted to Nate in the concise pill of that tiny three-letter word.

"W-Where are you from, then?" He knew from his mother that Southerners were sensitive about their accents, and he didn't want to let on that he had already zeroed in on hers.

"Georgia." Nate hesitated for a moment and then decided to play the kindred spirit card. It was a trump card that would win the trick for him.

"My family's from Tennessee. We moved up here eight years ago." There was a pause. Nate waited for more information about the girl's family, but it didn't come. "What's your next class?"

"Geometry. It's just across the hall there."

"Well, mine's chemistry, and I have to walk over to the next building. I guess I'll see you later." Nate broke into a huge smile that the girl years later would describe as both "beaming" and "winning" and then hurried down the hall and around the corner.

He was midway through his first chemistry experiment before he realized he hadn't asked the girl her name, nor offered his.

Nate awoke early, just as the sun came up, but he found his new visitor had already arisen and packed his small pack. He sat on a rock, sipping water and watching Nate as he set up his small camp stove, started boiling water and preparing a hot breakfast. The visitor studied all this in silence, making mental notes as his campmate meticulously measured out water into the pouch containing his dried food, and into a stainless steel cup containing his instant coffee. The visitor's breakfast was simple: two granola bars and water. Nate quickly began to feel as if he was on stage, becoming self-conscious of each motion and action he made. Back in Freeport, when he'd played golf, Nate understood the unwritten rule that you never offered advice or critiques of your partner unless specifically asked. His visitor must not play golf, as he began picking apart Nate's efforts like a bird taking apart carrion on a roadside.

"Why all the effort?"

"Excuse me?"

"Why all the work just to get some calories into your system?"

"You mean breakfast?"

"Yeah. Most through-hikers wouldn't do all this."

"How do you mean?"

Kenneth Knight gathered himself like a law professor about to deliver a Socratic exercise to a class of first-year students.

"Why are you on the trail?"

It was a question that reached much deeper than the faux professor realized, but his pompous tone and immediate answer to his own question kept him from discovering this.

"You're on the trail to get to the end, right?"

Nate nodded.

"So if your goal is to get to the end, you don't want to waste. Anything. You don't want to waste food, because food is calories that can fuel your journey. You don't want to waste water because it will keep you alive. You don't want to waste steps because you have so many to make. You don't want to waste hours of sunlight, because there's only a certain number of those in a day."

Nate soaked this in. It was making sense, but the condescending tone was making the message – and his now-finished breakfast – difficult to swallow.

"I've met quite a few through-hikers during my years up here. Since most of them were Northbounders, they're the ones who've made it. They didn't bail out. They know what they're doing, or else they'd be sitting at a McDonald's in North Carolina after quitting the trail. They don't waste time. By the time the sun's up, so are they. They stick a breakfast bar in the mouth, roll up their bedroll and they're on the trail as soon as they can safely see it. No Bobby

Flay cooking act all morning. By the time your scrambled eggs and ham are warm in the bag there, they've already clicked off another mile. By the time you're halfway to the shelter for the night, they're already there. They've gotten the best bunk in the shelter because they got there first. By the time you come dragging in, they've already had a nice hot dinner, cleaned up, and are in their bed so that when the sun goes down, they can get their sleep in."

Nate must have given a slightly confused look, which gave professor Knight the green light to continue his pontificating.

"Look, you can't hike in the dark, right?"

Nate nodded.

"So you want to be hiking as soon as you can see the trail. You want to finish and get all your gear dried out, food cooked, and bedroll set before the sun goes down. Night is for sleeping. This time of year, you're going to get almost a full twelve hours of night. You'll need every bit of it if you expect your body to carry you where it has to go. So don't waste time."

Nate considered what the visitor was saying, recognizing the truth of it. He wasn't making good time because he wasn't hiking more than five or six hours a day. His long breakfasts and camp breakdowns, his lunch breaks, and his general stops for rests after long climbs were holding him back.

"So Kenneth," Nate began, hoping to change the subject from his shortcomings. "Why do you spend so much time out here? Surely checking on trees can't require that much time."

Knight quickly smiled as the talk changed back to his favorite subject: himself. He settled comfortably back on his rock, his body knowing instinctively that it wasn't going anywhere until the subject of Kenneth Knight was completely exhausted.

"No, truth be told, I probably could come out here twice a year and be done with it," he conceded. "I enjoy it out here. I come out here in the spring because I run into greenhorns like you, although I admit I hadn't expected to see one out here this early in the year."

The term "greenhorn" grated, but Nate let him continue.

"Things back at the office are always … uncomfortable. It's usually that way in family businesses, but let's just say our family puts the "fun" in dysfunctional. Rather than be cooped up in a cedar-paneled office, I'd rather be out here with the real cedars."

"So you don't get along with..." he was fishing here, "your father?"

"Oh, heavens no. My father's a saint and worships me. It's my older brother who drives me to Thoreau distraction." Knight smiled at the pun he'd made in his head, while Nate remained oblivious.

"About eight years ago, we had the misfortune to fall in love with the same woman," he continued. "We were jailed in that small office, in the same town, and things understandably became rather heated. We battled over her, but in the end my brother won out. You'd think that would be the end of it – I was a good chap and conceded defeat. Even offered to be his best man at the wedding. Somehow, though, the things we said and did during that courtship poisoned the well. He still glares every time we see each other, and that tends to make things a bit uncomfortable. So I take it upon myself to 'check out the north forty' as often as I can. We could hire someone to go out and do it, but I just find it more … comfortable. Speaking of my job, it's time I got to work." Knight rose and slung his knapsack over his right shoulder in a single, casual movement that looked as natural as a rhododendron. "I'll walk with you as far as the spot I told you that's perfect for cleaning up, and then I have to head off on a side trail to start marking trees."

It took five minutes for Nate to mash all his gear down into his pack. He was determined not to keep Knight waiting, lest he get another lecture about speed on the trail. Once loaded up, the two began working up and the finally down the last ridge before the trail widened slightly and joined a rut-filled road that wound its way along the sides of the ridge as it gradually moved downward. A century earlier it had led to an iron works, but now it led deep into wooded forest. Finally, at a hairpin turn, a small trail split off to the left and Knight took it, with Nate following dutifully behind.

"It's only about a mile to this spot, but it's worth the extra 20 minutes," Knight explained. The access trail was less-worn than the main road, and Nate quickly found himself pushing still-barren low-hanging branches out of his way. He kept trying to stay close to the man in front of him, but every time he got close, Knight sped up. Finally, Knight stopped and turned.

"I know from what you said last night that you're planning to hike alone – which is a truly unwise strategy. But on those rare occasions when you hike with someone else, let me offer you some advice. Hike at least ten paces apart. Why, you ask?" Nate hadn't asked, but Knight had assumed he would. "First, if you hike closer, I'm likely to swing one of these branches back right into your face.

Second, if you're hiking up or down hills, if one of you stumbles and crashes to the ground, you're less likely to create a domino effect and send everyone tumbling. Understand?"

Nate understood, but again grew flush that he had to be lectured on how to hike a trail. Knight, in the first indication that he noticed anyone but himself, noticed the blood rushing to Nate's face. "Getting too hot? Do we need to stop for a minute?"

"No, I'm fine."

A noise rustled just off the right side of the trail. Nate startled, but Knight didn't even flinch.

"Swampdonkey."

"Excuse me?"

"Moose. There's a bunch of them in this area. They'll wander around and cross the trail occasionally. Give them plenty of room. They look stupid, but if one of them kicks you, it'll be the last thing you remember."

The spot Knight had spoken of was everything promised. The path paralleled a small and misnamed Pleasant River, which was barely large enough to be a creek. Finally, at a split in the trail they turned left and climbed slightly along a smaller brook. In the distance, a hissing sound gradually grew louder as they climbed, and eventually a twenty-five-foot-tall waterfall revealed itself, smashing into a boulder-strewn pool the size of a baseball diamond.

"Behold Maine's most beautiful shower, Screw Auger Falls." Knight said, beaming as if he'd built it himself. "Although you'll find the hot water faucet never seems to work."

Before beginning the hike, Nate had braced himself to the idea of six months of cold showers, so the prospect wasn't unexpected. Indeed, the thought of washing ten days worth of sweat off was quite appealing, regardless of the water temperature. Nate set down his backpack, then dug in a side pocket looking for the biodegradable soap.

"Since I'm no voyeur, this is the point at which I leave you," chimed in Knight. "I assume you can easily find your way back to the main trail?" This time the question seemed more peppered with genuine concern than condescension. Nate nodded. "Then good luck, greenhorn. Say hello to Georgia for me." With that, Knight scrambled farther up the trail into the tree cover and was quickly gone from sight and hearing.

4
INTRODUCTIONS

The water was freezing, but the force of the water pounding down on him after its steep drop was bracing, and Nate could feel the dirt and perspiration blasted off his skin. He lingered for a bone-numbing five minutes under the waterfall and then climbed out onto one of the boulders, stretching out his naked body so the sun could dry it. At first, his blue skin shivered against the air, but as the yellow rays began to beat down on him, he warmed and relaxed his muscles. When he was finally dry, he strolled over to his backpack and dressed, putting on his last clean shirt and a pair of hiking pants. He considered washing out his dirty laundry in the pool but remembered that he should be reaching Monson at the end of the day, and he was determined to give his clothes – and himself – a thorough laundering in town. Another reason to delay was that wet clothes were heavier than dry ones, and he didn't want any more weight on his back than he was already suffering. He quickly packed up his gear, slipped on his last clean pair of socks, and laced up his hiking boots. Just as quickly, he was back on the access trail heading back toward the AT.

The remainder of the day was more MUDs, although the waterfall shower had given him an unexpected burst of energy that helped him climb the ridges more effectively. Perhaps it was the knowledge that he would be dumping much of the excess weight once the day's hiking was done. In either case, his anticipated 6 p.m. arrival in Monson came more than an hour earlier. The feat was even more impressive considering Nate had to walk the two-mile stretch of Greenville Road from the trailhead into town. He had hoped to see a vehicle that could pick him up and give him a lift, but the road was unexpectedly barren in the late afternoon.

Monson at one time was considered part of the gateway to

Quebec, a stopping point along the long post road from Boston to Portland to Canada. Now, it was little more than a town of roughly seven hundred, with several ramshackle motels that catered to hikers. They were glorious testaments to the days in the 1950s and 1960s, when Americans took to their Packards and Chevrolets and explored, spending the night in whatever roadside motel appeared at dinnertime. As he walked through the town, he saw buildings that were unchanged from fifty years ago, and the paint schemes represented faded testaments to garish hues designed to grab the eye of passengers speeding down the highways. Hikers, of course, cared little for design or color charts. They wanted a hot shower, washing machines and a bed that was slightly cleaner and softer than hard ground. While the roadside motels couldn't compete with a Hilton or Four Seasons, they could provide those three basic needs.

The motel Nate chose was the first one he reached on foot, The Brown Bear. The motel's sign included its name and a rather poor artistic approximation of a bear, although fifty years of acidic rainstorms had turned the bear's color more gray than brown. The neon letters under the bear lit up "VACANCY" in red, and a wooden sign tacked underneath announced "Hikers Welcome." The desk clerk, a disinterested young woman who couldn't be more than eighteen, handed Nate a registration card and took his forty dollars cash without bothering to look up. She rattled off that the washing machines were at the north end of the building, that there were two places to eat five hundred yards farther down the road, additional towels were a dollar, and that checkout time was 10 a.m. – otherwise Nate would have to pay for a second night.

Nate loaded his clothes into the severely abused cream-colored washing machine, lined up his quarters in the slots and slid them in. From its abused appearance, it looked doubtful the Maytag was functional, but it began filling with water, and so Nate started walking down the street to find something to eat while the machine did its work. It had been more than thirty-six hours since he'd last eaten, so he was hardly discriminating. The first restaurant he came to was either out of business or simply closed for the night. It was difficult to tell which. The second restaurant looked like a small diner, with the unimaginative name "Kelly's Restaurant." Since the sign looked older than the motel's, Nate sincerely doubted he would find anyone in the restaurant named Kelly, but it offered hot food and was open, so in he went.

The restaurant was spacious on the inside, but that only added to the sense of emptiness. A quick glance around showed that twenty booths and fifteen tables were all empty, and there was no sign of a waitress or cook behind the eighteen-foot-long Formica counter that ran the length of the place. Nate settled into a booth, trying to make as much noise as possible to alert any hidden staff to his presence, but after two or three minutes it was clear no one was coming out of the back of the restaurant. Nate rose and tried to peer through the window opening between the counter and the back kitchen. He couldn't see anyone, so he walked behind the counter, and then through the swinging door leading to the kitchen. Glancing between the stainless steel pots and cookware hanging from hooks, he was still alone. A quick "hello?" failed to bring an employee out of hiding, and after a minute Nate considered turning and leaving. Just then, the back door swung open, and a brunette woman in her mid-twenties stepped in and was startled by Nate's presence.

"I'm sorry," he quickly explained, "I didn't know if the restaurant was empty or even open."

The woman slowly recovered herself and apologized. "I had to grab a quick smoke. The owner won't let us smoke inside." Nate quickly backed out of the kitchen and then to the front of the counter as the woman slowly followed him out, sizing him up and determining that the only danger he posed was the chance he might break up the boredom that had tormented her all evening.

Nate situated himself back in his booth, assuming the formality of the customer-waitress relationship. The woman quickly joined in the dance, grabbing a menu and presenting it to Nate along with a glass of water. "Here's a menu. Would you like some coffee or something else to drink?"

"Coffee would be great. Actually, anything hot would be great."

"You driving through?"

"Hiking."

"Wow. You're our first hiker of the season. A little early in the year, isn't it?"

"I guess I wanted to get ahead of everyone else." Nate had wanted to escape to the trail months ago, but had been forced to wait until the weather warmed. He didn't feel like sharing that with this young woman. "The temperatures have been fairly warm since my first day. Very unusual for May." Why am I suddenly so chatty, he thought to himself.

"Yeah, it's been quite warm," the waitress agreed. There was a brief pause as she studied him some more. Then she caught herself and backed up. "I'll get … I'll go make a fresh pot of coffee." She turned and headed back to the kitchen. A quick study of the menu and Nate ordered pot roast for dinner. It seemed the hottest and heaviest food he could find, and it was certain to alleviate the grumbling that had taken over his gut for the last day or so. The waitress took his order and then returned to the kitchen. Through the window opening, it was clear that she was the restaurant's waitress, cook, busboy, dishwasher and whatever other tasks needed to be done. Nate studied her as she went about her tasks in the kitchen. There was something about her that reminded him of someone, but he couldn't identify the trait that triggered the familiarity.

While he waited, he took a quick inventory of the restaurant. It was a testament to the glory of wood paneling, with every square inch of the dining room covered from ceiling to floor in spruce that screamed of the 1970s. The Formica countertop and fruit-colored tables and chairs completed the effect as Nate noted a jukebox tucked into the back corner. He walked over, curious if the songs inside matched the era of the décor, and was pleased to find that they did. Most were country songs, with one or two frighteningly garish disco tunes mixed in. He considered dropping a quarter in for a Loretta Lynn song, but decided against filling the quiet of the restaurant with the soulful and rambunctious "I'm a Honky Tonk Girl."

After a short wait, the waitress returned with his dinner. Nate built up his courage and asked, "Would it be all right if you sat down and joined me?" The waitress considered the request, shrugged her shoulders and then retrieved a pre-made salad from the refrigerated case.

"It's dinnertime anyway, and I guess I'm entitled to at least one break." She flashed a coy smile at him and sat down across the booth from him.

"I'm Nate," he said, grinning just slightly and trying not to feel awkward.

"I'm Julie," she replied.

"I'm not big on dining alone."

"Then why are you hiking alone on the trail?" she replied, and her logic was fresh and inescapable.

"Well … maybe I'm not big on eating alone in restaurants then. Do you live here in Monson?"

"Oh no. I live a few miles down the road in Moosehorn."

Nate stifled a laugh, trying to avoid losing the mouthful of pot roast in his mouth.

"No, really. It's called Moosehorn. It's where my folks and I live." She smiled, conceding his amusement about the name. "Moosehorn, Maine. When I used to travel out of the state for softball games no one believed there was such a place as Moosehorn, Maine either."

"It's a fine name," he said, trying to save some face. She apparently hadn't taken offense. "So you played softball?"

"In high school. My parents were trying to get me to work harder at it. Get a college scholarship and all that. I just enjoyed playing. I think they took it much more seriously than I did. My dad played minor-league baseball when he was young, and I think he always tried to live out his dreams though me."

"I'm guessing he had no sons to do this with?"

"Right. I was the oldest, so I ended up being the 'boy' of the family. My two younger sisters are much more girly."

"I don't think you're boyish." It came across awkwardly, and neither of them could tell if a line had been crossed. Why is just talking to women so difficult, he asked himself. Was it always this way?

The Colonel's class would always be Nate's most-loved and most-hated class. The duality was not hard to understand. The Colonel's paranoid ramblings were sheer torture, especially for teenagers who couldn't care less about why this militarist believed Martin Luther King was a communist, or why Barry Goldwater was the greatest American. The students were completely disinterested. Dr. King lived in the South. Goldwater was from Arizona. Both were as far from Freeport, the local Dairy Queen and the various after-school hangouts as Mars was from Pluto. The one saving grace was the Marine Corps wall clock perched above The Colonel's desk. The idea that Nate and his classmates could be forced to endure the class with no idea how long the torture would continue seemed far worse than the atrocities attributed to the Viet Cong. The tediousness of The Colonel's class had been tempered, of course, by the presence of the girl Nate had spoken to the first day of school.

On day two, he had corrected his oversight and formally introduced himself, learning in the process that her name was Marie Kirby. By the end of the first week, he had learned that her family had moved up during the summer from the tiny hamlet of Suches, Georgia, located in the northern part of the state. By the second week, the two had begun the slow, deliberate process of changing seats. The Colonel worshiped at the altar of order and consistency. To simply change seats and sit next to each other would have been too obvious, and elicited condemnation. Instead, much like the Viet Cong infiltration of South Vietnam that The Colonel deplored, each day one of them changed seats with a classmate so that within a week they were sitting next to each other, able to discretely whisper comments or pass notes during those moments when The Colonel had briefly turned his back on the class to raise a pointing finger skyward to illustrate a specific yet irrelevant point.

Marie's slightly upturned nose distracted from something Nate wouldn't notice until years later – a subtle sadness in her brown eyes. It's possible he had failed to notice because it had been camouflaged by his own puppy love and teenage lust. For her part, the attraction came from both his smile, which was almost constantly planted on his face, and his boundless energy, applied to everything he did. Whether it was playing a sport or simply writing on a piece of paper, Nate imparted a frenetic energy to the project that communicated confidence and certainty, something that Marie often found lacking in herself. People often connect with those who offer splints for their own failings. Nate found in Marie a quiet dignity that he sometimes lacked. She found his enthusiasm a deep well from which she could draw.

Marie would always remember the day Nate first referred to her as his "girlfriend." It was an overheard conversation in the halls between him and two of his teammates on the football team, and from his perspective it was forgettable and irrelevant. "My girlfriend is the same way," was all he said. To him, it was nothing. To Marie, it was everything, and she would always remember the feeling of lightheadedness and flight that she carried down the halls on her way to her physics class. When difficult times came, the memory of that moment would be one she would retreat to, seeking shelter and warmth in the simple title. Girlfriend.

Their conversations were always effortless, and the range of subjects was the full spectrum of experience that teenagers coming of age could hold. One day they would spend two hours debating which of their friends were the most obnoxious. That evening, they would sit on the hood of Nate's car and discuss the age of the universe – fourteen billion years – and how their lives and challenges were irrelevant in contrast to such a huge swath of time and space. Each conversation was a tango; each dancer knew what the other was about to do, each waited their turn and then stepped in, moving as one with words instead of footsteps. There was contentment there, and yet they considered their conversations as critical and historic as any Einstein lecture or speech from the floor of the United Nations. Each was like a wool coat to the other – comfortable, warming and familiar. Neither would notice the small holes in the coats' sleeves.

After forty-five minutes, Julie stepped out of the booth and returned to the kitchen. She brought back a piece of apple pie and placed it in front of Nate. "It's on the house," she smiled. "I enjoyed the chat." She walked back to the kitchen with his plates and began cleaning up. The dessert was a pleasant surprise, and Nate watched the vanilla ice cream slowly melt on top of the microwaved slice of pie. Once it had achieved the mushy consistency he enjoyed, he quickly shoveled it in, taking just a second to enjoy each bite before swallowing. He sat for a few more minutes, and then stood, remembering he had a date with a quarter-operated dryer back at the motel. He walked up to the end of the counter where the cash register stood. Julie caught a glance of him and came back through the swinging doors from the kitchen.

"Are you going to be all right here by yourself?" Nate asked, taking on a chivalrous tone.

"Oh yes," Julie supplied. "Actually, I get off in about thirty minutes." There was an invitation in the inflection of her voice, but Nate's ability to detect it had been damaged. He was deaf when it came to flirting and interest expressed by women, injured and impaired when it came to acting on romantic or sensual entreaties.

"Well, I hope you have a good evening, Julie. I enjoyed the conversation, too." He didn't say, "Hope to see you again soon," because he knew it would be untrue. It was well he didn't. She knew in an instant that she wouldn't be seeing him again, either.

5
NOTCHES AND A BELT

Checkout the next morning was relatively effortless. Nate learned from the clerk that a general store just past the restaurant catered to hikers, so he walked down the roadway, sticking his head into the door of Kelly's Restaurant. There was no Julie, so he ordered a bacon-and-egg sandwich to go, then continued down the road to the store.

Earlier that morning he had scattered his backpack's contents around his motel room, leaving two changes of clothes behind for the maid. Now he would go over his gear, trying to figure out where else he could shed pack weight. He had plenty of time to get to the end of the trail, but he knew what laid there, calling him. Still, every day away from that destination was another day of pain. He would lighten his physical load, but the psychic load wouldn't be lessened until he reached the end of his trail.

He walked into the store and noticed the tag sale atmosphere. Scattered amidst the newest and shiniest camping, hunting and backpacking gear was used equipment, clearly discarded by hikers like himself who found their benefits outweighed by weight. On the trail, every item on your back lives a Darwinian existence – only the fittest survives the cut once you'd taken your first thousand steps on the trail. During the past two weeks, Nate had plenty of time to perform the delicate balancing act of measuring an object's value versus its burdensome tonnage. While some of his cold-weather clothing was relatively heavy and bulky, he knew that the past few weeks' unseasonably warm weather was unlikely to last. He also had no desire to relive his near-death experience on top of Kathadin. So all of his warm clothing would stay. His stove was relatively lightweight, so it was a keeper. Everything else was on the chopping block, and as he rummaged through the store, he quickly took inventory of what other hikers had jettisoned that the shop had placed on the walls to resell. There were a dozen GPS receivers dangling from their strings on wall hooks. Apparently with a well-marked trail from Maine to Georgia, knowing one's latitude and longitude to the hundredths of a degree was an unnecessary luxury and a vanity. Nate had packed two cook pots, and within a day had realized the redundancy. He set out his two stainless steel cook pots to turn in, and grabbed a new lightweight titanium pot to replace them. That transaction alone would take a half-pound of weight off his back, and he quickly grabbed a scrap of paper off the counter to start adding up his weight savings.

"Whittle off the ounces and the pounds will take care of themselves," Knight had said.

Nate started adding up the ounces he was leaving behind in Monson, including calculations for the clothing he'd already abandoned at the motel. He replaced his heavy, hand-held flashlight for a lighter headband-mounted version that used lightweight, brighter LED bulbs. He added a generous tube of sunscreen while subtracting a second pair of loafers he had brought for walking around his campsite at the end of each day. His tent weighed more than seven pounds. He found one that weighed less than three. When he tallied it up, he had taken nineteen pounds off his back. The store clerk offered him thirty dollars off his purchase for all of his gear he was turning in, and Nate instantly understood how the owner managed to afford the expensive Lincoln he had parked out front.

Nate paid in cash, carried his purchases out onto the store's front landing and began repacking with his new, lighter equipment. Hefting the pack up onto his shoulder, he immediately noticed the difference and allowed himself a smile of satisfaction and comfort. He ducked back into Kelly's and picked up a wrapped hamburger and tucked it onto a side pocket of his backpack for lunch later in the day. He had hoped to find a car to give him a lift back to the trailhead, but instead had to walk the entire distance himself. Returning to the AT was a comfort to him, as the solitude and silence quickly embraced his soul. His pace, he noticed, was slightly accelerated, even on the uphill climbs. His back muscles felt better after a good night's sleep on a soft mattress, and even his sunburn – which had plagued him during the past week – wasn't as noticeable.

The trail seemed slightly different now that he was out of The One Hundred Miles. After hiking for several hours through a small canyon dug by a tributary, he crossed over a footbridge and then began hiking uphill along a second tributary. As he walked, the spruces seemed somewhat greener, and the boulders that littered the sides of the trail appeared to be growing in size. After six miles or so, the trail began winding through a forest of these boulders, forming arches and gaps – notches, to use the New England terminology. Over the next few days, a rhythm would develop. The trail first would wind around a large pond – with names like Bald Mountain, Pine Island, Pleasant and even to Nate's amusement, Moxie – then climb a ridge to provide a scenic view of the pond from above, as well as the next pond down the trail. Down to the pond, up to the ridge, down to the pond, up to the ridge. The cadence was consistent and reassuring.

At Caratunk, he had to cross the Kennebec River, the widest body of water he had walked over to this point. It was also unbridged, and he briefly considered trying to wade across the shallow but seventy-foot-wide swath of ice-cold water. Warning signs, however, advising him of extremely swift currents convinced him that doing so was reckless. A makeshift ferry service had been set up by the Maine Appalachian Trail Club, and Nate was able to see the small launch on the opposite side of the river. Signs directed him to raise a red flag tied to a long pole to alert the boat operator to his presence, and after doing so the launch slowly made its way across the river, with a long rope strung between the shorelines keeping it from being washed downstream. When it arrived, it did so with a sleepy white-haired boatman who at first didn't seem extremely conversational.

"Sign this," the operator spit out, handing Nate a release form that essentially said it wasn't the operator's fault if he dumped Nate into the currents to drown.

"Is it really that dangerous?" Nate questioned.

"Not so much right now, because we haven't had rains for the past few weeks. The melting snow has it up a good bit, but it's been much, much worse. We've had a few folk try to cross on their own and get washed downriver, but nobody's gotten killed in quite a while. Name's Ted. Ted Miller. And you are … ?"

"Nate. Nate Townsend."

"Nate, load your gear in the front of the boat and have a seat.

It'll take about ten minutes to get you across. Don't stand up in the boat. It will make both of us very, very wet and me very, very angry."

Nate had trouble imagining Ted Miller even more irritable, so he resolved to stay put in the boat. He carefully set his backpack in the bow, checking first to make sure there was no water inside. While he stowed his gear, Ted pulled out a small bottle of bourbon and took a quick swing.

"So are you a volunteer?" Nate asked.

"Sort of. The Appalachian Trail Club contracts with us to run this ferry during the season. I'm really a volunteer – I don't get paid – but at age seventy-two it's something to get me out of the house and away from my wife. She's a little over half my age, but I think that's because she's aging me twice as fast."

Nate was considering whether he should tip him, but Ted apparently read his mind. "No gratuities. They'd all end up with my wife, and she'd spend it shopping anyway."

"So how long have you done this?"

"Oh, a little less than ten years. Don't know what they did before the ferryboat was here. Maybe they drowned a few hikers and that's why they started it. Cindi – that's my wife – swears a high school classmate of hers drowned trying to wade across the river on foot, but I think she's making that up to make an old man feel important."

"So she doesn't mind you staying out here all day doing this?"

"Naw, not one bit. I keep thinking she's got boyfriends on the side, and that's why she's OK with me being out here. I mean, I'm seventy-two and she's twenty-eight, so I guess it's natural for me to worry about that." Ted took another quick swallow of bourbon and re-stowed the bottle in his back pocket.

Nate wondered what would prompt a twenty-eight-year-old woman to marry a seventy-two-year-old, and again Ted Miller was able to read his mind. "I don't know what my wife sees in me. I tell people she married me for my money, which gives everyone a big laugh, because I don't have any. Then I tell people she married me because I can lick my eyebrows, but only about half the people get that joke. As for the real reason? Who knows? Maybe a father complex. Maybe boredom. Maybe love. Love is always a possibility in a random world."

Nate took all this in, but couldn't come up with an appropriate response. Miller took the silence as a sign Nate was ready to cross, so he shoved off with his right foot, pushing the launch into the river and started yanking on the rope. He had a paddle stowed under the boat's gunnels, but it was clear this was only for use if the rope somehow snapped.

"How about you, Nate? Married?"

"No."

"Ever been married?"

Nate paused before answering. "Yes."

"So you know how it is then. Was your wife older or younger than you?"

"Neither. Same age." Nate kept hoping his staccato answers would send the signal that he really didn't want to discuss the subject. Miller's intuitiveness had suddenly vanished. Another quick swig of bourbon. With each shot, Miller became increasingly inquisitive.

"So, were you guys high school sweethearts or something?"

"Yeah, something like that."

"Didn't work out, huh?"

Nate paused for what seemed like eternity as he stared past the bow of the boat toward the cedars and junipers that lined the opposite shore. He exhaled slowly, then took a shallow breath and said the words.

Nate had always considered himself awkward in the presence of the opposite sex, but his relationship with Marie during high school gradually incubated him and healed him of that dread disease of adolescence. Each day at school walking through the halls together, each Friday night dance gradually bled the social gracelessness from him. He was a stronger, more self-assured and comfortable young man. The support and adoration that Marie gave him also allowed him to be more creative, and more gregarious, and by their senior year he found himself wearing multiple hats – class vice-president, editor of the school newspaper and president of the French club. He would not be class valedictorian or salutatorian – his energies were devoted more toward the extracurricular than the rigors of academia – but he would still graduate with respectable enough grades to gain admission to Boston College that fall.

Marie also drew strength from the relationship, but in different ways. Admittedly, Nate's affections helped dissuade Marie from her lifelong feelings of inadequacy, and she even found herself looking in the mirror and not reflexively hating what she found there. Nate's arm around her waist in the halls made her feel warm and needed, and she dreaded those times when a class project, student newspaper field trip or other activity kept him from escorting her to and from classes. Their weekends together were joyous, and her memories of the two of them rambling up and down the coastline in Nate's dented-up blue Mustang would be among her happiest. He was a more conservative driver than his classmates, yet his parking skills were atrocious, and as a result his car bore the traces of countless cement posts and guardrails. It mattered little to either of them. The Mustang was motion, it was speed, and it was freedom. It raced down the two-lane craggy coastal roads with an exuberance and recklessness shared by its occupants, sharing their adventures and triumphs. It bore witness to the dents and dings of their adolescence silently, a trophy for their successful navigation of those dangerous shoals.

After graduation, there was the inevitable drama of potential separation. Nate's decision to travel to Boston for college was a familial duty, similar to the forced marriages of medieval times in Europe or the present-day subcontinent. He would attend college because it was an opportunity his parents had never enjoyed but would do so vicariously through him. For Nate to be able – academically and financially – to attend Boston College was a triumph for his parents which Nate wouldn't dare take from them. The looming departure quickly created angst, though, as both he and Marie debated how their relationship might survive the physical separation. Freeport was a two-plus hour drive from Boston, and shortly after Nate began his classes, it was clear to both him and Marie that the distance was too painful and too inconvenient.

Within four weeks she had abandoned her courses at the University of Southern Maine and moved into Nate's tiny studio apartment in Watertown. Both sets of parents were upset, but apart from voicing their displeasure to their respective children, took no action to stop it. The new couple's lives quickly settled into a comfortable routine: Nathan would spend his days in class while Marie worked at a nearby coffee shop. In the evenings, they would lie in bed with his textbooks scattered amongst the sheets.

He would diligently study for his classes while she lay beside him watching their tiny ten-inch black-and-white television. They would take short breaks to make love, and then gradually return to their diversions. On top of their rickety twin-size bed, Nathan would study literature, statistics and advertising and marketing theory; she would study him. After a brief six months of living together, they traveled back to Maine for a modest wedding ceremony, which salved some of their parents' concerns and hurt feelings.

Money was nonexistent during that first year, but somehow they managed each month to scrape up enough for the rent and electricity. Food was whatever they could afford from the local market, usually fish sticks and vegetables. On occasions – usually in the winter when heating bills became unbearable – Nathan would pick up an evening job waiting tables at the nearby seafood restaurant for extra money. Marie appreciated the extra cash in their household budget, but after not seeing Nate all day, she resented surrendering him in the evening to others, even if they were tipping customers.

Their first fight had been, as often is the case, about money. Like all marital wars, however, the declared reason for the battle wasn't the underlying cause. For years, the subject of their fight, both would say, was fish sticks. It happened on a Saturday evening. Both Marie and Nathan had been working late, and they had agreed to eat dinner together after they had ended their shifts. Marie arrived at the house first, and dutifully fired up the oven to heat what had quickly become their staple meal – fish sticks and frozen french fries. The couple had found fish sticks to be the most cost-effective meal for them, and so night after night their dinners would consist of frozen fish sticks heated in the oven on a cookie sheet along with frozen French fries. No green vegetables, no salads. Just fish sticks and empty carbohydrates. It wasn't pretty, and it wasn't a great meal, but it boiled down to just $1.95 per person, and with their extremely tight budget, that was the meal they could afford. Nathan arrived home twenty minutes later, in a foul mood. He had been stiffed by his last two tables, and had managed to have a whole bowl of hot clam chowder dumped on his right leg earlier in the evening. He had determined that keeping his job was more important than railing at the kitchen supervisor who had spilled the soup on him, or the hostess who had double-seated the final high-maintenance, no-tipping couples at his tables. Unfortunately, he had only temporarily swallowed his anger, and it would be regurgitated shortly after he arrived home to Marie.

For her part, Marie had been nursing resentment of Nathan's busy schedule. He had found the business classes quite enjoyable, and while she appreciated him sharing his passion with her each evening, the mental stimulation he was enjoying reminded her of exactly what was missing in her life. She had been a good student in high school, and she slowly realized that serving coffee and wiping tables was hardly as challenging as statistics or business psychology. As she placed the tin tray in the oven with one dozen fish sticks and a handful of French fries, she touched the top of the oven opening and reared back after burning the top of her hand. She screamed and quickly rushed to the sink to run cold water across the burn. At that moment, Nathan burst through the door, still angry from the injustices heaped upon him at work.

Marie had expected sympathy and comforting from Nathan because of her burn, but he was too wound up to notice the injury. He noticed the empty fish stick box still on the counter and immediately exploded.

"Fish sticks? Again?" he screamed. "Good God, how many nights in a row can we eat fish sticks! When are we going to eat something else? I just spent six hours serving shrimp and scallops and high-price tuna steaks to these Massholes, and I get to come home to Gorton's-fucking-fish sticks!?"

Marie's shock at the outburst, coupled with her throbbing hand, instantly rallied her own anger. Her outburst was the kerosene that turned Nathan's flaming displacement of anger into a full-bore house explosion.

"You self-centered, cocksucking son-of-a-bitch!" she railed. "You think I fucking like fish sticks? You think I enjoy eating plastic-coated scrod every fucking night? For a goddamned college boy, you're slower than smoke off of shit!"

Nathan was briefly startled by both Marie's anger and the slew of obscenities, but his primal attack mechanism was fully triggered, and he and Marie continued to scream for ten full minutes at each other, rattling of litanies of each partner's personal traits that annoyed. Fish sticks. Fingernail clippings in the sink. Towels on the floor. Failure to shave on a daily basis. In one quarter-hour explosion all of Nathan and Marie's irritations rose to the surface, each raised to the level of capital crime and each quickly matched or bested by another housekeeping or grooming sin.

Eventually the true cause of the battle royal reared its head, and Nathan vented about his hatred over their poverty, and Marie exploded about her loneliness and emptiness. Revealing these base, underlying causes of their anger didn't assuage it, however. Rather, it accelerated it. With their fears and resentments bared, they reared back at each other with an emotional ferver usually reserved for the bedroom. Finally, the angry tit-for-tat back-and-forth reached a crescendo as Nathan returned to his hatred of fish sticks and Marie, unable to muster an effective retort, pulled a half-cooked fish stick out of the oven and then hurled it directly at his head, a slider that would have done Red Sox pitcher Bill "The Spaceman" Lee proud. Nathan was momentarily stunned as the fish stick slapped against his forehead and then plunked to the floor in front of him. He gathered his wits in time to dodge the second, third and fourth sticks launched his way. In his rage, he began picking up the fish sticks and flinging them back at Marie, and within seconds a full-fledged fish-stick war had broken out in their tiny ten-by-twenty-five-foot kitchen. After a few minutes of throwing and being battered by fish sticks, Marie ducked down behind their tiny two-seat table, while Nathan, attempting to dodge a particularly well-arced throw by his wife, slipped and landed on his left side. Both now on the floor, they continued to toss fish sticks back and forth until their ammunition had disintegrated from the abuse it had received. They stopped and simply stared at each other in silence, their respective rages now spent, their passions as dissipated and spattered as the breading that covered their kitchen floor, counters and walls. Both broke their steeled, steely, rage-riddled stares into each other's eyes and surveyed the room. The kitchen was coated in chunks of fish and spattered with brown breading. There was fish stuck to the light fixture on the ceiling, and breadcrumbs spackled across the spines of Marie's four cookbooks on the counter. Each surveyed the damage before their heads turned back to each other, breathing heavily in the silence. Both recognizing the absurdity of the scene began to smile slightly. Then broadly. As usual, it was Marie who would finally break the tension.

"I had no idea you didn't like fish sticks."

Nate had tipped the seventy-two-year-old Ted Miller a fifty when he reached the other side of the Penobscott.

"I know I don't have to," Nate said, cutting off the old man's objection. "I know I'm not supposed to. Lord knows it looks like you don't need any money. But I appreciated you listening to me. That bourbon you're drinking doesn't grow on trees, so go buy a fifth on me."

"Well, I appreciate it, and I didn't mean to be prying into your life," he said, truly regretting that he had.

"No problem. I hope things work out with your wife. They can be a source of great joy and great woe. The trick is navigating the river so you go down the right tributary."

With that, Nate slung his pack on and headed up the trail that cut upward along the side of the ridge fronting the river.

He had loaded up with plenty of food and supplies before crossing. His hunger in the One Hundred Miles was not an experience he wanted to repeat, but as he continued to work his way up and down ridge lines he found himself thinking about food less and less. His stops were shorter, and his snacks were quick and light. The routine of his hikes – climb the ridge, descend the ridge, cut through the notch, circle around the pond – became calming rather than monotonous. He clicked off the mountains in his way one after the other. Bigelow. Crocker. Sugarloaf. Spaulding. Saddleback. Old Blue. Baldpate. Goose Eye. After 16 days of waking at dawn, hiking all day and bedding down just minutes after the sun had set, Nathan was startled to see a wooden sign alerting him that he was crossing into New Hampshire. The suddenness of it – he hadn't pulled out a map during the entire two-week trek from Monson – shocked him. He stopped at the sign and pulled out his water bottle and nursed it as he straddled the imaginary state line, keeping his right foot in Maine while his left stepped into the Granite State.

He had rarely explored New Hampshire. His only experiences were relegated to exits along the seventeen-mile section of I-95 that sliced a corner of the state between Amesbury, Mass., and Kittery, Maine, as he and Marie had driven back and forth between Boston and Freeport. This portion of New Hampshire was far more challenging than the Welcome Centers Nate had frequented. He knew from his planning that New Hampshire would lay in front of him the most challenging mountain to climb in all of New England, worse than Kathadin and statistically much more deadly. The trail would only wind 181 miles through New Hampshire, a little over half the distance he had already traveled. But his chances of dying of exposure would greet him in less than twenty miles. The White Mountains were a formidable barrier, and getting caught on top of the mountains in a snowstorm was a possibility anytime in the spring or fall. By starting earlier than most, Nate had increased the likelihood that he could be trapped on top of 4,800-foot Mount Moosilauke, 5,249-foot Mount Lafayette or the worst of them all, 6,288-foot Mount Washington. Stories of hikers lost in snowstorms on top of Mount Washington were a regular occurrence, and rangers there could remember more years of pulling dead or almost-dead tourists and hikers off the peaks than they could mild winters where no rescues were needed. After his first day on the trail, Nate needed no warnings about the dangers, and as he hitchhiked into the city of Gorham to replenish his food supplies, he made sure the motel room he settled into had The Weather Channel on its cable lineup.

After an afternoon nap that ended up being fourteen hours of uninterrupted sleep, Nate woke to find the sun coming up outside his rustic motel room. He marveled that there were any trees left in the White Mountains considering how many had given their lives to create the paneling that surrounded him on every wall and even on the ceiling of the room. He staggered into the shower and enjoyed lingering under the hot water for a good twenty minutes. After that, a slow, steady-handed shave removed a good week's worth of whiskers and wear from his face. He constantly was amazed how one week's growth of beard could result in a totally different person staring at him from the mirror. Each time he left the trail and visited a motel to clean up and recharge, the person in the mirror that first morning would always be unrecognizable. But he would reappear the next morning, unveiled by a triple-bladed disposable razor. Nathan scoured the room for a small coffeemaker but found none. It had turned bitterly cold, and he had hoped to be able to hibernate inside the room all day. The call of caffeine was too great, however, and so he bundled up and braced for the fifteen-degree wind that greeted him when the door opened. Temperatures had dropped. The combination of biting cold and bright sunlight momentarily stunned him, but he recovered and looked left and right from the motel parking lot scouting for an appropriate place to sit and enjoy some heat and breakfast.

Gorham was one of those New England towns that labored hard – perhaps just a tad too hard – to earn the moniker "quaint." It boasted the required number of churches with painted white steeples, and several whitewashed inns for well-heeled tourists driving up from Providence, Boston or even New York. Most of the inns were overbooked in the fall, but below-freezing days in May meant empty rooms. Nathan had considered one of these inns when he'd first landed in town after the ten-mile hitch from the trailhead, but decided that all inns, motels and hotels looked the same once you closed your eyes and went to sleep. Also, he was always self-conscious when he first came off the trail, suspecting that his appearance and well-seasoned smell was detectable from miles away. Even though he had showered and shaved, he still felt "uncivilized" in the town. The small restaurant just a block from the motel looked promising, and once inside Nathan was able to enjoy a quiet breakfast without the unnerving stares of locals wondering about him and his life story. Shortly after his ham and eggs arrived, the front doors swung open, disgorging a blast of cold air from outside and a small, withered but aristocratic woman who gingerly stepped in, scanned the entire restaurant and then scuttled over to Nathan's booth and sat down across from him.

"Where are you from?" she blurted, matter-of-factly, staring straight through him with gray eyes that clearly had seen a great deal over many years.

"Ex-excuse me?" Nate managed to blurt out, nearly spitting out his eggs.

"You're not from here. So you're from somewhere else. It's a rather simple question, I think. Where did you come from?"

"Ah, em. I'm from Freeport."

"Maine?"

"Yes, ma'am. Just passing through town."

"Not from New York?"

"No, ma'am." Nate noticed his Southern upbringing was creeping out as he uttered his second 'ma'am' in less than a minute.

"Ever lived in New York?"

"No." He intentionally avoided the honorific this time.

"Good. I hate New York. Hate everything about the city. Hate people from there even more. If you grew up in one of the five boroughs, you're a hopeless cause in my book. The folks in Connecticut and north of Westchester County have a chance for redemption. Not the city folks. Certainly not those people on Long Island. They're as lost a cause as someone from the Bronx, Brooklyn or Queens. And don't even get me started about New Jersey."

After a remarkably long, painful pause with Nate and the woman staring across the table at each other, Nate's confusion reached a crescendo.

"Do I … know … you?"

"Well now, that's a pretty unintelligent question," the small, wrinkled woman spit back, with no animosity but with a bluntness that resembled a slap. "I just indicated I didn't know where you were from. Therefore it's clear we've never met. I've never lived more than fifteen miles from this spot, so unless you can prove to me that they've moved Freeport south and west through some miracle of plate tectonics, there is little doubt that you and I do not know each other at all, young man."

Another uncomfortable pause. Nate stole a glance around the restaurant, seeking a waiter, cook or bystander who could help explain the geriatric incursion into his breakfast. No one in sight. Clearly the responsibility for introduction would fall to him and not to this matronly local who continued to stare and study Nate in silence.

"I'm Nathan Townsend." He waited. And waited. "…and you are …"

"Allison. Allison Lollard. And that fact that you don't know who I am further reinforces the fact that you are not from here. For if you had been raised anywhere within 100 miles of this spot, you'd know Allison Lollard."

"And that would be because?"

"Because I'm incorrigible. I'm a scandal. I'm feared, loved and avoided. But most importantly, because I'm talked about. For there is no greater sadness in this world than a life lived that doesn't merit people gossiping about you."

Nate pondered this a moment as he saw that the proprietor – who had all but disappeared in Nate's moment of need – had now reappeared.

"Coffee, Allison?"

"Indeed, James. And a cruller, please."

"Is this going to be Number Six?"

"James, why don't you go give someone food poisoning and let me and the young man talk." The waiter smiled and moved off back to the far counter.

"Number Six?" Nate looked confused.

"A weak joke on James's part. He's an extremely uninspired cook. Still, his dishes are much more flavorful than his sense of humor. Our friend there was making allusion to the fact that I have – to date – had five husbands."

Nate startled and quickly wondered if James had sized up the situation correctly, and this woman of nearly sixty five was indeed hitting on him. As if reading his mind, Allison quickly slid into a sly grin.

"Fear not, boy. While I do enjoy the fact that I've made you nervous, you are clearly not my type. You are neither affluent, nor rich, nor politically powerful. You were not born and raised here in the mountains, and you are not – please forgive me – not overly rugged looking. Since you are none of those things – and my first five husbands were, in order, all of them – it is unlikely that you could rise to the level and be part of their pantheon." She took another small pause and the sly smile returned. "The last one, however, was quite a … riveting lover. Perhaps you may qualify on that score."

Nathan's discomfort forced him to squirm in the booth's bench, and this time Allison did not immediately move to relieve his discomfort.

"Ah, good to know I can still make men half my age nervous. My day is made, and I can now enjoy my cruller – which James slowly is approaching with from behind so he can overhear our conversation."

The proprietor, disturbed but hardly surprised at Allison's alertness to his approach, quietly placed her doughnut and coffee in front of her and retreated, making sure not to cock an ear as he backed away toward the counter.

"I am the town's scandal and its glory," Allison continued unprompted as she poured sugar into the coffee cup with the force and magnitude of a cement mixer. "My weddings were both social events and the subject of laundry line chatter here. I revel in Mr. Wilde's admonition that the only thing worse than being talked about, is not being talked about. In some ways, I pity many of the other women in this town because if being the subject of gossip were oxygen, they all clearly would have suffocated by now."

Nathan considered a question, but realized no prompting was needed to keep Mrs. Lollard talking.

"My first three husbands were all influential men about town," she began, as if rattling off the players on a baseball lineup card. "Number One was James. James's family owned the town's furniture store, and I married him because I was 18 and thought I was in love. After a few years, I decided it was because I was in lust. Shortly after that, I couldn't remember why I'd married him at all. He died in a mill accident, and let me tell you there were quite a few local hens who said he threw himself on the saw blade to get away from me." She paused briefly, her eyes lifting up to the right as her mind traveled back through time. "He didn't, though. At least, I don't think he did. No. I doubt he did something as dramatic as that. He was many things, but he was hardly dramatic. In any case, the money he left me made me extremely attractive, and it wasn't long before Gerard came sniffing around looking for me – well, looking for my money. Gerard was a politician. At the time he was the mayor, but he had higher aspirations. He told me he wanted to be President someday. He became Number Two, and he used me and my money to run for the Senate, but in the end both the voters and I rejected him. We were living in separate houses when he died in a plane crash. At least no one could accuse me of being responsible for his perishing in a plane."

"No." Nathan added an affirmation just to make sure his vocal cords were still working. It also allowed Allison to quickly move on to Number Three.

"Roland. Roland was the man I was married to the longest. Twenty years. He owned a department store in town, and I so enjoyed traveling with him on buying trips. We would drive to Boston three times a year – for obvious reasons, I refused to fly. Then twice a year we would venture to New York. Filthy place. Awful people. You're not from New York, are you?" Clearly she hadn't remembered asking earlier.

"No Ma'am." Another ma'am.

"Yes, well. That's good." She paused briefly, regaining her thoughts and gathering energy for her next verbal charge. "Roland was tall and very thoughtful. Every year I was guaranteed flowers on four dates: my birthday, our anniversary, the anniversary of our first date, and the anniversary of our engagement. Unfortunately, all four dates fell in February, so for the remainder of the year there was a drought of flowers. Roland passed away of a heart attack. A lot of the women in town started spreading the rumor that he died – how do they say it in Latin? – *Coitus interruptus?* No. *In flagrante delicto?* In the act. Supposedly it's happened to many famous people: Attila the Hun, Nelson Rockefeller. I didn't do much to dissuade that rumor from making the rounds. Thought it made me look more powerful. More dangerous. Some men reacted by being afraid of me. Others were intrigued. Needless to say, I was always attracted to the ones who saw it as a potential challenge and not the cowards who saw me as their potential killer."

She paused to nibble on her cruller as Nathan – stunned – took in the machine-gun pace of the multiple-marital tale.

"What about your fourth husband?" She was up to Number Four, right?

"Yes. Four. Rhymes with Theodore. That's the only way I can remember his name. His name was Theodore. Named after the first president Roosevelt. Sad, really. He had absolutely nothing in common with him. TR was a large, powerful swashbuckling figure. My Teddy was mousy to the point all he would eat during the day was cheese. I'm not kidding. He would have a couple of slices for breakfast and nibble on it all day until supper. Quite odd, actually."

"What did Teddy, er, Theodore do?"

"As little as possible. He had an accounting job at the bank here in town, but he was hardly a paragon of ambition."

"Well then, compared with all these other men of power and drive," Nathan stalled momentarily as he searched for the right words. "Why then, marry Teddy?"

"I had been widowed from Roland for four years and was, well, lonely. I was starting to doubt my abilities to allure. And indeed, the point in her life when a woman loses that skill is worse than if she loses a limb. Much more painful." She stopped, and imbibed in a brief moment of deeper self-reflection. "I was really cruel to Theodore. I think I resented that I'd married him in a moment of weakness. I blamed him for my growing old. I blamed him for many things that weren't his fault." She quickly snapped out of the moment and returned to her more dispassionate tone of narration. "Of course, I blamed him for everything that was his fault. And he had many. Kind of ironic that he had no ambition or drive, never would step out of the cocoon of comfort – until he made the decision to divorce me." She paused, almost sadly. "I supposed I helped him grow as a person. He finally developed the drive to do something." She paused for a good ten seconds. "How paradoxical. That something was leaving me."

James showed up to freshen both of their coffee cups. Nathan tried to quickly change the subject and the mood while he stirred sugar into his cup. "What about your most recent husband?"

"Geoffrey. He just passed away last year. Odd that he passed away too, since he was the only man I married younger than me. At the time, I figured I'd made a smart move picking a younger one. Figured we'd have the rest of our lives together. We only had three years. How odd." There was something different as she spoke of Number Five. It wasn't a story. It was a fresh hurt. A scab that had yet to harden. Nathan was familiar with that type of wound and easily detected the sensitivity to the not-yet-resolved pain.

"Why was Geoffrey different?"

At first, Allison protested that there was no difference. Her glance into Nathan's eyes, however, let her know he wouldn't believe her, and that perhaps he had some preternatural skill that gave him insight she hadn't initially detected when she first sat down.

"He was …" She drifted off. How to explain it? All her husbands were simply husbands, right? Their differences were merely ordinal, weren't they? Why were her feelings toward Geoffrey different? Was it merely the newness of it? Was it the usual pain of recent loss that eventually would give way to the cynicism she embraced regarding Number One through Number Four? Apparently not. "He was … different. I can't explain it." Nathan was startled that this firehose of opinion and certainty suddenly had been shut off. He waited in silence for her to regain her thoughts. "With each of my previous husbands, I held something back. There was a part of me that was sacred. I kept it to myself just as I kept one or two pieces of jewelry hidden under the bottom flap of my music box. They were there just for me, shared with no one. I think every woman holds part of herself back, unsure, protecting herself from the dangers and hurt that are out there. By the time I married Geoffrey, perhaps I was just too tired to do that, but I found myself sharing everything. I stopped censoring my comments, my thoughts, my emotions. What I said was what I meant, not what I thought needed to be said. I had spent a life hoarding – hoarding money, hoarding power, hoarding stories and a reputation that made me the darling and the villain of this town. But after a while, I stopped wanting to hold these things." After a moment, she paused, collected herself and reapplied the emotional facepaint that she obviously wore around town. "Not that I want to stop being a darling and a villain, mind you, dear boy. I think my one regret is that when I finally die, I won't be able to hear what everyone in the town says about me."

"Do you hear it now? I mean, isn't the point of gossip that you're talking behind someone's back so they don't know what you're saying?"

"One of the cruel traits of gossip is that the person you're sharing it with to loves to share it with others. And they especially love to share it with the subject – after appropriately attributing it, of course. When you have as much money and infamy as I do, dear boy, everyone wants you to know that everyone else despises you. Makes them think you'll make a leap of faith and believe that by reporting this insult they suddenly are your friend. Gossiping and spying are really the same thing, you know. There's espionage and there's counterespionage. Trust me. I know what's said about me," she delayed for effect and then leaned in and whispered, "… and I love it."

Her coffee and cruller finished, she popped up from the booth with a spryness that belied her sixty-plus years. "What was your name again, young man?"

"Nathan, ma'am. Nathan Townsend."

"I have enjoyed confiding some things with you that I wouldn't dare share with anyone else, Nathan Townsend. Since you are just passing though, I feel my secrets are relatively safe with you. You have an enjoyable and long life, young man." With that, she left three dollar bills on the front counter and quickly darted out into the cold.

6

WHITE MOUNTAINS, BIG GRAY AND A TEAPOT

Restocked and heavily loaded with two weeks' worth of food, Nate set out the next morning for the AT. He'd arranged for the motel's night clerk to drive him up to the trailhead after his shift had ended. Since the trail followed Hwy. 2 for several hundred yards, he made sure to begin his hike exactly at the point he had ended it. No shortcutting, he told himself. By 8 a.m. he was already well up the first climb, an extremely slow one as the trail paralleled the very narrow Rattle River. He passed his first wooden shelter and kept hiking upward, making a good twenty-five-minute mile despite the full load on his back. The climb had been so gradual that when he reached the ridgeline and pulled out his map, he realized he had ascended to Mount Moriah, the first of the several peaks he would need to pass over to get through the White Mountains. The air was bitterly cold but there was no wind, which was a blessing. With gloved hands he shoved the map back into his pack's side pocket and continued to take in the scenery. As he did so, he watched as a lanky young man with a goatee slowly emerged from the trail he had just walked, nodded and uttered a quick "hello," and then continued down the trail at a fairly brisk clip. Nathan had assumed he was the first southbound hiker of the season, but hadn't considered that there would be others behind him who might be hiking the trail at a faster pace. Over the next few days, there would be several who would meet up with him. A few would spend the night in a shelter with him and they would talk. Many would be interested in maintaining a fast gait than in having a conversation, and would either stop for a brief drink of water and a chat, or would only offer a nod and a hello before continuing on their way. As he worked his way along the ridge lines he evaluated the views he was enjoying. The cold air meant clear views for almost 100 miles. The first peak, Moriah, had offered the best views, but North Carter had provided stellar scenery to the East. There was still several of inches of snow on the peaks, and light dustings of snow on the lower elevations, adding to the panoramas. After taking in the view, Nathan descended the sharp ridgeline, stumbling four or five times on the patches of ice that littered the footpath before reaching a deep, carved gap in the mountains called Carter Notch. The entire gap was littered with thousands of boulders, and there was a large stonewalled hut located at the bottom of the boulder field. The hut was staffed during the summer months with a caretaker, but in the winter and early spring it was self-service. There were enough bunks to handle 40, and a kitchen that was, unfortunately, still shut down for the season. Nathan quickly slung his pack inside the hut, dug out his camp stove and sat down on the front stoop and began boiling water for a hot freeze-dried dinner. He had bought one food package that advertised it served two, and tonight – with the temperatures hovering around thirty degrees and a series of peaks behind him – was a good night to pig out and enjoy a huge dinner and a long sleep. He had just finished adding the boiling water to the package when he saw two figures tentatively working their way down the obstacle course of boulders toward the Notch he had traversed an hour earlier.

When the two hikers saw him on the front stoop of the hut, they were still three hundred yards away. They stopped and engaged in a conversation with each other. One pulled out what must have been a map or guidebook, leading to more animated discussion. After several minutes, they restarted their descent and slowly approached the hut.

"Hi there!" one yelled while still a good fifty yards away. From the timbre of her voice, it was clear it was that of a young woman in her mid to late twenties. Nate quickly determined that both hikers were female, and they both were not novice hikers. Their gear was seasoned and their clothing was dusty and worn. Nothing was shiny and new. Nothing screamed newbie. They were here to click off miles, not win fashion awards.

"Hi there!" Nate shouted back. "You're just in time for dinner."

The two women determined that an offer of dinner meant Nate was less of a threat than initially imagined, so they walked closer to the hut. After a visual inspection from 20 yards off, they decided he was safe. Both walked up and deposited their backpacks on the hut's front porch.

"I'm Nate," he quickly volunteered, hoping to allay any lingering concerns.

"Teapot," the long-haired brunette volunteered, instantly confusing Nate.

"Big Gray," the redhead added, injecting more confusion to the mix.

"You want … Earl Gray tea?"

Both girls laughed. "No, those are our names," the brunette explained. She pointed at herself. "I'm Teapot, this is Big Gray."

"Those are some interesting names," Nate smiled. "Your parents hippies or something?'

The two girls looked at each other for a second and burst out into giggles again. Nate's confusion had now reached epic proportions.

"No, no. Those are our trail names."

"Trail names?"

"You new to the AT?" the redhead asked.

"No," Nate said, a little stung. "I've been on it since Kathadin."

"Well, one of the unwritten traditions of the AT is trail names. After you've been on the trail for a while, you get branded with a trail name. It's usually something that helps people remember you or tell others about you as they meander up or down the AT. Plus, there are a few people who don't want to share their real names."

"So you chose Teapot for yourself?"

"Oh, heavens no. You don't get to choose your own name," Teapot explained. "It has to be given to you by another through-hiker. It's sort of a badge of honor. You have to earn it. We were camping in The One Hundred Miles when we spent the night in a shelter with this fast-walking guy from Wisconsin. It was bitterly cold, and I kept sticking my head out of the bag to make tea with my camp stove. I have a little teapot I brought with me, and after knocking it over for the fourth time in the middle of the night, he awoke rather irritated and announced that he was naming me Teapot because that's what he would remember about me."

Nate got it, finally. "And you?" he gestured to the freckled redhead, who was quickly screwing the fuel canister onto a campstove and firing it up.

"All of my hiking clothes are gray. So this guy stumbled upon me the next morning going out to do his business. Since I'm about six-foot-one and towered over him, he just started calling my "Big Gray." After being "Big Red" all through grade school, I guess it's a nice change." By the tone in her voice, Nate wasn't convinced she was that pleased.

"So that night we became Teapot and Big Gray," Teapot chimed in. I take it then you don't have a trail name?" Teapot asked, studying him more intently now.

"No. Quite honestly this is the first evening I've ended up in a shelter with any through-hikers so I suppose I haven't had the chance to get one."

"We'll have to give it some thought," Teapot said, casting a smile at her hiking partner. "Might take a few days."

Nathan waited gallantly until the two girls had prepared their dinners before he dove into his package of dehydrated beef and noodles. As the three ate, he learned more about their trek thus far. The two were graduate students from Indiana University. They had just finished their first year of classes – Teapot was studying history, while Big Gray was working on her MBA – and they had decided that six months on the Appalachian Trail would be the perfect diversion after four years of undergraduate work immediately followed by their first year of graduate studies. The idea had been Teapot's, and she had eventually persuaded Big Gray to join her so she wouldn't have to hike the trail alone. Teapot's parents had been campers, and three weeks each summer were spent in the back of their green, wood-paneled station wagon during the day and inside a World War II army surplus tent at night. By age eight, Teapot could start a fire with flint and steel, and at age eleven she caused quite a stir in her Fremont, California, community when she rebelled against the local Girl Scout troop and instead tried to join the Boy Scouts. "I found the local Girl Scout leaders less interested in camping and more interested in shopping." The brief legal skirmish had been unsuccessful, but it had given Teapot a firm belief in fairness and equity that had helped her easily navigate through the teenage years her friends had found so fearsome.

Big Gray's upbringing had been decidedly different. Born and raised just outside San Antonio, she had lived a more suburban, sheltered existence with divorced parents whose method of compensating for the guilt they felt was to take Big Gray shopping every chance they had. As a result, there was little the tall, lanky redhead lacked during her childhood, which led to a few spoiled mannerisms. There was an air of privilege in her voice, even though her rung was far below that of the Texas debutantes that she had always loathed, resented and mocked. Both girls had done their undergraduate work at public universities in their home states, and they became roommates upon their arrival in Bloomington. As it is with all relationships, they quickly recognized their similarities – a deep, abiding disrespect for authorities and patriarchy – as well as their differences. Teapot was more feminine, while Big Gray would admit that she had thrown away every dress she owned after slogging through and then bolting during the first day of sorority rush at the University of Texas. She had vowed one hot August Austin afternoon never to buy another dress or pair of heels.

The discussion about hiking the Appalachian Trail had begun shortly after Teapot and Big Gray had met a fellow grad student that Gray eventually slept with. The relationship never took off, but during the awkward intervals each morning, the grad student had entertained Gray and Teapot over breakfast with his romanticized stories of the trail. His tales of waking to see black bears had enthralled Teapot, who had a great love for bears, even though the only species she had ever seen up close was of the stuffed teddy genus. After the grad student and Gray had their falling out, Teapot kept suggesting that she and Gray hike the trail the following summer. All winter she worked to convince her roommate, and like water percolating through solid rock, she finally she wore down Big Gray.

Now, three hundred miles down the trail, it was clear to Nate that Big Gray was having second thoughts. After dinner, Teapot had walked the two hundred yards down the hill to a small pond to collect water for the night. Big Gray and Nate had gone inside the hut, and as he began spreading out his bedroll on a bunk, she turned and asked him, "Are you enjoying this?"

"The hike?"

"Yes. The whole Grizzly Adams, mindless walking up and down hills thing."

Nate considered. "Well, I'm sort of a loner, so I have to admit I've enjoyed the solitude for the past month."

"Oh, so you don't like having us here, then."

"Oh, no, no, no." he quickly corrected her. "Don't get me wrong. I'm not antisocial or anything. I'm enjoying the conversation. I'm glad you're both here. You just asked if I was enjoying the hiking, and I guess the part of it I appreciate the most is being alone with my thoughts for long periods of time. It sort of centers me."

"Hmm," she considered. "I guess it's a guy thing versus a girl thing. The thought of being alone – not having someone to talk with, to interact with, to socialize with – is horrifying to me. I think it would be to most women. But what about the actual hiking? My feet have been killing me since the first day, and every time I get to the bottom of a big climb, I keep wishing I had a gun in my backpack so I could whip it out and end this." She took a quick, furtive glance to make sure her friend was still down the hill. "Please don't say anything. It's her big thing. She's done nothing but talk about this hike all winter. And while I don't know if I can do the whole thing, I don't think now is the time to bail on her."

"Well, if it makes you feel any better, you're one-seventh the way done."

"Fourteen point two-eight percent done." She blinked once and stared hard at him, no trace of a smile. "My bachelor's degree was in statistics. Don't think that I don't do the math in my head every mile we walk."

Nate set his gear next to his bag, both on the opposite side of the hut from the two girls' gear, respectfully giving them as much space as possible. Teapot returned just as the sun dropped behind the peaks on either side of Carter Notch. All three climbed into their sleeping bags and chatted as what lingering light there was quickly vanished. Nate enjoyed their stories of tormenting undergraduates at IU as teaching assistants, but the long day's run along the ridge lines had taken their toll, and the darkness, now complete, enveloped them all.

He awoke the next morning to silence, a deep canyon-ish silence. There had been countless moments during his first month on the trail where he had heard no sounds, but there was always the background noise, be it a slight breeze, a far-off bird or some other natural phenomenon. This morning, there was nothing. He slowly peeled open his caked-shut eyes, rolled out of his bunk, looked out from the hut's windows and saw white. Lots of white.

During the night and his oblivious sleep, more than a foot of snow had managed to fall on top of Carter Notch, and more than likely there was even more on top of the peaks on the ridgeline. Snow coated the heavy boulders, and it was easy to calculate by looking at the top of the rocks that at least 18 inches of snow was outside, with more still falling. The white powder had done its work, muffling whatever sounds might be outside, and the silence was humbling.

"Morning, sunshine!" Nate startled briefly before remembering he had company in the hut. He turned to see Teapot lying on her side, swaddled in her black sleeping bag and resting her head on one arm as she smiled at him. "Who ordered the snow?" she asked, her green eyes twinkling impishly.

Nate took another look outside, trying to calculate how hard it must have fallen to rack up so much depth overnight. Nights had been getting progressively shorter as he hiked southward and as April had given way to early May, so the precipitation must have dumped at a rate of more than two inches per hour. Teapot spun out of her lower bunk while staying in her sleeping bag and began hopping across the hut floor, away from the still-sleeping Big Gray and over to Nate's side of the structure. Nate took his first real look at the girl and was surprised that despite what had to be a good five days away from a shower and a soft mattress, she still had a clean, wholesome glow to her face, and her long, straight hair, while pulled back in a ponytail, was unmatted and ungreasy.

"Pretty nice wake-up call, huh?" Teapot smiled as she took a glance out the window and then plopped down on a bunk across from Nate's. "I never saw this coming, did you?" Nate admitted he hadn't taken stock of the sky the night before, so he also had been caught unaware. He considered the trail conditions they might run into. As if mind-reading, Teapot chimed in. "You're not thinking of going out this morning, are you?"

Nate considered. The trail would be hard to find under a foot of fresh, untamped snow. White blazes painted on the large rocks along the ground would be invisible, and those on the trees would be hard to spot with splotches of blown snow sticking to the trunks. His sleeping bag was extremely warm and comfortable, the hut was one of the best shelters you'd find on the trail, and his bag held more than a week's worth of food. It wasn't a difficult choice.

"No, I think trying to push through would be pretty foolhardy today," he said, not unhappy at the idea of spending the day with Teapot and Big Gray. "I hope you two aren't going to try it."

Teapot tried to gauge if this meant Nate was genuinely worried for their safety, or if he was saying he valued their company.

Perhaps he was just being polite. Big Gray might have considered the comment paternalistic, but the California brunette simply took it for the polite concern it was intended to be.

"No, I guess not. Definitely a zero day." Zero day was a through-hiker term for a day you spent in town or sitting out bad weather in a shelter. It meant you clicked off zero of the 2,100-plus miles you needed to finish the trail. "I don't think Suzanne will be disappointed to take a day off." So Big Gray's name was Suzanne. One mystery solved. Nate wanted to ask for Teapot's real name, but decided against asking, not wanting to appear forward. "So let's find out a little about where we are." Teapot caterpillar-scooted back over to her backpack and dug out a small four-by-five booklet from the bottom. She returned, still encased in her sleeping bag and began leafing through the booklet, which Nate recognized as an Appalachian Trail Conference guidebook.

"Let's see here. We're at Carter Notch, right?" Nate nodded. "That puts us right in the middle of the White Mountains. Cool." She quickly read through several paragraphs, then paused to distill them for Nate. "All these boulders around here are called The Ramparts. They're part of a huge avalanche that happened here back in 1869. Carter Dome – which is where we were yesterday – is 4,832 feet high. We're down at 3,288 feet above sea level and when we get started back southbound we'll go over Wildcat Mountain, which is 4,422 feet. It's a shame we're making such good time. The caretaker is supposed to show up here in about two weeks, and as part of the service they offer a hot breakfast in the mornings."

Their current home was one of several huts and lodges maintained by the Appalachian Mountain Club throughout New England. Most were a good step above lean-tos, but anyone looking for any of the luxuries of a rudimentary hotel room would be disappointed. The rustic charm was unmatched, but these were stayovers for the true backwoodsers, not tourists. The fact that you had to hike in a minimum of four miles just to get to the huts let you know they were not designed for drop-ins.

Nate spent the morning listening to Teapot recite information about the trail ahead from the guidebook. Big Gray finally roused herself after smelling breakfast cooking on the campstoves. Nate had gathered snow from outside and melted it in the cook pots for water. It wasn't needed, but the thought of fixing instant coffee with melted snow had a romance to it. Nate spent the day doing a great deal of listening to Big Gray's and Teapot's stories, while spending as little time as possible sharing stories of his own. The scales of verbal give-and-take, however, didn't allow for complete reticence, and by mid-afternoon Teapot had learned of Nate's Southern roots, his upbringing in Maine and his college days in Boston. The inevitable question about Marie had been handled with tact and diversion, but he had made clear that she was no longer in the picture, and the absence of a wedding ring amplified the point to both women.

"What about children?" Teapot asked.

There. It was out there. He stared at her, then at the window. The snow – and her question – had him trapped.

"We had a daughter."

Four years of studies and hard work at Boston College had brought Nate several scholarships and grants, a degree and some level of respect from his professors in the business department. He had interned one summer with Gilchrist's, a large Boston retailer, in their marketing department and had demonstrated a preternatural understanding of buyer behaviors. The twelve-week intern program allowed him to spend a week with each aspect of the department store's operations, starting on the sales floor and working his way up to the executive suite. While his college professors had presented marketing as a science, he saw it more as an art, and not a terribly complicated one. Listening, he quickly determined, was the secret to success in sales and marketing. The customer knew what he wanted; it was just a matter of listening carefully enough to what he was saying.

Marie had quickly moved up from making coffee to managing the coffee shop. She enrolled at a local community college and picked up work at a substitute teacher in south Boston. Soon she was as busy as Nate, and the time they had to spend with each other grew more limited. While the quantity of time together had shrunk, both would have agreed the quality of those moments had improved. They had slowly migrated from the immature love of high school sweethearts to the more divine and truer caring that came with modest maturity. Interest in the events in the other's day wasn't feigned – each was truly involved in the small successes, failures and challenges that the other had confronted. The routine courtesies, such as opening car doors, had evaporated, not because of a lack of love or care, but more in the interest of convenience and speed. Both felt their lives were rushing by so quickly that those extra moments and courtesies were now luxuries. Occasionally, Marie would note and regret their passing, but more often than not their absence was as ignored as background music or a missed meal. It would be much later before other signposts warning of diminishing love and romance were missed as the two careened at high speed through their lives.

The moment of their daughter's conception was something in later years both would admit they had recognized the minute it happened. It was a romantic evening, by the fireplace, and afterward there was something different in the post-lovemaking moments, a warmth and intimacy that couldn't be traced to the red wine or warm afterglow of the fire crackling. Somehow, there was a supernatural feeling that this moment was a milepost on their journey, that after this evening of soft jazz on the radio and lying in each other's arms nothing would be exactly the same. There are many pivotal moments in one's life, Marie would later point out. It's rare when you can recognize them, even if on a subconscious level.

Although the moment was felt, it was almost six weeks later before it was fully understood. Marie's morning sickness was at first brushed off as the flu, and it was only after she described the nausea, soreness and other symptoms to a doctor that he suggested the obvious and provided the necessary testing. She left his office staggered by the enormity of the news, unsure how to share it with her husband and slightly unsure that he would react in the way she expected and hoped. He arrived home from work late, angry about surly customers and perceived transgressions by managers. Marie considered waiting to share her news, but Nate quickly picked up that something was worrying her.

"What's wrong?" he blurted out, immediately shifting into his customary male fix-the-problem mindset.

"Absolutely nothing. In fact, I'd say everything is very right, and I'm hoping you're going to feel the same way."

"You found a better job?" Finances had continued to be a challenge for the pair, and Nate was always hoping one or both of them would discover a more lucrative position.

"No, nothing as mundane as a job. Something much more important. More wonderful."

This halted Nate from what would have been a simple game of twenty questions. Clearly the answer was more complicated and more esoteric than he had imagined. He was struck silent by the combination of curiosity and fear as he awaited an answer. He knew it was significant, but couldn't muster the bravery to ask for it.

"We're going to be parents," she said, smiling one of her largest smiles and searching his face for the first glimmer of reflexive response that would telegraph his true feelings. "You're going to be a daddy."

Nate would in the months ahead find himself stumbling on the trail, tripping over a rock as his concentration vanished while remembering the joy of that moment. It was a touchstone of happiness, and even though there now was sadness also attached to it, he recognized it as one of the few moments in his life where he had experienced true joy. His father had once told him that there was little true joy and happiness in life, and the best feelings that one could hope for were contentment and satisfaction. But his father had been wrong – at that moment, when he first discovered he would be a father, Nate had known pure, undistilled joy, as pure and as powerful as the mountain liquor his grandfather had brewed in the woods behind the old family house. It was strong and warmed your insides. It was addictive, and at that moment Nate would drink it down.

Both Nate and Marie's parents were ecstatic at the news, and immediately began identical but uncoordinated campaigns to convince the two they needed to move back to Maine to strategically position their new grandchild closer to the grandparents who would dote on and spoil her. Marie was interested, knowing that she would shoulder most of the child's care now that Nate's retail job was taking up increasingly larger chunks of his time. In the end, they realized that his career required him to stay in the Boston area and so when their tiny baby girl was born, it would be in Boston, at St. Elizabeth's Hospital, just four blocks from the congregational church Nate and Marie attended.

Nate's recollection to his two cabinmates was interrupted by the arrival of a giant figure in the cabin doorway. Silhouetted by bright sun behind him, the six-foot-five backpacker was sporting an incongruous wardrobe of heavy parka above the waist and thin hiking shorts below. He sported a gray wool ski cap, but his wet brown hair was so long that it emerged and trailed down the sides of his head more than a foot below the edge of his cap. More notable than his apparel, however, was the trickling stream of blood running from his knees down past his shins and calves and into his wool socks and hiking boots. At first, Nate and Teapot were startled by the sudden appearance of the bloody stranger. After a moment, Teapot's Boy Scout Handbook-honed instincts kicked in and she bolted over to her pack to dig out her rudimentary first-aid kit.

"What happened to you?" she asked over her shoulder as she continued rummaging for the small plastic bag that held small tubes of ointments and a variety of bandages and tapes.

"Fell on the rocks trying to make my way down the mountain," the hiker admitted as he slung his brown pack off his shoulders and immediately slumped down on top of it. "It's ridiculously icy up there, and I really wanted to get down here to get in the shelter and get warm. Smarter thing would have been to pitch a tent and stay put, I guess."

Teapot returned with a white tube of antibiotic and a small roll of bandages and began tending to her patient. The man made a gesture offering to take care of his own injuries, but the almost Boy Scout would have none of it. "Just be still," she insisted. With nothing else to do, he returned to detailing the trail conditions Nate, Teapot and Big Gray had been wise to avoid today.

"There's ice all along the center of the trail," he continued. "You can try walking in the deeper snow on the sides of the trail, but you run the risk of sliding off the side of the mountain on the steeper cutbacks. I tried staying to the center, but without hiking poles or a walking stick, I kept losing my balance when I hit patches of ice on the rocks. You can't even see them half the time. Even if you don't lose your balance, your feet slide out from under you like you're walking on a treadmill. It took me three hours to walk two miles on those devilish black rocks. What a mess."

Teapot had finished applying the antibiotic and was now gingerly wrapping his shins with the gauze wraps. The kind efforts merited an introduction, and the thankful hiker provided one.

"I'm Franklin, by the way. Franklin Peterson."

"Named after Ben Franklin?" Nate chimed in, trying to inject himself between the newcomer and the girls. Lots of New England children were named John Adams this, or Benjamin Franklin that. Nate had shared a first-grade classroom with both a John Hancock and a Paul Revere.

"No, my full name is Franklin Pierce Peterson. Named after the only president from New Hampshire." Franklin's wounds hadn't sapped his energy, or perhaps the warmth of the cabin was reviving him from his semi-laconic state. His foot-long hair had now completely emerged from under the ski cap, and it continued to drip melting snow onto the cabin floor. "I'm one of the proudest products of The Shire since Mr. Pierce himself," he grinned as he continued to peel off wet, dripping clothing. "Mind you, I'm from the true New Hampshire, not those coastal pretenders like down in ManchVegas" he said, referring disparagingly to the bright lights of the state's largest city, Manchester. With no semblance of modesty, he had stripped down to a pair of white long johns, draping all of his wet clothing on top of any elevated spot he could find in the cabin – on top of vacant bunk beds, straddling the tops of doors, hanging from some of the loose nails stuck into the cabin's log walls. After parading around the cabin splaying his wet clothing around the building like a mad interior decorator working in undergarments, he returned to the main room, finally sizing up the three other hikers.

"Through-hikers?" he asked, waving his long bony finger horizontally to include Teapot, Big Gray and Nate. All nodded. "About time for the first of you to be passing through, I figured. Never did understand why I see more of you in the fall heading north than I do in the spring heading south."

The Appalachian Trail Conference estimates that roughly 2,000 attempt to through-hike the entire AT each year. Of those, all but about 250 start at Springer Mountain, the southern terminus in Georgia. Southbounders from Kathadin are rare, because most hikers prefer to start when the mild winter weather breaks in the South, usually in late March or early April. An early start means hikers can reach the trail's end in four to six months, well before cold weather begins to strike in Maine in late September. Waiting to leave Maine in May usually means hiking in North Carolina and Georgia in October, when hunting season is in full boil, and the risk of hikers getting shot by overeager and inexperienced hunters multiplies. There was another reason hikers from the Northeast chose to start their trek on the opposite end of the trail.

"Blackflies," Nate explained.

"Excuse me?"

"Blackflies." They're brutal in May and June, and anyone who knows about them would rather be in Georgia this time of year than Maine, New Hampshire and Vermont."

"Ayah, they're wicked. One nice thing about this late snow, I guess. Sure knocked them down a bit."

"They'll be back," Nate said dolefully.

"In any case, let me be among the first to welcome you to the greatest state along the trail, the Granite State." Given his enthusiasm, Nate and the two women wondered if Franklin was a rogue element from the state's chamber of commerce, but shortly he calmed down and switched his monologue to the subject of the weather.

"This storm is a wicked cocknockah," uttering an expression that Nate found more common in his old neighborhood in Boston than in rural New Hampshire. "I was expecting a nice couple of cool days on the trail, but this is idiotic." Franklin related that he enjoyed semi-monthly escapades along the various trails of the Green and White Mountains, spending on average three or four days a month away from his wife and two teenage children. His rather tactless explanation of this disturbed Nate and positively offended Teapot.

"My house is one constant Gilbert & Sullivan musical," he complained hollowly. "There's plenty of drama, lots of words and music and dancing around. In the end, whatever it is that everyone is shouting and carrying on about matters very little. So when it gets really crazy I just pull my pack off the shelf in my garage and head off to the hills for a few days."

"So you just run away from your family?" Teapot said, her voice rising, unable to hide her distaste for Franklin's almost disavowal of his wife and children.

"No, no," he said, starting to regret mentioning his wife and children to the two young women who he would most likely be spending the night with in the cabin. "It's not that at all. I just choose not to be part of the drama. It's a regularly scheduled play where I don't have an Actors Equity card. When I return, the crisis of the hour has usually been resolved with no input needed from me. By heading to the woods, I get to the end without having to waste valuable time and emotional capital on the process itself."

It was clear from Teapot's glare that this explanation had not salved her irritation with Franklin, and Nate took in her irritated looks with a mixture of amusement and empathy. Not wanting to spend the evening listening to a torturous debate, he attempted to switch the subject.

"So which direction did you come from?"

"I'm heading north," Franklin replied. "Parked my car 20 miles farther up the trail and got a ride back south to my starting point." He uttered "Pahked," "cahr" and "stahting" in the distinctive New England style. "I may stay here a day or two until the trail gets better." Nate considered asking when Franklin's wife would start worrying if he was late getting off the trail but speculated that she wouldn't miss him at all. While listening to Franklin pontificate on some issue of importance only to people in New Hampshire, Nate began to consider the unpleasant prospect of spending several days trapped in the cabin with this self-important section hiker. He didn't like the idea, and he knew his two female companions would like it even less. He considered bolting for the trail at first light the next morning, but Franklin's stories of icy trails and the prospect of skating up and down ridges alone sounded neither agreeable nor wise.

"I bring a gift to the party," Franklin declared, erupting in a grin that promised both pleasure and danger. "I've brought both fresh Green Mountain coffee – and aged Scotch. I guarantee you by the end of the day we'll all be wide-awake drunks."

The coffee was quickly brewed in a light camping percolator Franklin had attached to the side of his pack with a small clip. The Scotch, which apparently had been transferred from its original one-liter glass bottle to a plastic jug to save weight – sat on the hearth of the cabin's fireplace, which boasted a wet-wood fire that Nate had gathered and built while the coffee was being prepared. It was initially ignored except for Big Gray, who confessed an abiding love for Scotch, especially single-malt. The fire quickly knocked down the damp, cold air that had hung inside the cabin and Franklin's soggy clothing began steaming slowly as it dried.

After another half hour of Franklin talking about himself and his work, which in some way involved banking, finance and what he kept referring to as "shrewd and creative accounting tactics," the now-dried hiker suddenly found himself in a rare predicament – unable to continue a conversation about himself. He paused, momentarily confused, and then to assuage what for him was a rare awkward silence, turned to Big Gray and asked, "So where do each of you hail from?"

Gray's Texas nativity interested Franklin not at all, so he briskly turned his attentions to Teapot. He found the idea that she was a Californian, and thus in his simplistic mind a free spirit and perhaps even a hippie or the daughter of hippies somewhat interesting and even a tad sexually alluring. He tried to disguise this base interest, but as with most things in Franklin's life, he was anything but subtle.

"Is everyone in California as debased as they are reputed to be?"

Teapot was confused by the adjective. She understood its literal meaning but had no idea what Franklin was driving at.

"Debased?"

"Wild. Free. Unencumbered by more traditional morals and values."

Teapot thought the generality – like all generalities – absurd.

"Of course not. California has been the home of everyone from Jerry Brown to Ronald Reagan. You can't categorize Californians any more than you could say that everyone from New England thinks and acts the same. Do you have the same attitudes as people from, say, Rhode Island?"

"Oh heavens no," Franklin recoiled. "We try to think of Rhode Island as little as possible. Its descendants were kicked out of the Massachusetts Bay Colony for a reason," he said, curling the ends of his lips up slowly in a grin. Coupled with his narrow, pointed nose, Franklin's grin reminded Nate of a red fox eagerly contemplating his next kill.

"So why would you assume everyone from California is some type of hedonist?" Again, Franklin had scraped Teapot's sensibilities raw and couldn't fathom what he could have said to generate such a reaction.

"Perhaps 'hedonist' isn't the right word," he retreated, now apparently disappointed that he wasn't trapped in a cabin with two twenty-something female hedonists. "I have always had the impression, however, that people from the West were less reserved and more gregarious than their Eastern counterparts." He smiled, satisfied in his belief that he had strategically removed himself from a cul de sac that lessened his chances with one of the two women in the cabin. Nate's voice instantly reminded him that there was someone else sharing the space.

"So assuming you're correct and Californians are bohemian free-spirits with little regard for morality," Nate summarized, enjoying putting this pretentious pretender on the spot, "how would you categorize people from your native state?" Nate smiled, knowing he'd placed the last nail in Franklin's coffin, at least as far as Teapot's interest in the man was concerned. If Franklin realized that Nate was obstructing any opportunity at gaining the favors of either woman, he didn't betray it in his face or his response.

"We're solid," was his response, somewhat surprising Nate, who for the first time found himself wanting Franklin to elaborate on a point he'd made. "We're solid in our beliefs. Solid in our values. We accept responsibilities as if they were two-hundred-page contracts. We can be depended upon. I consider these all noble traits, and I think most residents of The Shire – at least those who were born here – would agree with me."

Now Franklin was in full preening mode, making him even more unattractive than his ideas and xenophobia had already done. Franklin had pulled a short stack of paper cups out of his bag and was now filling three of them with Scotch from the plastic jug. He refilled Big Gray's camping cup, then dispensed the drinks and offered a toast, "To David Thoreau. A bit of an anarchist for my taste, but as a native of Concord, Mass., and a lover of the wilderness, we drink to you!" At this, Franklin slowly swirled the Scotch in the paper cup and swallowed the ounce or two in one slow gulp. Nate and the others looked at each other, shrugged and did likewise. Cups were quickly refilled and another small sip was slowly imbibed, warming, Nate noticed, the inside of his throat even more than the fireplace, which was now crackling as the wet wood had dried out and stopped steaming.

"To David Thoreau—and Ralph Waldo EMERSON!" Big Gray said a bit too loudly. For the first time, Nate realized that Gray had drained nearly a third of the jug while they had been talking and arguing.

"Indeed," said Franklin, noting Gray's inebriation as well.

Franklin began talking with Gray about Emerson while Nate and Teapot moved into the kitchen area to fire up their stoves and started heating a midday supper for the group. Nate had a bag of freeze-dried stroganoff that served two he'd been carrying for more than a week. He'd bought it expecting he'd have a night where he'd be famished and could gobble down the whole thing, but each night he'd found his appetite far from ravenous. Teapot pulled out a homemade dried mixture that Nate wouldn't be able to identify until it was rehydrated and cooked. Pooling everyone's food stocks, they'd cobbled together a true backpacker feast. Both began boiling water and making coffee, which they agreed Gray would probably need shortly.

"She never was a big drinker in school," Teapot offered, making a modest apology for her friend and hiking partner. "I guess the Scotch is really getting to her."

"If you're not used to it, it can pack a wallop," Nate agreed. Later in life his wife had evolved into a Scotch snob, refusing to drink anything but single-malts and insisting that someday they would vacation in the Speyside and Highlands areas of Scotland so she could spend a week touring distilleries. For his part, Nate could never develop a taste for the stuff, and even now the lingering taste of it in his mouth was an irritation and distraction.

"On the few occasions when we did manage to get her to go out drinking, Suzanne would have one or two beers and then nod off to sleep. She's not a mean drunk or a funny drunk. She's just a sleepy drunk. I just hope she can stay awake for dinner."

She did, but just barely. Shortly after downing six or seven bites of Teapot's mystery dinner – which turned out to be chicken and rice – she staggered away from the fireplace and over to the far corner of the cabin where she and Teapot had staged their sleeping bags fifteen feet apart from each other. Never bothering to climb into the bag, she simply crumpled like a melting pile of snow onto the bag and stretched out into a prone position, immediately closing her eyes and then slowing her breath.

After cleaning up, both Teapot and Nate realized they had a choice between turning in early or listening to two more hours of Franklin. Each individually made the decision to adjust their respective bedrolls on opposite sides of the cabin, signaling they would be turning in shortly. With the girls at one corner and Nate in another, Franklin had chosen to begin unloading his backpack in a third corner, furthest from the door and about 20 feet from Gray's bedroll, quietly setting out a simple bedroll and blanket.

Although there was still sunlight outside, it was quickly dimming, and before long the tired but now dry King of the Shire joined the others in an early but well-earned sleep.

It was dark when Nate was startled awake by Teapot shaking him a few hours later. She had a headlamp flashlight on her head and gestured with one finger over her lips for him to remain silent. She carefully leaned over him, her black hair falling forward and brushing against his cheeks. At first, he misread the move as affection, but then realized she had been positioning herself to whisper in his right ear.

"We have to get out of here. Now. As quietly as possible."

7

VANISHING ACT

"Can you pack up without making a noise and meet us outside?" Teapot whispered.

The request confused the still-groggy Nate, but the urgency underlying the whisper gave the question a tone of desperation and demand, so he nodded silently and began carefully shoving items into his pack. He was slow and methodical about the cooking gear he recovered from the kitchen area, making sure his pot and stove didn't clang together as he gently slid them into a side pocket. Rolling up the sleeping bag was his last task and after jamming it into the top of the pack, he carefully hefted the pack and walked in his stocking feet to the cabin's front door. He waited until he was outside before he sat down on the cabin's front porch and slid on his boots. Finally, he pulled his headlamp out of his right jacket pocket, adjusted it over his stocking hat, and switched it on.

He immediately saw both girls standing thirty feet in front of the cabin, huddled together but neither talking. He tightened his pack straps and adjusted the belt as he walked toward them, but before he could consider questioning them he saw Teapot give him a look that said, "Don't." Rather than ask why they were about to start hiking in the pitch-dark, he chose instead a more innocuous question.

"Going South, I assume?"

Teapot nodded. Big Gray didn't even look at him.

It was difficult to decide which was more frustrating: the slow climb that was extended by the constant slipping and sliding that the icy trail caused, or the dead silence from Teapot and Gray. The hike was especially nasty, with the ice all but invisible in the dark. Their headlamp flashlights were unable to give any visible warning to the hikers before they planted their boots on it and they would suddenly find themselves dancing like cartoon characters to retain their balance. Nate congratulated himself for deciding to keep his hiking poles back in Maine when he was jettisoning excess equipment after The One Hundred Miles wilderness. Without the carbon-tipped metal rods that resembled ski poles, he would have fallen to the ground and perhaps broken an arm three or four times during the first two hours of ascent.

Their caravan was a silent, slow-moving but methodical one. Nate led the threesome, pushing the occasional ice-laden tree branch out of the way, or pointing with a pole at a particular obstacle and stating "careful" or "watch it" so that Gray, who was hiking behind him, could avoid it. Teapot was sweeping up behind the threesome, keeping a constant twenty-foot interval between herself and Gray.

Nate had avoided looking at his watch until they'd been on the trail for what he thought was two hours, but with no sunlight warming the dark horizon, he finally took a glance and saw it was now just 4 a.m. Doing the math, he calculated Teapot had initially awakened him around 1 a.m. Thanks to the early bedtime, he'd gotten at least five hours of sleep, so he didn't feel tired. Hiking at night was not something he was comfortable with, however, and the icy trail and steep ravines off one side of the trail made it positively foolhardy. He was thrilled when an hour later light started to flood the rock-strewn peaks they were walking along and he could see without the aid of his flashlight. After another thirty minutes, visibility was greatly improved, although low-hanging clouds and fog didn't allow you to see more than 100 feet in front of you. That was fine for the hikers, who all night had dreamed of just being able to see three feet forward so they could gauge the safest place to plant their next footstep.

Each member of the trio kept looking over their shoulders every half-mile or so. Nate kept checking back to make sure he wasn't hiking too fast for the girls. Gray kept looking over her left shoulder, presumably at Teapot. What confused Nate was that Teapot, who was at the back of the line, kept looking over her shoulder too. Nate stopped right after they'd descended out of the winds into a gap, and began digging out some food. "Anyone want to take the time for a hot meal?"

Teapot looked at Gray, who immediately shook her head violently no.

"Let's just take fifteen minutes to rest our feet and eat some protein bars and then we'll keep moving. We might make Mount Washington today," Teapot offered.

Amazingly, they did. Washington was the biggest landmark in the northern third of the Appalachian Trail. It was set amongst a family of mountain peaks called "The Presidentials" – Mount Washington, Mount Jefferson, Mount Madison and Mount Adams. The trail itself played a cruel trick on hikers, starting south of the daunting white mountain peaks, then turning due north, forcing hikers to scale 5,300-foot-high Mount Madison, then made a 180-degree turn at its peak, descending slightly and then scaling the even more painful Mount Washington, the highest point in the northeastern United States at 6,288 feet. A one-day eighteen-mile hike from where they started, up and down across two major peaks would be unthinkable, even without the added obstacle of unseasonably icy trails, but the trio had begun early, and it was clear that the two girls had no interest in stopping. Their first fifteen-minute break had ended in less than five, when Gray quickly slung her pack over her shoulder and gave the other two a look that was half panic and half impatience. Four hours later Nate had stopped for water, thinking the two would want to put their feet up for a few minutes and rest. Instead, both started walking down the trail and Nate found himself having to scurry to catch up. After a few minutes, the two slowed only enough to allow him to regain his position in the lead, but after that he decided he would wait until one of them called for a break before he would stop. They didn't, and by mid-afternoon they were descending Mount Madison and about to ascend Mount Washington itself. Sunset wouldn't come until almost 7 p.m., and Nate weighed stopping now versus the prospect of having to camp on the higher – and much colder – peak. By now, he'd figured out that the girls wanted to put as much distance between themselves and Carter Notch as possible. Every attempt he'd made to try to find out why they were fleeing the shelter had been met either by silence or icy stares from Teapot. After two tries, he stopped asking.

There was a hut just past the peak of Mount Washington called Lakes of the Clouds. It was popular with tourists visiting the mountain, but Nate speculated that the late-season snow and ice might have prevented many of the tourists from making it up the mountain in their comfortable heated-seat minivans and

SUVs. At their current pace, they most likely could make the top of the mountain and reach Lakes of the Clouds. As opposed to their previous stop, it was likely that this hut was staffed, which meant a warmer place to stay and a hot meal. The hut was huge, accommodating up to ninety hikers, so the chances of finding bunks would be good.

The first three hundred yards of climbing Washington was pleasant. Then it became painful. Nate's joints were sore, and a full 15 hours of hiking with few stops were now taking their toll. He kept looking over his shoulder to see some signal that the girls were in similar distress, but their pained expressions hadn't changed all day, so he couldn't tell if they were having any more difficulty than when they first started out. Neither had slowed, as if driven by an unseen force to plod on over every obstacle. As they continued their ascent, the number of plants and trees diminished, replaced by more and more rocks and boulders. The winds were high, but nowhere near the 231-mile-an-hour burst recorded in 1934 that gave Mount Washington credit for the highest windspeed ever recorded in the U.S. The air was cold, but because it hadn't changed much from the chilly high thirties they'd experienced at the base, Nate calculated that a warm front was moving in, raising temperatures in the region overall. That would bode well for melting ice on the trail, making tomorrow's hike better.

As they approached the peak, they saw off to their right train tracks scaling up the side of the mountain, evidence of the Cog Railway, a unique rack-and-pinion single-car railroad that takes tourists up and down the steep west slope of the mountain in an hour-long slow-motion thrill ride that would put any amusement park to shame. With a grade up to 35 percent, riders are both thrilled and frightened at the prospect that the aged railroad train might break and send them plummeting down the side of the peak to certain death. They saw no trains going up or down, reinforcing Nate's belief that they would have no difficulty finding a bed at the hut on the mountain's south face.

The top of the mountain itself was an anticlimax. There were a variety of cars near the peak, each spewing sightseers who felt smugness that they had managed to overcome the snowy automobile road through intestinal fortitude, chains and snow tires. Ignored were the three solitary figures who quickly plodded through the parking lot on their way to the trailhead on the other side of the flotilla of Ford Explorers and Chevy Trailblazers. Nate took a quick look to see if the girls wanted to visit a shop or step inside for something to eat, but both were scanning the cars and groups of tourists, as if expecting to see a familiar face. Their pace never slowed, and it was clear that they were more comfortable on the solitude of the trail than amongst strangers. Gray paused just a moment, to read the signs for the Cog Railway, then continued following Nate, who began stepping down the south face toward the Lakes of the Clouds Hut. He could see it from the mountain's peak, sitting like a tiny toy house on a shelf about a half-mile and a good thousand feet below their current location. At this point, with the sun nearing the horizon, Nate decided to take charge. "It's getting late and we've put in a hell of a day. You guys want to crash at that hut up ahead, right?" he said. Teapot looked at Big Gray for guidance. She offered none.

"Let's check it out and see what it looks like," Teapot offered.

When they reached the hut, it was more crowded than Nate had expected. Only a third of the hut's ninety bunks looked filled, but the late-winter storm had brought dozens of hikers out to enjoy the rare sight of snow on top of the Presidentials in early June.

Big Gray whispered something to Teapot, which set off a brief animated discussion between the two at hushed volumes. Finally, Teapot looked at Nate and stated "It's a little too crowded here for us. We're going to go on another half-hour or so and just tent along the trail." There was a brief pause. She looked briefly at Gray and then added, "You're welcome to join us if you want." This elicited a brief flash of anger from Gray, which subsided almost instantly. Nate didn't know how to read this, but didn't feel good about abandoning the two in subfreezing overnight weather on the side of a windy peak.

"I'm OK with hiking a little further," he said with a wan smile that failed to camouflage the dishonesty of it. "Heck, at the rate we're hiking, we could reach Virginia by the end of the week." The joke fell flat, and the familiar silence returned.

The last half hour of hiking was the least difficult of the entire day. The sunlight had melted or broken up much of the ice on the trail, and since most of the hiking was downhill, the three were using leg muscles that had seen little action for most of the past sixteen hours. When they found a brief curve in the trail that allowed the next mountain – Mount Monroe – to block most of the direct wind, they located a relatively flat section devoid of large boulders and began to set up camp. As Nate began unloading gear next to the girls, Teapot began pantomiming a plaintive gesture and pointing toward another flat section of ground a good fifty yards beyond where they were unpacking tents. Nate, now thoroughly confused, needed an additional head nod from Teapot toward the far-off section of ground before he realized she was asking him to give the two of them the open area they were standing on and move his tent site further down the trail. He quickly jammed his still-rolled tent back into his back, and carried the pack with both hands to his private site down the hill. That evening, the girls quickly slid into their tents, positioned with the vestibules facing each other so the two could share a common cooking area while still laying inside their respective tents. Nate quickly cooked a chili-macaroni dish, drank a cup of decaf coffee and settled into his tent for the night, making sure to tear open a chemical heating packet and jam it inside his sleeping bag so his now-aching calves, shins and feet would stay warm during the night. He was infuriated at the silent treatment he'd endured all day, and resolved in the morning to demand answers.

The morning brought bright light and silence. Exhausted from the grueling previous day, Nate has slept well past dawn, one of the rare times he'd done that since taking to the trail a month and a half ago. The silence was not unexpected. He figured the girls would be just as exhausted, and admittedly they had been anything but noisy during the past twenty-four hours. When he unzipped his vestibule, he fired up his camp stove and began heating water for some coffee and instant oatmeal. He kept all of his body except two arms and his head inside his sleeping bag, waiting until after he had finished his breakfast before sliding his pants back on and puling himself out of the tent. The bright sun momentarily blinded him, and it took a moment before he could turn and clearly focus on the area where Teapot's and Big Gray's tents were located.

Except there were no tents. There was nothing except bare ground and boulders.

Where was his wife? Nate had searched the house twice upon his arrival from work, calling out her name constantly. Marie rarely left the house now that she was nine months pregnant and less than a week away from her due date. When at work, Nate rarely stepped far from his desk to ensure that if she called to report she was in labor, he could instantly dart out of the store's headquarters and be at their house to pick her up in precisely 17 minutes. He'd timed the route. Repeatedly. He'd made it a point to drive it at differing times of the day – during morning rush-hour, at midday and during the plodding afternoon traffic. Going into labor during the afternoon rush would clearly be the most problematic, as it would take him almost forty-five minutes to get from his desk to the front stoop of the twenty-year-old Somerville duplex they'd bought earlier in the year.

Nate had earned a respectable promotion and raise from Gilchrist's, a position that made their run-down apartment seem somewhat inadequate. The inside of their new duplex was not much bigger than the apartment, but it did provide a second bedroom that would serve as their soon-to-arrive daughter's nursery. More importantly, they owned it, and by renting out the downstairs floor to an employee and friend from Marie's coffee shop named Jeff Shippman, they were able to achieve a level of financial security unusual for a couple just in their mid-twenties.

Decorating the nursery had been accomplished on a single sunny Saturday afternoon, with Marie and her visiting mother picking out all the decorations, a changing table, crib and rocking chair. Nate had spent the day painting and hanging wallpaper borders while his wife was out of the house, to prevent her from inhaling any of the paint fumes. Both had agreed they wanted their first child's gender to be a surprise to them, so Marie had chosen a soft green color for the room, with a matching wallpaper border of flowers encircling the top four inches of the walls.

Now searching for his wife, Nate opened the door to the nursery and took a quick glance around. Seeing nothing but oblivious aardvarks, bears, cows, ducks and all the other animals whose names ran from "e" to "z," he continued on to check their bedroom, the bath and then back to the living room and kitchen. The house was deathly silent, and he picked up speed as he ran out the front door, down the stairs and then around the back to the door that led to Jeff's tiny downstairs rental. He rang the bell and then knocked on the door loudly, in case Jeff was taking one of his post-workday pre-carousing naps. No answer. He returned to the front of the building, taking the front stairs two at a time and bounded back into his house. Now what? He considered calling someone, but who would he call? He would never dial Marie's parents and worry them. Perhaps still resenting Nate's role in moving their daughter four hours away from them, they had always worked subtly to give Nate occasional twinges of inferiority. Letting them know he'd lost their nine-months-pregnant daughter wasn't going to raise their esteem for him. He felt an urge to call his father for advice, but decided that other than worrying him perhaps unnecessarily, it would accomplish little. He tried calling his wife's obstetrician to see if she had headed to the hospital, but since it was now after 5 p.m., the office was closed and all he got was the answering service.

"If it's an emergency, I'll be happy to try to reach the doctor," the polite but curt operator told him. Telling the doctor that he'd lost his wife was no less attractive an idea than telling his in-laws, so he decided not to leave a message.

Finally, he decided to start calling hospitals, beginning with the one he and Marie had selected for the delivery of their baby. St. Elizabeth's was just a five-mile drive from the house.

"St. Elizabeth's," the receptionist sharply answered as he nervously and carefully fingered the magnet attached to their refrigerator.

"Yes, I'm trying to find out if my wife has been admitted to your hospital," Nate blurted out, his concern clearly telegraphed by his voice. "Marie Townsend." For a moment, he gave way to thoughts that she might have been admitted for something more sinister or devastating, such as a traffic mishap, but he quickly brushed those irrational fears aside. "She is expecting a child at any time."

There was an interminable pause as the receptionist rifled through her records.

"There is a Marie Townsend here. She just checked in twenty minutes ago. Shall I …"

But Nate had already hung up the phone and bolted through the front door, not even taking the time to lock it from the outside.

Rush-hour traffic turned the five-mile drive into a forty-five-minute nightmare, and Nate congratulated himself for not taking their narrow pale-blue car down the sidewalks to avoid traffic-clogged Prospect Street and Western Avenue. After crossing over the Charles River and clearing the entrances to the Massachusetts Turnpike, the logjam cleared, and he quickly wheeled into the hospital's parking lot and into the emergency entrance.

When he met up with Marie, he learned his frantic battle with trucks and cars was unnecessary. She was only in mild labor, several hours at least away from delivery. Jeff was there, and from the two of them he learned the details of her disappearance.

"I've been walking in the neighborhood, the past three weeks," Marie explained. "It's something the doctor insisted was not only healthy for me, but he said it would speed up the delivery both in terms of when it happened, and how quickly it progressed once childbirth began. Well, you know how I've felt the last month or so, Nate. Anything to speed things up is a winner with me."

Nate smiled at this remark, finally able to calm down after the past hour of panic and hyperactivity. Nate had no doubt that Marie had taken the doctor's suggestion to heart with the radical obsession that had become her trademark.

"As you know on the days I've been working at the coffee shop, I've been getting up before dawn and walking for a mile before heading off to work," she continued. "You've been going with me on those, love, and I've really enjoyed us spending that extra time together in the mornings. What you don't know is that on days when I don't work, I've been taking two-hour hikes – I like to refer to them as 'long-distance waddles,' around the neighborhood. I've gone down in and around the neighborhood, and then all the way down and around Cambridge. Then in the late afternoons, regardless of whether I worked or not, I've been making sure to get in another mile or so before you returned home."

Nate looked at her in astonishment, trying to understand why a nine-months-pregnant woman would be parading all around the West Boston suburbs for hours at a time. As if reading the question in his face, Marie smiled.

"I really want this baby to hurry up and come."

As if agreeing with her, a contraction began, and her story had two wait for the minute or two it took the pain to pass.

"So today I was on my afternoon mile-and-a-half route and I started feeling some pressure just after starting. By the time I returned to the neighborhood, it was clear I was having full-bore contractions, strong enough to double me over. I didn't have a watch on, so I couldn't tell if they were coming ten minutes apart or ten seconds apart. I tried counting seconds, but that didn't work too well. It sure felt like they were coming every ten seconds. The nurse here (she gestured to the elderly RN replacing her IV bag) thinks I'm a big baby, though, and they couldn't have been more than fifteen minutes apart.

"That's what you're doing now, sweetie," the nurse smiled. "You're going to be here for a while, so don't rush."

At this point, Jeff picked up the narration from his corner of the hospital room, where until now he had simply been listening and beaming at Marie.

"When she pounded on my door she looked really scared. I just tossed her into the front seat and raced here. It was only after we got here that she realized she didn't have her bag of belongings, her purse, her ID or anything. We also remembered we hadn't left a note or called you. She tried to phone your office but they said you'd left. We called the house twice but didn't get an answer. I guess we're glad you figured it out."

Nate's relief that his wife was safe and healthy overruled any minor resentment he might have felt about Jeff being the one to drive her to the hospital. It wasn't the scenario he had envisioned, but now that she was safe and their child was on the way, he was able to crack a smile and clap Jeff on the back as a way to say thanks for his role in bringing her here. Jeff stayed for several hours, never taking repeated subtle hints that it was time for him to retire and let Nate and Marie get on with the birth of their baby. Finally, when Marie reached eight centimeters, a nurse shooed him out and sent him to the waiting room downstairs.

The delivery had been a frenetic, hectic affair, with minor complication that had taxed both Marie and Nate, and at one point they were minutes from having to wheel Marie into an operating room for a C-section. In the end, however, a soon-to-retire seventy-two-year-old obstetrician arrived amidst the chaos, surveyed the situation, and calmly stepped in to deliver the baby with little fanfare and even less drama. Pink and mottled, she was a quiet baby moments after her arrival, and after the customary inspections, the doctors and nurses left the new family of three alone in the giant delivery room, turning down the lights since it was now 2 a.m. The sudden change from bright, crowded bedlam to a silent, darkened and empty room was disquieting to Nate and Marie, who had been parents for all of thirty minutes. Father, mother and daughter quickly nestled together, the tiny infant bundled tightly in a blanket almost as pink as her new skin. Their new child was safely wedged in the crease between Marie's arm and ribs, while Nate stood alongside the hospital bed and rested his head on Marie's shoulder. *Yes, dad, you said there was no joy in the world, but you were wrong. There is joy in the world,* he told himself. *I have found it. I'm nestled in its bosom and I don't want to go anywhere else.* Naming their new daughter was a simple task. They called her Joy.

"This is the greatest accomplishment of my life," Marie cried as she stared down into the seven-pound, ten-ounce package wound tightly in a white-and-blue hospital blanket. "I used to think things like graduations or test scores or promotions mattered. They don't mean anything. I've knitted a scarf and a sweater from scratch. How silly and simple those creations are compared to this."

Nate didn't know what to say. Marie was rarely one to wax philosophical, so he merely listened.

"I have a confession to make," she continued. "Until today, I've always felt a little inadequate compared to you, Nate. You're so much smarter than I. You're college-educated where I'm not. You've got a great career ahead of you, while I just manage a coffee shop where people come to light up their neurons for the day's drudgery ahead. I'm really not much more than a glorified drug pusher, while you're on your way to become a big retail hotshot."

Nate tried to discount what she was saying, but she interrupted him.

"Honey, you wear a suit to work. I wear an apron. I know you don't see it this way, but it's how I feel. At least, that's how I felt until tonight. I did something you could never do. I did something amazing today. I know it's something women have done since time immemorial, but I created a life today. We have a daughter, and I helped make it happen. I'm just amazed at myself."

Nate was amazed at her creation too, and told her so.

"I don't know what else I'm going to do in this world, but I know whatever it is will probably pale in comparison to what I did tonight." She smiled. "It's all downhill from here, kiddo," she cracked.

Downhill? Uphill? Which way should Nate go to look for the two girls? The bright morning sunlight reflecting off the snow coating the side of the mountain made him almost blind. Why would they leave in the middle of the night and not let him know? If he'd found their tents still pitched and empty, he would suspect foul play, or the possibility that they'd simply hiked back up to the top of the mountain to use one of the restrooms in the tourist area. But their camp was completely broken down. No tents. No camp stove. No packs. No sign that they'd even been there a mere eight hours earlier. Why would they leave ahead of him?

He quickly dropped his tent and shoved his gear into his backpack, slinging it over his shoulders and stomping back from the Mount Monroe campsite down and then back up the large hill to the Mount Washington tourist area. It was a fairly difficult climb, and took him Northbound instead of Southbound, but he needed to make sure nothing sinister had befallen the pair. What had happened to force their long march of the day before? Clearly they didn't want to stay in the cabin with Franklin, but who would? Were Big Gray and Teapot worried he would catch up with them and they'd have to endure another evening of his posturing and preening? Why abandon Nate too just a day later? When he returned to Mount Washington's top, he checked first at the small snack bar.

"Did you see two female hikers come through this morning?"

"We just opened," the bored twenty-year-old clerk sighed. "You're the first person in here today. If it's worth anything, I didn't pass any cars coming down the mountain on my drive in."

So no one drove them off. That left only one other way to get off Mount Washington.

"Yeah, they were here before I even opened," the bearded ticket agent at the railroad office said. "Two hikers. One tall redhead and brunette, right?" Nate nodded. "They must have gotten cold up here and decided to call it quits," the clerk said. "Can't say as I blame them. I think any of you folks that go hiking out here before it warms up are nuts. Anyway, they left about an hour ago, which means they're already at the bottom. You want a ticket to follow 'em down?"

Nate had to consider the question. They clearly didn't want to speak to him or they would have let him know they were leaving. They had a one-hour head start, which meant it was likely they would have hitched a ride at the bottom and already were gone.

It was clear from yesterday's silence and today's disappearance that they didn't want to be on the trail anymore. It was equally clear they didn't want to be with Nate anymore. They were safe, he had discovered, and at this point there was nothing more he could do. He walked over to the snack bar and ate a hard cinnamon bun and weak coffee. As he sat, a familiar tune again reverberated in past recesses of his memory. It was the tune he'd recalled at Kathadin, and this time he only remembered a partial verse:

Oh they tell me of a home where my friends have gone.
They tell me of a land far away …

He couldn't remember any more. He sat at the snack bar and stared out toward the white and brown horizon. After 20 more minutes of quiet he loaded up and headed southbound back down the hill. As he passed the site of their former joint campsite on Mount Monroe, he took a quick look around, and then continued down the slope. Ten miles later, he laughed out loud when he saw the sign indicating the mountain top he had just climbed, part of "The Presidentials" despite the fact that its namesake had never been a president: "Mount Franklin. 5003 Feet."

<h1 style="text-align:center">8</h1>

SMALL HILLS, BIG CITY

The rest of New Hampshire, and the entire state of Vermont were mostly a blur to Nate. He had clicked off all 161 miles of the trail in New Hampshire in just twelve days, running ridges that hovered at the 4,000-foot elevation and occasionally peaks that raised him to about a mile above sea level. Shortly after crossing I-93 in the mountains, he found a beautiful waterfall and spared himself an extra twenty minutes for rest and reflection, but for most of the next four weeks his routine would be up before dawn, hiking all day with no more than a ten-minute break, and then finishing at whatever cabin or shelter was near just as the sun set. Warmer weather had made the hiking easier, and all remnants of snow and ice had vanished by the time he crossed the Connecticut River into Vermont on June 15, his birthday. He sat that night at the Happy Hills shelter just a few miles away from the lights of West Hartford, Vermont, treating himself to a double-serving bag of ravioli before setting into his sleeping bag for the night. Before drifting off to sleep, he took time to listen to the sound of crickets and other insects, whose numbers had been increasing exponentially with the warming weather. As he lay there, it suddenly dawned on him that this was the first birthday he'd ever spent alone. He tried to think back to where he was and who he was with from the first birthday he could remember – his sixth – all the way to this year. Mercifully, he drifted off to sleep before revisiting the most recent birthdays, and when he awoke in the morning he had neither the interest nor resolve to continue reflecting upon it.

Vermont was much the same as New Hampshire, with the Green Mountains substituting for the White Mountains. The ridges were equally rocky, and the peaks equally majestic and daunting. Nate managed to traverse Vermont's 146 miles of trail in only eleven days, and it was clear to him that his strength and stamina were increasing, aided perhaps by the discipline that solitude and singleness of purpose provide.

Crossing into Massachusetts came as the trail continued its due-southward traverse of New England, and with only ninety miles of trail in the state, Nate found the trail no challenge. Even Mount Graylock, the highest point in Massachusetts, was a mere 3,491 feet. Connecticut was an even easier section of trail than Massachusetts, just fifty-two miles, most of those an easy stroll through the Houstatonic River Valley. By the time he entered New York State, greening ridges, hills and flower-laden rises had become routine, and he was easily clicking off twenty miles a day. With shelters placed strategically every ten to twelve miles, he was able to ignore every other rest stop.

When he came to an unusual wooden structure ten miles past the Connecticut-New York line, and just one hundred yards from Highway 22, he had to stop and study it. It was wooden like a shelter, but more like the deck off the back of a house, and straddled a train line. A huge white and blue sign blared "Appalachian Trail" in a block typeface. A bulletin board – similar to the ones at shelters and road crossings that displayed topographic maps and various inane warnings and bears and wildlife – instead showed timetables and a map with a different trail, one that lead from Wassaic, New York southward all the way into New York City. It finally sunk in that this was a commuter railway, and there was a train station right there on the Appalachian Trail. Admittedly, "station" was a bit of an exaggeration. It was nothing more than a ten-foot by forty-foot wooden deck with railings on the three sides not abutting the train line. Nate scanned the horizon looking for a store or restaurant to grab a bite and resupply. He hadn't replenished his foodstuffs since Massachusetts, and he was down to several granola bars and a small bag of raisins. He also hadn't had a chance to go off trail and shower, shave or do laundry in weeks. He was sure he was beyond aromatic. Perhaps a brief return to civilization couldn't hurt him. New York City was a wilderness all its own. From experience, Nate knew it was easy to be alone and anonymous in that city of 8 million people, as anonymous and unacknowledged as if he were camping off a remote cliffside in the Berkshires.

As he contemplated this, he heard a train horn off in the distance to the North, and quickly decided he would hop on board. He waited as the gray and blue ten-car train pulled by a diesel engine came roaring around the corner. He fished through his backpack pocket for his Ziplock bag filled with the thousands of dollars he had hidden away to finance his trip. As the train closed on the platform, he hoisted the pack around his shoulders and back on. He stood and stared patiently as the train roared toward the platform – and then raced at full speed right past it.

Nate stood bewildered as the train – which had never slowed – raced southward and then turned another corner heading out of view. Confused, he went back to the bulletin board and studied the train schedule. Apparently the commuter train made stops throughout the day at every stop on the line – except the Appalachian Trail platform. It only stopped there once a day, at 4:20 in the afternoon. Nate's watch had stopped working during a particularly horrific rainstorm along a ridgeline in Vermont, so he didn't know the time. Still, he deduced from the sun's position that it was sometime in the early afternoon. He plopped his backpack down on the wooden platform, and using it as a pillow, decided to catch a nap until 4:20 arrived.

Three times northbound trains blew by the platform as he slept on and off. On two occasions southbound trains did their part by ignoring the dirty but willing passenger standing on the platform. Finally, a southbound train appeared and slowed to a stop at the tiny wooden stage. Only the first passenger car opened, as the platform was the length of a single train car. Nate climbed aboard and scanned the car's interior, eliciting quite a few stares from the well-dressed people scattered among the fifty or more seats in the car. Each looked at the scruffy, bedraggled mountain man with the same thought: "Please, smelly man, don't sit next to me." Nate extended the courtesy of walking between cars until he found an empty row of three seats and sat down. He paid the conductor the full peak fare to New York City and slumped back to sleep, knowing it would be an hour and a half before he reached his destination.

The jarring of the train cars as they pulled into the underground train station woke him. He hadn't opened his eyes once during the ride, despite the noise of opening and closing doors, conductor announcements and one set of noisy teenagers traveling from Brewster to the big city to see what trouble they could get into that evening. Nate shook off the initial disorientation and pulled his backpack down from the overhead rack. Walking onto the indoor platform, he slowly made his way up the ramp with the other passengers and entered the huge atrium of Grand Central.

Grand Central was without question Jacqueline Kennedy Onassis's greatest contribution to New York City. When the historic epicenter of the Vanderbilt family's Grand Central Railroad was literally falling down in the mid-1970s and in danger of being lost – just as New York's Penn Station had vanished a decade earlier – she and an army of preservationists rose to the task of fighting to not only save it, but restore it to its past glory. It is a marvelous structure, a time machine trip into a previous century where you can imagine yourself in a scratchy wool suit, wearing a fedora, and listening to an FDR fireside chat on the radio while you await your train to Albany, Buffalo, Chicago, or just about any point in the country. The soaring ceiling has star charts embedded in it, with lights that twinkle and illuminate the constellations at night. At the center is the terminal's giant, gold clock, and although its value has been estimated in the millions due to its gold plating, it is without question priceless. While most misname the building Grand Central Station, it is technically a terminal, because unlike most train stations, all tracks enter it from one direction and terminate inside Grand Central.

Nate had never visited the terminal, because most of his business trips had involved flying the Boston-to-New York shuttle out of LaGuardia. The stature of the building was unmistakable, and he lingered long enough to take in its giant schedule board, brass ticket windows and even passed by the "whispering corner," where tourists could stand on opposite sides of a thirty-foot arch and whisper to each other, their voices funneled overhead to their friend diagonally across the corridor.

Nate had expected strange looks from passersby because of his unkempt appearance and dirty, musty backpack. He received few. In a building vagrants frequently haunted, there was nothing in his grungy appearance that was extraordinary. The nonchalance continued after he hit the sidewalk on 42nd Street. It was now afternoon rush hour, and the street was packed with a volatile mix of tourists and suit-clad professionals. The tourists walked slowly, necks tipped back as if they wanted to catch falling raindrops in their mouths. They gawked at the tall buildings – including the Chrysler and Empire State, with their art deco design and impressive architecture – as well as other less-imaginative brass-and-glass boxes that towered over the masses they imprisoned from 9 to 5 each weekday.

Nate walked north, not because he had any particular ending point in mind, but because the swarming, oscillating, jostling crowd had pushed him in that direction, up Park Avenue and the street's rare-for-New York greenbelt median. He passed the headquarters of Chase Bank, a giant, block-like fortress lined with vehicle barricades and threatening security guards more numerous and ominous than any security he'd seen on the passenger train. He crossed the street and walked in front of the Waldorf-Astoria, the city's historic hotel and still the preferred refuge of United Nations heads of states and U.S. presidents when they came to the city. As he gawked at the giant flags that hung overhead to announce whatever country's leader was visiting – the hotel always flew the flag of the powerful visitor's nation – a surly doorman with think black-framed glasses crowned with a single eyebrow gave him a quick once-over and menacingly barked "Get a move on, buddy. Keep going." Nate at first thought he was talking to someone behind him, but quickly realized his shabby appearance had given the doorman the perceived right to run him off from the front of the hotel. He considered arguing the point but calculated that the guard had fifty pounds on him, and Nate really didn't want to spend his first night in New York in a holding cell. He moved on up Park Avenue but quickly cut westward two streets to avoid similar incidents in front of the other fancy hotels he knew lined the subsequent blocks of Park Avenue along the Upper East Side. Unfortunately, his westward jog hadn't allowed him to escape the city's materialistic core – rather, it had put him in its epicenter. Walking northward now along Fifth Avenue, he marveled at the windows of jewelry, electronics and opulence once familiar, if not comfortable to him. Now, after several months in the sparse, quiet and primitive world of the trail, he found them jarring and gaudy. The things that at one time seemed necessary extravagances or toys were now insulting, base and offensive. A pearl necklace couldn't be used for warmth, for cooking or for shelter, so how could it have value?

The buildings grew taller as he worked his way through midtown, and then suddenly they vanished. Like Lewis & Clark suddenly stumbling onto the Pacific Ocean at the mouth of the

Columbia, Nate had suddenly walked into a verdant field of green amidst the towering hotels and office buildings. His response was exactly the one Frederic Law Olmstead and Calbert Vaux had intended when they'd designed Central Park in 1858. The jarring pastoral setting cast amidst the city noise had immediately created a sense of the familiar, the natural. A more humanistic sensation.

As he walked northward, he strolled through the park's zoo, catching a seemingly knowing glance from several of the seals sunning themselves upon the large rocks in their enclosure. He passed innumerable statues, to war heroes, poets, writers and even a dog – a statue commemorating Balto's saving of the sickened children of Nome, Alaska. Finally, as the sun began to turn the landscape yellow and then orange, he bought two hot dogs from a cart vendor and sat down on a green wooden bench overlooking a small lake near the center of the park. He ate quietly and slowly, eavesdropping on the dozens of discussions that strolled past him, clouds of conversations enveloping the tourists and nearby residents that passed him. All were banal, and yet each was a matter of great import to the speaker. The difficulties of finding a dependable dog walker, how poorly a coworker was treated or which restaurant was offering the most affordable sushi seemed to be of critical import to each respective passerby. To Nate, it was all triviality. These sincere tones focused on the trivial annoyed him, so he wandered off the paved walkways and into a green, grass-carpeted field, strolling near several two-story boulders.

"What are you doing here?" The voice reverberated like a gunshot, and it startled Nate enough to cause him to drop his water bottle. "I've already got this spot staked out, so you'll have to find another!" Nate now had a chance to size up the man who had fired off the verbal shot, and was surprised by what he saw. From a quick glance he looked like many of the homeless Nate had passed on the city's streets, but this one had an indescribable air of elegance that wasn't obvious from the brown and black unwashed clothing layered over his body. His graying beard contrasted sharply with the dark, mocha skin of his face, pockmarked with scattered facial blemishes and several scars across his neck and right cheek. Despite his rough appearance, however, he held his frame in a regal posture, holding a stand-up wireframe shopping cart with his left hand and a wooden staff that years earlier had done duty as a mop handle in his right. He used both to keep his balance, and holding his seventy-ish frame in such an upright posture clearly required effort and concentration.

"I'm sorry," Nate stated. "I didn't realize."

The response was clearly not the one the elderly man expected, and he took several seconds to try to size Nate up.

"You clearly don't belong here," he finally said. He craned his head to inspect Nate's backpack. "You're not homeless, and you sure as hell are too old to be a student or a runaway." He considered other possible options but couldn't find a mental file folder in which to place Nate's paperwork. "Who the hell are you, boy?"

Nate misunderstood the question and did his standard trail introduction. "My name's Nate," he said, sticking out his right hand. The old man stared at it, not warily, but rather with a dismissiveness that made it clear he had no interest in shaking hands with anyone.

"No, I mean who are you? Why are you here, white boy? Shouldn't you be in some fancy high-rise or loft or wherever the hell you white boys live?"

"Well, I ..." Nate was genuinely confused and off-balance.

The elderly man eased off his guard slightly, as he realized he'd put Nate on his. He knew the confused were less of a threat than the certain.

"Actually," Nate began, "I guess I am homeless. I don't have a home."

"Shit," the man spat, continuing to keep an eye on Nate as he slowly turned to keep an eye on another man who at fifty yards distant was also starting to encroach into his safety zone. "Not having a home don't make you homeless any more than not having water makes you a sand dune. Where you from, cracker?"

"Maine," Nate replied.

"Shit, they grow cotton in Maine?" Nate was now genuinely confused. "You may not have much of a cracker accent, but you got enough that I can smell the grits in your mouth. Where you really from, Southern boy?"

"I was born in Tennessee."

"Den that's where you from. So you one of those hillbilly crackers." Nate found himself getting defensive.

"My family moved to Maine when I was eight," he protested.

"Don't cry to me about it, cracker boy. I don't care."

Nate immediately wondered why he'd gotten so defensive with

a homeless man.

"Besides, cracker boy, don't matter where you've been. It's where you're going that counts. If you think you're going to be sleeping in my spot, you'd best keep thinking."

"That's fine, that's fine," Nate waved him off, now irritated. "Plenty of park for everyone."

"Yeah, you'd think so, Maine cracker boy. If you planning on sleeping in this park, you might want to take a couple of tips from old Philly here. You spot me some crackers or a candy bar from your bag there and I'll tell you where you can sleep and not get rousted by the greenleaf cops."

"Greenleaf cops?"

Philly laughed, and when he did Nate was quickly able to inventory all four teeth the old man had left in his mouth. "Shit. Now you know you gotta give me a bite. You don't even know about the greenleaf cops."

Nate thought for a moment, and figured both the information and conversation were worth a granola bar. "Done," he said.

Both men found an exposed piece of rock and settled down for a lesson.

"The greenleaf cops are the Central Park police. Got a green leaf on their uniform. They really aren't police, but you have to treat them like that, cause if you don't do what they say they'll radio for the NYPD and they'll crack you up ugly. So when one of the park employees rousts you and tell you to move or leave the park, you pretty much do what they say. If an NYPD wakes you and tells you to move on, you'd best do it fairly quickly. Most of them are OK, but you'll find a few that don't like being part of the Central Park Precinct and they're just looking for an excuse to take it out on you."

"So sleeping in the park isn't allowed."

"You right, Maine cracker boy. It ain't the '70s no more. Most of us don't stay here during the day, because the cops like to keep the place all prettified for the tourists. Once the sun goes down, you can settle in and find a place to bunk down. The trick is to find a place where you can't be seen, but you can still see what's around you. The cops are bad only because they'll force you to bundle up your things and go find another place. What you really want to be scared of are the kids."

"Kids?"

"The teenagers. They wild. If they catch you alone with no one around, at best they'll just beat you up to show you and each other how tough they are. At best." He stopped, staring off into the distance.

"And at worst?"

There was a long pause, and Philly kept staring out further and further, as if trying to see a ship on a distant horizon.

"I had a buddy they caught one night. After they beat him up ... they had some lighter fluid on them ..." Philly stopped talking and kept searching for the ship. Nate quietly watched the sunset over the buildings of the Upper West Side while Philly stared.

Marie stared blankly out the window into the backyard of her Boston house. Nate was busy cleaning up after a dinner of tiny Vienna sausages – not his and Marie's favorite, but little Joy had just moved from bottled baby food to adult food, and she'd quickly fallen in love with the taste, texture and playfulness of the mash-able food. Joy was in the backyard rocking up and down on the rusting metal swing set that Nate had tried with limited success to cement into the ground just outside their back door. The yard was small, and the five-foot white wooden clapboard fence gave the illusion of privacy but also made the space seem even more confining and small. Joy was focused on pointing her toes skyward just as she reached the apex of her forward swing. Marie at first seemed focused on Joy, but as Nate was finishing the last of the dishes he began to realize that Marie's eyes were fixated past her to a horizon far beyond their tiny backyard.

Jeff, their neighbor, had just left. He blew out the front door and around to his back entrance the same way he entered – with noise, energy and unfocused childlike playfulness. He was animated and always smiling, but as always every question, comment and discussion had focused on Jeff and his world. Jeff had the remarkable gift of being completely narcissistic and charming at the same time. After his departure, the silence in the house was palpable.

"Are you OK?" Nate had taken to asking Marie this question a great deal in the past year. Like most new mothers, Marie had believed motherhood and parenting would provide her with the sense of accomplishment and completion she had been missing in the working world. The accomplishment of creating a new life was indeed sobering and empowering. "I've done something you can never do," she had joked often with Nate during the first few weeks of her recovery. The first few months flew by, with Joy's 18 hours a day of on-and-off sleeping quickly diminishing to eight consecutive hours of quiet. Sleeping through the night had come relatively quickly, and Nate and Marie had spoken to enough parents to know that was a blessing to be counted. It was quickly determined – both by her parents and by both sets of grandparents, who had happily and regularly made the pilgrimage down I-95 to see her – that she was the spitting image of her mother, and that Nate's contributions to her appearance would be minimal. "She doesn't know how blessed she is," Nate would smile at this, issued both as a self-deprecating joke and as a mild but intentional compliment to his wife. Joy moved from scooting to standing to walking relatively quickly. Her intelligence manifested itself in many ways, most notably in how she constantly challenged and thwarted any effort her parents made to childproof the house. There wasn't a cabinet latch or safety device that she couldn't defeat, and she giggled uncontrollably each time her mother or father let out a heaving sigh upon discovering her latest victory over the best thinking of child-safety engineers.

Tonight her focus was not on latches, but on toe-pointing, and the late northern summer day meant an extremely late sunset, and plenty of time to sync her foot extensions to her swinging. Her efforts were missed by her mother, who continued staring blankly beyond her.

"Marie, are you OK?" Nate hadn't received a response to his initial query, and he moved into her line of sight to get her attention.

"Yes, I'm fine. Just thinking."

"About?"

"Nothing in particular. Just trying to clear my head. It was a busy day today, with the doctor's appointment, grocery shopping and all the other errands. Tell me about your day."

"Not much to tell," Nate said. "They may finally be ready to decide on store closings." Gilchrist's had expanded during the past decade, trying to open stores in the Boston suburbs where most of their clients had fled during the 1960s and 1970s. Now many of those very stores were barely holding on, as a recession and changing shopping trends had made the giant malls less attractive. Where just a decade before shopping malls had provided convenience and comfort to shoppers, now they found them too complicated and inconvenient, and traffic and sales at the chain's mall stores were plummeting. As a key player in the chain's marketing department, Nate was feeling pressure from the executives to come up with plans to reverse inevitable trends that even the best advertising and marketing couldn't prevent.

"I had another call from that headhunter again," Nate volunteered, carefully studying Marie's response. Her expressionless gaze out the window never changed. "It seems the people I talked to really want me to join them. They added another $20,000 to the offer."

Marie turned slightly at the mention of such a large sum of money, but then turned back to the window. "That's a lot of money," she volunteered, noting the obvious. She knew what was coming next but refused to broach the subject.

"If we took it, we'd be much closer to our folks. And they're not getting any younger." As with any life decisions, Nate had considered the initial offer from the Maine retail giant by drawing a long vertical line down a piece of paper and then listing the pros and cons of the offer. Along with the money and the career opportunity, he had placed proximity to his and Marie's parents in the positive column – finding a reliable babysitter for Joy had not been easy or inexpensive, and their neighbor Jeff had proved himself incapable of paying attention to the subtle signals that a toddler might need food, a changing or a hug. The possibility of imposing on two sets of grandparents – not imposing, really, since all four would be excited at the prospect of doting on their only grandchild – made sense. While Nate had missed his wife's reluctance to the move when he first mentioned it, this time he correctly read her silence as at best disinterest and at worst flat-out rejection of the notion.

"I don't understand, Marie. The first couple of years we were married you were homesick for Maine. We drove home as often as we could afford. Now, I sense you don't want to go back. So why don't you tell me what's changed?"

"Oh Nate, it's not that I don't want to go back. It's just ..." she paused, unable to find the right words for what she was feeling, finally settled for other words. "It's just that I fear it."

"Fear it?"

Marie would never express her true feelings, because in part they were selfish ones. She had initially enjoyed working and was challenged by her management role, but eventually she tired of it. Only her employee and friend Jeff's company made her days in the coffee shop tolerable. Joy's arrival came at the perfect time, allowing her to abandon the workaday world for that of stay-at-home mom. This, she believed, would be her highest calling. After two years, however, the joy and fulfillment were unrealized. If she wasn't happy with a career and wasn't happy as a wife and mother, what was out there that would make her happy? How could she explain these feelings to Nate, who clearly knew what made him happy? She had grown slowly to resent his certitude. He was certain about his career, about his role as a father. She didn't envy him his professional success. She didn't envy his comfort with Joy. It was the certitude that she coveted.

"I just don't know what I'll do if we move back to Freeport," she said. "If I want to go back to work, there's plenty of options here in Boston. Back home, there will be fewer. Here, I can write my own course. There, everyone's assumptions about me were fixed back when we were in ninth grade."

"Do you want to go back to work?"

She didn't. But she didn't not want to go back to work. What did she want? She had no idea. Surrender always was an acceptable option to Marie, so she took it. She had surrendered back when they were first married, abandoning Freeport and school for a life with Nate in Boston. Why not surrender again and sail with the tide?

"If it makes sense for us as a family — more money, better opportunity for you, better schools for Joy, then I guess we'd be crazy not to do it," she said, turning to look into Nate's eyes so she could sell her insincere acceptance. Whether she was that good an actress or he simply saw what he wanted to see would be debated for the remainder of their marriage.

In Central Park, Nate had moved a good 200 yards away from Philly and found a spot to spread out his sleeping bag, partially covered by a rock overhang. It was shaded by a canopy of small trees hanging just five feet over the ground, and with the temperatures still in the eighties even an hour after sunset, Nate accepted that he'd be sleeping on top of his bag rather than in it. He had a clear line of sight toward the spot where Philly had been resting, and was surprised to see the stooped black figure slowly working his way across the lawn toward him. He was dragging a beat-up wheeled suitcase along with him, and when he arrived at Nate's location, Nate couldn't help but crack a joke.

"Late for your flight?"

"Oh you're funny, Maine cracker boy. Amazing how many people in this town throw these out just when they get a little scuffed up. Never understood that. I thought the point was for the suitcase to get scuffed up so your belongings inside didn't."

"Well, you look very fashionable."

"I am fashionable. I'm the biggest trendsetting urban camper on the island of Manhattan. Don't you forget that, amateur." Philly took a quick glance at Nate's spread, and then cut a glance back toward his spot across the field.

"Thinking I got a better spot?" Nate asked.

"No, I'm very happy where I'll be staying tonight, Maine cracker boy. I left a blanket to hold my spot, but some people can't take a hint, that's why I'm keeping an eye on it. No, I'm here because you got me thinking."

"About?"

"About why you're here. You obviously ain't lived on the streets, because you got all your teeth and still look in pretty good shape. You ain't poor, because that gear you're carting there hasn't been scavenged. You're not some young kid backpacking across the country. You ain't near my age, but you're not 18 either so that makes no sense. So I kept sitting there after you left wondering what a Maine cracker boy would be doing in my park?"

"Just passing through. They didn't like the looks of me at the Waldorf."

"Ah, they should love you. You're white. That's about all you need to make them happy."

"That and some money."

"Money ain't nothing. I had it once in my life. Didn't bring me nothing but pain. I tell you, Maine cracker boy, there's lots of measuring sticks in this life, and money's a shitty measuring stick. In fact, it's the shittiest."

"You think?"

"I walk the streets of this city every day. I see the guys in suits on Rector Street and the guys in rags up on 252nd Street. I'd trust the guys in rags long before I'd trust a suit. A guy in rags might take some of your food, but he'd only do it if he was hungry. A guy in a suit would take a million dollars out of your pocket even if he didn't need it. Now which one's the evil one?" Nate just nodded.

"You know what my favorite days of the week are?"

"No."

"Saturday and Sunday."

"If you haven't got a job, isn't every day a weekend?"

"No, it ain't for that. My favorite thing to do is to set myself up with a donation cup outside a synagogue on Saturdays and a big church on Sundays."

"Why? Do you clean up?"

"Not any more than I do downtown or at Times Square on a weekday. It's not that I make more money, it's just that I make the people coming out ... uncomfortable. They've been listening to somebody inside telling them to look to heavenly things and give up belongings. Then they come right outside and bang! I put them to the test. Either they give me something so they can feel good about themselves for a few minutes, or they don't and then they spend the rest of the day questioning themselves. I prefer the ones who don't give me something, especially when they pretend they don't see me. I know I tie them up in knots trying to explain to themselves why I don't deserve anything. Truth be told, maybe I don't. But that's not the point. I just like that a dirty, aging shell like me can make the richest, most powerful person in town uncomfortable. I make him think. I make him question what he believes. I either make him rethink his life, or make him decide that he likes mammon more than man. That's power. From where I'm sitting, you don't have a lot of power, so you take it where you can."

Nate considered this, admitting that on occasions he'd walked past street beggars in Boston, speculating – or was it just rationalizing – that they were professional hucksters who made a good living begging for cash.

"That's the best part of it, and why I feel like I'm just a little better off," Philly continued. "They're judging me, and they think I'm judging them by whether they hand me a dollar bill or not. I don't judge them. I don't care. I really don't. I don't have to live their life, so whatever they do is fine with me. If I get enough to buy a meal, great. If I only find enough to get a cheap snack, that's fine too. Philly doesn't care. They goes crazy thinking I'm judging them. That's power too."

"But you were sitting back there and judging me by what I looked like and what I was carrying," Nate noted.

"Not judging, Maine cracker boy. Taking inventory. I don't care if you're some mid-life crisis ex-hippie, a murderer on the lam or just some unemployed Wall Street type who's getting a comeuppance. I don't care. I may find it interesting, but I don't judge. That's the secret. Don't be a judge. I see judges sometimes when they run me in. They don't seem terribly happy being a judge. Sour people. If they don't like it – and they get paid to do it – why would you do it on your own."

Nate considered the logic of that. "Judge not, lest ye be judged, right?"

"Oh, it's beyond that. I judge not, and I don't even care if I'm judged. Everybody's caught up in measuring everything, putting it on a scale. Where's the point that determines whether you're good or evil? If you've done ten evil things and twelve good things, is that the break-even point? Five-to-one ratio what gets you into to heaven? What have you got to put up on the scoreboard? Judging is measuring, it's keeping score. Keeping score is looking back. You can't walk forward while you're looking back. You're guaranteed to trip on something doing that. Just walk forward, Maine cracker boy. Don't be so caught up in keeping score, of judging, of looking back."

The last thought hit Nate hard, and he took on a serious tone.

"Let me ask you this, Philly. What if there's something back there that you can't leave? What if you've got something so awful that you don't even want to go forward, you just want to stop?"

Philly tried to take this in. He wasn't sure what Nate was driving at, but he plunged forward.

"You're always going forward. You take a breath, that's a step forward in life even if you're sitting still on the ground. This globe's spinning at thousands of miles a second around the sun and the galaxy. You can sit perfectly still and you're still flying faster than any airplane can. You're moving, cracker boy. You just need to decide whether you're going to drive the bus or whether somebody else will."

"What if you just want to get off?"

Philly considered this. Eventually, he understood what Nate was suggesting.

"One day, back when I worked at a garage, I just couldn't take it anymore. I was supposed to get off in Williamsburg, but I just couldn't take it anymore. So I stayed on my bus. Smelled the ocean. Didn't know where it was going, but I didn't want to go forward no more. Well, the bus took me to Far Rockaway. I finally got off. Didn't know nothing about the place, but when I got there it was clear I didn't belong in that neighborhood. Got roughed up by some toughs, and then the police came and tossed me in jail for a few days." He leaned in close and stared hard at Nate. "Yeah. If you don't know what it's going to be like when you get off the bus, my advice is just to stay on."

Nate managed to sleep well in the park, despite the occasional late-night dog walker strolling by within fifty feet or so. The dog would sniff and occasionally let out a bark, but the owners never saw him and would have avoided him had they known he was there. In the morning, the early sunrise woke Nate just as it had done for the past hundred or so days on the trail. He gathered up his gear, cinched his pack and wandered back toward Philly's spot. The old man was still sacked out, lying on his back and snoring, with his suitcase propped under his head like a huge, black rectangular pillow. Nate studied him, then pulled a New Hampshire-Vermont trail map out of his pocket, along with three one-hundred-dollar bills. He folded the map into a makeshift envelope, and wrote on the back with a pencil:

"Money may be a shitty measuring stick, but no one says you have to measure anything with it."

He signed it,
Maine Cracker Boy

Nate placed the note carefully on top of the suitcase near Philly's head so he couldn't miss it when he woke up. Then he headed east toward Park Avenue. He splurged on a cup of coffee and a scone at a corner Starbucks – the barista initially confused him for a street person just wanting to use the bathroom – and then continued southward through the Upper East Side. He passed four high-end brass-and-glass hotel buildings but waited until he reached the Waldorf. He moved quickly, at his four-miles-per-hour hiking pace, made a sharp ninety-degree turn and entered the revolving brass doors before the doorman out front could say anything to him. By the time the doorman had time to respond and scurry into the hotel lobby, Nate had already bounded up the stairs and reached the check-in counter.

"Need a room please. Something very nice. Maybe a view. Don't have a reservation, though."

The clerk was initially confused. Nate's appearance screamed "kick me out," but the officious tone hinted at both power and money. It was still morning, usually check-out time rather than check-in time, but the hotel had plenty of vacant rooms.

"I have a couple of smaller suites that are available this early in the day, but that's about it." He didn't volunteer the room rate, curious if Nate would ask. Nate didn't. "Do you have an ID and credit card?" This would be the moment of truth, the clerk thought. Nate pulled out his Maine driver's license and a Platinum American Express card, both of which had been sitting untouched at the bottom of his pack since the start of his odyssey. After running the card, the clerk returned with a room key and was rewarded with a $100 bill and a question.

"Can you arrange for a barber to be sent to my room? And do you have an arrangement with any men's suit stores who can send someone to my room with some off-the-rack offerings? Size 42 long and 34/32 slacks."

"Yes sir, Mr. Townsend. I'll take care of both personally."

"Thank you."

Nate turned and walked past the doorman who had accosted him yesterday to the bank of elevators. Nate tried very hard to neither judge nor measure him.

Nate had finished showering by the time the barber from around the corner arrived. He had an arrangement with the Waldorf, which often had a head of state or celebrity who needed grooming but didn't want to expose himself to the crowds of New York's streets. Likewise, the nearby men's clothing store was occasionally prevailed upon to provide a repair, alteration, jacket or even custom job for a bigwig. Once, a U.S. President staying at the hotel had ruined the trousers of the suit he was scheduled to wear to the United Nations, and a new pair had to be measured, sewn and delivered in less than an hour.

Nate had to admit that the attention being heaped upon him was enjoyable, even though he knew it was the huge wad of bills with Benjamin Franklin's likeness and not him that these people were eager to see. He obliged, and both the barber and tailor smiled with the false belief that the now well-groomed and well-dressed man had an unlimited supply of the bills. Nate's secret was that he had a limited supply, and only he knew the demand for them would eventually vanish. Now decked out in a dark blue suit, hair groomed, fully shaved and scented, Nate had given all his hiking clothes to the bell man with orders to have the hotel laundry deliver them back to him by the next morning. A laundry used to tuxedos, ties and evening gowns was going to be scratching their heads as they cleaned wool socks, zippered hiking shorts and water-wicking shirts.

Nate took the elevator to the ground floor and stepped out onto the street. The doorman who twelve hours earlier had all but evicted him now didn't even recognize him. He whistled for a cab and Nate climbed in.

"Where to?"

Nate realized he hadn't even considered where in New York he wanted to visit.

"If you only had one day in New York, where would you go?" Nate asked the driver.

"Anywhere else," the cabbie snapped back.

"Great. Let's start with an early lunch. What's a good lunch place in midtown?"

"Got a good one. Right between Times Square and Rockefeller Center." Nate was there in six minutes. He ate his meal in silence, avoiding every attempt by the waiter to engage him in friendly banter intended to ingratiate and earn a larger tip. Nate mentally mapped the city in his mind, trying to decide where he would spend his last day there before heading back to the trail. In his mind, he started north and moved south. Yankee Stadium. A baseball game? No. Some tourist mecca like the Empire State Building? Hell no. Walking the neighborhoods? A little to warm for that, especially in a suit. As he sat alone, his sense of loss began to build once again. As it grew, it instantly occurred to him where he needed to go.

"St. Paul's Church downtown," he told the cab driver after leaving the restaurant.

Nate didn't know the street address of where he wanted to

go, but he knew what was next door. An old high school chum had become an Episcopal deacon and had told him stories about St. Paul's, especially its finest hour in September of 2001. When he arrived, he walked through the church, out its back door and through its ancient and historic graveyard. As he exited onto the corner of Vesey and Church Street, he stared at the giant blue plywood walls and listened to the construction sounds coming from the other side. He gradually worked his way around the huge construction site to its west side and entered an office building whose escalators took him to a second-floor overlook where he could see clearly into the site.

The gash in the ground was astonishingly symmetrical. It was a giant hole in the face of New York City, and yet it was perfectly square. The stories-deep hole was slowly being filled with rebar and concrete. Structures slowly tried to rise from the empty pit of unimaginable loss. The efforts of the construction workers interested Nate not at all. It was the emptiness of the square plot that stirred him. This was an epicenter of loss. Its enormity helped Nate feel a kinship, a brotherhood. He was a member of this club, and while his loss was far different, and much less newsworthy, he knew he belonged to the club. He had a membership card. He wondered if such complex feelings as loss and pain could be measured. How could one person's loss be scaled against another's? Was the loss of a child more painful or less painful than the loss of a spouse? A parent? What about the loss of friends? Did they matter less? Was the method of loss important? If there is such a thing as a recovery period for loss, was it shorter? If the death of loved ones put a hole in your soul, how did you measure it?

An hour passed and Nate continued to stare at the World Trade Center site. Office workers and the occasional tourist passed by. The latter would occasionally stop next to him to share the view of the scene, or snap a picture, while the former rushed on, disinterested. Some may have been deeply affected on that day, but today their attentions were elsewhere. Finally, Nate disconnected and walked back down to the street level, walking south and east several blocks before entering a nondescript tower. He checked in with the security guard, using a downstairs phone to call an old college friend, Daniel Reeve, who was shocked to receive the call but immediately cleared him to head up to the 23rd floor.

"What in the hell are you doing in town?" Daniel asked,

offering him a plush seat in his office. "We haven't talked in years. What have you been up to? Still peddling wool shirts and boots?"

"Yeah, I'm still with them," Nate said. "I'm just in the city for one day, so I figured I'd drop in and pay a social call, as well as throw a little business your way."

"I like the sound of both of those," Daniel smiled. "Business before pleasure, though. What can I do for you?"

"Well, I need some help setting up a will and a charitable trust. If something happens to me, I need someone from your office to serve as executor and clean up everything, putting the balance into some type of charity."

Daniel didn't ask about next of kin or family members. He had heard through the old high school grapevine why Daniel was having to rework his affairs. "We can do that. If you outline your assets and liabilities, along with what specific charity or charities you have in mind, we can draw up the papers."

"Already ahead of you," Nate said, handing him a sheath of paperwork that had been sitting inside a waterproof bag for the past two and a half months. "Here's the deeds and documents, as well as the three charities I have in mind."

"Wow, you've thought all this through, haven't you? I wish all our other prospects thought this far ahead and knew what they were doing."

"I just like being prepared."

"Be prepared? What are you, a boy scout?"

He thought about some of his foolhardy mistakes along the trail during the past two months. "Hardly."

Daniel scanned the information. "We can set this up for you. How about I have my people draw up a first draft and I can bring it tonight when I take you to dinner."

"You don't have to take me to dinner."

"I kind of have a rule: Friends I haven't heard from in years walk in and give me business get a dinner. Don't make me break my rule."

"Fair enough. How about one of those New York steak houses I keep hearing about. I haven't had a good steak in months."

"Done."

"Here's the address I'd like you to send the final documents to when they're done so I can sign them."

Daniel looked at the address. "Virginia? You living in Virginia now?"

"No, but I'll be passing through about the time these get done. They'll hold my mail for me until I show up."

"Fine. Where are you staying tonight?"

"Waldorf."

"Nice. I'll come pick you up at seven and we'll have a great meal and many vodkas."

The dinner was magnificent and cholesterol-laden, and Nate enjoyed catching up on Daniel's life in New York. He admitted that being a Red Sox fan deep in the heart of Yankees territory was a purgatory, but the huge salary his legal firm was paying salved his pain sufficiently. They talked about high school days, and he questioned Nate just twice about Marie. Both times Nate was able to deflect the questions with clever and subtle lies. When they parted, Nate chose to walk the 20 blocks back to his hotel, where he slammed down two extremely overpriced drinks in the hotel bar and then went upstairs to sleep.

In the morning, he left his suit spread out neatly on his bed, donned his hiking clothes and caught the Harlem Line train from Grand Central back to where he'd last left the trail.

9

SHARP ROCKS CUT DEEP

Crossing the Hudson River over the Bear Mountain bridge meant his days in New York State were numbered, and three days later the trail made a left-angle turn from west to south and he entered New Jersey, a state with comparatively few AT miles. Despite its proximity to New York City, the New Jersey section of the trail was remarkably remote and mountainous, and twice Nate spotted black bears roaming near the trail. He gave both wide berth, making enough noise that they were aware of him and quickly scurried away. Bears didn't like humans but loved human food. The process of protecting your food – and thus yourself – from the bears was a nightly ritual. Bears have horrific eyesight, but their sense of smell is so attuned that they can detect food from more than ten miles away. A neighbor of Nate's had such a misguided desire to see bears that she would regularly place sardines in her backyard in hopes of luring them within sight of the picture windows in the rear of her house. On the rare occasions when her baiting worked, it resulted in three or four days of the bear lumbering around the neighborhood, upending trash cans until someone called animal control to either shoo off or capture and relocate the creatures.

On the trail, bears were rarely a physical danger. On the few occasions when black bears attacked humans, a quick investigation usually revealed either the bear was trying to get to food the camper had foolishly kept with him in his tent, or that a hiker had unwittingly placed himself between a mother and her cubs. The proper procedure for avoiding an unwelcome meeting on the trail was to be just noisy enough to alert the bears in advance to your presence, and to use a bear bag. A bear bag was a simple device, quite simply a waterproof sack – Nate used an old bag once used to hold his sleeping bag – and a thirty-foot section of rope with a small lead washer at the end. Each night after dinner Nate would place all his foodstuffs, and any clothing that might have spilled food or even the scent of food on it, inside zippered plastic bags. He would then place these items inside the bear bag. He would throw the rope over the highest tree branch he could find and hoist the bag well out of the reach of any bear. The tree had to be of substantial diameter, or else the bear would use its enormous weight to bend the tree to the ground – and enjoy a midnight snack at Nate's expense. On occasion, Nate would hear rustling during the night near his bear bag. In the vacant darkness of the wilderness the reverberating sounds made him think a pack of bears were ransacking his gear, but in the morning the evidence suggested it was likely a single raccoon.

His short excursion into the city had allowed several southbound hikers to catch up with him, and each night he found himself sharing the shelters with one or two of them. At Rutherford Shelter, he met with his first northbound hiker, a marathon runner with the apt trail name "Lightning." A sinewy figure carrying nothing but a three-by-three-foot knapsack, Lightning wandered into the campsite shortly after Nate arrived, with just over an hour of sunlight left. He had momentarily hesitated as he saw the shelter, trying to decide if it was time to stop or keep hiking. Seeing Nate, he took a quick glance at his watch and decided some conversation was in order. He strolled down the hill toward the shelter. After introductions, he took a quick glance skyward and then, deciding that rain was possible, tossed his knapsack inside the shelter and pulled out a lightweight down blanket.

When he noticed Nate marveling at how little gear he was carrying, he explained himself. "Lightpacker." As if that was all the explanation that was required. The word meant nothing to Nate, and his face apparently transmitted that fact. "I try to hike with as little weight as possible." A hiker named Ray Jardine had been among the first to popularize the philosophy that enjoyment of the outdoors and hiking was inversely proportional to the amount of weight you carried on your back. Hiking the AT (or the Pacific Crest Trail, Continental Divide Trail, or any of the hundreds that Jardine had clicked off) was much more fun, Jardine argued, if you were focused on nature and not the pain in your back, feet and shoulders that carrying a forty- or fifty-pound backpack required. Nate thought back to his purging exercise after he had slogged through the One-Hundred--Mile Wilderness, and the advice that Kenneth Knight had given him, but he quickly realized this hiker was taking the philosophy to the extreme. Nevertheless, Nate pressed Lightning for pointers.

After boiling a small tin of water with his homemade alcohol stove and dumping in a small amount of dried food from a plastic bag, Lightning dumped out his knapsack, spilling out very little gear. Nate saw little more than two pairs of lightweight socks, a thin plastic tarp which he presumed served as a tent, and a small bag with some toiletries. Yes, he noticed, Lightning, like Knight back in Maine, had sawed off half the toothbrush handle to save weight.

"What do you do on the trail when it gets cold?"

"My blanket," Lightning replied, pointing to the quilted down blanket he'd laid out on one of the shelter's bunks. "It's very warm but extremely light. I use it to sleep with instead of a sleeping bag, and if I get cold while hiking I just wrap it around myself and keep walking."

Nate had heard this song before. "No poncho," Nate noticed.

"I use this," Lightning smiled, pulling out a small collapsible umbrella.

"You're kidding."

"Nope. Got nothing to do with my hands while hiking anyway, and it also does a great job keeping the sun off of me on hot days."

All of this was a bit much for Nate. Unlike his previous meeting with Knight, he didn't feel a driving urge to dump out anything he was currently carrying. Some of the items in his bag seemed like creature comforts compared with Lightning, but he was very happy to keep them.

"You're the first northbounder I've passed."

"Really?"

"The first through-hiking northbounder, anyway."

"Awesome! There was a guy who started out ahead of me in Georgia in February, but I haven't heard about him for a long time. I think he dropped out somewhere in the Smokies. I'm not racing to be first or anything, but it's always great to know you're the first." In 2011, runner Jennifer Davis raced from Kathadin to Springer in 46 days, 11 hours and 20 minutes. Lighting was a fast hiker, but hardly the fastest.

"So what have you seen so far?" Nate said, hoping for a scouting report on his next few weeks of hiking.

"Seen? Rocks. Rocks, rocks and more rocks. You're about 20 miles from the state line, and then you'll be in Rocksylvania. If God lives in that state, he hates hikers."

"I hate to break the news to you, but the whole trail is nothing but rocks."

"Yeah, but not like this. Back in Georgia, Tennessee and Virginia, the rocks are fairly smooth and they're all laying on their flat sides in the middle of the trail. Sure you have a jutting edge sticking out here and there, but in a large part of the trail it's like hiking on a tile floor. In Pennsylvania for some reason – maybe that's as far as the glaciers got – all the rocks are turned edge-up, so it's like hiking for weeks and weeks on top of razor blades. I had a pair of boots that made it all the way from Springer Mountain through Maryland, but after just five days in Pennsylvania, I had to get off the trail, go buy a new pair and then go through the painful process of breaking them in. I just now got them to where I don't think about them every single, painful step."

"How was the scenery?"

"Dunno. Was too busy clicking off miles. And bitching to myself about my feet."

"So any towns worth stepping off the trail and visiting?" said Nate, still recovering from the disorientation that his brief off-trail visit to Manhattan had caused.

"Nope, couldn't tell you. I went off trail for about two hours to pick up food and supplies, but that was it. Don't remember the name. Cleared Rocksylvania in ten days. That means I was averaging over 22 miles a day. Not bad, but I think I can do 25 a day until I hit Vermont."

Lightning was racing through the trail, but clearly it was little more to him than an unpaved marathon route. He was oblivious to anything more than two feet to either side of the trailbed. Nate finished his dinner and stared at the orange sunset that was developing over the western horizon well below him. The sun had already passed below the ridge line, but the orange and red hues it was spewing skyward morphed and slowly darkened for a good 25 minutes. Nate watched it all. Lightning was already on top of his quilt, snoring soundly.

❖ ❖ ❖

Nate had missed it all, but it would be years later before he'd had time to regret it. Joy rolled over for the first time six weeks after coming home from the hospital. Nate had been at the office. Her first word was a slurred version of "good," and Nate had been on a buying trip to Wisconsin. Her first steps came while he was attending a company wide retreat in Florida. Increasingly, he had stepped into the role as a provider, because Marie told him she wanted to be able to stay at home full-time with Joy. He also fell back on the old-school work ethic with which his father had infected him. In his mind he was living the 1950s lifestyle of driving to the office, putting in a ten-hour day, and then returning home for dinner, an after-meal drink, a little television and then quickly to bed so he could begin the merry-go-round again early the next day. His only meaningful interactions with his family came when he found time to feed Joy dinner and give her a bath, and all of his memories of her infancy were of these two nightly events. Her playtimes were during the mornings and afternoons while Nate worked, trying to establish himself at his new employer and understand the political hierarchy that is common to retail – and must be mastered if you're to remain part of it. On the weekends, Nate tried to find time to play with Joy, but his responsibilities fixing up the aged, worn shoreline house they'd purchased to save money took up much of his time. Nate would never be the home-repair expert his father was, but he was handy enough that he could make most of the needed repairs himself without making the mistakes that required you to tear down your efforts and start over. Jeff, their old neighbor and tenant from Boston, often made weekend trips up to visit at Marie's insistence, a link to their previous life in the city that she insisted she didn't want to sever. Nate found Jeff to be somewhat of a bore, and his self-centered attitude continued to grate, but as Marie kept trying to pan her new surroundings for happiness, Nate was eager to allow her every nugget she could find. Happiness seemed to be more and more elusive for Marie, something both of them found surprising. Her depressions became more common, and Nate considered it his personal responsibility to relieve them. Both quickly rejected the notion of a second child as a panacea.

Marie's bouts of melancholy led her to barricade herself occasionally in the bedroom with the lights out, leaving Joy to play in her crib or in her living room playpen alone. Some nights

Nate would come home to discover this, and as Joy became more mobile it began to worry him. One late afternoon he arrived home to find Joy blissfully playing outside of her playpen with a trail of blood leading along the carpet from the playpen back to a corner of the hallway where she had apparently toddled and then fell into the corner of a wall, cutting a small gash just above her right eye. Whether she had cried out when it happened was unknown, but regardless Marie had never emerged from her dark cavern to tend to her, and Nate barged into the bedroom with Joy in his arms, the gash now dried shut.

"What happened?" he shouted, already knowing that Marie would have no idea what had taken place outside her emotionally clouded retreat.

"I don't know," she cried plaintively, a look of guilt and horror flashing across her face. Both the of them quickly bundled Joy into the car seat and off to the emergency room, Marie sitting in the back with Joy trying to comfort her while at the same time crying incessantly.

The scar was deep enough to require eight stitches, and while the pediatrician conceded the scar was permanent, he assured the parents that as Joy grew up, it would gradually migrate upward so that by the time she was a teenager it would be hidden under her hairline.

The drive home was in silence, Marie guilt-wracked and Nate searching for what to say to her once Joy was safely asleep in her own bedroom.

"What is the matter with you, Marie?" he asked later that night as they prepared for bed. "You keep getting worse and worse, and now you're putting our daughter at risk. What am I supposed to think?"

"I don't know, Nate," she exploded in a mixture of tears and rage. "I know I should be happy and content, but I can't find it. I thought I'd love working, but I didn't. I thought I'd love being a stay-at-home mom, and while I love Joy dearly, I'm still not happy. I just feel so sad all the time. Everything about my life seems empty to me."

"Including us?"

"Yes, but it's not because I've fallen out of love with you. I feel empty about everything. Breakfast. Playing with Joy. Having lunch with my friends. Playing music. Riding a bike. Whatever I do, it seems so empty and meaningless. I feel the same way about us, but it's not because of anything you've done. I'm as empty about that as I am about everything else in our life."

Nate was hurt by this but tried to work past that to find a cure. Nate was a man. Men didn't explore feelings; they immediately looked at such things tactically seeking quick solutions and resolution.

"What about seeing a doctor?" He paused before next saying, "Or a therapist."

It hung there.

"I've talked to the doctor, and he tells me there's nothing physically wrong with me," she said. "He said if this had happened right after childbirth, he might have diagnosed it as postpartum depression. Now he just thinks its depression. He wants me to talk to someone, too."

"Then why don't you?"

"I don't want people in this town seeing me talking to a psychiatrist. This seems like a big city, but it's not. Everyone seems to know everyone else's business. I don't like it. Your folks would know about this and I don't want them to think any less of me."

"Honey, my parents adore you."

"You say that, but I think they worry I'm dragging you down."

He put his arms around her, a gesture meant to comfort, that instead only made her more uncomfortable. "Honey, you're not dragging me down. I love you. I just want to help you feel better about yourself. You can't love others if you don't love yourself."

Nate continued to try to solve the problem.

"What if you saw a therapist from out of town? You could drive to Portland."

Marie was quiet for a long time. "Portland's still too close. I'd rather drive the two hours to Boston. Probably better doctors there."

Nate considered the idea. He wasn't thrilled with the thought of Marie driving the long distance regularly, but he was pleased that at least she appeared to be interested in dealing with the problem. "Do you need me to try to find someone? I could discretely call some of my old co-workers at Gilchrist's and find someone.

"No, don't. I'll take care of it all, Nate. I really don't want to share this with anyone. And please don't talk to your mom and dad about this." She hugged him, somewhat mechanically.

He hugged back. Hard. "Of course I would never do that, sweetie."

"I appreciate you wanting to help, dear. Hopefully going to Boston will make me feel better." She squeezed him harder as they hugged, and she looked blankly over his shoulder out the living room window, across the road and far, far away into the distance. It was yet another weathering signpost Nate had missed.

The three weeks Nate spent on the trail in Pennsylvania were a mixture of heavy rain and boot-slicing rocks. Four days after parting company with Lightning, Nate began to notice his feed getting wet, from holes cut into his boots by the razor-sharp shards he kept pounding his feet on top of. He left the trail near Lehigh Gap and hitched a ride with a delivery truck to Allentown to buy replacement boots. His new blue-gray fabric trail shoes were lighter and billed as more waterproof than his previous pair of traditional leather boots. He wisely held onto his old pair for the next few days, alternating between the two pairs so he could gradually break in the new boots and avoid the blistering that new shoes cause. Even with the new footwear, the rocky trails were excruciating, and an awkward ankle turn as he tried to scale down the side of a near-vertical section of the trail forced him to take two zero-mile days in a row – the first time he'd done that during the entire hike. A few days later, the old pair was donated to a trash receptacle he passed at a roadside trail crossing. As he battled with his bleeding soles and still-tender ankles, he was barely able to click off five miles a day, severely extending his stay on the Pennsylvania segment of the trail. The views continued to be outstanding, and while the mountains were less angular than those he had crossed in New England, he made sure to appreciate the soft-edged, rolling beauty of the green tree-shrouded mountains that stretched for twenty to thirty miles off to the horizon.

After a few days of good weather, his final week in Pennsylvania was a wet one. As the number of slicing, painful rocks began to diminish, the rain picked up. It ranged from light, misting sprays to torrential downpours, and the cloud formations that he would see ahead and the western horizon gave him no indication of which type of precipitation was coming. Despite the rain, he enjoyed the break from the steep up and down climbs that had characterized most of the Keystone State. At the second shelter after crossing the Maryland State Line, he squandered the first sunny day in a week by splaying all of his gear outside a shelter trying to dry out tent, sleeping bag and clothes, and washing everything in a nearby spring to try to scrub out traces of mold that had started to grow everywhere. This zero day was at the Ensign Cowall Shelter. Nate had no clue who Ensign Cowall was, but the structure did boast one amenity: a two-foot by three-foot polished piece of metal designed to serve as a mirror that some hiker had mounted to the side of the shelter. The mirror gave Nate the first detailed look at himself in months, and the changes the trail had made on him were noticeable and shocking. His face was obviously dirty, and he expected that. He had a good six days growth of beard on his face, and he had anticipated that, too. What he hadn't counted on was the gauntness of his cheeks and chin. When he left Maine, he had carried chubby cheeks and the suggestion of a second chin with him into the woods. Now, both were gone, replaced by angular cheekbones and a pointed chin that included a slight cleft he hadn't seen since high school. He stepped back and saw that his upper body was more narrow than he remembered. He had noticed his legs had gotten thinner and more muscular on the trail, but hadn't considered that the rest of his body and his face would reflect the staggering number of calories he was burning off each day both due to the exertion of hiking and the energy needed to generate heat to keep him warm at night. Nate resolved to find a scale the next time he went into a town to discover how much weight he'd lost.

The next day, as he ascended what his topographic map said was South Mountain, he spotted a dark gray figure sitting on a large rock beside the trail. As he closed in on the figure, he noticed that the gray came from his clothing – he was wearing a gray wool uniform from head to foot, with brass buttons, a sash, sword and black belt. It was a Confederate Civil War uniform, and Nate marveled as much at the meticulousness of the design as he did the absurdity of it appearing along a remote, mountain trail in modern times.

"Good afternoon," Nate offered when he came upon the soldier. Back in high school, The Colonel would have identified the uniform's military rank instantly, but having no military experience and a grade of B-minus in The Colonel's class, Nate was unable to address the stranger by whatever rank he might have claimed to possess.

"Hi there," the stranger offered. Nate dropped his pack and pulled out a packet of crackers and water, offering it to the stranger with a gesture.

"No thanks," he smiled. "I have my own." He then pulled out a small skin of water and a giant brown cracker that looked like a square of hardened bread.

"Hardtack," he explained. "Staple of soldiers during the War Between The States."

"The Civil War?"

The soldier blanched. "Well, if you think about it, 'civil war' is a contradiction of terms. An oxymoron. Kinda like 'jumbo shrimp' or 'military intelligence.' My friends and I prefer the more accurate 'War Between the States' or 'War of Northern Aggression.' 'War for Southern Independence is quite popular too."

Nate remembered his mother preaching the same semantic gospel during the family trip from Tennessee to Maine, and he just smiled. He took all of this in, trying to think of a tactful way of asking this bizarre little man why he was out in the woods dressed in a uniform from a century-old war. He couldn't come up with one, so he just waited.

"You through-hiking the trail?"

"Yes."

"Heading south. That's unusual. Most hikers go the other way."

"Yes. I started running into them a couple of weeks ago."

"Never really understood the purpose of hiking two thousand miles just to say you did it. Seemed like a waste of time to me." Nate didn't challenge him. "Me, I like to spend my time doing something productive. Like keeping history alive. Me and my friends preserve the history of the war by costuming ourselves, holding camps and giving demonstrations to tourists and schoolkids."

The light began to dawn on Nate. "So you're one of those people who dress up and re-create Civil War battles?"

The solider blanched again. "War Between the States. And we prefer to be called 'historical re-enactors.'"

"Sorry. I'm Nate, by the way."

"Vince. Vince Yeomans. No big deal, Nate. There's plenty of people that are involved that give us re-enactors a bad name. On both ends of the scale."

"How do you mean?"

Vince leaned back onto his rock to explain more comfortably. "Well, I'm pretty mainstream. But you've got folks who take it too seriously, and those who don't take it seriously enough. On one end, you've got the folks who in my view don't take it very seriously at all. They'll just go out and buy a uniform at a costume shop and show up at an event. Might just wear store-bought hiking boots like yours, or a simple T-shirt underneath. They might even wear blue jeans. We call those guys 'farbs.' Don't know where the term came from. Some say it was from 'far be it from authentic,' but I like the acronym 'Fast And Researchless Buying.' I think if you're going to try to live historically, you need to be serious about it."

"All right," Nate said, noting the small man's passion.

"But not too serious," Vince continued. "You've got people on the other end of the spectrum, the ones who take it too seriously and will point out any flaw. They call themselves 'progressives,' but I call them 'stitch-counters' or 'stitch-nazis.' People who will obsess over any flaw in your costuming, your actions, your campsite or even what you eat. They'd look at what I'm eating and if it wasn't in season during the war, they'd turn their noses up at me. At many events, they go off and set up their own camps. I love what I do, but I'm not obsessive about it."

Nate watched him trickle hardtack crumbs all over the front of his wool uniform and immediately questioned the statement. He moved on to the more obvious question.

"So what are you doing out here in the middle of the Appalachian Trail?"

"Visiting battlefields. Monuments. There's tons of monuments around here. If you're coming down from Pennsylvania, then you just crossed the Mason-Dixon Line. You've entered into Civil War Central, buddy." Nate caught the incongruity and considered jokingly correcting him as to the war's name, but halted himself. "There was only one major battle that took place in the northern states: Gettysburg. All the rest of the battles took place on southern soil. Most in took place in Virginia. Tennessee had the second-highest number of battles during the war. Maryland, being a border state, saw a lot too. There's a monument to Reno nearby." Vince clearly felt Nate should know who Reno was, and equally clearly, Nate had communicated his ignorance through his facial expression. "Union General. He was like General Omar Bradley in World War II. He liked being amongst his men and fighting with them. He was killed by a sharpshooter right here in Fox Gap back in '62, so they put up a monument to him just down the hill there," he said, pointing to a dip in the ridge line a quarter-mile farther down the trail. "They've got monuments for everything here. There's a monument just a few miles ahead on the trail to George Washington – built long before the one in the nation's capital was built. Heck, two miles down the trail they even erected a monument to war correspondents!"

"Interesting," Nate politely offered. After finishing his snack, Nate strapped on his gear, said a quick but polite goodbye and began walking southward again, but in less than a minute Vince had picked up his knapsack and had caught up to him.

"Hey. I'll be happy to serve as your tour guide through the area," Vince said, half volunteering and half begging. Nate didn't see that he had a much of a choice, so he smiled, nodded and walked single-file just behind the Confederate anachronism.

"I don't think people learn enough from history," Vince volunteered after he had spent twenty minutes telling Nate far more about General Jesse L. Reno than he ever knew or wanted to know. "Looking to the past gives us a sense of perspective and peace, don't you think?"

Nate didn't think so. All looking backward brought him was confusion and pain.

"I think you have to constantly be focusing forward," Nate offered. "If you're always looking back, you miss the present. Or what's coming down the trail in the future." Nate suddenly realized that throughout his hike thus far, he had rarely looked over his shoulder, and in a subconscious way had avoided looking back down the trail in the direction he'd traveled.

"I disagree," Vince continued to push. "If you don't know your history, you're condemned to repeat it. That's what they say, isn't it? Do you really want to make the same mistakes you made in the past?"

"Oh, I've made mistakes. I'm not sure there's always something to learn from them."

"There's always something you can learn from them." The pitch in Vince's voice was rising to an annoying squeak. "A mistake is a mistake, and only through self-correction do we as a species improve."

"Maybe so," Nate said. His irritation was rising, and he clearly was not enjoying the debate. "Even with a good grounding of history, though, we as a culture seem to be making the same mistakes we've made since primitive times. We're a savage race. We covet each other's things. We fight. Burn people at the stake because their God isn't like our God. We're selfish. What makes you think we've learned anything in the tens of thousands of years we've been on this planet." Nate wasn't talking now, he was shouting, and the outburst startled and slightly scared Vince, who fingered the three-foot scabbard that hung on his right hip. Nate collected himself, and calmly restated his point. "I mean, when you look at history we still fight wars, we still torture. Maybe Dick Cheney is just the Marquis de Sade with a high-tech heart pump."

Vince didn't want to delve into politics, and was still unsettled by the nerve he'd apparently touched in Nate.

"We used to think war was a glorious thing," Vince said, taking on the tenor of a philosophy professor. "It was a noble game. Aristocrats lived to wear sashes and swords and go riding off to lead troops in maneuvers and battles to be recounted later by poets. By 1865, that changed. We learned. Through photographs and the deaths of half a million people, we learned that war wasn't something to be admired. It was something to be feared. It was brutal. Savage. It was a meat grinder. So yes, I think the history of that event taught us something, Nate. It made us a little more reluctant to enter into one. Did we fight future wars? Sure. I don't think we ever walked into it again deluding ourselves into thinking it was a quaint game, however."

Nate realized he and Vince had been jousting about the issue from two totally different perspectives, and while they agreed on the evils of war, neither could possibly understand the lens the other was peering through. It was as if they were marveling over the same mountain peak, but from different valleys. Vince saw human failings from a full-campaign standpoint. Nate viewed it from the microscope of his own limited, personal skirmishes. Vince eventually would be proven right. Before he left the trail, Nate would learn the lessons from his history. It was much too early for that yet, though.

For the next three days, Nate found himself walking with Vince through Maryland. Vince had left the trail briefly to get more supplies, because his small knapsack didn't hold as much food as Nate's pack, but as promised he'd met up with Nate again at the next crossing and continued to serve as tour guide. During the brief separation, Nate had hoped he wouldn't see Vince at the next trail crossing. But like the next inevitable uphill climb, Vince was calmly waiting at the road crossing sipping on a large antique canteen. What at first had seemed annoying gradually became endearing. Nate realized Vince had little in the way of friends, family or career to keep him occupied. He learned that the small soldier's love of the nineteenth century came from a deep-seated, childish wish that he'd lived back then, when connections were more permanent and life seemed less complicated. Nate couldn't criticize that desire. Wasn't his entire journey a similar effort?

Vince had wanted Nate to repeatedly leave the trail to see various Civil War sites and markers. He had relented just once – to see the Antietam Battlefield. Vince insisted on calling it by its preferred Confederate nomenclature, Sharpsburg, but otherwise proved an admirable guide, doing such a good job telling the story of how the battle progressed that a nearby tour group stopped listening to their National Park Service guide and moved closer to hear Vince's story. The fact that Vince was doing so in costume didn't please the National Park Service ranger, but he politely and wisely held his tongue. He did, however, after the crowd cleared ask Vince if he was carrying any ammunition, which Vince insisted he was not.

"What was that all about?"

"National Battlefields are federal property. Can't carry loaded weapons without their OK," he said, patting the empty ammo box attached to his belt at the right hip. You notice I left my musket locked up in the trunk of the car," Vince explained. "The Park Service likes us coming around and demonstrating, setting up authentic camps and so forth. Makes things more interesting for visitors. Occasionally they'll let us do a firearms demonstration where we'll set up a firing line and show how long and difficult it was to load, discharge and reload our weapons. What they don't allow is skirmishes and fake battles."

"You mean when some of you dressed as Confederates fire blank charges at others dressed as Union soldiers and re-create a battle? Why not?"

"Nate, this battlefield is sacred ground. People died here for a noble cause. There might be bodies still buried here. Might not be.

Even if there aren't, it's the equivalent of a cemetery, and you don't play games in a cemetery."

The next day they made it all the way to Harper's Ferry, another key Civil War lynchpin, and one of the few places where the Appalachian Trail wove straight through the center of town. The headquarters of the Appalachian Trail Conference was on Washington Street, and Nate dutifully wrote his name in the logbook of through-hikers. His pilgrimage was halfway done.

10
BIKES AND BATTLEFIELDS

Later that afternoon, he said goodbye to Vince, who clearly had extended his stay longer than his current employer wanted. He confessed that he would be driving 18 straight hours in order to report for work the next morning in St. Louis and keep his job.

Nate had opted to spend the night in Harper's Ferry's old Hilltop Hotel, an aging white structure that overlooked the confluence of the Shenandoah and Potomac rivers. In the 1920s and 1930s it had been a luxury retreat for those driving up from Washington or Philadelphia to visit the area's historic sites and escape the summer's sweltering malarial heat, but like so many great hotels its slow death was presaged by the Eisenhower Interstate System in the 1950s. It had survived to this point solely because of nostalgia and inertia.

Nate checked in late in the afternoon and decided to eat an early dinner in the hotel. He dined alone. The only other customers in the restaurant were a frail couple in their late '80s sitting across from each other in silence as they worked to move the food from their plate to their mouths, using shaking utensils held by shaking hands covered with translucent skin. Nate studied the couple and found some comfort that each had someone with which to share their octogenarial years. While there was little conversation, it was clear the company of the other provided comfort, and Nate found that prospect strangely saddening.

The next morning Nate awoke more stiff than usual. Clearly sleeping on the hard ground had become the norm, and the comforts of a soft bed – albeit one topped with a two-inch, fifty-year-old mattress, was something his body found unnatural. He looked out the lace-curtain-lined windows and saw a steady rain and heard the occasional peal of thunder. This is a zero-mile day, he said to himself instantly. It was not a tough decision, and he immediately rolled back over in the bed.

When he awoke, he was disoriented. It was still raining hard outside, and the darkness confused him. Had he slept through the entire day? A quick glance at the clock indicated no, but it was nearly 1 p.m., far later than he'd expected to sleep. The long rest was apparently needed, and a twenty-minute hot shower was also welcome, although it clearly had taxed the capabilities of the hotel's hot-water heater to its limits. Nate walked down to the hotel lobby and had the desk clerk call a cab to take him to a nearby grocery. He returned with a good 12 days inventory of supplies, and two beers, the first alcohol he'd consumed since New York City. Since the hotel didn't serve alcohol, he sat in the lobby and drank both. While there, two men darted in, wearing running shorts and drenched from the still-continuing rain.

"Jim, when you landed in that puddle you went all the way up to your thigh!" the taller one laughed.

"Well, thanks for warning me about it ahead of time," the shorter, thinner one laughed back. "They ought to put a diving board on that thing."

Both sat down in high-back chairs opposite Nate in the lobby. Catching their breath, they gave Nate a once-over and tried to figure out if he was a tourist or business traveler. Everyone who stayed at the Hilltop was one or the other. Nate didn't appear to fit into either category.

"Visiting?" the one named Jim asked him.

"Just passing through," Nate responded. This didn't help Jim in the least.

"Traveling on business?"

"Oh no. Hiking along the AT."

"Really?" The shorter one piped up. "Where did you start?"

"Maine."

"When?"

"Back in early May." It was now late July.

"That's great. I've always wanted to do that," the shorter non-Jim continued, still failing to introduce himself. "Jim, what's that thing the hikers do around here? What's it called? The forty-in-twenty-four or something?"

"Four States, One Day," Jim replied. "It's when hikers attempt to hike in four different states all during the same day. They start at midnight, across the river right at the Virginia border with West

Virginia. Then they race from Virginia through West Virginia, Maryland and try to get to the Pennsylvania line by midnight. Then they can say they hiked in four different states on the same day. It's about 45 miles, if memory serves."

"Well," Nate smiled, "I've already passed through Maryland, so I guess I won't be trying to set that mark." I also don't need to salve my ego by running some macho marathon on the trail, he thought to himself.

"Too bad," Jim said. He turned to his friend. "Mel, we're going to have to do that someday. I hear most of the hikers leave their packs at the start and just carry water and a little food to make it easier. We could do forty-five miles in twenty-four hours easy."

His friend, now clearly defined as a Mel, nodded. "Piece of cake."

"Well, good luck, friend," Jim said back to Nate. "This rain is supposed to end tonight, so you should have a good day on the trail tomorrow." Despite the conversation's inanity, Nate thought, at least it ended with some useful information.

"Take care," he said politely as the two jogged up the staircase toward their rooms.

The next morning's weather was ideal, but the topography was not. Leaving the river valley, Nate had to climb Loudon Heights, a steep ascent which afforded him a spectacular view of the valley he'd just left, but hardly worth the pain on his knees, he thought. The previous day's rains had made the trail extremely muddy, and he had to be careful with his footing as he ascended and descended hills. His hiking poles sunk a good six inches into the muck each time he placed his weight on them and moved forward. After the initial climb-up, however, the trail for the next few days was comparatively flat, with only the occasional peak to climb. As he continued deeper into northern Virginia, he discovered an annoyance once he crossed Interstate 66. The trail paralleled, and in many cases ran along the shoulder of Skyline Drive, a two-lane highway that wended its way through Shenandoah National Park. While commercial trucks were banned, the road was favored by cars that liked racing down winding roads. More dangerous in Nate's view were the huge motor homes each filled with a withering retiree driver who needs to use every inch of the roadway and much of the shoulder as well. The rural aspect of the trail was lost, and in many cases Nate leapt back as giant Winnebagos suddenly roared inches away from him. The first two nights he tried to camp on sections of the trail at least a few hundred yards away from the roadbed, but even those didn't shelter him from the sound of cars roaring down the parkway late into the evening.

After five days of hiking, he reached Pass Mountain Shelter an hour before sunset. The open-faced cabin shelter was only a few hundred yards from the roadway. Nate considered skipping the site, but the next shelter was a full day's hike away, and the prospect of finding a campsite anywhere away from traffic was slim.

There were already four Northbound hikers in the shelter, which also boasted a good-sized open camping area that could be used for overflow hikers' tents. As was customary, they introduced themselves by their trail names. The tallest of them was Doc, a reedy dark-haired and bearded hiker who said he'd gained his trail name due to his first aid skills. A much wider and younger blonde-haired hiker had told Nate his trail name of Cookie was bestowed upon him after sharing three consecutive shelters with a group of hikers who had been enraptured by his ability to whip simple ramen noodles and local plants into delicious and filling meals. The third northbounder, Reeve, was less thrilled with his trail name, which he said came from his passing resemblance to the late Superman actor Christopher Reeve. The remaining three including Nate all conceded the tall, square-jawed hiker favored the actor. Nate was fast discovering that trail names had a side benefit: With such unique monikers, it was almost impossible to forget a through-hiker's name. Nate confessed to the group he had made it halfway to Georgia without picking up a trail name, a testament to how much he'd avoided interacting with other hikers during his pilgrimage. All vowed to make an effort to come up with a name for him before they parted company the next morning.

Nate broke down his pack, pulling out his sleeping bag to air out, and then rummaged for dinner. His cookstove lit and his titanium pot of water on its way toward a rolling boil, he suddenly heard a distant rumble that at first he mistook for thunder down in the Rappahannock Valley. Rather than fade out however, it built, and he quickly recognized it as road noise. As it grew louder, he was able to look a good mile and a half down the side of the mountain to a section of the Parkway that would eventually wind its way up to him. He saw a caravan of 18 motorcycles enjoying the corkscrew twists and turns the Parkway had to offer. The noise would briefly fade as the snaking line of bikes ducked behind a ridge, but return as it emerged and a clear line-of-sight materialized. When the caravan finally approached the widened overlook parking area near the shelter and campground, they slowed and began pulling off the roadway into the parking lot. One motorcycle. Then two. Then six. Then all 18 flooded into the parking area. Nate and the three other hikers cut glances at each other, sharing a look of concern but not outright panic. The bikers were all clad head to toe in black leather, but that's where the similarities ended. Some wore full jackets. Others sported vests. Each had unique emblems embroidered or stamped on the back. Most favored winged creatures, ranging from the popular eagles to hawks and – in once case – a griffin. A few sported fringe on their sleeves, and about half had small American flags on the back of their Harley Davidson and Indian motorcycles. While there were 18 bikes, there were 22 who straddled off the seats, as four of the chrome monsters had boasted passengers. Three of the riders were women, and one was a young man about 12 years of age. The women were somewhat overweight, in Nate's eyes, and all had long hair that they apparently enjoyed flying behind them as they cycled down the road. As one of them hopped off a heavily chromed bike ahead of her driver, Nate noticed her boyfriend – husband? – had a T-shirt emblazoned with the words "If You Can Read This, The Bitch Fell Off."

Nate found the rider with the twelve-year-old boy the most interesting. The man had a build and appearance that reminded you of Santa Claus, with a white, wispy beard topped with plumped sunburned cheeks. He could have been the boy's grandfather, but after toeing down the kickstand and turning off the bike told the boy to "find a good campsite, son."

This was the first indication that the bikers weren't just taking a break, but intended to stay at the shelter for the night. Nate and the other hikers shared another glance of concern. There was a small, non-authoritative sign indicating the shelter was for the use of through-hikers only, but none of the four could muster the courage to point this out to the almost two-dozen bikers about to share the evening with them.

Cookie decided not to wait, quickly stashing his gear into his pack and walking back to the trail, acting nonchalant as if that had been his intention long before the cast from The Wild Bunch arrived. Nate considered doing the same, but since the southbound trail was on the other side of this horde of bikers, he didn't relish the thought of running a gauntlet through them. It was a simple gesture that gave him a sense of sudden comfort. While the bikers' dress, demeanor and vehicles had presented a menacing tone, their initial behavior wasn't threatening. Indeed, as the Santa Claus biker caught Nate's eye, he gave a very slight and respectful head nod, a look that told Nate that while sharing a campsite with 25 strangers was going to be challenging, it wouldn't be dangerous. Nate returned the nod, and the Santabiker slowly strolled over and stuck out his right hand.

"Gil. Gil Shipman."

"Nate. Nate Townsend." He pointed at the young man now tramping around a flat area ten feet away from the shelter, inspecting it to see if a tent would fit in the space. "Your son?"

"Yeah, that's my boy Andy. How we doing on that campsite, Andy?"

"This seems pretty flat, Dad. I like it."

"Then make a tent appear. Remember how I showed you." The boy dutifully returned to the motorcycle, pulled a small rolled-up tent, and began spreading it out in the space.

"You guys riding the Parkway?"

Gil was polite enough to ignore that the answer was obvious. "Yeah. We started on the Blue Ridge Parkway all the way down in Asheville and have been winding our way up. When we get to the Interstate we're going to cut over to Washington, D.C. Big rally up there next week. Plus, Andy's never seen the nation's capital so his mom thought it would be a good idea for him to tag along. He's had a great time."

"Nice." Nate's water was rapidly boiling away. "Let me grab my dinner while you guys get set up."

"Copy that." The phrase had a clipped precision. "Let's chat later."

Nate walked back to the shelter, where Reeve and Doc gave him an odd look.

"Friends of yours?"

"Naw, they're OK," Nate said, trying to soften their continued concerns about the sudden invasion. "At least, that guy and his son are."

"They aren't supposed to be camping here," Doc protested, pointing to the hardly readable sign.

"Yeah, I told them you'd be over in a few minutes to run them all off," Nate joked. Doc didn't find it that humorous. "Hey, no big deal. Plenty of room. Plenty of water. There's a bunch of them, but they seems nice enough."

"Are you planning to stay in the middle of all this?" Reeve asked.

"Hey, I'm already set up and my dinner's waiting. I got a good night's sleep last night, so even if they keep me up, no worries. You guys do what you want."

The other two cut wary glances at each other and decided they also would stay put.

After sunset, the bikers decided a campfire was in order. With half the contingent scouring the area deadfall and the other half pooling their pyromaniacal skills, a large roaring campfire was crackling in the fire pit within minutes. No one in the group had chairs – neither backpacks nor motorcycles had enough room for such luxuries – most in the group had been able to round up small rocks to keep their rear ends off the dirt. The wide circle surrounding the fire pit was roaring with four or five conversations all taking place at the same time, and it was clear the backpacker and biker cultures were rubbing together with little friction.

Nate learned most of the biker group were veterans, with Gil the unofficial "senior officer" of the group. All had served either in the U.S. Army or Air Force. Most of the younger bikers talked about experiences in Afghanistan and Iraq. Two older bikers were in heated conversations with their younger counterparts, comparing their experiences in Iraq during the 1991 Gulf War versus the country's second invasion of that cradle of civilization. The consensus was the older soldiers had been luckier in their one-week cakewalk than those who'd had to endure multiple one-year rotations into the IED-littered country. As Nate talked with Gil, he discovered why the quiet-spoken bearded vet engendered the entire contingent's respect. He hadn't necessarily outranked all the others, but the length of his service stretched far beyond them. As a sixty-year-old helicopter pilot, he had flow over battlefields in Vietnam, Panama, Afghanistan and both conflicts in Iraq. Two bikers joked that he was pushing a stick ten years before they were born. Gil wasn't just any pilot, though. He usually flew medevac missions. To any foot soldier, those who braved flak and incoming fire to airlift the injured were the highest level of hero. During World

War II, most combat infantrymen despised pacifists. But many conscientious objectors enlisted as medics, and endured horrific mortality rates trying to scramble across battlefields to retrieve and save the wounded – and they quickly gained other soldiers' respect and loyalty. While hardly a pacifist, Gil's lifetime of service saving ground-pounders' lives engendered the same respect, admiration and appreciation.

"I still think you were the pilot who lifted me out after I got nailed in the Korengal," one young biker kept shouting at Gil, apparently restarting an argument that the Santabiker had thought long resolved. "That chopper's driver looked like somebody's grandpa, so it had to be you!" he shouted, creating a peal of laughter that rolled around the campfire.

"If you were as shot-up as you claim, you probably couldn't see past your fat nose," Gil smiled back. He had spent a lifetime with screaming young men behind him after making countless landings, hot and not, and he wasn't that interested in revisiting those moments or places.

"You won't let me thank you for saving my life?" the boy insisted, a slightly more serious tone creeping into the conversation.

"If I'd done it, I'd take the credit – or in your case, the blame!" That prompted another round of laughs. "Truth be told, I don't remember you and I don't remember making that many pickups in that valley. Plus, I never drove the model of bird you claim dragged your sorry ass out of there. If you want to write me a check for twelve-thousand dollars, though, we'll call it even." More laughs. And finally, to Gil's relief, the subject turned to the three hikers in their circle.

"So what makes you guys to want to hike all the way from Georgia to Maine," one of the women asked Reeve. Since the bikers were obeying the Parkway restrictions by not drinking beers, she must have been inebriated by Reeve's good looks.

"Why do you guys straddle a hot bike for 500 miles? For the experience, the views and the challenge." Reeve wasn't picking up on the woman's nonverbal cues, which was a good thing with her thee-hundred-pound canon-armed husband lurking on the rock to his left. "I've had days where I've thought about quitting the trail, and even had one cold wet day where I went down and spent three days in a Franklin, North Carolina motel before I conned myself into going back."

"So why did you go back?"

Reeve already knew the answer, because he'd answered the question for himself many times during his subsequent weeks on the trail. "Because all my life I've bailed out when things got hard. I took easy classes in high school because I didn't want the pressure of not getting good grades. When I went to college, I wanted to be a doctor, but I quit my junior year because I was afraid I'd do all that work and not get into medical school. I took jobs I was overqualified for because I didn't want to find out I couldn't cut it. Finally, I told myself it was time for me to do something from start to finish. So this is it. Either I finish this, or I live the rest of my life knowing I'm nothing more than a quitter." His eyes were starting to water and burn a little, and it wasn't just from the smoke from the campfire blowing smoke into his eyes. "I don't think I can go through life knowing I'm a quitter. I don't want to be one. How can you live the rest of your life knowing you'll never complete anything you start?"

The discussion had quickly moved from rollicking laughter to serious silence, and the transition made everyone around the fire uncomfortable. Reeve finally sensed this and tried to lighten the mood. "Anyway, can one of you guys give me a lift off the trail tomorrow so I can go home?" This brought laughs, but they were little more than efforts to break the tension.

Doc decided to help diffuse the moment.

"I just starting hiking because I heard it was a way to meet chicks." This also brought peals of laughter. Doc had to admit that he had seen only three other women during his four months on the trail.

As the evening continued, the conversations constantly shifted as the participants came and went. Some would wander into the woods for a bathroom break, while others would retreat to their tents, calling it a night and gradually nodding off to sleep despite the din of continued talking and shouting. Nate noticed that Gil's son Andy was doing his best to stay awake with the adults and his father, but was quickly fading. He would startle each time his head started to nod, bringing his chin onto his chest. Finally, he moved over to the tent but kept his head poked out the doorway so he could listen in to the conversations. After 20 minutes, he was fast asleep, and once his dad noticed this, he briefly excused himself and walked over, gently moving his son fully into the tent and lovingly placing his head on a small inflatable camp pillow before returning to the campfire.

"He really wanted to hang with us, didn't he?" Nate asked.

"Yeah," Gil smiled. "He loves hearing stories about his dad's old job. I don't talk about it at home. Let's be clear. I'm not a hero, just a guy who did what he was ordered to do. It's no big deal, but when he comes with us and hears all this hooey from the ground-pounders, it makes dad sound 200 feet tall. He likes that."

"What son wouldn't?"

"Yeah, I guess. I just don't want it to sound too romantic. When we get to D.C., I've got about 20 friends I have to go visit on the wall." He paused, thinking of his apparitional friends and comrades, forever young in his memory. "The people who make war sound fun have never been in one. The more some politician tells you how noble war is, the more likely he took a deferment. War's a horrible thing, and we've had far too many of them lately. If my son grows up to fight for his country, no one will be more proud than me. I also pray he never will."

"I appreciate your service." This important phrase was almost a cliche now, but from Nate it was meant sincerely.

"Thanks."

"Is he your only child?"

"Yeah. I waited very late to have kids. I didn't think I wanted any. When I was in the service, I had a hard enough time leaving my wife. I saw my fellow soldiers shipping out and leaving small kids behind, crying every eight to twelve months. I just couldn't do that to them – or myself. So I vowed I wouldn't have kids til I mustered out. I know my wife wanted one, but I couldn't do that. Was kind of a jerk about it to her, I'm afraid. So after I did my 20 and then some, my wife and I adopted Andy."

"How do you like being a father?"

"Best job I every had. You know, I'm never going to have a statue erected to me. I won't created any great work of art that will live forever. Children are your one legacy. When I'm dead, he'll be the only monument to my life here on earth. That's a big responsibility, so I take it seriously."

"You don't think all those lives you saved on the battlefield are a nice monument to you, too?"

He considered this. "Maybe. But a son or daughter is different. They know you. When they're this age and younger, you're perfect to them. You can't be wrong. You can't make a mistake. Even when they get older and know you're a flawed human being, they're willing to overlook so much because you're the person that raised them and loved them unconditionally. You and I are monuments to our fathers."

"Yes," Nate said. "Whether we want to be or not."

Juter Townsend was standing in the rain. It was no more than 40 degrees outside, and the raindrops were starting to soak through the black cloth hat we wore, as well as the polypropylene jacket Nate had bought him for Christmas at the company store. Nate's dad was proud of the jacket, not because of its quality, but because of the corporate logo on the front. It allowed him to brag about his son's increasing importance with the company at his weekly get-togethers with his fellow plant retirees at the local McDonald's. Juter's retirement had come just at the right time, four weeks after the birth of his granddaughter, who he told everyone was "as cute as a box full of puppies." He worked to strike the right balance between helpful grandparent and overbearing parent who failed to give his children the space they deserved as parents. He and his wife were always available when Nate or Marie called needing someone to watch Joy, or pick her up from daycare on the days when Marie made her weekly unexplained visits to Boston. Nate had told his father that Marie had friends in the city she didn't want to separate from, but Juter thought it unusual she made a point of visiting them ever Wednesday like clockwork. Still, his mountain upbringing had taught him keeping out of others' business – even family members – was a good policy, and he stuck to it with the fervor of a religious pilgrim.

Likewise, he was respectful about Nate and Marie's desire for Joy's health. Since he had been unable to beat his three-packs-a-day habit, they had asked that he not smoke in the house or around his granddaughter. It was an easy enough request to honor, except in the dead of winter or when it was raining or sleeting outside like today. As he stood shivering in Nate's driveway, only partly sheltered by the trees that shaded the front of the house, he cursed himself, as he often did, for the weakness of his addiction. "Quitting smoking's not hard," he would joke with his coffee buddies. "I've done it hundreds of times!"

This Saturday they were celebrating Joy's second birthday. The rain had been somewhat of a disappointment, as Nate and Marie had arranged a pony ride for their daughter and her four invited friends, plans now scrapped and replaced by Nate's friend David bringing over a neighbor who happened to do amateur magic. Some of the illusions were beyond the interest of toddlers, but any critical displeasure with the performance were quickly forgotten when he pulled away a large black cloak and reveals a giant blue-and-white sheet cake and paper bucket of ice cream. Juter was hailed from the front driveway just after the cake was revealed, and stubbed out his cigarette and returned in time to join in the singing of "Happy Birthday." His voice was the lowest and scratchiest among the singers.

Joy's birthday presents included several dolls and assorting clothing, and two stuffed elephants. Elephants had become a personal favorite, and Nate and his dad had spent an afternoon three weeks earlier stenciling her bedroom with the outlines of various elephants, all marching in a counterclockwise parade around the room. Marie had wanted to get her a set of elephant earrings, but Nate had convinced her she was far to young for jewelry or ear piercings.

After the last party guest and their parents bid goodbye, Sarah helped Marie clean away the plates and clean some of the spilled cake and ice cream from the wall-to-wall carpeting. Nate stepped outside with his father onto the driveway. The rain had stopped, but the cold air still provided a small level of instant penance for Juter's lighting up.

"How you doing, dad?"

"If things were any better, I'd have to hire someone else to help me enjoy it."

"Hang on a minute, dad." Nate returned a moment later wearing a jacket identical to his dad's. "It' freezing out here."

"Cold as a banker's heart."

Nate smiled at the expression he'd heard hundreds of times.

"Work OK, son?"

"Busy as ever." Nate rarely shared specifics about his job with his dad. He assumed his father wouldn't find it interesting. His father secretly longed for Nate to share it all with him. Instead, he was forced to settle for generalities.

"Your boss still giving you trouble?"

"No more than usual."

"I swear, son. From what you tell me, in a battle of wits that guy is unarmed. Why's he giving you a hard time? I heard the new children's store is outselling the main store."

"Finally overtook them five months ago. Suspect it'll always outsell the main store now. You retirees have more money than everyone else."

"Yeah, we earned it though. Greatest generation and all that."

"Yeah, well I think you're great." Did Nate mean his generation, or was he paying his father an individual compliment? Juter didn't fish for clarification. Where a mother or daughter might probe to investigate the exact meaning of such a statement, fathers and sons were just happy to be in the moment. That they were together and talking was, in some ways, more than enough.

"I heard mom say you might be going on a vacation next month. You two have never been on a vacation."

"That's not true."

"Dad, all the time I was growing up we never went on a vacation."

"Vacations cost money," his dad said. "Didn't we take you on vacation to Boston?"

"That was to check out my college. I don't think that counts."

"Did we drive to Boston? Did we stay in a hotel room?"

"One night. Oh, and where did you find that cheap a hotel room in Boston? Our pantry in the kitchen is bigger than that room we stayed in. You were always tighter than the bark on a tree," smiling as he used one of his dad's expressions against him.

"Picky, picky. I remember you had a good time."

"It had a swimming pool. I'd never swam in a pool before."

"When you were little you had the best swimming pool in the world. You got to swim in a beautiful creek and a pond right in front of the house."

"Don't really remember it, dad. Plus, I don't think a pond counts as a swimming pool."

"You're just too picky."

"Heard your friend David's gonna have a baby, too."

"Yeah, his girlfriend's expecting next year."

"They gonna get married?"

"Dunno."

"That's like eating dinner before saying grace."

"Great, dad. I'll tell him."

Juter stubbed out his cigarette, exhaled his last cloud of smoke, and then father and son smiled at each other as they walked back to the front door.

Joy's bath that night was especially difficult. She had wanted to bring her stuffed elephants into the tub with her, and when Marie had tried to explain the water would ruin the toys, Joy had thrown a tantrum. Nate had to step in and take charge, providing a semi-threatening tone that persuaded Joy to disengage from the battle she now realized she was not going to win. While he was drying her off, the phone rang. By the time Nate had bundled her up in the oversized towel, slung her over his shoulder and carried her out of the bathroom, Marie had hung up and met him in the hallway with an ashen face.

"You need to go to the hospital," she said, slowly and carefully. "It's your daddy."

By the time he made it to the hospital, the theatrics were over. His father had suffered a massive heart attack shortly after returning home. Sarah had ridden with him in the back of the ambulance, and had been standing just on the other side of a not-opaque-enough curtain as they tried reviving Juter with a mixture of drugs and electric current, all to no avail. By the time Nate arrived, the hospital had courteously wheeled his father's body into an unused private room with the lights turned off. Nate stepped in to find his mother sitting stoically in a chair, staring without visible emotion at her husband of forty years. Whatever grief she had expressed – if any – was gone, at least visibly. She was a statue, and rose only to give Nate a firm hug and kiss on his left cheek.

"It was quick, dear, and they say he wouldn't have felt anything. He may not have even known it happened. He just collapsed. I'm sorry, sweetie. I'll leave you alone with him for a moment."

It wasn't something Nate wanted, and he started to turn and protest. His mother, however, had already stepped out and let the door close behind her. Nate stared at the lifeless husk now lying in the bed, covered to his neck with a white sheet. His eyes were closed and he was at peace, as if his father was simply sleeping, but absent the telltale rising and falling of the sheet where his chest was hidden. Nate stared at him for several minutes, slowly realizing there would be no more motion coming from him. No more colorful sayings, or advice. No more expressions of parental pride or debates about politics or friends or family. Nate had always knew his parents would die, but he hadn't expected it to be this soon. He'd always assumed he'd have an opportunity to say goodbye, to settle unfinished business, to share true feelings and appreciations. Now he would have none of this, and he wept not because of death or his love for his father, but rather mourning these lost opportunities.

The next morning, Nate studied carefully as little Andy and his father raked the campfire, exposing still-warm coals covered by ash and using them to restart a fire. This one was much smaller than last night's, and they used it to start cooking a small skillet of eggs and link sausages, smells that instantly drew the attention of the other campers still lingering in their tents. Most of the other campers had planned on a breakfast of Pop-Tarts, plastic-wrapped pastries or cold Krispy-Kreme doughnuts, so Gil and Andy's hot breakfast drew a great deal of attention and envy. Showing a good heart, Andy took a couple of the sausages and cut them into bite-size pieces, sharing them with the other riders. Gil didn't protest, pleased and proud of his son's generous instincts. After breakfast, Gil cleaned up while Andy was put in charge of breaking down the tent and repacking the motorcycle's storage compartment. Father and son had a long conversation over the motorcycle as the father helped his son rearrange their gear so that it would all fit inside the small space. A couple of times while Nate packed up his own gear, he saw the boy gesturing in his direction. Finally, he strolled over to Nate while Gil continued to check out their bike before starting it up.

"I have a question," the boy asked, in a simple staccato tone that befit the son of a soldier. "What advice could you give me if I wanted to hike the entire Appalachian Trail? I asked my dad, but he said when you have a question, you should always ask someone who's gotten their hands dirty. I figure since you're doing it, you could give me a tip or two."

Nate considered all the things he'd learned thus far, and rattled off a couple.

"Pack lighter than you think you need. Always wear dry socks.

Always know where you're going to put your hands, your feet and your seat." The boy smiled at the last one.

Andy thanked him and said goodbye, then started walking back toward the parking lot. "Andy?" The boy turned and looked back at Nate. "Can I give you one piece of advice that doesn't have anything to do with hiking?

"Sure."

"Tell your dad that you love him far more than you think you should. Tell him until you think he's sick of hearing it. Because I assure you. He never will be."

11
BLACK AND BLUE RIDGE

Nate waved a goodbye to the bikers but didn't wait for them to pull out, as he'd already burned a good two hours of daylight. He worked slowly along the roadway, and mercifully after a few miles the trail made a respectable departure into the woods. Within a half-mile there was a ridge between the trail and the Parkway, which satisfied Nate's wish for a more remote journey. After crossing Thornton Gap, the climbs along the Blue Ridge Mountains became more intense, as he worked his way from 2,000 to 3,000 and even 4,000 feet. He scaled and rambled over peaks such as Mary's Rock and The Pinnacle. He took a few hours one afternoon to go off-trail and visit one of the many tourist attractions that allowed visitors to descend into the deep caverns and grottoes honeycombing the narrow Shenandoah Valley. He kept confusing stalactites and stalagmites, but was suitably impressed with the massive structures of calcium and other minerals constructed over tens of thousands of years. Nate got to spend one night in a hotel just off the trail called the Skyland Resort, a quaint, rustic spot that provided little more than a soft bed, marginal history and great views.

Each evening he was camping alongside more and more Northbounders. The bulk of them had begun at Springer Mountain back in March, and they were now flooding the trails of northern Virginia, winnowed down from the optimistic many who had begun their journey. Almost half of those who started their journey at Springer Mountain had dropped out before leaving Georgia. By the time the trail reached the Great Smoky Mountains National Park straddling the Tennessee-North Carolina border, seventy percent of those who left with full intentions of making it to Maine had given up. Nate knew the stats: Less than one in five of those who start the trail complete it.

The conversations with Northbounders each night took on the sameness and tone of a legal deposition, or the interrogation of a spy. How was the trail up north? Were the rocks in Pennsylvania as bad as they say? Were Northern drivers as likely to pick up a hitchhiker as Southerners? Had the lack of rain caused any of the springs to dry up?

Nate answered all of their questions, but never asked his own. He wasn't too concerned with trail conditions ahead of him. He was hiking south regardless of what was ahead of him, so questioning the Northbounders was like fast-forwarding to the end of a movie.

After another week of hiking, he neared the end of Skyline Drive. At the point where the roadway crossed I-64 its named changed to the Blue Ridge Parkway, which would, like its predecessor, wend and wind its way along the crease of the Blue Ridge. It would do so for 469 miles, past Asheville before it ended in Cherokee, North Carolina. I-64 would take you either east to Charlottesville or west into Waynesboro, but Nate had no interest in visiting either town. As the sunlight began to duck behind the mountain range on the other side of the Shenandoah Valley to the west, he stopped to review his current topographic map. There were no shelters up ahead. He used his hand to calculate how much time he had until sunset – a trick Lightning had taught him. By holding his hand at arms length toward the horizon, he could measure the distance between the sun in the sky and the point where it would set. All four fingers represented an hour of sunlight left. Each finger meant he had an additional 15 minutes until sunset. With the sun only two fingers away from the horizon, he knew he'd have to make a decision between pitching a tent and night hiking. He had only night hiked twice – once on his bizarre escapade with Teapot and Big Gray, and the other time when he was unable to find a comfortable tent site in Massachusetts. Both occasions were less than enjoyable, so he started looking for open stretches of ground as he hiked down the ridgeline, slowly losing altitude as the trail began to close on its crossing with the Interstate highway.

Finally, Nate chose a clear area near Beagle Gap just 200 yards from Skyline Drive's roadway. It was a mere ten feet off the trail itself and slightly lower than the road, which he hoped would shelter him somewhat from the noise and headlights of any cars that might be racing up or down the Parkway at night. Another benefit of his solitary tent site was that there were no other campers, so he would not have to endure the endless questioning of Northbound hikers. He had easily passed 25 of them on the trail today, and he knew the shelters both to the north and south of him would be teaming with loud, noisy through-hikers full of questions and stories. Nate was too tired and too disinterested to stay up and chat with other hikers, so his tent along the side of the trail suited him fine. He was so exhausted he chose not to cook dinner, and instead wolfed down three granola bars and then settled into his tent. He slipped on his headlamp and looked around the small enclosure. He unzipped the bug screen and popped out of the tent briefly and walked over to his backpack, which was leaning up against a signpost. He rummaged through it, looking for something – anything – to occupy his thoughts while he waited to drift off to sleep. He found a plastic bag with photographs at the bottom of his pack, but knew he didn't want to pull those out. Finding nothing, he resolved to buy a couple of cheap paperback books the next time he was in a trail town. He folded the bug screen back open and slid back into his tent, then his sleeping bag. He laid there on his back staring up at the peak of his tent, trying hard to keep his memories from joining him. He finally gave in and tried to visualize the cabin of his childhood, even though his memories were scant. He would use his imagination, he told himself, and create whatever he couldn't remember. Finally, about an hour after the last trace of sunset had evaporated, he nodded off.

He awoke to pitch darkness and the sound of something rattling just a few feet from his tent. Damn! In his haste to get to sleep, he hadn't considered bear-proofing his pack. True, there were no trees nearby he could have hung it from, but he at least could have moved it further away from his tent for safety's sake. He heard something dropping his cook pot on the ground, and listened to it roll downhill over several rocks. Then he heard a sound that truly scared him.

"Bill, there ain't shit in here."

The first time Nate had experienced true fear was on a cross-country business trip five years earlier. He had lived a pleasant, sheltered life, he admitted, and his parents had protected him well from most of the world's uncertainties and cruelties. True, he'd taken risks as a teenager, but for the most part he had enjoyed the false illusion of immortality imbued into all adolescents. He had never experienced raw, unfiltered panic.

On his third visit to the Outdoor Retailers Conference in Salt Lake City, Nate had overextended himself. He had scheduled way to many visits with way too many manufacturers, trade reps and fellow retailers. He had been asked to speak about his initiatives to market sporting goods and apparel to children, and his preparations for the talk had extended into the wee hours of the morning. He had represented the company and himself well, but the rigors of three days of breakfast meetings, walking the trade show floor, lunch conferences, visiting show booths, cutting deals over dinners and late-night drinks had sapped his energy and reserves. The brutal cold and wind on the streets of Salt Lake City had only made things worse by giving him a massive, skull-contracting head cold. When he arrived at the airport for his nonstop flight back to Boston, he had nothing left as he slumped into a chair in the Delta Crown Room. "May I have a vodka and tonic, please?" he smiled at the attendant. While his Southern-bred accent was all but gone, his Southern-bred manners had never escaped him. He never demanding anything from a waitress or assistant. It was always "Could I trouble you for ..." or "If you don't mind, I'd like a ..." The result was always a smile and what he needed, usually because it was so rare to hear a polite request in the service industry these days. "If I fall asleep, is there someone who can wake me so I don't miss my 11 p.m. red eye?" he asked again with an honest mix of exhaustion and pathos.

"I'll take care of it sir," the sylph-like redheaded attendant smiled. She'd seen it before, and knew not to wake him when she returned two minutes later with his drink to find him already slumped snoring in the chair. She set the drink on the table beside him, knowing it wouldn't be touched. An hour later, when he was awakened and pointed in the direction of his gate, he sleepwalked through most of the boarding process. Once safely in seat 14A, he tried to again nod off. Sadly though, sleeping on a plane was a skill he'd never quite mastered. He asked for a plastic glass of caffeine-free soda and some pretzels, and took only eight minutes to read the in-flight magazine cover-to-cover. After an hour of staring at some inane movie flashing four inches in front of his nose from the seatback ahead of him, he decided to just stare blankly out the window at the darkness that wouldn't change to light for another three hours and three thousand miles.

Then he heard the bang.

He had always joked he preferred window seats because if the plane was going down, he wanted to be the first to know. Now he'd instantly gotten his wish, and it wasn't amusing. He was seated just five rows in front of the left engine, and looked out to see huge shards of aluminum jutting out in all direction from the tubular engine, an unnatural display that indicated that something inside the engine had wanted to get out, and wasn't going to let an eighth of an inch of thin-pressed metal get in its way. There was flame shooting out the back, but almost instantly some type of water or foam spewed out from inside the engine, killing the flame and any smoke that might have trailed out. Nate noticed the fan blades next. What blades were left were not spinning. Nate wasn't a pilot, but you didn't need flight training to know it wasn't good.

The jet had only two engines, but the captain quickly came on the intercom to calm fears of the passengers, none of whom were sleeping anymore. "Ah, we just had a malfunction on our port engine, folks. Rest assured this jet is fully capable of flying our entire route on a single engine, but just to be safe, we're going to talk to air traffic control and see if they want us to set down somewhere. We'll be back with you shortly and keep you informed." Either the pilot was correct, and the emergency was run-of-the-mill, or Nate was going to nominate him for an Academy Award if they made it down safely. The wait for a further announcement took just five minutes, but every passenger would have sworn under oath it was two hours.

"Folks, another update from the flight deck. We've got bad weather below us so air traffic control wants us to continue on toward Boston. More than likely they'll want us to put down at the first airport along the way with good visibility, and it sounds like that might be someplace like Indianapolis or Columbus. We'll keep you informed, but for now there's nothing to worry about. We would like you ..."

No one got to find out what the pilot would have liked them to do, because at that moment the plane jerked hard to the left and began to nosedive downward at a remarkable rate. The passengers had been told to keep their seat belts on, but two flight attendants standing in the aisle were slammed against the ceiling of the cabin and then flung over a row of seats. The male attendant would later find our he'd broke two bones in his leg when he landed in a twisted position on the seat backs, and the female attendant would be bruised for weeks, leaving the airline after her disability payments ended to sell real estate in Tucson. For 30 seconds, however, they all shared the same thought as the other 161 passengers on the plane: We are going to die. Right now.

Investigators would later determine that the earlier engine explosion had sent shards of metal into the plane's lower fuselage, and two of those shards punctured the airframe just inches below the passenger section. The bureaucrat that wrote the report for the National Transportation Safety Board would remark that it was a miracle no shrapnel had gone through that section and the bodies of passengers seated inside. What they had punctured, however, were two hydraulic lines and a nearby pressure sensor. Thus the pilots had assumed all their systems were unaffected by the engine explosion, and didn't realize they had lost the precious fluid that moved the plane's controls until almost all it had leaked out.

To his credit, the pilot had spent 20 years with Delta and four years before that dodging flak and missiles during the first Gulf War. He'd had the good – or was it bad? – fortune to have a flak burst sever the hydraulic system of his F-15 over Iraq. It had almost cost him his life in the skies over Baghdad but on this day it saved it. When the 767 had reacted the same way as his fighter jet had two decades earlier, he instinctively knew what had happened. Officials would later credit the pilot's quick response with saving the airplane, along with his physical strength in strong-arming the controls without the aid of hydraulics to bring the plane out of its dive. As the plane was plummeting, Nate did what the majority of passengers did: Prayed and considered his loved ones that it was likely he would be leaving behind. He worried his death would push Marie over the edge of her depression. He questioned whether his daughter – now four – would even remember him. During the final 12 minutes as the plane was quickly redirected to a just-long-enough airstrip in Nebraska, he made a list of the changes he would make in his life. None were earth-shattering – no joining the priesthood or moving to live in Paris. He did, however, resolve to work harder to help Marie overcome her demons, and to spend more time with Joy.

The fear never fully left his body. Even after the pilot had seemed to right the still-jerky plane. Even after bracing for impact and landing with a hard thud on the runway. Even after the plane came to a stop and he and other passengers had barreled down the inflatable slides in the darkness and rushed quickly across the Tarmac to the tiny private airport waiting area that was now overcrowded at 2 a.m. with hundreds of unexpected visitors. The next morning when he was bused to Lincoln for a flight home, he still retained much of the fear. It sat next to him now like a close friend, and accompanied him on the drive home from Logan Airport. Every car he passed was a potential killer, capable of swerving headfirst into his lane. Even when he got back into his house and was holding a pleased but confused Joy in his arms, enjoying the sheer happiness of the moment, Fear was there to share it with him.

Nate's campsite was being ransacked not by possums or bears, but by humans. That was much more frightening. Animals were predictable and their needs were natural and noble, even when they conflicted with those of humans. The disembodied voices Nate heard sounded anything but noble. Nate would have found this scenario comical except for the arrival of his old friend Fear, who now joined him in the tent. He laid quietly in his sleeping bag dressed only in a T-shirt and underwear while at least two strangers were standing a few feet away, hidden only by the thinnest layer of polypropylene. Getting out of his bag and then the tent would be an awkward event, and in the end he'd be standing in the dark with unknown thieves in his underwear. It was unlikely to be very menacing.

He made a rustling noise inside the tent.

It was intended, not accidental. He had decided a noise might frighten off the intruders. Instead, it only drew their interest.

"Well, let's see who we got inside tonight," the other one, apparently named Bill, said. The comment was terrifying both because of the promised action, and the implication that this might not be the first time this pair had attacked hikers on the trail. A flashlight suddenly sent light surging into the tent opening just above Nate's head. Like a possum, he was blinded and unable to see the features of whoever was wielding the light.

"Just a guy," Bill said to his partner. "No fucking for you tonight, Zac." The idea of Bill and Zac raping hikers on the trail sickened Nate. It also imbued him with a sense of outrage that produced bravado that was uncharacteristic, and in this situation unwise.

"You guys need to get the hell out of here," he shouted, now scrambling to extract himself from the bag and tent that prevented him from defending himself. He was met with a boot in the face, Bill swinging his leg back and kicking him repeatedly while he was still in the tent. Suddenly the opening vanished. Bill apparently had grabbed the entire opening in his two hands and clamped it closed, like clinching the opening of a burlap sack.

"Oh, you're not going anywhere tonight, hiker-boy. We're just gonna have some fun." Nate's good friend Fear was now screaming in his ears. Robbery was now off the agenda. Ironically, Nate had his wallet in the tent with the thousands of dollars he'd brought with him on the trail to buy food and equipment at trail stops. He would have gladly parted with it at this moment to have the brutes leave, but he knew doing so wouldn't change the cloud of sadism that infested their souls.

"I'm pulling out my gun!" It was a bluff, a last desperate one. There was silence outside the tent as the at least two trespassers considered this. Carrying a gun on the Appalachian Trail – indeed all National Parks property – was until recently illegal. The NRA had bullied legislators into allowing it, but very few of the deep woods hikers were gun owners. You still couldn't hunt there on National Park land, so most gun owners preferred instead to visit private reserves or National Forest Service land. Apparently Nate's visitors were familiar with the fact that backpackers rarely carried anything as heavy as a gun, and called his bluff.

"Fire away, hippie. We'll wait." The seconds of silence that followed quickly demonstrated the pathetic nature of Nate's threat. "Thought not," Bill finally answered. A second later, Nate was stunned by a blow that creased the right side of his jaw, breaking the surface of his lip and leaving a ringing sound in his right ear. A second later, another blast of pain in his stomach and solar plexus. From Nate's point of view, the tent was attacking him, with the walls and roof raining blows down on his body. His attackers had decided to take a solid two-inch think oak branch and beat Nate repeatedly from outside the tent, never bothering to open it up to see who they were beating. After three more blows the pace of the beating doubled, with Bill's partner apparently finding a branch to use and join in the fun. There were occasional war-whoops of joy, but no conversation as the beating continued for at least five minutes. It might have lasted longer, but after five minutes of blows, a clear shot to his head sent Nate swimming into a lake of black and merciful unconsciousness.

12
PAIN KILLERS

The first sense to return to him wasn't sight, or even sound. He felt a biting, harsh sensation in his nostrils – one he hadn't experienced for several years. It was a scent he had spent a great deal of time with, but he still couldn't place it. A familiar smell can bring comfort, but this one brought on an unusual emotional response: Sadness. What was it? The scent was so memorable, like a childhood friend, and yet he still couldn't identify it. It might have been because of his semiconscious state, or even the possibility that the beating had caused brain damage. After a few minutes, he began to emerge from the fog and realize who he was, that he was alive. Shortly thereafter, he realized he was in tremendous pain.

"Aaauuauuuuuuuugh!" he screamed out. He tried to open his eyes, but only blackness surrounded him. He screamed several more times before the sound of other voices came nearer.

"Mr. Townsend? Mr. Townsend! Listen to me. Are you in pain?"

It was an inane question given the screams Nate kept belching out. They sounded unnatural, and to Nate they certainly didn't sound like him. It was a disembodied scream, and yet he pulled air into his lungs harder so that he could scream even louder.

"Three milligrams of Dilaudid IV stat," a second, male voice said in the dark as Nate inhaled for another scream. He cried out four more times, and then the pain began to rush away from him. His body seemed to sink where it lay, as if a giant elephant had sat on him. He stopped screaming and heard himself make a sound he hadn't made since infancy. A whimper.

"Mr. Townsend, can you hear me?" the male voice asked. Nate concentrated on his breathing, as if he had to relearn how to time his inhaling and exhaling so that he could speak. His diaphragm felt as if it was on fire, so it was difficult for it to push air out of his lungs in a controlled way to allow speech.

"Yes," he croaked. This sounded even less like him than the screams.

"My name is Doctor Sonerstein. I'm a physician here at the University of Virginia Hospital in Charlottesville. You're in the hospital right now because you were severely beaten. Do you understand that?"

"Yes," Nate croaked.

"You've been in a protective coma and we've just now brought you out. There's going to be a good deal of pain, but we need for you to be conscious now. We'll give you painkillers to mitigate the pain, but we can't give you so much that you drift back off to sleep. Do you understand that?"

"Am I blind?"

"No, your optic responses seem find from what we can tell. The reason you can't see right now is both your eyelids are still swollen shut. They're better than they were when we brought you in, but it will be another day or two before they get to the point where you can see past them. You're very lucky."

Nate found the last comment to be the most absurd thing a doctor had ever told him.

"Despite all you gashes and bruises, it doesn't appear that you're going to need cosmetic surgery. Most of your injuries were internal. We had to remove your spleen and appendix and we're going to have to run a battery of tests to determine any long-term brain injuries, but I think putting you into a therapeutic coma was the right call."

Nate said nothing. The pain was still there, but back in a corner of his consciousness and behaving itself for now.

"We'll talk more tomorrow. For right now, do what the nurses tell you. We're going to send you for another CT scan later today. Now that you're awake, I think the sheriff's office people will want to talk to you about what happened. Do you remember what happened out there?"

"Yes," Nate croaked. He found himself in the odd position of wishing his beating had given him amnesia.

"Very good then. There's a call button right next to your right hand. You won't have to yell if you need a pain killer or anything from the staff. Just press the button."

Nate pressed the button often during the next 24 hours. The

next morning, the nurses switched him to a system where he could self-medicate with painkillers when needed. The system was set on a timer so he couldn't push the button and dose himself more than once every two hours. He had just awakened from a nap and hit the button when he discovered two things: First, that his eyelids had shrunk enough that he could see his hospital room, albeit through a blur and haze. Second, that two rather large sheriff's deputies were sitting in chairs just to the left of his bed.

"Good morning," he croaked, sounding only slightly better than the previous day.

"Good afternoon, actually," said a large black officer in a green uniform and a hat that made him look like Smokey The Bear. Sitting to his left was a rather young, thin wisp of an officer who looked more like a Cub Scout than a peace officer, and made one question if he had the strength to carry all the weapons and accouterments attached to his black service belt. "I'm Sheriff Denton Wilkes of the Abermarle Sheriff's Department, the larger man continued. "This is Deputy Benton. You've had an interesting experience, Mr. Townsend."

Interesting. Maybe absurd comments were a local phenomenon, Nate thought.

"Can you tell us what happened to you up on the trail?"

Nate related as much as he could about the incident, which for the law enforcement officers was extremely unhelpful. Nate couldn't identify his attackers, apart from the voice of the non-Bill. He had no idea what they looked like, indeed didn't even know if there were more than two people involved. He wasn't sure what he had been beaten with, and couldn't remember anything of how he came to arrive in the hospital. After listening to Nate's story and asking a few questions – all of which elicited "I don't know's" from Nate – the sheriff was kind enough to fill in some of the details.

"You're very lucky to be alive, not the least of which because of the severity of the injuries. Apparently your attackers, once done, took your entire tent and flung it over the side of a crevasse with you still inside. You were found 600 feet below the trail in a gap between two large rocks. If you'd hit either of them, you'd be dead. You'd also be dead except for the fact that a hiker came upon your campsite the next morning, saw all of your gear strewn about and in a beeline pointing down the crevasse. The hiker reversed course, hiked the three miles to road and then flagged a passing car. That's when we were called. It took a team of 20 people to get you out of there and evacuate you to Charlottesville. The Park Service collected all of your belongings, and I think they're safely stored in the administrator's office here at the hospital. Not that you're going to be getting out of here tomorrow, from what they tell me." There was a long pause that made Nate uncomfortable. "Mr. Townsend, can I ask you about that?"

"About what?"

"One of your belongings you'll be happy to know we found was your wallet, which made it easy to ID you." There was another long pause. "Mr. Townsend, why were you hiking on the Appalachian Trail with over four thousand dollars in cash?"

Nate carefully parsed his answer.

"It's expensive to buy food along the trail, and I didn't want to set up trail drops. Until last week, I felt safe along the trail."

"Last week?"

"Yes, when I was attacked."

There was another long pause, with both law enforcement officers looking at each other.

"Mr. Townsend, because of your concussions and other head injuries ... you are aware they put you in an induced coma when you came in, right?"

"Yes, they told me."

"Do you have any idea how long you were in a coma?"

Nate realized he didn't. He didn't have to ask. Likewise, the law enforcement officer had done enough interrogations to know what his subjects were thinking.

"You've been in this hospital bed for two months."

Nate suddenly felt dizzy, as if dropped from a great height. It wasn't a reaction to an IV medication, though. It was the shock of realize he'd lost eight weeks of his life. The silence continued as Nate tried to process this. The law enforcement officers, both of whom were trained to make interrogation subjects uncomfortable, were now themselves uncomfortable.

"Is there someone we should contact Mr. Townsend? A family member? In our calls back to the authorities in Maine, to your employer, no one there could give us any information on that. Who should we call?"

Suddenly the smell that he had detected as he came out of his coma came back to him. This time, he recognized it. It was the smell of pure alcohol, used to sterilize hospital rooms and equipment. It was a unique scent, one he associated with both cleanliness and death, with the death of both germs and people. Nate pressed the painkiller button before he answered the sheriff's question.

"There's no one to call."

Boston General was a larger and older facility than the University of Virginia Hospital. Although Nate had spent the past four weeks wandering its halls, he still found himself turning down corridors and suddenly facing closed doorways with "Hospital Personnel Only" signs. He preferred being here late at night, because there were fewer people. The night nursing staff was more tolerant of family members staying with sick relatives, because they appreciated those sharing their vampire-like hours and existence.

Nursing, like all professions, involved trade-offs. True, the night staff didn't get enjoy the creature comforts and traditional lifestyle of their 8 a.m.-to-8 p.m. colleagues. They rarely, however, had to interact with physicians except on the phone, and many appreciated that. Nurses respected doctors, but wished that respect was reciprocated more often. While Nate still found the hallways a confusing labyrinth, he had mastered the snack machine in the third-floor waiting area. He knew that the corn chips on row A were a far better value per ounce at 50 cents than the candy bars on row E at $1.25. He avoided the overpriced chewing gum on row L as a legacy of his Scot-Irish frugality. Nate knew that the diet soda always ran out on Thursday nights, since Friday was the day the vending machines were restocked. He knew exactly how to feed the dollar bills into the machine so they wouldn't be regurgitated out repeatedly.

After grabbing a bag of chips and what was likely to be the last diet soda of the week, he took the elevator back up to the oncology floor and stuck his head inside room 724, listening to the slow, rhythmic breathing pace of sleep. He walked down to the nurses station to chat.

"She still asleep, Mr. T?"

"I am NOT Mr. T.," he said with a grunting voice. Nate smiled at what now had become a running joke between himself and Nell, the large and always-grinning floor nurse.

"That's the joke, dear." She enlarged her grin, nearly blinding him with teeth. "With a thin, white, unflashy stick like you, you're the most UN-Mr. T-like person I can imagine!"

"I pity the nurse who says that to me!" he fake-bellowed. Nell erupted with laughter.

"Mr. T., I sure am sorry that you're here under the circumstances you are. I'm also glad you are, though, since you've made this boring floor a little more interesting."

"Well, better to keep you entertained than some stiff nurses at the hospice."

"I'm sorry they couldn't discharge her," Nell said, flipping the switch to serious nurse mode. "We just can't seem to get her stabilized enough to discharge her. Darndest thing I've ever experienced. I know Dr. Kyle is totally confused about it. I saw him on the phone calling some doctor up in Minnesota trying to come up with a reason."

"I guess she's just old fashioned, and wants to die in a hospital rather than at home or in a hospice," Nate said.

"You really shouldn't talk about dying so much."

Nate didn't have a problem with it. He'd gotten past the stages of denial and anger. He'd live with regrets, but he'd accepted that his mother's pancreatic cancer, discovered late, was a medical death sentence. The fact that they couldn't get her to a point where she could be transported was complicating Nate's life, but not in a way that remotely concerned with. He had fallen in love with the Peabody-born nurse during a particularly heated phone call with his insurance company. Although the time between when the cancer was discovered and her admission was short – they'd only found the cancer three weeks ago – the insurers were threatening not to continue paying the expensive hospital charges, while Nate was explaining that the hospital itself wouldn't allow her to leave. At one heated point, Nell pushed a slip of paper into his hand. He opened it to find a numbered list of forty-two of the most obscene, offensive and foul names your could call anyone. In his frustration, he started using the list, until the insurance supervisor hung up after the creatively scatological number twenty-seven.

"Where did you get this?" Nate marveled after slamming down the receiver in the floor's waiting area.

"Dad was in the Navy. He felt swearing was an art form that should be perpetuated and expanded upon. He was the Cezanne of Cursing."

The insurance company was still telling Nate it wouldn't guarantee paying the bills. He didn't care. When someone you've loved all your life is dying, leaching ticks like health insurers are problems for another day.

Tonight, Nate smiled one more time at Nell as he turned and walked back the hall. This time, the breathing in room 724 was more erratic, more labored. Nate stepped in and saw the patient was awake.

"Hi Mom."

"Hi darling boy. What time is it?"

"Two o'clock."

"AM or PM?"

"Does it matter?"

"Yes." A beat. "Would like to know whether I need to put on my evening dress or something less formal."

"Gee, and I forget to bring your pearls."

"Guess we'll stay in, then."

"For the record, it's a.m."

"Why are you here at two in the morning? You've got a wife and daughter ..."

"Who are blissfully asleep over at Jeff's. In the state they're in, they don't know I'm not there. You, on the other hand ..."

"I was just dreaming about your late father."

"Did you tell him he owes me $20?"

"You always used humor to push away things you didn't want to deal with, Nathan." His mother was the only one left who called him Nathan. Even his wife had dropped using his formal name years earlier. "No, it was like he was right here in the room with me."

Nate hoped this wasn't going to be one of those supernatural experiences that he placed little stock in. His mother was an extremely rational woman, however.

"I mean, I know he wasn't here, and I know it was a dream. We dream either things we want to see or things we're afraid of. It was comforting to see him again."

"Was he smoking?"

"That's not funny, Nathan." Both Nate and his mother blamed his father's smoking for his death from a heart attack five years earlier. For Nate, he was still angry that his father had died so soon after the birth of his first grandchild. While he understood on a cerebral level that his father had taken up smoking in an era where the dangers weren't known, he had never forgiven his dad for the perceived weakness of not being able to quit.

"Do you think you'll see him again?" Nate asked. He and his mother hadn't had religious discussions in years. The family had been Presbyterians when they left the hills of Tennessee, but within months had begun attending a Congregationalist church in Freeport. Religion was rarely discussed in the house, but his parent's dutiful Sunday ritual of making sure he attended church with them indicated it held some importance with them.

"Like everyone else, I don't know, Nathan," his mother sighed as she looked out the hospital room window at the city lights flickering off in the distance below them. "I've tried to take a pragmatic approach. If there is an afterlife, then I think I will see him again. I've tried to do everything right by everyone else in this world, and for that I hope I'll be looked upon kindly by the Creator. If there isn't anything, then I guess it's like going to sleep and just not waking up. I handled nothingness before I came into this world. I guess I can handle it after I leave."

Nate found the thought of nonexistence to be scarier than anything else he could imagine. He loved his existence, even with the marital problems he and Marie had been experiencing for the past few years. The thought that he could go from a living, breathing self-aware organism to nothingness was something he could fathom, but didn't want to accept.

"What would you say to him if you did get to see him again?"

"Oh, I don't think there's anything I'd say. It's more just the comfort of having someone with you that you've spent most of your life with." She considered for a moment. "I guess I'd say, 'Thank you.'"

"Thank you?"

"Yes. Your father gave us all a good life. He worked very hard for us. He looked at the limited prospects we had back in Tennessee and made a brave choice to leave everything – his friends, his family – everything he knew. You have no idea how hard that was for him."

"Why did he do it?"

"He said for you and me, and I think that's most of it. I also think, though, that your father resented the way the company always treated people from the hills that worked in the plants. He knew he was better and smarter than they gave him credit for. He wanted to prove that to people. Do you remember your father reading to you?"

"Every night."

"Do you remember how he read to you?"

"What do you mean?"

"Your father had a very distinct accent."

"No, he didn't. That was one of the things that I thought made the company willing to promote him up here to Maine. He didn't sound like he was from the hills."

"Yes, dear, he did. Your father had as hillbilly a twang as you ever heard. Worse even than mine."

"No, he didn't."

"Yes, he did, Nathan. But he knew that the people up here would never accept him with it. He trained himself to mimic them. He listened to the radio, repeating back what he heard trying to copy exactly the inflections and tone. He didn't take on the extreme Maine accent, because he knew they'd think he was mocking them. He worked very hard to bury the Southerness in his voice. The only time you'd hear him talk about 'singin' and 'dancin' was when he and I were alone. Even at the dinner table, and certainly while he read to you, he used is 'work voice,' as we called it. He used that voice so you would grow up without a Southern accent too. He knew it would hold you back, just like it would have held him back."

Nate was stunned at this vocal secret his father had kept and taken with him to the grave. He cried as he thought about it, and even let his mother reach up from her bed and dry his eyes as she did when he was little. That only made him cry more. He cried now for the father who'd done more for him than he'd appreciated. He cried in forgiveness for his father leaving shortly after Joy's birth, now fully appreciating that such a selfless man would never leave them purposely. He cried too for the loss about to happen.

"Mom? Do you think daddy's using his 'work voice' in heaven?"

"Oh goodness no," his mother said with angelic earnestness. "God has a beautiful Southern accent."

She died only hours after he'd left the hospital to catch a few hours' sleep and see Marie and Joy at Jeff's house. His head had barely hit the pillow before the phone rang letting him know his mother had passed away peacefully in her sleep. By the time he returned to the hospital, his mother's body had already been removed from her room and the cleaning crew had been through the place, bathing it in rubbing alcohol, a smell he would forevermore associate with loss.

The open-casket funeral was a blur to him, and he remembered nothing from it except young Joy's confusion about why everyone was sitting around watching her grandmother sleep.

It took two weeks of convalescence before UVA Hospital would discharge Nate. He rented a room at an extremely unremarkable Charlottesville motel and spent the next week watching TV, building his strength and reassembling his hiking gear. His doctors had insisted he should not return to the trail, and he had gracefully given the false impression that he would heed their advice. His walks around Charlottesville started slowly, barely more than a block the first day, but after a week he was able to go for an hour before he needed to stop and rest. He decided that he would get to Georgia faster hiking one hour and resting an hour, than he would sitting in a hotel room.

Ten days after he was discharged, he made his scheduled followup visit to his doctor, who counseled more rest and recovery. He had told the doctor where in Freeport to transmit his medical records, knowing he'd never be making a follow-up visit. He walked out of the office and hopped into the passenger seat next to the University of Virginia student he was paying $50 to drive him back to the trail.

13
PENITENCE AND PERSISTENCE

South of its crossing with I-64 near Charlottesville, the trail still paralleled the Blue Ridge Parkway, and it and the AT would do a convoluted dance with each other for over a hundred miles, until their paths separated just north of Roanoke. The Parkway would continue down the Blue Ridge, while the AT would dart westward to snake along the spine of the Appalachians through large swaths of the George Washington and Thomas Jefferson National Forests. Nate now viewed the roadway even more warily, sleeping fitfully each night and making sure he camped miles away from the road, even if it took him dangerously far off the trail. Some nights the road noise was loud enough that he couldn't sleep at all. When their paths finally diverged, he slept slightly better, but not well. The combination of fear, coupled with the discomfort of his still-tender internal organs laying on the hard ground made sleep difficult. He was able to hike for more than two hours before he had to stop. He used the increasing intervals between breaks as a yardstick of his recuperation, and when he reached three straight hours of hiking somewhere south of Roanoke, he celebrated by heading into town the next day and having a beer.

After heavily loading up with foodstuffs in Roanoke – and deciding not to spend the night in a more-comfortable but more-noisy Roadway Inn – he hitched his way back to the trail and began working his way along the crease of the Appalachians. To his right, he would see the rippled rises and peaks of West Virginia, while to his left he could see the green pastureland of the Shenandoah Valley stretched like a green belt northeast to southwest. Beyond that shone the sheer blue-and-gray wall of the Blue Ridge, paralleling the valley off on the horizon.

Nate was now clicking off more than eight miles a day, but was still far from the 12 to 20 he was hiking before the attack. He'd lost two and a half months in a hospital bed, so he was mindful that he was way behind schedule. His hiking was now completely solitary. Southbound hikers, of which there are usually precious few, would be well ahead of him. Northbound hikers had for the most part already finished their journeys by either scaling Kathadin or giving up somewhere short of the peak that had almost claimed Nate's life on the first day. While he would occasionally meet a day-hiking couple, he was truly alone with the now-browning mountains. It was just two weeks until October, and Nate was considering what he would do if he couldn't make the Tennessee line by that date. As he slogged along the mountaintops, he calculated the 450 miles he'd still have to hike in Tennessee and North Carolina before he'd even get to Georgia, where he'd still have another 90 miles or so to click off. Suches was the last town on the trail, just 20 miles from its end at Springer Mountain. Nate made a mental note of it and reminded himself to pick up the final trail guides for Tennessee, North Carolina and Georgia the next time he headed into a town for supplies.

That side trip came soon after he'd taken a right-angle turn due south, climbing down off one ridge, crossing I-81, and then making another sharp turn on top of another ridgeline. Soon afterwards, he found himself walking out of the woods into the small south Virginia city of Damascus. The town has a unique relationship with the AT, and with through-hikers. It's the only city where there trail literally passes down the town's main street. Damascus has made the most of its geographic location, hosting a Trail Days event each spring timed to coincide with when the majority of northbound hikers reach the city. The festival in recent years has attracted more driving tourists than hikers – since those with their eyes firmly set on the trail's end in Maine are usually unwilling to rack up three consecutive zero-mile days to enjoy the event. For a southbound hiker, especially one like Nate arriving in late September, Damascus was just another town.

By the time he reached Damascus, however, the sun had already set. The hiking days were much shorter this late in the year, another challenge created by his two-month medical hiatus. During the past two weeks, he'd found himself arriving at a shelter well after sunset or trying to break camp before sunrise to get in as many hours of trail time as possible.

Damascus, like most small Virginia towns, had no nightlife. By the time he arrived, all of its storefronts were closed. Nate realized he would have to hold up in town for the night and buy his supplies the next morning. As he walked slowly down Laurel Avenue, he saw a thirty-foot tall illuminated sign for The Hikers Inn in the distance. Normally packed to capacity in the spring, this late in the season he had no difficulty securing a room. After a quick shower in a cramped pink bathroom no doubt older than Nate, he decided to continue walking down the street to find a hot meal. After a much-appreciated fourteen-ounce-steak dinner, he stepped outside and began the slow walk back to the hotel. As he crossed the street mid-block, he saw a figure dressed in a black shirt and light blue jeans sitting on the steps of a small brick building identified as St. Bernard's Catholic Church. Once closer, he saw the man, easily in his late sixties, was wearing a clerical collar and watching him intently. The gate to the white picket fence that separated the church from the sidewalk was open, and with the church steps only twenty feet from his path, Nate felt the obligation to nod and say a polite hello.

"Where are we off to this fine night, lad?" the priest asked, with a winning smile, a severe Scottish brogue and a booming tone that clearly served him well as a leader of a religious flock.

"Off to rest after a tiring day," Nate politely responded.

"Physically or spiritually?" the priest asked, knowing it was likely the former but hoping for professional reasons it was the latter.

"Physically. Lots of miles walked."

"A hiker! Glory! And just three days short of All Saints' Day! Either you must be the slowest hiker in history or you got a very late start."

"Neither, actually. I ..."

The priest interrupted him, holding up his right hand to halt his story. "Wait, wait. Don't go away." He lifted himself from the steps and pivoted back into the church. After a tedious six-minute wait, he returned with two small coffee cups and offered one to Nate, inviting him to step inside the fence and join him on the steps. "It's cappuccino. It was the final birthday gift from me now-late brother. I rarely have a chance t' use it. The fine people of rural Virginia aren't coffee snobs." He then whispered conspiratorially, "But I am." Nate settled in on the steps and took a sip of what now was a warm, albeit unexpected after-dinner drink. "I'm sorry, young man. I interrupted your story."

"Not much of a story," Nate said, realizing the falseness of this as he said it. "Just had a little medical emergency up in northern Virginia that put me behind a couple of months. Still hope to finish before the end of the year."

"Well, you'll never make it to Maine this year. I hope you're heading south. Are you now … ?" he said, trailing off his sentence, holding out for a name.

"Nate. Nate Townsend."

"So you're heading to Springer Mountain, then, Nate?"

"Yes, Father … "

"Cousin."

"Excuse me?"

"It's my first name. Cousin. Cousin Manciple's my full name."

"Father Cousin?"

"Yes, yes. Everyone enjoys that," he smiled impishly. "In seminary, I had a classmate named James Lover. We so enjoyed calling him 'Father Lover' after his ordination. So you're a Southbounder. Last Southbounder we had here was six weeks ago. Think you'll make it all the way before the end o' the year?"

"Hope to. I have a date."

Cousin couldn't determine whether this was a joke or there was meaning there, so he chose to ignore it.

"So what have you learned on the trail, lad?"

"How do you mean? Learned about hiking techniques? Equipment?"

"No son. You've spent close to half a year on the trail enjoying a very solitary experience. Similar, I'd say, to a monastic life. Few in this high-tech age of electronic gadgets and televised jibberish get to partake in such an experience. I speculate few even would choose to if they could. You've met people on the trail. You've hiked alongside some of them. You've crossed their paths. You've been alone with your thoughts for months. Your ghosts. Your demons. Your joys. Your dreams. It's Walden in motion, my boy. What have you brought out of the woods with you?"

"Nate wasn't expecting an esoteric discussion, and as always wasn't eager to delve into his feelings. Common courtesy, however, required an answer.

"I've found some exceptional souls and some horrific ones," he admitted, surprised for the second time on his trip by his sudden candor.

"Ah, an experience not unlike my own. Except, of course, I've never set a foot on the trail. Excluding the section that goes down the sidewalks in town, of course. I've said mass for thousands of them, of course, especially during Trail Days. So what travels with you when you're by yourself, Nate Townsend?"

"Travels with me? When I'm alone?"

"Yes, lad. We're never truly alone, even when we are alone. We carry those people and experiences we've left behind with us. It's true on the trail, and it's true in life. We carry the souls of those who've touched us in our packs as certainly as we carry canteens of water or tent poles. I walk the streets of this town with my parents, God rest their souls. I walk and talk with friends long departed, and especially my late brother. He lived here with me for the last ten years of his life, and he's constantly whispering impish things in my mind's ear about the things I see."

Nate considered the many ghosts who were hiking with him.

"Honestly father, I like the isolation. I like not thinking. I find I do it a lot."

"That requires a tremendous amount of energy. To not think. Because you're really not *not* thinking about them. You think of them, and then you work instantly and very hard to suppress them. Am I right now, lad?"

Nate knew the priest was right, but didn't want to agree.

"So how many hikers come through here in the spring?" he said, desperate to change the subject. The priest recognized the verbal parry, but like a Highland cavalry unit, decided to circle around before reengaging.

"Hundreds. They start getting here in early April, the fast-moving ones. They tend not to stop. Later in the month, the number of hikers hit their peak. By May most have passed on through, except a few stragglers. Southbounders like yourself rarely get noticed, because there's so few of you. There's a hostel in the back of the Methodist church for hikers, but I think they've closed it for the season. I could make a call, but you'd be the only one staying there tonight."

"Thanks, but I already have a room at the hotel up the street."

Most hikers tried to conserve money, so Father Cousin found this interesting. Hiking the entire trail wasn't an inexpensive proposition, so Nate's use of a hotel room, while not completely out of the ordinary, added to the priest's peaked interest.

For his part, he found the idea of a Catholic priest in backwoods Virginia equally intriguing. In an area that seemed to have Baptist and Methodist churches scatter across it as if God had dispensed them with a pepper shaker, finding a Catholic, much less a Catholic priest, was unusual in such a remote area.

"How large is your parish?"

"Oh, not large at all. Truth be told, the archdiocese would have shut me down long ago were it not for my desire to live here, and the persistence of so many of my flock. Driving to Abingdon or Bristol for mass would be such a hardship for them."

"Bristol." Nate had forgotten he now was so close to the state of his birth. "How far is Bristol?"

"It's just a 30 minute drive."

"So I'm just 30 miles from the state line?"

"Oh heavens, no, my lad. On the trail, you're only five miles from Tennessee."

Nate knew that once he left Virginia, he would be enter the state of his nativity, the settings of his earliest childhood, part of the reason he had chosen to take this unusual path to Georgia, but still something he approached with a sense of uncertainty.

"Are you heading out on the trail in the morning?"

"I was planning to, but I need to get supplies."

"Bart Sinks runs the outdoor supply store that caters to hikers here," the priest began. "He comes across as rough as a corn cob, but secretly he's a very saintly man. Tomorrow's Monday, and Bart usually closes the first two days of the week once the hiking season finishes up. I'll make you a deal. He's one of my flock, so I'll call him at home tonight and ask him to come in and open up for you at 7 a.m."

"I appreciate that very much, Father Cousin." Nate smiled again at the sound of the name.

"Ah lad, but there's a quid pro quo," the priest said. "After you're done, the trail runs right past my doorstep here. I expect you to join me for breakfast at my rectory in the back there," he said, gesturing to the even smaller building behind his tiny church. "I expect at least 30 minutes of good conversation about your experiences on the trail. Ay, and the conversation had better be good, or you get none of my biscuits and gravy." The last sentence was delivered with a stern, paternal tone befitting a priest.

Nate wasn't crazy about the deal, but also wasn't interested in waiting two days for supplies before he renew his already delayed pilgrimage. He nodded his agreement, thanked the priest again, and then strolled down the sidewalk back to his hotel.

After a shower, he sat down in a poorly upholstered chair in the room and began dreading the invitation to breakfast. He wasn't Catholic, and had no interest in making any confession to a man he'd just met, formal or informal. Would talking about his pain be therapeutic? No, he said to himself, therapy was overrated. It hadn't helped Marie.

The weekly therapy sessions in Boston at first did seem to help. Marie would come back in a much better frame of mind, Nate saw, and he didn't mind coming home from work on time each Wednesday so that he could have dinner waiting for her when she returned from her long drive. Like everything he touched, Nate attacked his once-a-week cooking duties with a vengeance, filling the top cabinet with a slew of cookbooks. First there was his obsession with Chinese cooking, developed after he'd bought a heavily blackened wok at a garage sale. Then after Marie had begged him not to cook any more stir-fried chicken or sweet-and-sour pork, he moved on to French cooking, complete with several books by the patron saint of American/French cooking, Julia Child. Each dish seemed to take hours to prepare, and the results were hardly spectacular, he felt. Nate then spent a lamentable four weeks trying to master Cajun cooking, which resulted in a huge unused container of cayenne pepper in the pantry and an equally large container of PeptoBismol in the medicine chest. After his doctor during his yearly checkup suggested his cholesterol level was starting to tweak into the borderline range, he bought a set of Graham Kerr lowfat cooking guides and began trying to wrestle flavor out of food without the aid of tasty fats and sugars. He felt he had succeeded. Those who ate his meals without complaint were enablers in that delusion.

Often his mother would come over for the Wednesday night suppers. After picking up Joy at daycare, she would drive her over to Nate and Marie's house, staying to play with her granddaughter and talk with Nate until his wife returned. At first, Marie seemed pleased to arrive to a home filled with Nate, his mom, her daughter and a hot meal. After a few months, though, her sessions in Boston seemed to be less productive. Her mood was less joyful, and Nate's mother, sensing on the tension, soon stopped staying for dinner. On the weekends their friend Jeff from Boston sometimes came up, but the tension was palpable.

Relationships are never static. Most think of time as linear, but when it comes to the relationships between a man and woman, they spiral. They either spiral upward or downward, and Nate and Marie's, which had begun like a pirouetting stunt plane racing to the heavens, was now slowly but steadily descending silently toward the hard ground. Both knew it. Both didn't want it to happen. Each felt their efforts to halt the descent were at first rejected by the other, and eventually each felt any additional effort was useless. Then, after a full year of emotional and physical isolation, they stopped trying to pull the plane out of its descent. After they stopped trying, they stopped talking. Not completely, of course. Still, both conversational intimacy and physical intimacy both vanished. Talking to each other was no longer about the other's feelings, cares, concerns or aspirations. It was now only logistics. Who would pick up Joy today? When would one or the other be home for dinner? Could you pick up some potatoes on the way home from work? Unimportant things were discussed. The critical subjects lay silent. Nate and Marie now were alone together.

Morning in Damascus dawned bright and clear. A thick sheen of gray popcorn clouds filling the open sky had vanished overnight, and the entire area was bathed in bright, unfettered blue. Nate's supply shopping was fairly effortless. Mr. Sinks had boxed up some of his inventory to await next spring's arrivals, but while he grumbled about opening on a Monday, he was still willing to dig the boxes out of his basement without a major complaint. Selling backpacking supplies had its advantages – unsold freeze-dried food could be packed away easily and held for a year or more without fear of spoilage. Now that he was heavily loaded, Nate worked his way down the sidewalk back past the Hikers Inn. He found a small bookstore tucked away next to an office building and stepped in, inadvertently ringing the small bell attached to the front door and drawing the attention of the clerk behind the counter, who quickly returned to the yellowed, scruffy paperback he was reading. Nate had avoided reading on his hike, partly because of the exhaustion each evening that quickly put him to sleep, as well as the extra weight that books – even paperbacks – added to his load. He walked back and forth through the eight-foot tall corridors created by the black oak bookshelves, filled with used, heavily read books. He finally selected two small books from the "regional" bookshelf, written by two revered authors of Appalachian birth – Thomas Wolfe and James Agee. He had read neither, and was only familiar with Wolfe, but the titles had struck a chord with him. After paying 50 cents each for the books, he tucked them into the side pocket of his backpack. He returned to the street and quickly walked the two minutes needed to bring him to the side door of the rectory.

"I didn't think about asking last night, but I hope you eat meat," the priest said as he opened the door, before offering a belated and out-of-order "good morning."

The bacon-and-eggs were delicious, as was the promised biscuits and gravy. "Me father emigrated here from Scotland just afore I was born," Father Cousin said, a fact that his accent clearly telegraphed. "He told me half-jokingly he was the only Catholic in Scotland, so being one of the few Catholics here in the backwoods was no different. Fortunately, most of the people here are from a Scot-Irish background. He married a mountain girl, and thanks be to St. Lorenzo, she taught her beloved sons how to make drop biscuits and sausage gravy. Otherwise it would have been haggis and eggs for ya this morning. And I dinna think you'd like that."

The coffee made with Father Cousin's espresso maker was luxurious compared with the freeze-dried coffee Nate drank on the trail. He looked around, finding the walls of the frenetic priest's one-room rectory filled with photographs, crucifixes and small plaques with various sayings. A giant sign hung over a rolltop desk in one corner with the one word: Simplify. Another sign over the side door that led outside read *Amor Vincit Omnia* in a flourished, gothic script. The priest was a consummate host, and Nate soon found a sense of familiarity that allowed him to open up more about his trail experiences.

"I've seen beauty and ugliness out there," he told the priest after relating the details of both his first days on the trail and the vicious attack that nearly ended his journey. "That duality has made the hike interesting. I can stand on top of a mountain and see colors and wisps of fog dancing across the surrounding peaks. Then I can hike down to a trail crossing and see vile, fetid piles of trash dumped along the roadway. I've met kind people who have given me food, water and attention selflessly. I've met evil who would maim strangers just to be entertained, too."

"So you're saying you've seen creation, and you've seen man."

"I suppose so."

"Every coin has two sides, me boy. To put it in more appropriate terms, laddie, every trail goes two directions. You can't look at the natural world and only expect to see beautiful things. Coyotes are beautiful creatures, but they kill sometimes in a way we would see as cruel to survive. Human beings, being part of God's nature, are the same. You can't have holiness without having evil to counterbalance it."

"Sure, sure. Still, it seems to me the natural world represents all that's beautiful, kind and worthy. Man on the other hand, represents selfishness, pain, ugliness and destruction."

The priest shifted in his chair. "I can understand why you might feel that way considering what happened to you ..."

"I've felt that way for much longer, though." Nate interrupted. "Human beings for the most part are self-centered, and willing to hurt others to get what they want. Sometimes what they want are the most insignificant things. Yet they'll destroy everything to get those things. Look, I see clear skies today, and that represents to me a day on the ridges where I can see the quiet solitude of nature. Whenever I see stormclouds, they and the thunder, lightning and rain remind me of the loud, brash, destructive and uncomfortable things that are man."

"Nate, let me suggest the biggest stormclouds are inside of you, not outside in the world."

Nate blinked at the observation. "Excuse me?"

"The storms you fear aren't outside. They aren't from human beings and what they may or may not have done to you. Storms are turbulence. The storm you're dealing with, lad, is a turbulence in your soul. External forces have done damage to your heart, the same way high winds can down a tree. Is there a wind-downed tree that's blocking the trail for you? Maybe that is what's keeping you from finishing your journey."

"My journey to where?"

"Ah, where indeed, laddie. That's something only ye know. You've been very clear you don't want to share your moral destination with me. That's fine. You need to find a way to clear that tree from your trail, though. Or at least, find a path around it."

Nate sat in silence, soaking this in. Like a performer who knows when to leave the audience on a high note, Father Cousin rose from his chair. "Now it's time for you to get back on that journey, me boy. The trail awaits." With that, the priest stood, walked to the side door, pushed open the screen door with one hand and gestured outside theatrically as if to show Nate where to exit. Nate shook his hand and, once outside, slung his pack over his shoulders and began walking back down the street.

"Be happy while you're living, Nate Townsend," the priest shouted, intoning a proverb his Scottish father had brought with him from the Old Country. "Because we're a long time dead."

It took Nate less than five minutes to travel from the center of the still sleepy Virginia town to the deep woods. The sky was still bright blue and empty, and he could still taste the priest's bacon an hour later when he crossed into Tennessee. He also could still taste the breakfast conversation in his head. Trails go two directions. Trees down. Emotional stormclouds. Nate knew what his stormclouds were, but the last thing he wanted to do was stand out in that storm. Then, just at the point he crested his first peak of the day and saw clear blue open sky to both the east and west, taking his first expansive look at the Tennessee Valley, Nate recalled the second verse of the song from his childhood – the song that had first visited upon him in Maine:

"Oh, the land of cloudless days,
Oh, the land of an unclouded sky.
Oh, they tell me of a home where no stormclouds rise.
Oh, they tell me of an unclouded day."

14
REUNIONS

The return to Tennessee soil had triggered a desire to remember moments from his earliest childhood. Mining those memories was as difficult as drilling a water well in granite. Once his family had left the state, they had never returned. A combination of distance and dollars had made visiting family left behind impossible. Nate's father had returned for his parents' funerals, but he had not been able to bring his wife or son on the journeys. Nate's childhood recollections of Tennessee were only vague ones. Running up and down the hills to and from their cabin on the day they left for Maine. After the move north, he had tried several times to remember his life in Tennessee. He had blocked many of those memories on a subconscious level, however, trying to sublimate the sadness and disappointment he felt leaving his grandparents and friends behind. He had expected the scenery as he entered the northeast corner of Tennessee would be instantly familiar, triggering lost memories and fanciful recollections. The steep climbs and mountains with slowly changing colors were no different from those left behind in Virginia, however, and they held no magical properties. His first few nights in the state of his birth continued to be uneventful and solitary, with no hikers out this late in the season, despite unseasonably warm temperatures in the mid-sixties. Three days in, he had stumbled across a pair of hunters. They were polite and friendly enough, but a bit skittish as they knew hunting in along the trail was illegal. Nate ran into a day hiker the next afternoon, who told Nate he was only two day's away from Roan Mountain. While he had enough supplies to keep hiking for another four days, he made the decision to head down the mountain to resupply and see if he could find any trace of his infancy and childhood. His only remaining aunt and uncle had moved out the area when they retired more than a decade ago, moving closer to Knoxville and the medical care the larger city supplied. He might have cousins in the area, but he didn't know their names or addresses. He wasn't interested in a soppy family reunion, anyway. His childhood friends wouldn't recognize him, and he suspected they wouldn't remember their childhood games and activities any better than he did. Nate did want to see his family cabin one last time, but that was the only reunion he sought. He was as disinterested in engaging with people off the trail as with those on it.

He was shocked when stumbled onto the side trail that led to his childhood cabin. He hadn't expected to recognize it, given decades of growth that had elevated and expanded the trees and mountain laurel. He failed to consider that he had grown in height also, so his relationship to the tree canopy hadn't changed much. He even recognized a large tree stump that had been a landmark during his childhood rambles that he had arrived at the peak of the ridge. He nostalgically sat down on the stump and ate his crackers-and-granola lunch, just as he had wolfed down the bacon-and-egg sandwiches his mother had packed for him years before. He scanned the horizon eastward into North Carolina, appreciating its the beauty much more than he had as a child. He considered his ancestors, now gone, and how much they had loved this land. He also recognized that as natives of the hills, he and they had never fully appreciated the beauty and magnitude of the mountains. The mountains were his stage, the set of his genealogical play. It was the backdrop he performed in front of as a child, but like an actor he faced the audience, not the scenery. Nate had never fully recognized the inherent beauty and majesty of the geologic wrinkles that dwarfed the tiny people scattered among them. He was glad he was taking the time to do so now.

He stood, slowly pivoting his body in a three-hundred-sixty-degree arc, like a human panoramic camera taking a mental picture of the scene, and then began walking down the side trail. The passage was narrower and steeper than he remembered, and the covering brush had to be pushed aside, again something he had not remembered from childhood. Like all backpackers hiking downhill, he leaned further and further back, to keep his center of gravity aligned and keep him and his heavy backpack from toppling forward. As the trail grew steeper, he leaned back more, and soon the his calves were feeling the strain of the effort. The hike to the cabin, which was little more than a mile, seemed shorter to him than it had as a child. He chalked that up to his longer adult legs, but when he reached the clearing, he was realized that more had changed than his stride.

The cabin, which he recalled was built with seasoned timbers, was darker than he remembered. It was black, the black of wood scarred with flame and fire. The cabin had burned. There was a huge chestnut tree that had blown over onto the left side of the 30-foot long cabin, breaking through the roof and leaving the structure essentially uninhabitable. He dropped his pack at the edge of the clearing to one side of the cabin and slowly and carefully stepped on the unburned section of the front porch, holding on to the doorway to maintain his balance as he poked his head inside.

There clearly had been a fire. Looking inside, he immediately saw its origin. Someone had been cooking in one of the four stone fireplaces scattered around the cabin and something had gotten out of hand. Shortly after his father had married Sarah and bought the old homestead for $150, he had built a cookhouse addition on the right side of the structure. Juter Townsend had heard too many stories of cabins burning to the ground from cookfires, so he had built a separate structure next to the cabin, connected only by a small wooden overhang. The cookhouse was on the downwind side of the cabin, so that if a fire occurred, only that small ten-by-ten structure would be lost. He had insisted that the only fires built would be in the cookhouse. The other fireplaces in the house, used only for heat, would be fed by warm coals from the cookhouse fires. Each night, Juter would carefully scoop up the remaining red cookhouse coals in a bucket and carry them to the house, cautiously shoveling them into the stone firebox so that none could roll out accidentally. He had taken sections of window screens from houses down in the valley and fashioned them into fireplace screens to prevent sparks from popping out onto the dry wooden cabin floor.

Apparently the residents who had followed the Townsends were not as cautious. They might have been the people Juter had sold the cabin to when he left Tennessee decades earlier, or they might have just been squatters. Regardless, they had built a large fire in one of the main cabin's fireplaces, and it had gotten out of hand. Nate speculated the fire must have broken out during a rainstorm, which would have kept the blaze from simply razing the entire structure. As it was, the interior walls were charred black and the inside of the roof was pocked with the fragrant carbon ruffles of burned wood. Still, the exterior of the structure, while coated in soot and pockmarked with charring, had not been lost. Walking to the left side of the cabin, Nate looked in to the small room that had served as his parents' bedroom, and the even smaller one that had been his. He suddenly remembered that this was seen as a luxury. Most of his childhood friends lived in single-room cabins where parents, children, aunts and uncles all slept in the same room.

He slept that night in his tent, listening to the burbling stream of his childhood off in the distance. It was a tranquil sound, and just as it had decades earlier, it quickly lulled him to sleep. The next morning, he went to the trouble of cooking himself a full breakfast of freeze-dried eggs mixed with chunks of ham, and not one or two, but three cups of coffee. He was eager to empty some of his supplies, since he knew he would be restocking down in the city of Elizabethton 17 miles away. He started walking down the winding dirt road – barely wider than a trail – that his father had driven each morning so long ago. Mountain laurel and fallen trees now made it impassible by a car, and somewhat awkward for a hiker. Nate finally wended his way around the hills to the main road and began walking westward.

Only a couple of cars passed him on the road as he walked along the narrow shoulder. U.S. 19E had once been a major, if treacherous road for those seeking to cross the mountains from East Tennessee to Western North Carolina. Since Tennessee was dry, but alcohol was available in Asheville, many drove over the winding roads seeking illicit booze. Sadly, many couldn't wait until they returned home to sample their evil spirits, and drunk drivers plummeting off the side of a winding mountain curve was a monthly event. Tennessee eventually voted wet, ending the carnage, and the opening of Interstate 26 in the early 1990s had slowed traffic on the once-bloodstained road to a trickle. Now the road was used only by locals traveling from their hilltop homes down the winding curves to Elizabethton, or on to Kingsport or Johnson City. Nate walked downhill on the right side of the road, his back to oncoming traffic and his left thumb extended in the traditional backpacker/hitchhiker salute. After 30 minutes and four cars, a large red pickup truck pulled over to the side. "You're welcome in the back if you're just going to town," the burly unshaven driver said over his shoulder, never looking fully back at his new passenger. Nate dutifully hopped into the truck bed and kept his head down as the winds whipped his shocks of hair left and right.

Nate recognized nothing of Elizabethton, a testament either to changes made in the area since his departure, or the fact that his father had rarely brought him into town. It wasn't a large city, but neither was it a one-street town. There were several fast-food restaurants, but Nate decided his modest lunch would hold him over dinnertime. There was no outdoor outfitter in town, so he headed to the town's only grocery store to stock up on Lipton Cup-a-Soup and other lightweight foods. He noticed a small run-down motel that clearly hadn't thrived even during its 1950's glory days, and decided a hot shower and a quick nap might be in order. The motel had a washing machine which kept him from having to search for a laundromat. Nate thought the clerk at the hotel had raised his eyes at his name when he signed in, but if he was somehow distantly related to Nate he didn't say anything. Indeed, the clerk said nothing more than his duties required, and barely managed a curt "thank you" as Nate left with his room key. After dropping his gear in his room, Nate took a short walk to a nearby bank to pick up a roll of quarters for the washing machine, and once his clothes were safely tucked away in the rusting, jerking Maytag, he plopped down on his twin-size bed for a short nap. He awoke after an hour, and stumbled back to the laundry room to move his clothes to the dryer. He returned to his room and after entering, stepped on a yellow sheet of notebook paper that apparently had been slipped under his door while he was at the opposite end of the building.

"Bill Leonard's Barbecue & Bluegrass – 9 p.m." the note said. Nate stuck his head out the door and looked around the building and the parking lot for the person who might have written the note. No one. He closed the front door and went to the motel room desk. He pulled out a phone book and looked up the address. According to the map it was a half-mile north of his motel on the opposite side of the Watauga River, a slow-moving, rock-filled river beveling directly through the center of town. He tried to lay down and continue his nap, but his curiosity now had him awake and alert. The writing was a soft cursive, not likely to have been from the hand of his detached and sullen check-in clerk. Nate tried to figure out who might have left the note, but his imagination left him no suspects other than some distant relative with a secrecy fetish. No one knew he was here, though. How could any distant aunt, uncle or cousin have tracked him down? It was only 4 o'clock. He needed a distraction until time to walk to the restaurant and satiate both his hunger and his curiosity. He rifled through his backpack for one of the two books he had bought back in Damascus. He pulled out the Thomas Wolfe. *You Can't Go Home Again*, the title lectured him. "Don't I know it," he said out loud to himself. He sat in a worn upholstered armchair and read the book for two hours before it began to lose his interest. He flipped through the worn pages, wondering about "Jackie Earnest," the book's previous owner who had felt compelled to write his or her name inside the book's front cover. As he flipped toward the back of the book, he saw a long passage illuminated with pink highlighter. You can't go home to your family or your childhood, Wolfe insisted in the tinted text.

"No, Thomas," Nate thought to himself. "No, you can't." His unfamiliarity with Wolfe kept him from realizing the town of which the author spoke was less than 60 miles from where Nate sat.

By 7 o'clock, Nate was already famished, and decided he would walk to the restaurant and eat before whoever had left him the note arrived. As he entered Bill Leonard's, he saw the red clapboard building housed not just a restaurant, but a restaurant that doubled as a music hall and dance club. The lighting was low, and there were long rows of picnic tables in a giant U-shape, leaving a huge area in the center of the building open for couples to dance. Behind the open space was a slightly-raised stage where a five-piece bluegrass band was warming up in preparation for what would be an evening of country dancing, beer drinking, and for the people of Carter County, Tennessee, assorted misbehavior and drama they would be able to gossip for the next seven days – until the following Saturday night. Nate followed the rope line – made of real rope, not the felt variety – inside the front door to a raised counter where you were supposed to order your meal. The person in line in front of him ordered a beef barbecue plate, and was immediately chastised. "We don't have beef barbecue," the portly woman behind the counter intoned. "No such thing. If it ain't pork, it ain't barbecue." The patron, who might have been visiting from Texas, took this news hard but quickly settled on a pork sandwich and large beer, the latter likely to smooth out any hard feelings over the porcine faux pas.

Nate ordered ribs and took his food and beer to an open spot at one of the long lines of picnic tables that encircled the band and dance floor. Just as he began gnawing on the first rib, the band fired up with "Black Mountain Rag," a speedy acoustic number designed to both get the audience in the mood for the evening and stall for time as they awaited their lead singer, who apparently was running late. The group's fiddle player, the only female member of the group, sawed quickly on her instrument while the guitarist, banjo player, bass and mandolin player followed along. Like most bluegrass groups, there was no percussion and no electric instruments. The large bass and the mandolin alternated providing rhythms to the songs by plucking away, while the electricity was provided by the fervor at which the group attacked each traditional folk song. After playing another fast acoustic number, "Hell Among the Yearlings," by Sam & Kirk McGee, the singer arrived with his own large guitar in tow, and sheepishly joining the group and adding background to the first guitar player.

They fired up a song called "My Little Georgia Rose," introduced as a Bill Monroe tune, and Nate couldn't help think of Marie, his own Georgia rose. Nate had never appreciated country music, and as a way of hiding his heritage, insulted it regularly while growing up in Maine. Country music always seemed anti-intellectual and unrefined to him. The combination of twanging steel guitars and rhinestones seemed "hickish" to a teenager more interested in rock and roll. As he listened, however, this music was different. It was more honest, more genuine. Gone were the pretensions of overdressed, garish Nashville celebrities. Gone were the ubiquitous outfits all country musicians seemed to sport these days. No rhinestones. No ridiculous cowboy hats. This was music nurtured in the poverty and simplicity of the hills that were his home. He respected that. Bluegrass music had come from the highlands of Scotland, was seasoned by a single-generation exodus to Ireland, and then migrated to America. It had grown into its own once the white man's music was mashed together with the black man's blues coming up from the Delta, and developed into a pure music that was uniquely American. As the group quickly transitioned from song to song, talking about the joy of the hills, of family gone and hard work in the fields, Nate found it speaking to him on a cellular level. Something genetically called to him in the music, and he became enthralled with its simplicity and structure. Each verse was separated by an instrumental break. During these intervals, each performer would get four or eight bars to showcase their musicianship. The structure was consistent: Verse. Guitar solo. Verse. Banjo breakout. Verse. Focus on the mandolin. Verse. The bass player showed off. Each musician would show their skill and then would unite during the verses to mesh into something pure and harmonious. All of his pompous pretense about country music was forgotten. The music was speaking to him in the same language as his retreat to the woods.

After ninety minutes, the band took a quick break to refortify itself with barbecue and beers before returning. After an uptempo Stanley Brothers number, the mandolin player stepped up announced their next number was the lead guitarist's favorite, a "Roy Acuff tune called 'The Precious Jewel.'" He alerted the band they would be starting off in the chord of G and then quickly plucked the opening notes. The guitarist stepped up to the microphone and the lyrics immediately stabbed Nate like a post-hole digger shoved directly into his chest. He froze in his seat staring with a pained expression, unable to take his eyes away from the stage.

> *"Way back in the hills, when a boy, I once wandered*
> *Buried deep in her grave lies a girl that I love*
> *She was called from this earth, a jewel for heaven*
> *More precious than diamonds more precious than gold."*

Nate stared at the band during the instrumental break, frozen, certain that the band was staring straight at him and studying him as it began the next verse:

> *"When a girl of sixteen, we courted each other*
> *She promised someday to become my sweet wife*
> *I bought her the ring to wear on her finger*
> *But the angels they called her to heaven one night."*

By now, Nate was stricken. It was if the seventy-year-old song had been written for him, and none of the 80 or so listeners inside the bluegrass and barbecue joint were there. Pain that he had spent almost a year and 1,800 mile repressing had now risen to the surface like water from a saturated spring, and the water from that spring began dripping from his eyes. The guitarist continued stabbing Nate with his words.

"A jewel here on earth, a jewel up in heaven
She'll brighten the kingdom around God's great throne
May the angels have peace, God bless her in heaven
They've broken my heart and they left me to roam."

Nate could take no more. His flight reflex was triggered and he quickly disentangled himself from the picnic table and clumsily began stumbling over patrons trying to fight his way to the exit. The song had two more verses, but Nate heard neither of them. His ears were now ringing with remembrance and pain. The patrons he slowly pushed by were blurs, faceless furniture standing between him and the escape hatch from his pain. When he got to the door, one blur stepped into his way, preventing him from bursting out of the building. He tried to sidestep the blur, but it kept blocking him. Through the ringing, he suddenly heard his name.

"Nate! Nate!" The blur's voice was now yelling at him. It was familiar and forgiving voice, and he struggled to bring the blurred face into focus. It had long brunette hair. Finally, the haze cleared.

"Nate!" *Teapot* was staring at him, and holding him by both shoulders. She shoved him back and forth, trying to snap him out of his disorientation. "What's wrong?"

The memorial service had been awful. All funerals were painful, but given the extenuating circumstances, Nate's discomfort was almost unbearable. He was grateful in a small way that Marie's parents had insisted on an interment at the family cemetery back in Georgia. Nate still had to suffer through the service in Maine, however, one crafted to placate their local friends and family. If funerals were for the living and not the dead, Nate felt whoever designed the idea was either cruel or insane. Forced to accept the sincere condolences of his coworkers, friends and family members, each offering the same words, intended to heal but words instead that tore the same scab off the same wound. The pain of the tearing was repeated, over and over, for more than an hour, before finally the minister arrived and the service began. There was a mixture of both contemporary and traditional songs from a small choir, neither providing any true consolation but providing a slight amount of emotional anesthetic as a result of their banality.

Nate had chosen to sit on one side of the aisle, alone, while his in-laws sat in the front row of the opposite row of pews. There were reasons for this, with each side of the aisle racked with both recriminations and guilt. Nate couldn't help but notice the seating mimicked that of a wedding, with the friends and family separating almost instinctively between his side of the aisle and Marie's. The minister, once he began speaking, proved his training made him much more effective at inflicting emotional suffering than the choir. His intent was to provide comfort, but the words he chose unwittingly only managed to remind Nate of his loss and sorrow. The usual Bible verses were cited, and on this day their familiarity rendered them ineffective and discomforting. Nate sat stoically staring forward, focused on nothing in particular, certainly not any human being in the small wooden church. He was remembering his father retelling the story of his grandfather's mountain funeral, where Nate's grandmother had employed professional wailers, a mountain custom where the widow sat emotionless while a chorus in black was paid to cry, moan, pull their hair out and express the grief that the spouse was forbidden by custom to convey. Nate wondered what his friends from Maine would think if he had employed such a bizarre custom for this event. As it was, the church's choir was unwittingly and accurately expressing his current emotional state, which was numbness and disinterest.

After the service, Nate endured more condolences as he watched the caskets, one large and one small, wheeled down the aisle and outside to two hearses that would drive them to the airport for their flight to north Georgia. Nate's decision to not accompany them was questioned by some, but in his mind he'd already said his goodbyes. In the back of his mind, there was a kernel of belief that he would see them both again.

His first night back in his house, freshly cleaned for him, was horrific. The silence created a ringing in his ears that grew louder the more he focused on it. He tried turning the television on to distract him, but no channel, no diversion could gain his attention. Reading also was of no help. Two days later, his friend David called and then came to the house to check up on him. It wasn't a good visit, since David's sarcasm and joking were useless in salving Nate's wounds. Like an electrician sent to fix a leaking water pipe, David quickly found he was incapable of making the spiritual repairs

Nate needed.

Nate waited three weeks before returning to work. His coworkers were sympathetic and supportive, but their distance and the caution they used around him only served to remind him that everything had changed. His fight-or-flight reflex had been triggered, violently so.

Nate shared the story of the funeral with Teapot that night, back at his hotel room. They sat up until five the next morning as he told her most of it. When he talked about the deaths of his wife and daughter, he made clear to her they'd both died together, but repeatedly balked at providing details about how they'd died. Was it a car accident? A robbery? Teapot didn't know, and it was clear from how Nate repeatedly brushed over this detail that it was an area too painful to probe, so she finally began to avoid it. Indeed, she asked very few questions as Nate related the tale, allowing him to share only what he wanted. Her questions focused less on the painful loss that had brought him to the trail, and more of his thinking about how running away to the woods would bring him peace. His answers didn't provide much clarity.

"After the funerals, I felt truly and deeply alone for the first time in my life. My parents were both gone, and now I'd lost my wife and my little girl," Nate said. "The house was so empty I could hear the ringing in my ears all day long. I took long walks but that didn't help."

"Didn't you talk to anyone?"

"No, not really. I don't think men have the type of supportive friendships that women enjoy, and so I was unable to find any comfort there. My friends from work were cautious to the point of avoidance – I could feel their fear that they might say or do the wrong thing and trigger suffering on my part. They didn't understand that by doing this, they were just reminding me of that suffering."

"So you already were alone in Freeport. Why go to the woods to be alone?"

Nate paused to consider his answer. "There are plenty of reasons. I thought about Thoreau and his escape to the wild. I thought that might help me recover. I will admit part of it was simply me being a coward, and running away from all those things that caused me pain. I'm not proud of that, but I don't apologize for it either. There's something to be said for solitude as a way to discover your true self. When you're alone with your demons, you have to confront them. There's no one else on the trail with you in large part, so you and those thoughts have to have conversations."

"You've been talking to these demons since Kathadin?"

"We're old friends by now," Nate nodded, starting straight into her green eyes.

The sun was now starting to brighting the thin white drapes covering the hotel room's high square window. Both were exhausted now, Nate especially from the release of feelings he'd allowed to escape for the first time since his family's death.

"What about you?" he asked. "Why did you vanish back in New Hampshire? What happened? Where were ..."

She cut him off with a finger to his lips. "You shared a lot tonight, she smiled. "Get some sleep, and when you wake up it'll be my turn." He was so exhausted, he didn't argue. She shut off the light in the room and quietly closed the door as she left. He stared at the door, laid his head down on the pillow and instantly fell asleep without even crawling under the bed's garish red-and-green plaid comforter.

15
ROOTS AND REMEMBRANCE

He awoke after five hours of sleep feeling more refreshed than on days he'd slept ten. The red light on his motel room's rotary phone was blinking, and he dialed the front desk for his message. Teapot had suggested he meet her at the Silver Skillet, a local breakfast place around 11 a.m. "Bring your gear," she'd added. He looked at the clock. 10:30. He had 30 minutes to shower and shave, he did it in ten and then jammed all his clothes and gear into the top of his backpack. He walked to the front desk, found directions to the Silver Skillet, and arrived just five minutes late. Teapot already had her cup of hot tea steaming in front of her as he sat down in the restaurant's wide booth.

"They have Earl Gray here?" he smiled.

"Lipton. A perfectly acceptable compromise, since we're roughing it," she smiled back. "I'm going to try to do the Southern thing this morning. I will be experiencing grits for the first time in my life. I think they're illegal in California – at least I never saw them growing up. I refused to consider eating them when I went away to college. This will be my tip-of-the-hat to your birthplace, Nate. My first exposure to the grit.

Nate laughed. Her chances of finding granola and wheat germ here in rural Tennessee were somewhere between slim and none, so she might as well embrace the local fare. For his part, Nate ordered country ham and eggs, anticipating he would wolf down every bite. He requested so many refills of coffee that the waitress finally relented and left him a carafe filled with hot Maxwell House. Teapot pronounced her scrambled egg whites excellent, but the grits quickly turned into a science experiment.

"How do you eat them?"

"With a fork."

"No, dummy. What do you put in them? Or do you eat them plain?"

"There are many schools of thought here," he began, pontificating on grits as a university professor might lecture a hall of undergraduates. "Yes, you could eat them plain, but I knew very few who do that. Some just have butter. Some have sugar. Some do both. I've known people who mix jelly into them. Some like salt, some not. It's your choice."

Teapot used her spoon to divide the pool of yellow-white corn grits into five small pools. On one she added butter. The second just sugar. Butter-and-sugar on the third. Butter and salt on the fourth and she opened her packet of strawberry jam and stirred it into the fifth pile. She then dutifully tested each option, slowly savoring each bite as if she was back in Sonoma Valley at a wine tasting. "I have a ruling," she said after finishing the last of the five samples. "They're all exquisitely ... bad. You can't add anything to these things to make them taste good."

"Now you know how I feel about granola," Nate smiled back.

"At least that's healthy for you."

"Yes, but who wants to live a life where you eat cardboard-flavored food for 90 years?"

She smiled back again. How long had it been since Nate had coaxed a smile out of a woman?

"OK," he said as the waitress removed his empty plate. "Your turn. What happened to the two of you back in New Hampshire?"

She paused as she handed her plate back to the waitress and asked for the check. She batted her eyes and flashed green at him again. "I'll make a deal with you. You're still heading Southbound, right?"

"Yes."

"I'm back to hiking, too. Let me tag along with you, and I'll share everything with you." Was that a double-entendre? Nate didn't think so, but he wasn't sure.

He thought for a minute. "Fair enough. Are you stocked up or do we need to stop somewhere?"

"Not only am I ready, I have us a cab set up to take us back to the trailhead. If you're waiting on me, you're behind."

They were off. Within 30 minutes, they were back on the Appalachian Trail, heading southbound at a respectable clip. Nate was pleased that he didn't have to alter his stride to keep up with

Teapot, or allow her to keep up with him. While she was a good four inches shorter than Nate, apparently her legs were the same length, and so she was able to match him stride for stride. In most parts, the trail was too narrow for them to walk alongside each other, so he took point and listened as she followed directly behind him and explained their strange night hike and her and Big Gray's vanishing act.

"When we woke you up that morning, my friend Gray was in shock," she began. "All she kept saying was that we had to get out of there. That it wasn't safe. She kept whispering that to me, but I couldn't understand what she meant. I tried to find out what had her so upset, but all she could do was keep pointing at Franklin, who was sleeping about ten feet away from her. It was frightening the way she stared at him, so I quickly decided to get us up and get out. I remembered the talk about ice on the trail, and quickly decided we needed a third hiker to help us in case someone got hurt. That's why I woke you.

"But what happened?"

"I didn't find out until later in the day. During one of the points where you were well up ahead of us and out of earshot, I asked Gray what happened. She told me the whole story. Apparently while she was sleeping, Franklin over the course of an hour crept closer and closer to her in his sleeping bag. She awoke at one point and found him inside his bag right up against her bag, but figured he had just been rolling around in his sleep and didn't think much of it. The next time she awoke, he had both his hands inside her sleeping bag, one hand down her pants and the other grabbing her breasts. She was so shocked and disoriented she laid still for a minute, not believing what he was doing to her. Finally, she grabbed both his arms and with great force pushed his hands away from her, she said. He was apparently resisting strongly, and she'd been smaller like me I don't know if she'd have been able to fight him off."

"Why didn't she scream? Or say something?"

"She couldn't explain that to me. Shame? Fear? Worried that if she raised the alarm he might do something violent to all of us to cover up his actions? Trust me, she was second-guessing her actions all that next day on the trail. She was ashamed, too. Deeply ashamed. Which just kept pissing me off. If I'd known what the bastard did before we'd left the cabin, I'd have taken my handy Boy Scout knife to his pecker."

"How did she get him to stop? Or did he?" This story was turning uglier by the minute, and Nate kept finding himself wheeling his head around to look back at Teapot as she continued the tale.

"After she got his hands off her, she curled up in a ball and wrapped the top opening of her sleeping bag under her. She was in a cocoon. He couldn't get to her any more, and after trying for a minute or too, it was clear he wouldn't be able to lift her off the opening so he could get back in her sleeping bag. So I guess he decided he'd just go to sleep, and in the morning deny anything she said about it to the two of us. After she was sure he'd gone back to sleep, she slid slowly and quietly over to where I was in the cabin and let me know we had to get out of there."

Nate was furious at the pompous and privileged New Hampshire hiker. Nate's instincts, which he had never learned to fully trust, had been right about Franklin, and he felt some semblance of guilt regarding Big Gray's molestation. It wasn't the first time Nate had felt guilt for a crime for which he'd had only a cursory responsibility.

"So I understand why we had to leave in the middle of the night," Nate said. "That explains why you both kept looking over your shoulders the next day. You could have told me what had happened."

"She wouldn't let me." Teapot was crying now. Nate could hear it over his left shoulder. "She was so ashamed, and she made me promise not to say anything to you. Or anyone. What do you do when your closest friend has had such a horrible thing happen to her and makes you promise such a thing?"

Nate stopped in his tracks and turned to her. He put his arms around her and hugged her, to let he know she'd done all the right things. "I understand. You did what you had to do for your best friend. But why abandon me on the middle of the trail that next night?"

Teapot gently pushed away from him and looked down at her boots as she answered. "I'm not happy about that, Nate." she said, tears rolling down her now-swollen cheeks. "I don't know whether it was the shock of fear or what was going on with her. She woke up that night in the tent thrashing. She kept mumbling "No, no, no," over and over again. "She was petrified that Franklin would catch up to us and attack her again. I was afraid for her, Nate I made the decision we had to hike back up to the tram and get her off the trail and off the mountain. You have to know that as we were packing up that night, I started to walk over to you and have you join us. But she freaked out. She kept pointing at your tent and crying, plaintively saying 'no, no no.' I was afraid she was so damaged she'd throw herself off the mountain."

Teapot started walking again, this time taking point but continuing her story. "I had nothing to leave a note for you. My first thought was that I had to get her to safety, though. I'd make the same decision again, but I knew you'd be hurt and scared by what happened." By now she was sitting on a large rock on the trailside, weeping uncontrollably. Nate kneeled down and instinctively and hugged her, the way he had in the past for both his wife and daughter. His strong hug comforted both Teapot and Nate.

"It's OK. I was just afraid for you. I had no way of knowing if you were safe. When I backtracked to the tram and the operator told me you'd gone down the mountain earlier that morning, I assumed you never wanted to see me again."

"Oh no, Nate. I appreciated what you did. It's one thing to be kind when you know why you're being kind. It's a higher level of selflessness when you do something like that and you don't even know the reason. You have a good heart, Nate. It's been scarred and scraped up so much, but it's a good heart."

Both leaned back from the hug, still grasping each other but now looking into each other's eyes. It was that universal yet unexplainable look humans share that electrically communicates what comes next. They slowly leaned in, wordless, and kissed each other. It was soft and sensitive at first, then grew longer and more passionate. They grasped each other harder as they kissed. After their lips parted, they held onto each other for what seemed like hours.

"I've decided on your trail name, Nate."

"Really?" He had never received one, even from the hikers who'd spent the night with him and his motorcycling friends. They had promised to create one for him, but in the excitement and with the large crowd, the promise had been forgotten.

"Yes. I'm going to call you 'Rescue.'"

"'Rescue.'"

"Yes."

"My trail name is 'Rescue.'"

"Yes."

"Because I rescued you and Big Gray?"

"No." She smiled, hugging him harder. "Because I'm going to rescue you."

Each stared out onto the horizon. They were on the top of the world, one looking at pastures and mountains to the east of them, the other looking at small towns and farms to their west. They were in the middle of nowhere, and yet they felt as if they were everywhere. He was close to someone again. After too long a time, he finally had someone with whom he could talk. With meaning.

He had spoken to no one after the funeral. With both parents gone, he had nowhere to express his grief. His friends, David and others, had tried to console him, but were by their own admission not up to the task. How could you explain and soften the deaths of someone's wife and daughter?

His return to work had been equally awkward. His colleagues were clearly uncomfortable, unsure whether to strike a supportive, sympathetic tone or act as if everything was back to normal. Their intentions were good – they loved Nate and wanted to aid in his healing. Their awkwardness around him, however, only made him more self-aware, and kept his pain alive. The flowers that had been sent to his office on the first day of his return quickly wilted in the dry heat of his building, but his pain and remorse stayed fresh.

He discovered his only respite from the pain came on long, solitary walks along the trails that worked their way along the cliffs near his home. The trails were worn from the 15 or so residents in the area who would walk along the high shelves of granite, gathering in lungfulls of fresh sea air, or hoping to burn off calories from an excessive meal. Nate sought therapy for his soul rather than his body, and found the concentration required to keep his footing distracted him from the remembrances that pained him. He couldn't focus on his anguish while staring down at his feet to make sure he didn't slip into the cold, salty abyss. When he did stop, he was focused on the swelling and rocking wavetops near the horizon, or on the noise and violence as the waves crashed into the man-sized boulders that littered the shoreline below him. The trail was just high enough over the breakers that the sound of the waves breaking would reach him just a second after seeing the shattering, foamy action below. Time seemed briefly displaced to him, and the disconnect was, in some ways, comforting.

Oh, he had considered just flinging himself off the cliff. It might have been unnatural for him not to. For the most part, however, the hikes provided a necessary intermission from his grief, if not true escape and comfort. That intermission was welcome.

It was during one of these walks along the coast that he had decided on his pilgrimage down the AT. Once the idea popped into his head, he instantly saw the wisdom of it. If a twenty-minute walk above the shoreline could provide him with a brief respite from his suffering, a six-month hike would be a godsend. He would travel south to where it all began, the land of his and Marie's nativity. He would abandon fir trees and rediscover chestnuts and hickories. He would leave scrub and return to Rhododendron. Along the way, he would sort things out and in the end complete his pilgrimage.

He returned to work the following Monday and immediately began planning his escape to the wilderness. He would go through the motions of interacting with people only for as long as necessary to plan, supply and organize his escape. After four weeks, he informed the CEO of his need for the leave of absence. Given the circumstances, his boss thought he understood the request and granted it on the condition that as his head of marketing, Nate wait another six weeks to finish the summer and fall ad campaigns. Since it was still late-winter, Nate readily agreed. He was intent on fleeing human interaction, escaping humanity and all of its inhumanity. What would another six weeks matter?

Nate had missed an opportunity to show Teapot his family's cabin in their haste to return to the trail. In the subsequent days he kept telling her about it. He was back home, in the familiar mountains with soft, smooth curves along their peaks. As a child in school, he had drawn smooth lines that looked like the oscillations of ocean waves. By pulling out his pine green, yellow green and forest green crayons from his huge Crayola box, however, they were transformed into a portrait of the very mountains he spent his days roaming. He shared with her his feelings about leaving, and what few memories he could assemble. Walking among familiar groves, he'd remembered playing football on one of the balds – the cleared areas on top the mountain peaks created by grazing animals that farmers would lead to the mountaintops in the heat of summer. He also remembered taking piece of cardboard and using it as a sled one snowy winter, the excitement of the downhill speed suddenly tempered when he collided with a ten-inch wide hickory tree, losing two of his baby teeth in the process.

Teapot was sharing too, telling Nate stories of growing up in northern California, trying to find a place amidst the many cliques that the area's diversity created. There were the techies, the skiers, the surfers, the outdoor types, sailers, the car freaks and the hippies. She had gravitated toward the outdoor types, but because of her friendly nature said she could count among her friends all the different circles that intermingled in the classrooms of Sonoma Valley High School. She admitted her eyes had glazed over whenever the techies or the car freaks started waxing passionately about circuit boards or carburetors. She thought it humorous that both talked about their respective toys with the same reverential and loving tones. She had a good friend from early childhood, Charlotte, who had gravitated toward the hippie culture shortly after reaching her teenage years. She had pulled Teapot with her in that direction, at least for a year. Teapot found the selfless and nonmaterialistic aspects of the culture appealing, but as the movement became marred by overdoses and violence, she moved away from it, and from Charlotte. She had received a phone call from Charlotte several years later, a 2 a.m. call from a pay phone in Tulsa, asking Teapot if she could wire her $60 for a bus ticket home. The next morning, Teapot had ridden her bike to the Western Union office and sent her old friend all the money she had, which wasn't much, but the girl never returned to Sonoma and Teapot never heard from her again.

The hiking along the rippled ridges separating Tennessee and North Carolina was quite different from the first 1,800 miles of the trail now behind them. Nate had hiked most of the trail in silence. Now, he found he was enjoying conversation again. He still preferred listening over talking, a bias that his father had preached to him was admirable and noble. "You learn more by listening than talking," Juter had often told his son. "That's why God gave you two ears but only one mouth." When he was 13, his father and he had been forced to spend 90 minutes on a train sitting next to a man his father would have called a "know-it-all who doesn't."

Nate never heard his father get a word in during the Downeaster train ride to Exeter, where the man finally departed. After the train started up, Juter enjoying four solid minutes of blessed silence with his eyes closed before quietly stating "If dumb was dirt, that man would cover half of Vermont."

His father always had succinct statements like that, and whenever Teapot was looking for a laugh on the trail, she would ask Nate to recount some of them. Her favorite was his descriptions of Nate's befuddling friend David, who Juter had once described as "as confused as a cow on Astroturf." Like many sons, Nate as he grew older tried in vain to not be a carbon-copy of his father, but Marie pointed out to him on the occasions when he used expressions that clearly had come from his father and the hills. She had asked a store clerk at a resupply shop in Marshall if she looked good in a woolen flannel top she was trying on to replace her now-threadbare cold-weather shirt. The commissioned salesclerk told her it was beautiful on her, and she'd bought it. "Never ask a barber if you need a haircut," Nate smiled, and Teapot had immediately began teasing him, calling him 'Juter' for the rest of the day.

Since both of his parents were dead, and both of hers were still alive, he asked her why she didn't call them each time they stepped off the trail to resupply.

"My parents raised me to be obscenely independent," was her explanation. "Are they concerned about me? Sure, what parent wouldn't be? They would take it as a tremendous insult to the work they did as parents, though, if I felt I constantly needed to check in with them. They raised me to be my own person, and able to survive on my own. I've mailed a couple of postcards, but that's because my mother collects them, not because they need to check up on me."

Nate found the idea odd. He had been a parent, and knew that the thought of your children popped into your head hourly. Did that change when your children became adults? Nate thought not.

As they entered the northern end of the Great Smoky Mountains National Park at Davenport Gap, they had developed a predictable hiking routine. If the trail was wide enough, they would hike two abreast, with Nate always on the downhill side in a chivalrous position to prevent Teapot from slipping down any steep section of trail. He also served as a windbreak when needed, preventing the cold brisk winds racing up the mountain face from the valley below from chilling her. In narrow sections, he would always take lead, pointing out occasional obstacles, large roots, low branches or other minor dangers. When they camped for the night, they would each set up separate tents, with the openings facing each other so they could continue talking into the evening. While they'd kissed several times after their first outside of Elizabethton, and held hands sometimes when walking side-by-side, they had stayed chaste throughout the following weeks. While each had grown in their affection for the other, neither felt it appropriate or wise to step up to a higher plateau of intimacy. She had clearly fallen in love with him. Their relationship had begun by chance. It had reconnected only because she had felt guilty about abandoning him and felt an urgent need to find him and explain herself. Or was there more to it? Perhaps she had already known deep down from their first meeting, that he was someone damaged but savable, someone hurt but helpful, someone she wanted to share the next mile and the next walking alongside.

Nate was confused. He felt the same. Did he love her too? He didn't know. He was expressing himself and caring for another in a way he thought was long dead inside of himself. Teapot was stirring something inside of him that was as cold as the hearth in his family's burned-down cabin. He wasn't sure he was capable of feeling love. As they began to hike the steep downhill switchbacks that signaled the southern exit from the Smokies and presaged their approach to the trail's end, however, his mood began to change. And not for the better.

16
DISCOVERIES

The next few weeks moved quickly, both in terms of miles hiked and in their affection for each other. There continued to be no consummation of that affection – Nate didn't feel comfortable progressing beyond kissing and hand-holding, although by the time they reached Nantahala Gorge, Teapot would have welcomed such an advance and on one occasion, had dreamed about it while sleeping alone in her tent. While he was enjoying Teapot's company, Nate also began feeling a familiar fear of loss. Each time he made an effort to move forward and explore his warming feelings for her, he was pushed back by the swelling panic that anything gained could be easily lost. For her part, she was trying to probe and find an opening into the rock wall surrounding his heart, with limited success. He would speak about the funeral, and about the pain of the loss of Marie and especially his precious Joy, but any attempt to extract details about their deaths was met by walled silence. She wanted to move closer to him, but as they got closer and closer to Georgia, she realized his true pain was still has obscured from her as the distant hazy peaks seen from Wayah Bald. For five days they hiked in relative silence. Both knew what was causing the silence, but only one of them could break it. Nate knew he was unable – or was it unwilling? – to share his betrayal, the cause of his loss and, ultimately, his pain. As they crossed the park's southern border and began the ten-day up-and-down that would take them through North Carolina and to the border with Georgia, Teapot was becoming less sympathetic and more upset with Nate's silence. As they camped at the Sassafras Gap Shelter, they silently went through what had now become ritual: He began unloading pots and food while she walked down to the spring for water. No words were said, but as she scrambled back up the side trail from the spring she had decided she'd had enough.

"Why do you think I'm here?"

He was taken aback by the tone, and responded reflexively. "Hiking? I don't know," he responded somewhat sullenly, taking the water from her and filling the cook pot.

"I don't know either. I made quite an effort to be here, though. You have no idea."

"What do you mean?" Her now-angry tone was again triggering his defensiveness, but instead of flight this time he was opting to fight. His voice raised in timbre and he felt anger welling up inside him – something he'd suppressed for years.

"How do you think I found you, Nate?"

Nate blinked. He'd been so focused on revisiting the incident with Big Gray in New Hampshire, funerals and past segments of the hike that he hadn't considered the logistics of how Teapot had managed to be in Elizabethton at the moment he arrived.

"Do you think I parked myself in your hometown for three months just waiting for you to show up late?"

How had she known when he'd arrived? The attack in Virginia had set him two months behind. She was right. Surely she hadn't waited for him that long.

"Were you ever going to tell me about what happened to you in Virginia? Or is that some other burden you figured you should just keep to yourself?" Nate was now both angry and confused.

"You know about ..."

"OF COURSE I KNOW ABOUT IT! You blithering, self-centered idiot! Who do you think found you on the trail?"

Nate was too shocked to speak. He had been told a hiker had found him, but had never received any other details of his rescue.

"After I got Big Gray back home to her parents in San Antonio, I came back. I wanted to finish the trail. Why? I don't know. Maybe I wanted to finish what I started. Maybe I felt bad that we'd just bailed out on you. I tried to catch up. I figured you had a one-week head start on me, so I jumped ahead and waited. Apparently you were further than I thought, because on several occasions I had someone drive me to trail crossings where I'd wait in hopes of seeing you, and after several days I'd figure out you'd already passed. Finally, I gave up and just started hiking. At Harper's Ferry, I talked to a northbounder who told me you were just four days ahead of me, so I picked up the pace, hoping to catch up. When I got to Charlottesville, I saw your pack along the trail and thought I'd finally found you. Your gear was scattered all along the side of the trail, though, and when I looked over the side I saw more gear and your tent at the bottom of the ravine. Nate, I climbed 200 feet down that cliff to find you. You were alive but in bad shape. I couldn't drag you back up, so I had to climb back up and rush down the trail to alert the authorities.

"You were the one who found me."

"Yes. I didn't expect you to live, quite honestly. A deputy brought me into the city and after questioning me, brought me to the hospital. I had thought you'd fallen off the trail, but they later told me you'd been attacked. You looked horrible. I waited for a week until the doctors said you might not come out of your coma. Then I had to leave to get back to school in Indiana."

"You left?"

"I had to. I called the hospital every day, though, to see if you'd come out of it. Kept telling them I was your cousin so they'd share the information with me. At one point they wanted to know if you had a living will, so I lied and told them you didn't ever want to be unplugged. I called all the time. After two months, I called one day and they said you'd finally come out of your coma. I hung up the phone and cried for two solid hours. I made plans to fly back there during a class break, but by the time I got off the plane to Charlottesville, you were gone. I knew you'd started back on the trail. Don't ask me how I knew, but I knew. I remembered where you'd said your family was from, so I calculated how long it would take you to get to Roan Mountain. I dropped out of my classes and got there three days before you did. I told all the motel managers to look for you, and promised them fifty dollars if they were the one to call me if you checked in.

"Why did you do all that?"

"Do you really need me to say it? Are you that dense?"

Nate knew the answer, but didn't want to say it. He was afraid of the words, but found himself wanting to hear them.

"Because I care for you, Nate Townsend." She paused another two seconds before she said it. "Because I love you."

Nate stood silently. Dinner was totally forgotten now. He didn't know what to say, and the best he came up was "Teapot, I owe you my life."

"She glared at him, hating and loving him at the same time.

Her eyes fixed on his with a passion and furor from deep in the soul.

"If you owe me your life, maybe it's about time you shared it with me."

He sat there in silence. She was right. She had shown her loyalty. He would share with her his betrayal.

Nate had called Marie from Seattle that Tuesday when he'd arrived for the four days of meetings he'd scheduled with various outdoor manufacturers. He had booked a flurry of meetings and dinners with key executives at Columbia Sportswear, K2, Tubbs Snowshoes and three other companies wanting to increase their presence in his stores. Normally they would come to him, but he wanted to jam a high number of meetings into a single week, and he also wanted to tour several manufacturing operations. Also, unknown to his employer, he also had a meeting with a competitor who wanted to hire him away from his current company. REI, headquartered just south of Seattle in suburban Kent, was romancing him about possibly jumping ship and moving across the country to run their retail operations. His plan was to spend four days on the West Coast and take the red eye flight back so he would be there Saturday morning to wake up six-year-old Joy and take her to her 10 a.m. dance class. The week had gone well, but early Thursday he received a call that both of his Friday appointments had to bail out on him. Rather than be annoyed, he was thrilled. He could reschedule for a 3 p.m. Thursday flight and be home late that night, East Coast time. He rushed through his final appointment and then dashed to the airport to drop his rental car and make the flight. He'd had no time to call and alert Marie, but even if he had it was doubtful she'd express any happiness about it. Her depression and misery in the marriage were no longer camouflaged, and the relationship was now operating on two things: Inertia, and a joint desire to provide a stable environment for Joy.

The flight into Boston Logan arrived at 10 p.m., thirty minutes early thanks to a strong tailwind. The drive up I-95 would take two hours, and he put himself on autopilot as he drove the familiar route. He knew he would be enjoying a bittersweet early reunion. While his wife wouldn't care that he'd managed to come home a day early, his daughter would be thrilled. He would make sure she had her favorite breakfast waiting when she woke up – blueberry pancakes with the Maine blueberries arranged in the batter to make a smiley face. She would come down the stairs to find her father unexpectedly holding a spatula and a plate of smiling pancakes, he imagined. His anticipation of her smile and the hug that would follow kept him warm as the cold, fall air raced outside his car window when he crossed the Merrimac River.

When he pulled into the driveway just past midnight, there was an extra car in the driveway. It took a minute to recognize it as their friend Jeff's from Boston, and Nate immediately worried that something was wrong. Had Marie been hurt and called Jeff to help? He would have been just a few hours away, while Nate was on the other side of the country. Why wouldn't she have called, though? Things between them were bad, but if there was a true emergency surely she would have called. If she could.

The house was dark. Were they home? Had they taken Marie's car to the hospital? No. It was here, he saw through the window in the garage door. He opened the front door and walked in. The house was dark. He walked down the hall to Joy's room and looked in. She was asleep curled up in her bed, encased in pink blankets, pillows and her wearing her favorite cartoon pajamas. He leaned in to check her breathing and found her healthy and sleeping soundly. He felt relief.

There were voices on the opposite end of the house. A man and a woman's. Talking softly. A laugh. That was Marie, and Nate realized he hadn't heard her laugh in several years. Despite this, his instincts – his oft-ignored instincts – were telling him something was wrong. He slowly walked down the hallway, past the kitchen, dining room and family room. He stood at the door to the master bedroom and heard another laugh. He slowly and carefully tried the doorknob. It was locked, something he and Marie never did. He reached on top of the door frame and found the flat-faced key that unlocked the door. Just before he tripped the lock and shoved the door open, he heard a voice – Jeff's – whisper, "Did you hear something?"

When he flung the door open, he instantly became part of a scene that was a sickening combination of tragedy and comedy. When he opened the door and saw his wife and their best friend together, naked, in his bed, there was no comedy or even drama to the moment. Only shock. Pure shock. There was no attempt at denial. How could there be? There was no recriminating comments from Nate. The only words spoken were Marie's: "What are you doing here?" Her meaning was, "Why are you home a day early?" but the phrase "What are you doing here?" held more meaning than she'd intended.

Nate wanted to roar at them. He wanted to scream in rage. He knew instantly that Marie's trips to Boston each week for the past two years hadn't been to see a counselor. They had been to see Jeff. He knew that as she had grown more distant from her husband, she'd moved closer to Jeff, and Nate's cuckolding was a dual betrayal by both a friend and his high school sweetheart. He wanted to yell, to scream, to throw things. He felt the pressure of his rage ringing in his head. He had a handgun in the dresser and pulled it out, awkwardly removing the trigger guard left on to protect Joy. He waved it at both of them. "I ought to kill you both right here, right now," he threatened. Jeff was clearly more afraid of this possibility than Marie. At that moment, she considered that death would be a welcome relief from the pain she felt, but she also knew her husband well enough to know the threat was likely to be an empty one. Even with the trigger guard, she knew he never kept bullets in the gun because of the danger to Joy. They would be in a separate box in the same drawer.

"Nathan! Nathan! Nathan!" Jeff had always been the only person besides Marie and his mother to use Nate's full name, which until this moment had been the trait that annoyed Nate the most about him.

"Shut up!" Nate said *sotto voce*, trying to express rage and anger while still keeping the noise level low enough to avoid waking Joy and having her wander into this horrible scene. At least Marie had the courtesy to lock the door so their daughter couldn't have wandered in and accidentally witnessed her mother's adultery.

Marie suddenly responded with an uncharacteristic and, given the circumstances, unjustified response: Anger. "Just get out of here, Nate. Get out!" Nate took this for more than what it was intended. Marie had simply wanted the curtain to fall on this particular scene. He took it as a demand that he leave her and Joy's life forever. That he would not do. He slammed the gun down on top the dresser and glared at them both. Jeff had drawn the covers over him higher and higher, thinking somehow that a down comforter was adequate protection for a .38 bullet.

"I will be back in the morning. Make sure he's gone. Have Joy ready. I'm taking her with me."

He stormed out of the room, out of the house, violently backed his car out of the driveway and began roaring down the two-lane road back toward town. At the time, he was glad he hadn't scooped up his daughter and left with her immediately. The way he was venting his anger by roaring down dark, winding roads at high speed was nothing short of reckless.

He had shared it with her. He had been honest with her and himself. His wife had cheated on him, but he was no innocent. They had begun a downward spiral years earlier, and he hadn't done enough to reverse it.

"I didn't make her cheat," he explained, "but I created the emptiness in her heart that she felt she had to go somewhere else to fill."

Teapot didn't agree and told him so. "You can't make someone else happy if they don't want to be." Nate wouldn't hear it. "I drove out of that driveway knowing I'd failed as a husband. I failed as a husband, and I failed as a father, because I didn't provide my daughter with a loving, stable family. I drove out of that driveway knowing Joy was going to be a child of divorce, something I'd vowed would never happen."

Marie felt he was still being too hard on himself, and kept telling him so. This disclosure made her feel maternal and closer to him. She wanted to love him, but also protect him. She had seen his pain, and had discovered the knife that had made the scars she couldn't see. There were still unexplained scars, but this went a long way toward explaining Nate's escape to the trail. It also explained his fear of new emotional involvement.

"Go to bed, Rescue. I'll see you in the morning," she smiled.

During the next few days, they talked in spurts. He worked hard to learn more about her and her life growing up in California. She would occasionally ask him for a detail about his past life or about that fateful night, but always with great care. She still had no idea of how soon after the events of that night his wife and daughter died, but this was still a depth she was afraid to plumb. Still, there had been a breakthrough, and she felt Nate finally was released from the ghosts that haunted him. She thought the disclosure had brought them closer. In his mind, it only made him more eager to reach the end of the trail.

It was clear things had changed when they reached Bly Gap. The wooden sign there had two arrows, one pointing north into North Carolina, the other south into Georgia. This was their last state line, and Nate's entrance into Georgia caused another noticeable change in his demeanor. He quickly retreated back into himself again, and Teapot noticed that while he still continued to ask her about Northern California and her college experiences at the University of Texas, he was using them to deflect her questions rather than the previously obvious genuine interest.

The Georgia mountains were now cold. It was November, far to late for most to be out on the trail. While the deep South is hot, many of its peaks in north Georgia rocket to more than 4,000 and 5,000 feet above sea level. Until recently, one peak even had an extremely modest ski resort. On the trail, more signs began counting down the mileage to the trail's end at Springer Mountain. There was just seventy-five miles of Appalachian Trail in Georgia, but the state boasted some of its highest peaks and many of its most difficult climbs. Tray Mountain and Blue Mountain were particularly wicked, as temperatures continued to drop. As they reached Chattahoochee Gap, the headwaters of the river that provided downstream Atlanta with most of its drinking water, the pair was just 46 miles from the end of the trail. They scrambled along the razor-thin ridgeline that separated the Tennessee River Valley from the rest of Georgia. The steady winds along the ridgeline were easily thirty-five-miles-an-hour, and with temperatures even at midday only in the forties, exposure was a real danger. Both their faces were red and chapped, and there was no way to determine whether it was from sunburn or windburn. The next day they were in pain, but both knew the other wanted to finish their respective journey. Teapot assumed the end would come at Springer Mountain.

Nate knew his terminus was elsewhere.

17
WALKING ON ICE

Ice storms are common during North Georgia winters, but usually don't strike until January and February. The storm that descended on the mountains that early December morning started out as a slow, steady rain. The temperatures were in the low forties, which made the hiking uncomfortable, but not life-threatening as long as you had layered sufficient clothing and wore a rainsuit over it all. Moisture was the most efficient way to suck heat from your body, so keeping dry was paramount. Polyester and hydrophilic clothing to wick moisture away from your skin was imperative. You didn't wear cotton clothing hiking. It kept water close to your body, dried slowly, and became heavy when wet. It sucked the heat out of you. "Cotton kills," the hiking maxim insisted.

As they finished the slow, painful climb to the top of Blood Mountain, they lustfully eyed the twenty-by-twenty-foot cabin perched on its peak. One of the oldest shelters on the trail, it had been build by the Civilian Conservation Corps in the early 1930s, and at 4,458 feet was the highest point on the Appalachian Trail in Georgia. A Canadian front, which normally didn't make an appearance this early in the season, had pushed in over the Tennessee Valley, and as a result the temperature continued dropping rapidly. Unfortunately, because they were overheated from climbing almost 2,000 feet in less than three miles, they failed to note the temperature drop. After a ten-minute break for a cold lunch, they began working their way back down the trail. Springer was now just 28 miles away, and Teapot began to wonder what the two of them would do after reaching the peak. Would Nate want to travel with her to Indiana? Or California? Would he want her to return with him to Maine? Would they stay in Georgia? She wanted to know what came next, but each difficult step up and down the steep peaks forced them to continue focusing on the now, the point of the trail they were on. Nate again was almost silent, and looking at her during lunch Teapot felt that he was looking past her, not at her. Distant Nate was back, she thought. Hadn't she'd left that guy in North Carolina? Hadn't he bared his soul to her? Hadn't he shared his most embarrassing and painful moment? What could he be holding back? She knew he'd lost his wife and daughter soon after he'd caught his wife cheating on him. Divorce and death were horrible things, but he'd shared that pain with her. Could he not move beyond the loss of his daughter and his marriage? If he couldn't, it didn't bode well for them having a relationship after the reached the end of the trail.

They were fortunate the rain didn't turn to sleet and ice until after they had descended the slick western face of Blood Mountain. Had the ice storm hit an hour earlier, they easily could have slipped down a crevasse with little hope of discovery or rescue. There was little monitoring of the Appalachian Trail this late in the season. The last outpost before Springer was five miles back at Neels Gap, where the trail passes through a structure housing the Mountain Crossings store, the only point on the 2,100-mile hike where the trail goes through a building. The outfitter's store was dark, already closed up for the winter. The U.S. Forest Service, which controlled the narrow dirt road that snaked its way up to within a mile of the trail's terminus, shut down the road in late October, blocking it with a metal gate that prevented even joyriders with ATV's from accessing the mountain. This late in the season, the two of them were on their own, and they knew it.

The ice was sheeting down now, and the pellets were coming in with the western winds, slamming into their faces like sharp shards of glass. It was painful and forced them to keep their eyes pointing downward at their feet, slowing their progress. The impact on the AT was immediate and dangerous. The trail bed itself, two-feet wide, was sheeted with ice patches randomly scattered and invisible to the naked eye. Each step on the trail was a Russian Roulette trigger-pull. You could land on a rare dry stone, in which case your footing was assured. You might land on an iced-over rock, but plant yourself solidly and vertically so you could continue with no difficulty. More likely, you'd hit the icy rock at the wrong angle and begin an awkward, comical dance that could only end with you and your gear splayed along the trail. Try to catch yourself as you fell, and you were certain to shatter a wrist. Slowly, the ice turned to a hard snow, with large flakes limiting visibility to one hundred yards or so, quickly blanketing the trail. Within an hour, they were hiking on solid ice covered by a camouflaging layer of snow. To try to compensate, Nate began walking along the left or right sides of the trail edge with Teapot following in his footsteps to avoid the slick rocks. Regardless of the track you chose, the plodding was slow, laborious and exhausting. Nate spent two more hours searching for the right path. Indeed, this entire journey had been for the right path, and it was beginning to look like he wouldn't find it. Twice Teapot suggested they stop, and twice Nate had gruffly insisted they continue plodding on. He acted as if he had a train to catch, and Teapot knew the ground where they stood was just as hard as the ground five miles further down the trail.

Finally, after taking three hours to hike a half-mile, they gave up and found a small clearing next to the trail. The snow was still falling, but visibility improved just enough that they could see the small town of Suches, Georgia, 2,000 feet below them. Nate confirmed the city and their location on his topographic map, and then quickly began setting up their tents. A huge campfire would have been extremely welcome, but fires were expressly prohibited here, and in any case the wood was soaked thanks to the ice and snow, making it unlikely even an Eagle Scout could get a blaze started. He did the next best thing, getting Teapot's gear quickly into her tent, unrolling her sleeping bag, and quickly opening and tossing three chemical hot-spot heating pads inside her sleeping bag. By the time she climbed in and peeled off her wet clothes, her bag was extremely dry and extremely hot. She was extremely grateful, and let him know as he finished pitching his tent next to hers.

"You hungry?"

"Not at all," he said. "You?"

"I was going to suggest we just stay in here until the storm passes. We probably have only an hour of light left, so let's just hibernate and hope that things are better in the morning."

He agreed and once in his bag, listened as her breathing quickly snowed and he knew she was asleep. He reached deep into the side pocket of his backpack and pulled out the plastic bag with two photographs, a notepad and a pencil. It had traveled 2,075 miles in the bottom of his pack, and he had avoided pulling it out once.

He reached in and pulled out the second paperback he'd bought in Damascus and used it as a backing while he wrote a note. He stopped momentarily and stared at the two pictures. One was his and Marie's wedding picture. He stared at the two faces, trying to divine what each of them were thinking. What would the bride in the photograph think if she'd been granted the ability to peer into the future? What would the groom do? Would the young, naive man in the tuxedo have fled the church if he'd known what the future had in store for the happy couple? He started at the second photo, a snapshot of him with Joy as they both slept on the sofa. She couldn't have been more than eighteen months old. There was a football game on the TV, but Nate had fallen asleep stretched out across the couch, and Joy had climbed onto and fallen asleep curled up on his chest, her right thumb firmly planted in her mouth. Nate's father had taken the photograph and given it to him two weeks later. It was slightly bent, as Nate had kept it unframed in his briefcase to take with him on business trips. He stared at the photographs and then returned to the notepad. Occasionally he would look out and see the snow still falling outside the tent. There was already three inches on the ground, and Nate marveled at the rate it was accumulating even as the sunlight outside failed.

It was dark when he finished the note. He climbed out of the tent and arranged his backpack just outside the tent, leaning on one of his tent poles. He neatly placed the note – now placed inside the plastic bag that had housed his two pictures – on the floor of the now-empty tent. He shoved the photographs, a small flashlight and a pocket knife in his pants pocket. He looked at the James Agee paperback's title again, laughed a hoarse and saddening laugh, then tossed it back into the tent. He pealed off his coat and rainsuit and hung them neatly on his other tent pole. He stared briefly at Teapot's tent, then stepped off the trail and slowly began walking down the hill through the raw, untrampled woods.

There were only two lights in Suches to march toward, both back porch lights on a pair of small houses in the town. The lack of a trail made the trip slow, and the ice and snow made it treacherous. There was a great deal of ground cover, thorns and overgrowth to work his way through, and it took him more than two hours to work his way to the edge of the tiny town.

To call Suches a town was to pay it a generous compliment. It was little more than a small cluster of houses. It was quaint, but there was no downtown or main street to its credit. Residents who needed groceries or other supplies had to drive 20 miles either north to Blue Ridge or south to Cleveland. The town sat in a small narrow valley less than a mile long. Besides its 15 houses, its only other assets were a small elementary school and a tiny church. The valley wrapped around a small mountain, and as a result you couldn't see any of the town from the church and vice versa. Residents liked this, as it gave the church more of a "chapel in the mountains" feel. Situated behind the church, backed up to the mountains that rose all the way up to the Appalachian Trail, was a cemetery.

Nate had no difficulty finding the cemetery. They were popular landmarks on topographic maps, and Mt. Lebanon Cemetery was so clearly marked that Nate could even read its exact elevation above sea level. Finding the tombstones was more difficult. The cloud-covered night sky made reading the stones difficult, even with a headlamp flashlight. He had expected to be able to locate the graves easily, since they would be covered with freshest-dug dirt, but the snow and ice had foiled that plan. The snow up on the trail had changed back to ice and sleet now that he was at a lower elevation. He was shivering and growing colder now that he had stopped hiking. Rather than feel discomfort, though, he found the cold sensation to be an old friend, a friend he remembered from the start of his journey back on Kathadin. His friend Cold had visited him on that peak, but he wasn't ready to dance with him there. Now that friend was back, and Cold would be Nate's comfort and his deliverance. Cold would help him defeat his two other old friends: Fear and Pain.

The light bounced from tombstone to tombstone as Nate jerked his head to each, trying to read the writing. His shivering caused the light to jerk and shake, which also made his task difficult. Some of the stones were more than one hundred years old, but in a few minutes he found two modern ones, one large and one small, and knew he was at the right place. The sleet was falling harder now, sticking to his arms and caking in his hair. The heat from his head was no longer melting the ice immediately, which Nate took as a sign that his body temperature was starting to drop dangerously low.

He slowly lowered himself down and shined the light on the larger tombstone:

MARIE KIRBY TOWNSEND

The all-capital name added impact in the dark, and Nate studied the dates below the name. He had memorized them both. As her dutiful husband, he had never forgotten her birthday. He didn't now. The date of her death was so recently burned into his soul it also was unforgettable. He looked over at the smaller tombstone.

JOY CATHERINE TOWNSEND

The two dates chiseled into the granite marker were so close together, he thought to himself. So wrenchingly close. "How wrong that is," he found himself saying out loud to the ice spitting from the sky. The graves were next to each other, separated only by a few feet. He noticed his in-laws had placed the graves in a spot flanked by other family members. They did so to ensure there was no space for Nate to eventually lie next to his wife and daughter, he noted. He laughed. "How little they know," he said. Again, the ice had no response.

He was tired now. The ice was everywhere, in the air, all over the ground, on his arms, in his hair. He could see his breath passing through the beam of the flashlight each time he exhaled. With the porch lights of the houses far off and hidden around the bend, the headlamp was his only direct illumination. He switched it off and then tossed it away. The lights of far-off Atlanta, more than 100 miles away, were still bright enough to reflect off the cloud cover and prevent pitch-blackness. Nate carefully took his two pictures out of his pocket. He was very tired now. He had been shivering and shaking earlier from the cold, but that had now stopped. He gently placed his wedding picture up against his wife's tombstone, placing it at an angle so the ice wouldn't collect on it. He stepped over and did the same for the photograph of Joy sleeping on top of him. Now, he would sleep too. He laid down on his back in the space between the two graves, staring up at the ice as it raced toward him from the upward cloud-filled sky. It gave him the optical illusion that he was racing skyward, and in his now-delusional state that gave him comfort. He sang out loud, singing the verses of the song that had haunted him since Mount Kathadin. This time, however, instead of stalling after the second verse, he was able to sing through third, and it gave him comfort as the cold embraced him:

"Oh they tell me of a home where my friends have gone
They tell me of a land far away,
Where the tree of life in eternal bloom
Sheds its fragrance through an unclouded day.

He closed his eyelids so the ice pellets wouldn't stab his eyeballs and then rolled over to face Joy's grave, balling up into a fetal position. Sleep is the only escape from pain, he had learned after their deaths. In the weeks and months after his wife and daughter were buried in the cold Georgia ground, he had learned that the only peace he'd found was when he slept. Six or eight hours of escape a day wasn't enough, he'd soon decided. Eventually, he would crave total escape. He didn't want to leave little Joy and his wife alone in Georgia, though. He wanted to sleep alongside them one more time. He'd walked almost 2,100 miles to sleep with them again. And now he would.

Nate wouldn't learn what had happened at his house after he'd stormed out until early the next day. After roaring out of the driveway, he drove back toward Freeport. His mind raced trying to figure out the proper thing to do in this situation. He had made a career of thinking strategically. But how often did situations like this occur? There was no guidebook. No common wisdom on how to proceed. At work, he was called an "organization genius." He was a logical, organized expert in logistics and planning. How do you plan for this? How do you organize something that is so disorganized?

He would take Joy. That was a given. He loved his daughter, and couldn't imagine living his life without her. He would fight for her. He refused to be an every-other-weekend father. Why should he be punished when the fault wasn't his? He was realistic, however. Courts would always side with a mother over a father. How could he convince a judge he was a better father? It didn't seem fair. A judge would award Joy to a mother who'd committed adultery just 40 feet from her daughter's bedroom door? Was adultery still a criminal offense in Maine? He wondered.

When he reached town, he pulled up to a phone booth. He

needed some proof that his wife was alone with Jeff if he had any chance of gaining custody. By morning, it would be his word against hers. He didn't know if adultery was a crime, but having some record that the two of them were together alone in the middle of the night would go a long way to helping him make his case. He dialed 911.

"911 emergency," the voice quickly responded.

"I need to report a domestic disturbance," Nate said. "I was driving by a home at 843 Manning Drive and heard a lot of shouting, what sounded like a fight. I don't know what it was about but it might be a good idea to send an officer."

The operator at the other end of the line confirmed the address and then asked "and what is your name, sir?"

"I'd rather not get involved," he said, then hung up the phone. Even without identifying himself, he felt sure that a patrol car would be dispatched, and with a report filed he would have some documentation of what had happened and who had been in the house. Still angry but slightly satisfied, Nate drove to a motel along I-95 and checked in. He had left his suitcase back at the house, but in the morning he would return and pick it up, along with Joy. It took him two hours to calm down enough to sleep, but at 4 in the morning he finally nodded off.

Less than two hours later, there was a knock at the door. Groggy, he stumbled to the door and opened it to find a very erect state trooper standing just outside.

"Nathan Townsend?"

"Yes?"

"Mr. Townsend, I'm Sgt. Walter Thomas. I need you to come with me." Nate instantly thought he was in trouble for hanging up on the 911 call, and wondered how they'd tracked him down.

"What's this all about?"

"Please come with me, sir."

"How did you find me?"

The officer thought the question suspicious, but answered. "Tracked you down from your credit card. You used it to check into the motel."

Nate sat in the back of the trooper's car as it drove back down the winding roads back toward his house. He wasn't handcuffed, so he figured he might not be in too much trouble. Maybe Marie had sent the police out looking for him. When he got to his house, he saw a half dozen police cars parked on the street and in his driveway. He saw an ambulance parked down the street, with its crew quietly sitting on the back bumper, apparently unneeded. He felt his sense of panic rising as they opened the patrol car's back door. He started to bolt toward the front door but a large police officer standing at the doorway stopped him.

"Sir, you can't go in. Please wait for the detective. Detective!" he called in to the house. A short mustached man in a poorly fitting brown suit emerged from Nate's front door.

"Mr. Townsend?"

"Yes! Yes! Where is my wife? What's happened to my daughter?"

"Mr. Townsend, I need to let you know this is a murder scene. I know it's difficult, but I need you to go with me and help me identify who's in the house if you can. Please don't touch anything."

Nate was no longer paying attention. When he heard the word "murder," his consciousness altered and he began sleepwalking through the next five minutes of horror. He walked into the house led by the detective, who turned right into Nate's bedroom. He saw Jeff on the floor lying face-up in a pool of red blood that had soaked into the carpet. He had a dark red circle on the right side of his head and Nate's gun was lying three feet to the side. There were tiny cards of official-looking folded white paper all over his bedroom, looking like tiny wedding invitations, each with black block numbers printed on them.

"Do you know who this is?"

"Jeff Shippman." Nate heard himself saying. "He's a friend ... a friend of my wife's."

"Yes sir. Would you follow me?" He led Nate down the hallway. Nate knew instinctively where he was leading him, and he knew he didn't want to follow. He had no choice. He was sleepwalking now. Sleepwalkers never get to control where they go. He stepped into Joy's bedroom. Marie and Joy were both lying on Joy's bed. They were curled up together. Their eyes fortunately were closed, but it was obvious from the blood and the scattering of numbered cards that they both were dead. Nate started crying, managing to mutter through the sobs that it was his wife and daughter. An officer gently took his right arm and led him back outside where he collapsed on the front lawn sobbing.

The detective followed and studied Nate's reaction for several minutes. Like a theater critic, he evaluated the performance and, deciding Nate's shock and grief were genuine, gently led him to the back of a patrol car. Nate sat down sideways on the seat, his legs still outside the vehicle talking to the detective, who knelt down in front of him.

"Can you tell me what happened here tonight, Mr. Townsend?"

"I don't know. I can only tell you what happened up to the point I left here a couple of hours ago." Nate then related everything about the confrontation, sparing no detail, no matter how embarrassing and emasculating. He admitted the gun on the floor was his. He made a point of insisting that while he'd taken the trigger lock off, it was unloaded when he stormed out. When he was done, he sat there waiting, still in shock and unable to collect himself. It took him more than five minutes to build up the courage to ask the question.

"What happened here?"

The detective sighed, then looked at the various police resources deployed across Nate's front lawn. Did he think Nate had somehow killed everyone in the house? He'd thought about shooting Jeff and even Marie at the height of his anger that night, but of course had not. Still, it would be a very logical conclusion for the police to draw.

"We're obviously still investigating, but here's what we know, Mr. Townsend. We received a 911 call about 1 a.m. from someone in town, who based on what you just told me was most likely you. We dispatched an officer to the house shortly afterwards. When the officer arrived and came to the door, he heard yelling and arguing going on inside the house. He rang the doorbell and pounded on the door trying to get the attention of the people inside. He heard the male voice say something to the effect of "I won't give you up. If I can't have you then nobody can." He then heard three shots. He reports that he pulled his service revolver and kicked down the front door. As he entered the house, he saw the male suspect rushing down the hallway away from your daughter's bedroom toward the master bedroom. When he saw the officer he apparently panicked and fired a shot in the officer's direction, missing wildly. The officer returned fire, but the suspect had already passed down the hall to the bedroom and closed the door. He warned the officer off, and the officer retreated as he was trained to do, thinking he had a hostage situation. Before we could get anyone down here to negotiate, the officer heard a single shot. Concerned that hostages might be at risk, he re-entered the house and carefully made his way to the bedroom, where he found the suspect dead, apparently of a single self-inflicted gunshot wound. We currently believe this to be a double-murder and suicide, but obviously we have a long way to go in our investigation."

He paused, eager to find something positive for Nate at such an horrific moment. What he came up with was quite inadequate:

"Quite candidly, if we hadn't had an officer on the scene, we might have assumed you killed them all."

"He killed them. Because he couldn't have them?"

The detective softened, knowing that it was impossible to explain the logic behind murder-suicides. "I've been doing this long enough to know you can make sense of the senseless, Mr. Townsend. If it helps at all, the officer testified that the woman's voice kept saying that she wouldn't leave her husband."

It didn't help at all. Nate kept replaying the scene over and over in his mind. He would do so for months. He would do it every day on the trail. Each time he rewound the scene, it was more gruesome, more painful than the time before. He had set the events in motion himself, both in souring his wife's love for him, leaving a loaded gun in the house when he left, and then sending the police to the door which may have set Jeff off. Nate hadn't pulled the trigger, but he might as well have.

He spent the next four hours at the police station. Spouses are usually suspect number one when someone is murdered, but as the detective said, given that an officer was on scene to overhear everything, Nate was considered a victim. He knew in his heart, however, that he was an unindicted co-conspirator in the crime.

When he left the police station, he didn't know where to go. He couldn't go back to his home. He wouldn't go back there until well after the funeral and after the carpeting had all been ripped out and the bloodstains cleaned. Even when he returned, he never stepped foot in his and Marie's bedroom. He curled up and slept in Joy's bed each night. Each night he waited for the sleep, blessed sleep, to come and rescue him from the pain and tears. The icy sleep that now blanketed him as he rested on their graves.

When Teapot awoke, she rested quietly in her tent listening to the silence. Snow in the woods muffles and absorbs all sounds, and the silence after a snowfall is magical. She laid comfortably in her sleeping bag for several minutes enjoying the quiet and calm. She heard no wind, no animals moving, no distant stream or spring gurgling. Quiet. Then she realized there was a sound she should have heard but didn't. Nate's tent was 24 inches from hers. Why couldn't she hear him breathing? She unzipped the flap and bolted out of her tent. Standing, she called out. "Nate? Nate?" No answer. She saw the now-drenched backpack leaning up against the side of the tent, and his heavy coat hanging from the opposite tent pole. She knew instantly he had left her, just as she had left him in New Hampshire. This was no tit-for-tat, though. He'd left all his gear, including his tent and pack. He wasn't wearing critical clothing needed to survive the now sub-freezing temperatures. She looked inside the tent and found only a note and a book. She grabbed the note.

It wasn't her fault, he'd written. He had planned to end his trip and his life at his wife and daughter's grave even before he'd taken his first step on the AT. His pilgrimage wasn't an escape. It was a journey home. A journey back to the South. A journey back to his family. A hike that would bring him back to his daughter's side. He had never intended to return to Maine, and had deceived his coworkers, his friends and now, unfortunately, Teapot into thinking this hike was a way for him to convalesce. It wasn't. He had taken a 2,100 mile pilgrimage as his last journey. He had fled humanity because he doubted there was any such thing. He had seen the ultimate acts of selfishness and inhumanity, acts that had taken away the only things he truly loved. His only regret he expressed in the note was that Teapot had begun to restore his belief in love and humanity, and he wished that he could have been swayed from his original purpose. Sadly, he said, he could not. The demons had been with him every day on the trail. They had been whispering in his ear every night as he laid down and they spoke to him every night just before sleep came to provide him its blessed escape. He begged her forgiveness and wished her well. He even signed it, "Love, Nate." She folded the note and stuck it in her pocket. Then she picked up the James Agee book that had grabbed Nate's attention way back in Damascus and now sat alone inside his empty tent: *A Death in The Family*.

Without the cold front that had turned the ice to snow, she wouldn't have had a chance of finding him. Had the precipitation stayed freezing rain or ice, she would have no idea where to look. The three-degree drop in temperature on the mountains had changed the falling ice to falling snow, however. And as the sun slowly rose, she could easily see the footprints Nate had left hours earlier heading down the slope of the mountain. She broke down her tent and jammed it and all her possessions in her backpack in less than sixty seconds. She stumbled downhill, moving fast. At times she was running, other times she was simply sliding. The thorns and undergrowth scratched her arms and face, but she didn't notice. She kept her eyes focused on the footprints, partially covered by snow that had fallen after Nate had passed through. Thank God they're still visible, she thought. The descent was rapid, but still seemed maddeningly slow to Teapot. It was still well below freezing, and with her rapidly pumping exhalations she resembled a locomotive racing down a steep grade under full steam.

She neared the bottom of the hill, where the lower elevation had prevented the ice from changing to snow. Nate's tracks had disappeared. When she got to within one hundred yards of the Suches Valley the trail was completely gone. Ice was still falling. Where had he gone? There was a road off to the left, but because of the curving valley, she couldn't see the houses that were just around the bend. To the right, she saw a small wooden church. On instinct, she raced the five hundred yards toward the church carrying her full pack. When she got to the red front doors, they were locked. She kicked them in on the third try, after twice throwing the full weight of the pack and herself against them. She quickly scanned the five pews in the tiny church. No Nate. She ran back outside and scanned the horizon. Nothing. She looked to the side of the church and from where she stood saw a single tombstone. She slowly moved around, revealing more tombstones. Then the full cemetery. In the middle of it, a single figure lay on the ground, dressed only in green hiking pants and an orange shirt.

When she found him, she shook him and was elated to see he was still breathing. They were short, labored breaths, though. His skin was blue, and although she tried to wake him, he was unresponsive. She tried slapping him to wake him, but his eyes remained closed. She lifted his eyelids but there was no focus. Now in a full panic, she started dragging him into the woods, trying desperately to get him back to his tent up at the top of the mountain. She finally came to her senses, realizing there was no way she would be able to drag his limp body all the way back up the mountain. She looked around for shelter, and saw nothing. Should she reverse course and drag him all the way back to the cold, unheated church?

During her brief two weeks as the only female Boy Scout in Fremont, California, Teapot had carefully studied and memorized the first aid merit badge pamphlet. Hypothermia. She called on her memory from more than a decade earlier. Lowered body temperature. Right. Danger of death. First signs are uncontrolled shivering. Followed by disorientation. Followed by sleep. Followed soon thereafter by death. OK, she was remembering this. Treatment: Placing body in warm but not hot bath water to rewarm it. She glanced around. OK, that's not gonna happen. What else? In worst case, use skin-to-skin contact to warm the body. OK, that's what we're going to do. We're going to get you out of this ice and try to warm you up.

She quickly set up her tent and poked her sleeping bag inside. She looked for chemical heating packs but knew that if there were any, they were in Nate' pack back at the top of the mountain. No good. His clothing was drenched and she quickly stripped it off of him. Modesty matters very little when you're about to die, Nate, she thought. She dragged his now-naked blue-and-white body inside the sleeping bag. OK, she thought. He doesn't have enough internal body heat to warm himself up. Great. She knew what she had to do. Modesty matters very little when you're trying to save a life, Teapot, she told herself. She stripped all her clothing off and climbed naked into the tent and then slid into the sleeping bag next to him. His body was colder than any cold shower she'd ever taken, and she prayed he didn't die on her, since she didn't want to end up lying naked next to a cadaver. She hugged him hard, harder than they'd hugged weeks earlier back on the trail. She moved around, working to make sure every possible inch of her body was in contact with his. She pressed first to his chest, where she knew his vital organs were inside. She entwined her arms and legs around his, trying to touch as many square inches of skin she could. Occasionally she would shiver herself, and she rubbed her hands gently over him, trying to create friction that would generate additional heat. She grasped the opening of the sleeping bag closed so no cold air could enter. She shivered uncontrollably as she pressed harder and harder against him, but refused to let go. Dammit, Nate, warm up!

18
THAWING THE FROZEN

They would lie together in the sleeping bag for more than four hours before she saw any movement. She constantly listened to his breathing, fearing that each breath he took might be his last. It was labored, and it was shallow and slow, but at least it was steady. She tried to remember if the first aid merit badge pamphlet had said anything about brain damage, or if that was something she'd dreamed up. The danger of frostbite concerned her. She had gradually started warming up his torso by transferring her body heat, but his extremities remained ice cold. Thanks to millennia of evolution, the human body rarely gave up without a fight. As hypothermia took hold, the heart would stop pumping blood to arms and legs, trying to save what dwindling warmth was left for the critical organs such as the brain and heart.

"Boy, I should have had your trail name today, kiddo," she whispered to him, knowing Rescue couldn't hear her.

The first movement was a flicker of his eyelids It would take an hour after that before he would start moving his body at all. His extremities were still cold to the touch, but his trunk was clearly warmer than it was when she'd first pressed up against him. Wake up, she kept thinking to him. I'm cuddled up against you completely naked. The least you can do is wake up.

She left him only once, and that was because she had to sneak out of the tent to go to the bathroom. She tossed a fleece over herself, rushed out and then rushed back in, climbing back into the sleeping bag. He never moved, but his breathing was still regular. He felt warmer, but that may have be misleading since she had just been out in twenty-eight-degree weather in only a fleece. Shortly afterwards, the snow returned, this time a soft, downy snowfall with flakes gently drifting down and landing gently on top of the now-iced-over grass outside the tent. The silence was blanketing, giving the illusion that Nate and Teapot were the only two souls in the world, locked in embrace of survival and salvage. She loved him completely now, she knew. She loved him not because he was damaged, not because he was a repair project to which she could devote herself. He was a soul needing love and forgiveness, and she had been raised by parents who had stressed the importance of giving both unconditionally. He wanted to die; she wanted him to live. He wanted to escape. She wanted him to find the spark of confidence and assuredness she had seen inside him. He made her feel needed, certainly, but he also had shown during the past four weeks that he cared for her. His gestures, his generosity, his willingness to share so much of the pain that had stabbed at his psyche were clearly an effort. He had made them for her, though. That he hadn't been able to share it all was her only concern. Her only fear.

After another hour, there was a good sign: He moaned. Soon afterwards, he started slowly moving about inside the tight confines of the sleeping bag. Then he did something unexpected: He moved his arms and wrapped them around Teapot, embracing her. His eyes were still closed, but there was no mistaking he was steadily warming and reviving. After another half hour, he pressed harder against her and slowly opened his eyes. He was disoriented, but he lacked the energy to communicate it, either verbally or with a facial expression. He stared at the woman lying next to him, her face two inches from his. He slowly became aware of his location. Feeling was gradually returning to his extremities. He finally became aware he was in a sleeping bag without clothes. Then he felt that Teapot was also there, and also naked. They looked closely at each other's eyes and he raised his right arm out of the bag just enough to brush the brown hair out of her eyes so he could see them better. He hoped his facial muscles were working now, because he was trying to smile. They were, and in response she smiled back at him.

There were no words. She was there. She was warm. She was comforting. She was the peace he had been seeking in the icy graveyard, and he immediately realized it. He had thought he was at the end of his trail, but now he had decided they were only at the beginning of theirs. It was as if he'd died on ground of Suches, and been reborn here in this tented heaven. She saw this epiphany in his eyes. The peace. The understanding. Most importantly, the acceptance. She kissed him.

They made love slowly and carefully. He was still weak and she was still nervous. She gently climbed on top of him and brought him inside her. He was warm there, and while every other part of him that touched her on the outside was cold, where it mattered she felt his warmth. They moved slowly, deliberately and in unison. Their eyes locked as they alternated pushing closer and further from each other. Neither closed their eyes as they slowly rolled over in the tiny tent, remaining connected physically and spiritually. Nate continued to caress her as he pressed his now-warm torso against her soft flat belly and chest. There was no need for words – their feelings, their happiness and acceptance of each other was communicated by mutual glances just two inches away. She felt the warmth inside her suddenly grow and swell, and respecting the silent snow blanket covering the valley outside, she softly whimpered and sighed. Moments later, Nate's body shuddered, but he also remained silent. They continued to look at each other for several minutes before Nate's blood-starved arms began to give way, and they rolled back over beside each other. They stared at each other wordlessly. He felt that he needed to tell her the words "I love you." He did so, but she already knew. He slowly drifted back into sleep, this time at finding the peace he sought well before the peace of unconsciousness reached him. Teapot stared at him for a long time before she too drifted off.

They must have slept most of the day. By the time they awoke, the stormclouds had passed, replaced with a solid gray ceiling in the sky. It was still so cold that the fog of the breath and its condensation hung heavy inside the tent.

They kissed again, for a long time before speaking. Nate explained it all. He told her the entire story, with no shame and this time no guilt. He related his unwitting role in his wife and daughter's death and his reaction to it. He shared his true feelings, his true pain, his loss. This time, there was no flight reflex. He didn't want to run away from it. He had found someone willing to share his pain, to help carry the load from that heavy pack. He explained that Jeff, after Nate had stormed out of the house, apparently had insisted Marie leave her husband. By the time the officer arrived at the door, he was able to overhear their rapidly escalating argument, as Marie apparently was insisting she couldn't bring herself to split her family apart. She expressed true regret, which apparently only raised Jeff's anger. "I have destroyed my relationship with both you and your husband for nothing?" he had screamed, loud enough to prompt the officer outside to make his first knock on the door. The knock at the door apparently only escalated Jeff's fear, jealousy and anger, and by the time the officer was pounding on the door, he had grabbed the gun and a handful of bullets from the dresser, jamming several into the revolver. He waved it at Marie, forcing her to retreat down the hall. Perhaps her instincts drew her backwards in a move to protect their daughter. Unwittingly, by bringing a threatening Jeff down the hall and into the room, she had only staged the final scene. "If he can't have you, no one can!" were the last words Jeff would speak. The police wouldn't know whether Marie or Joy were shot first, Nate explained to Teapot, not that it mattered. That question for many weeks had haunted him. He finally realized that in the end, it mattered little. They would both be a long time dead. Nate's only satisfaction was that Jeff had quickly retreated to the bedroom and killed himself. Visualizing what a trial might have been like was unbearable.

"So you decided to walk the entire Appalachian Trail, knowing you would kill yourself on your wife and daughter's grave?" Teapot asked, still trying to fathom the depth of Nate's half-year pilgrimage of grief.

"Yes," he admitted. "I left last night with a pocket knife to slit my wrists, but the ice and exposure presented itself as a much less messy way to join them."

"Do you ... do you still want to join them?" she asked, making sure of what she had felt while they had made love. She was as afraid of the answer even as she asked.

He thought long before answering. He knew the answer was no, but verbalizing the reasons took longer.

He brushed her hair out of her eyes again, even as he was struggling to explain how he felt. "Ever been bitten by a snake?"

"What?"

He smiled. "It's a fairly simple question, I thought."

She smiled back, confused. "No."

"The creeks up where I was born are filled with water moccasins. When I was six, one bit me. Bad. By the time I'd run screaming back to my family's cabin, my left leg was swollen to twice its normal size. My dad didn't waste a second. He grabbed a big hunting knife, held my thrashing body down with one hand and cut my leg with the other."

"Cut your leg?"

"He made an incision connecting the two slashes where the fang-marks were. Then he put his lips to my leg and started drawing out venom. By running, I'd probably helped circulate the venom around my body more quickly, which didn't help, but he did manage to draw and spit out a good bit that was still pooled just under my skin. It's chalky white, by the way."

She remembered some of this from her first aid pamphlet, but stared at him, both horrified at the recollection and wondering how this answered her question.

"I was snakebitten a year ago ago, Teapot. That venom has been sitting under my skin, leaching into my blood and into my heart and brain. By going out in an ice storm and saving my life, by coming to my rescue in Virginia, you drew out the poison. You showed me what love can be again. Marie and Joy's deaths are a painful part of my life I'll never recover from. But someone willing to risk their own life for someone who doesn't want theirs ... well, how can I not fall in love with that person? How can that not change my view of whether there's any good in the world?"

"I love you Nate. I don't want a relationship with damaged goods, but I want to be with you."

"I understand that," he said, suddenly worrying that his baggage was too heavy for her to help carry. "No. No, I don't want to die."

She took this in and thought hard.

"You may be damaged goods, Rescue," she whispered, but you're good. You're a good person. Never doubt that."

He smiled. They looking long into each other's eyes, kissed and made love again.

Before the sun set, they finally emerged from the tent and packed up Teapot's gear. He did the gentlemanly thing and carried her pack all the way back up the side trail to where he had left his tent and backpack on the side of the AT. With the sun setting over Springer Mountain 20 miles to the west, they re-pitched her tent and stored all their gear inside to start drying. After camping apart over the past four hundred miles, they would share his tent tonight.

The next morning, Nate was up well before Teapot. His joints were still screaming at him, and he gulped down four ibuprofen – he grinned remembering that one Northbound hiker months earlier had referred to it as 'Vitamin I' – and then fired up the small stove to heat water for their breakfast. The smell of coffee and now-hydrated bacon and eggs drifted into the tent and woke Teapot. As she started to rustle around in the tent looking for dry clothing, Nate appeared in the opening, holding a collapsible metal cup of coffee and a small bag of food with waves of steam rising out of its top opening.

"Breakfast in bed?"

"Now you're just trying to seduce me."

"A little late for that I think, but I'm willing to continue the seduction."

"Let me climb out. I feel like I've spent a year inside this tent."

They sat amidst a forest coated with six inches of snow. Through the leaf-bare trees they could look down into the northern valley and see small squares of fallow fields and an occasional wisp of smoke drifting out of a house's fireplace.

"So what do we do now?" Teapot wasn't sure of the answer, but she knew Nate's response was important.

"We finish the trail, I guess. We're just another day from Springer. Let's finish this journey together."

"That's sweet of you, considering you made most of it alone. Even when I was with you." That came out a little stronger than she'd intended, and she regretted it as soon as she'd said it.

He didn't take it wrong. "Well, I think my days of hiking alone are over." He paused. "That is, if you're willing to hike the trail with me."

"You know I am, Rescue."

She took a bite of the eggs and immediately wished she had some salt.

"So," she continued. "Where do we go after Springer Mountain?"

"Dunno," he said candidly. "Someone once told me on the trail you only worry about the next step in front of you. If you look too far ahead, you're likely to stumble. I'm beginning to think that makes sense." He smiled at her, and she beamed back.

They made sixteen miles that day, despite the snowy trails and their desire to hold hands when possible, even when the trail didn't accommodate it. They talked during those final miles about possible futures. They couldn't immediately decide where to live, or what to do. They knew, however, that they would be on the trail together. Always. After their last night of camping on the AT, it took just two hours to reach the end of the trail and stand on top of a giant granite outcropping of Springer Mountain. That final morning the front broke, and with no more stormclouds it was bright, sunny and warm as they stood together on the stone outcropping as large as a baseball diamond. They looked west at the foothills crowned with blue sky and hugged and kissed.

After adding their names to the spiral-bound notebook hidden in a tiny drawer carved into the rock on top of Springer, they looked at each other and then began walking carefully down the steep approach trail that would take them back to civilization.

Nate never learned that the song that had haunted him throughout his 2,100-mile hike had a fourth verse. It would have given him comfort, though, as he and Teapot began their descent from Springer:

"Oh they tell me that he smiles on his children there
And his smile drives their sorrows away.
and they tell me that no tears ever come again
Oh, they tell me of an unclouded day."

"We still haven't decided what we're going to do next, Nate Townsend," she smiled at him, glad the trail was wide enough that they could hike side-by-side.

"I don't know," he said. "But I do know the first thing I'm going to do when I get off this trail, Teapot."

"Yes?"

"I'm going to find out your real name."

She smiled, and then told him.

Darren Drevik, a native of Oak Ridge, Tennessee, worked as a newspaper journalist for 20 years, serving as an editor, publisher and bureau chief for newspapers in Georgia, Tennessee and South Carolina.

Mr. Drevik moved to New York City in 2010 and documented the city through his humor blog, ManhattanHillbilly.

He currently lives in Montgomery Center, Vermont, where he continues to write while he and his wife own and operate a bed and breakfast.

Appalachian Trail is his first novel.